DECALOG
5 WONDERS

Other books in this series:

DECALOG
DECALOG 2 – LOST PROPERTY
DECALOG 3 – CONSEQUENCES
DECALOG 4 – RE: GENERATIONS

TEN STORIES
A BILLION YEARS
AN INFINITE UNIVERSE

Edited by
Paul Leonard
&
Jim Mortimore

First published in Great Britain in 1997 by
Virgin Publishing Ltd
332 Ladbroke Grove
London W10 5AH

Poyekhali 3201 © Stephen Baxter 1997
King's Chamber © Dominic Green 1997
City of Hammers © Neil Williamson 1997
Painting the Age with the Beauty of our Days
© Mike O'Driscoll 1997
The Judgement of Solomon © Lawrence Miles 1997
The Milk of Human Kindness © Liz Sourbut 1997
Bibliophage © Stephen Marley 1997
Negative Space © Jeanne Cavelos 1997
Dome of Whispers © Ian Watson 1983, 1997
Waters-of-Starlight © Stephen Marley 1997

The right of each of the authors listed above to be identified as the author of the story whose title appears next to their name has been asserted by them in accordance with the Copyright, Designs and Patents Act 1988.

ISBN 0 426 20515 4

Cover illustration by Colin Howard

Typeset by Galleon Typesetting Ltd, Ipswich

Printed and bound in Great Britain by
Mackays of Chatham PLC

This book is sold subject to the condition that it shall not, by way of trade or otherwise, be lent, resold, hired out or otherwise circulated without the publisher's prior written consent in any form of binding or cover other than that in which it is published and without a similar condition including this condition being imposed on the subsequent purchaser.

CONTENTS

THE PLACE OF ALL PLACES
based on an idea by Nakula Somana — 1

POYEKHALI 3201 by Stephen Baxter — 4

KING'S CHAMBER by Dominic Green — 21

CITY OF HAMMERS by Neil Williamson — 55

PAINTING THE AGE WITH THE BEAUTY OF OUR DAYS by Mike O'Driscoll — 84

THE JUDGEMENT OF SOLOMON
by Lawrence Miles — 112

THE MILK OF HUMAN KINDNESS
by Liz Sourbut — 153

BIBLIOPHAGE by Stephen Marley — 184

NEGATIVE SPACE by Jeanne Cavelos — 212

DOME OF WHISPERS by Ian Watson — 265

WATERS-OF-STARLIGHT
by Stephen Marley — 278

THE PLACE OF ALL PLACES
based on an idea by Nakula Somana — 309

Acknowledgements

The editors would like to thank Andy Cox of *The Third Alternative* and David Pringle of *Interzone*, without whose help the collection would have been impossible in its present form. Also many thanks to Paul Barnett for assistance above and beyond the call of duty, not to mention hospitality, free advice, etc. (if anyone ever does Paul's biography, we think it ought to be called *The Man Who Was Too Helpful*). Thanks also to Mike Ashley for very useful and timely advice given over temperamental email connections, to Rebecca Levene at Virgin for patience and understanding, and to Barb Drummond for listening when it mattered most.

Finally, Jim wants to say thanks to Paul (for doing most of it) and Paul wants to say thank you to Jim (for inspiring most of it). And, most important of all, both of us want to say thank you to all the writers, both the ones we published and the ones we couldn't find room for, because without their time, effort and imagination – well, you'd just have blank pages to look at, wouldn't you?

The Place of All Places

Based on an idea by Nakula Somana

Oasis is full of the sun. It lies over everything: cloying, clanging, a golden cloth. And not just gold but saffron, cadmium, zinc, amber, apricot, parchment, ochre, tan, bronze, all the yellow that God ever made lies here. The land and the sky are so full of colour that there is scarcely room for Boy.

Boy hides among the palm trees, squeezed into a narrow strip of ground between wetland and desert, life and death; near enough to the dhobiis ghat *to taste the moisture in the air with the* harijans *songs as they beat dirty clothes in dripping arcs against sloping rocks to clean them.*

The harijans *work, an untouchable machine endlessly building the foundation of a culture which will only ever mark them with non-existence. And yet they smile, these human mirages, and their faces glow like mountains in the sun: dark, gnarled, rivers of sweat mobilizing the geography of their faces.*

As always they are singing about Desert.
Desert and existence.

> The River of Stars is dying. Desert is all that remains.
> Desert remembers the universe but Desert, too, will pass away.
> The country of Man is dying. Oasis is all that remains.
> Man remembers Desert's stories but Mankind, too, must pass away.
> Every night there are fewer stars. Every day there are fewer stories.
> Desert is dying. Man is dying.
> Who will remember? Who will remember?

Boy listens, the song's ignorant prisoner; he listens but does not understand. The harijans *sing of Desert's stories as if they were real. But the stories aren't real, are they? Boy stays among the palm trees and considers this until the sun stands high upon Oasis and the yellow land has turned salt-white, but cannot conceive an answer to the question.*

Later that day Uncle comes to the dhobiis *ghat. He comes with a thing Boy cannot name. Uncle plants the thing in Oasis. It has silver leaves that chase and catch the sun, oiled arms that work without rest in metal sleeves, mouths that drink from Oasis and punch the dirty clothes with fists of water.*

For the first time that Boy can remember, the harijans *stop work.*

-What is it?- Boy points excitedly. -What does it do?-

-It is a machine,- Uncle responds proudly. -A machine for washing. I built it.-

Boy does not understand. -But the harijans *do washing.-*

Uncle sees that Boy is confused. -It has been my life's dream to build this machine for the harijans*. This mechanism will ease the burden of their work.-*

Boy still does not understand. -But what will the harijans *do if they do not have to work?-*

Uncle laughs. -Anything they want.-

The harijans *are laughing too, shouting their thanks above the voice of machine. Already it has done a day's work.*

Boy is angry. -Do you love the harijans *so much more than me that you give them this gift and me nothing?-*

Uncle smiles sadly. -But you already have what I have given the harijans.-

Boy is confused. -But I have no machine that does washing.-

-That is because you are the Last Born; you do not need to work. Time is precious now. I have given the harijans *time to dream, to wonder.-*

Boy sighs impatiently. -You say you have given them time and wonder, but I see only a machine.-

Uncle takes Boy's face in his big, dry hands and turns so they are both looking at the desert. -Think of the stories Desert tells. They affect you even though you cannot see their cause.-

-I don't understand. The harijans *say the stories Desert tells are real.-*

Uncle smiles wistfully. -Is a story less wonderful because it exists only in your mind?-

Boy stands in the grey rushes and considers his Uncle's words. He thinks until the sun is gone and night stands black upon Oasis, until Uncle has returned to his home to contented sleep and the harijans song has gone from the night, but cannot conceive an answer to the question.

And so, as the sun chases night from Oasis, Boy faces Desert and begins to walk. He walks until Oasis is gone, until only the sand and the sun remain, until the days and weeks and years make a desert rock of him, skin dry-scoured and full of mouths greedy for moisture.

And as his skin thirsts, so too does his heart.

He has but one question, and no answer.

Desert tells stories.

Are the stories real?

Poyekhali 3201

By Stephen Baxter

It seemed to Yuri Gagarin, that remarkable morning, that he emerged from a sleep as deep and rich as those of his childhood.

... And now, it was as if the dream continued. Suddenly it was sunrise, and he was standing at the launch pad in his bright orange flight suit, his heavy white helmet emblazoned 'CCCP' in bright red.

He breathed in the fresh air of a bright spring morning. Beyond the pad, the flat Kazakhstan steppe had erupted into its brief bloom, with evanescent flowers pushing through the hardy grass. Gagarin felt his heart lift, as if the country that had birthed him had gathered itself to cup him in its warm palm, one last time, even as he prepared to soar away from its soil, and into space.

Gagarin turned to his ship.

The A-1 rocket was a slim white cylinder, forty metres tall. The three supporting gantries were in place around the booster, clutching it like metal fingers, holding it to the Earth. Gagarin could see the four flaring strap-on boosters clustered around the first stage, the copper-coloured clusters of rocket nozzles at the base.

This was an ICBM – an SS-6 – designed to deliver heavy nuclear weapons to the laps of the enemies of the Soviet Union. But today the payload was no warhead, but something wonderful. The booster was tipped by his Vostok, shrouded by a green protective cone: Gagarin's spaceship, which he had named *Swallow*.

Technicians and engineers surrounded him. All around him he saw faces: faces turned to *him*, faces shining with awe. Even the *zeks*, the political prisoners, had been allowed to see him today, 12 April 1961, to witness as the past separated from the future.

They were right to feel awe. Nobody had travelled into space before! Would a human body be able to survive a state of weightlessness? Would cosmic radiation prove lethal to a man? Even to reach this deadly realm, the first cosmonaut would have to ride a converted missile, and his spaceship had just one aim: to preserve him long enough to determine if humans, after all, could survive beyond the Earth — or if space must for ever remain a realm of superstition and dread.

Gagarin smiled on them all. He felt a surge of elation, of command; he basked in the warm attention.

... And yet there were faces here that were strange to him, he realized slowly, faces among the technicians and engineers, even among the pilots. How could that be so, after so many months of training, all of them cooped up here in this remote place? He thought he knew everybody, and they him.

Perhaps, he wondered, he was still immersed in his dream.

... For a time, he had been with his father. He had been a carpenter, whose hands had constructed their wooden home in the village of Klushino, in the western Soviet Union. Then the ground shook as German tanks rumbled through the village. His parents' home was smashed, and they had to live in a dugout, without bread or salt, and forage for food in the fields ...

But that was long ago, and he and his family had endured, and now he had reached this spring morning. And here, towering over him, was the bulk of his rocket, grey-white and heavy and uncompromising, and he put aside his thoughts of dreams with determination; today was the day he would fulfil the longings of a million years — the day he would step off the Earth and ride in space itself.

Gagarin walked to the pad. There was a short flight of metal stairs leading to the elevator which would carry him to the capsule; the stairs ran alongside the flaring skirt of one of the boosters. White condensation poured off the rocket, rolling down its heroic flanks; and ice glinted on the metal, regardless of the warmth of the sun.

Gagarin looked down over the small group of men gathered at the base of the steps. He said, 'The whole of my life seems to be condensed into this one wonderful moment. Everything that I have been, everything I have achieved, was for this.' He lowered his head briefly. 'I know I may never see the Earth again, my wife Valentia, and my fine children, Yelena and Galya. Yet I am happy. Who would not be? To take part in new discoveries, to be the first to journey beyond the embrace of Earth. Who could dream of more?'

They were hushed; the silence seemed to spread across the steppe, revealing the soft susurrus of the wind over the grass which lay beneath all human noises.

He turned, and climbed into the elevator. He rose, and was wreathed in white vapour . . .

And, for a moment, it was as if he was surrounded by faces once more, staring in on him, avid with curiosity.

But then the vapour cleared, the dreamlike vision dissipated, and he was alone.

'Five minutes to go. Please close the mask of your helmet.'

Gagarin complied and confirmed. He worked through his checklist. 'I am in the preparation regime,' he reported.

'We are in that regime also. Everything on board is correct and we are ready to launch.'

Swallow was a compact little spaceship. It consisted of two modules: a metal sphere, which shrouded Gagarin, and an instrument module, fixed to the base of Gagarin's sphere by tensioning bands.

The instrument module looked like two great pie dishes welded together, bristling with thermal radiation louvres. It was crammed with water, tanks of oxygen and nitrogen, and chemical air scrubbers – equipment which would keep Gagarin alive during his brief flight in space. And beneath that was the big TDU-1 retrorocket system which would be used to return the craft from Earth orbit.

Gagarin's cabin was a cosy spherical nest, lined with green fabric. His ejection seat occupied much of the space. During the descent to Earth inside the sphere, small rockets would hurl Gagarin in his seat out of the craft, and, from seven kilometres above the ground, he would fall by parachute. In case he fell in some uninhabited part of the Earth, the seat contained emergency rations of food and water, radio equipment, and an inflatable dinghy; thus he was cocooned from danger, from the moment he left the pad to the moment he set foot once more on Earth.

There were three small viewing ports recessed into the walls of the cabin, now filled with pure daylight.

At Gagarin's left hand was a console with instruments to regulate temperature and air humidity, and radio equipment. On the wall opposite his face, TV and film cameras peered at him. Below the cameras was a porthole mounted with Gagarin's Vzor optical orientation device, a system of mirrors and optical lattices which would enable him to navigate by the stars, if need be . . .

'Three minutes. There is a faulty valve. It will be fixed. Be patient, Major Gagarin.'

Gagarin smiled. He felt no impatience, or fear.

He reached for his controls, wrapped his gloved hands around them. There was a simple hand controller to his right, which he could use in space to orientate the capsule, if need be. To his left there was an abort switch, which would enable him to be hurled from the capsule if there were some mishap during launch. The controls were solid in his hands, good Soviet engineering. But he was confident he would need neither of these controls, during the launch or his single orbit of Earth.

The systems would work as they should, and his body would not betray him, nor would his mind; his sphere was as snug as a womb, and in less than two hours the adventure would be over, and he would settle like thistledown under his white parachute to the rich soil of Asia. How satisfying it would be, to fall all but naked from the sky, to return to Earth on his own two feet!

'Everything is correct. Two minutes more.'

'I understand,' he said.

At last, he heard motors whining. The elevator gantry was leaning away from the rocket, power cables were ejected from their sockets in the booster's metal flanks, and the access arms were falling back, unfolding around the rocket like the petals of a flower.

Gagarin settled in his contoured seat, and ordered himself to relax.

'Ignition!'

He thought he heard a sigh – of wonder, or anticipation. Perhaps it was the controllers. Perhaps it was himself.

Perhaps not.

* * *

Far below him, sound erupted. No fewer than thirty-two rockets had ignited together: twenty main thrust chambers, a dozen vernier control engines. Hold-down bolts exploded, and Gagarin felt the ship jerk under him.

He could feel vibration but no acceleration; he knew that the rocket had left the ground and was in momentary stasis, balanced on its thrust.

Already, he had left the Earth.

Gagarin whooped. He said: '*Poyekhali!*' – 'Off we go!'

He heard an exultant reply from the control centre, but could make out no words.

Now the rockets' roar engulfed him. Acceleration settled on his chest, mounting rapidly.

Already, he knew, strapped to this ICBM, he was travelling faster than any human in history.

He felt the booster pitch over as it climbed. After two minutes there was a clatter of explosive bolts, a dip in the acceleration. Staging: the four strap-on liquid rocket boosters had been discarded.

He was already more than fifty kilometres high.

Now the main core of the A-1 burnt under him, and as the mass of the ship decreased the acceleration built up, to four, five, six times gravity. But Gagarin was just twenty-seven, fit as an ox, and he could feel how his taut muscles absorbed the punishment easily. He maintained steady reports, and he was proud of the control in his voice.

Cocooned in the artificial light of his cabin, exhilarated and in control, he grinned through the mounting pain.

Swallow's protective shroud cracked open. He could see fragments of ice, shaken free of the hull of the booster; they glittered around the craft like snow.

At five minutes the acceleration died, and Gagarin was hurled forward against his restraints. He heard rattles as the main booster core was discarded. Then came the crisp surge of the 'half stage' which would, at last, carry him to space.

Gagarin felt his speed mount, impossibly rapidly.

Then the final stage died. He was thrown forward again, and he grunted.

The automatic orientation system switched on. *Swallow* locked its sensor on the sun, and swivelled in space; he could feel the movement, as gentle and assured as if he was a child in the womb, carried by his mother's strong muscles, and he knew he was in orbit.

It was done. And, as the ship turned, he could see the skin of Earth, spread out beneath him like a glowing carpet.

'Oh my,' he said. 'Oh my. What a beautiful sight.'

That was when the voices started.

... Much was made of the fact that Yuri Gagarin was an ordinary citizen of the Soviet Union. He was born in the Gzhatsk District of Smolensk and entered secondary school in 1941. But his studies were interrupted by the German invasion. After World War Two Gagarin's family moved back to Gzhatsk, where Yuri resumed his studies. In 1951 he graduated with honours from a vocational school in the town of Lyubersy, near Moscow. He received a foundryman's certificate. He then studied at an industrial technical school in Saratov, on the Volga, from which he graduated with honours in 1955. It was while attending the industrial school that the man who would be the first to fly in space took his first steps in aviation, when he commenced a course of training at the Saratov Aero Club in 1955 ...

Voices – chattering and whispering around the capsule – as if he was dreaming. Was this some artefact of weightlessness, of the radiations of space?

The voices faded.

... And yet this *was* dreamlike, voices or no voices. Here he was falling around the Earth, at a height nobody had approached before. And objects were *drifting* around him in the cabin: papers, a pencil, a small notebook, comical in their ordinariness, pushed this way and that by tugs of air from his life-support fans. This was weightlessness, a sensation no human had experienced before.

Briefly, he was overwhelmed with strangeness.

And yet he felt no ill effects, no disorientation; it was remarkably comfortable, and he knew it would be possible to do good work here, even to build the cities in space of which the designers dreamt.

He would complete a single orbit of the Earth, passing across Siberia, Japan, the tip of South America, and west Africa.

He peered out eagerly, watching Earth as no man had seen it before. There were clouds piled thickly around the equator, reaching up to him. Over the baked heart of the Soviet Union he could see the big squares of the collective farms, and he could distinguish ploughed land from meadows. It would take twenty minutes, of his orbit's ninety, just to cross the vast expanse of his homeland.

The Earth seemed very near, even from two hundred kilometres.

... And again he heard a voice – this time his own, somehow echoing back at him, from somewhere beyond the hull of the spacecraft: *We are peace-loving people and are doing everything for the sake of peace. The Soviet man – be he a geologist, polar explorer, builder of power stations, factories or plants, or space engineer and pilot – is always a seeker*...

The voice, echoing as if around some gigantic museum, faded and vanished.

He felt irritation, mixed with apprehension. Strange voices were not in the flight plan! He had not been trained for this! He had no desire for his mission to be compromised by the unexpected!

The voices could not, of course, have been real. He was cocooned in this little craft like a doll in wood shavings. The padded walls of his cabin were just centimetres from his gloved fingers. Beyond that, there was *nothing*, for hundreds of kilometres...

And yet it was as if, briefly, he had no longer been alone. And still that feeling refused to leave him; suddenly the Vostok seemed small and absurdly fragile – a prison, not a refuge.

As if someone was watching him.

For the first time in the mission, he felt the breath of fear. Perhaps, as the psychologists had warned, the experience of his catapulting launch from the Earth had affected him more deeply than he had anticipated.

He put his uneasiness aside, and fulfilled his duties. He reported the readings of his instruments. He tried to describe what he saw and felt. Weightlessness was 'relaxing', he said. And so it was: with his restraints loosened, floating above his couch, Gagarin felt as if he was flying his favoured MiG-15, low over the birch trees around Star City.

He recorded his observations in a logbook and on tape. His handwriting had not changed – here in space it was just as it had been on Earth, just as he had learnt so long ago in the schools of Klushino – but he had to hold the writing block or it would float away from his hands.

And he maintained his stream of messages, for the people of Earth. '... The present generation will witness how the free and conscious labour of the people of the new socialist society turns even the most daring of mankind's dreams into reality. To reach into space is a historical process which mankind is carrying out in accordance with the laws of natural development...'

Even as he spoke, he studied Earth through his Vzor telescope.

White clouds, curved blue sea: the dominant impression. The clouds' white was so brilliant it hurt his eyes to look at the thickest layers too long, as if a new sun was burning from beneath them, on the surface of the Earth. And the blue was of an extraordinary intensity, somehow hard to study and analyse. The light was so bright it dazzled him, making it impossible to see the stars; thus, the Earth turned, as it always had, beneath a canopy of black sky.

It was easier to look at the land, where the colours were more subtle, greys and browns and faded greens. It seemed as if the green of vegetation was somehow filtered by the layer of air. Cultivated areas seemed to be a dull sage green, while bare earth was a tan brown, deepening to brick red. Cities were bubbly grey, their boundaries blurred. He was struck by the land's flatness, the way it barely seemed to protrude above the ocean's skin ... There was truly little separating land and sea.

But it was hard to be analytical, up here, on the ultimate flight; it was enough simply to watch.

He flew into darkness: the shadow of Earth. Reflections from the cabin lights on the windows made it hard to see out, but still Gagarin could make out the continents outlined by splashes of light, chains of them like street lights along the coasts, and penetrating the interiors along the great river valleys. The chains of human-made light, the orange and yellow-white spider-web challenging the night, were oddly inspiring. But Gagarin was struck by how much of the planet was dark, empty: all of the ocean, of course, save for the tiny, brave lights of ships, and great expanses of desert, jungle and mountain.

Gagarin was struck not so much by Earth's fragility as by its immensity, the smallness of human tenure, and the Vostok, for all the gigantic energy of its launch, was circling the Earth like a fly buzzing an elephant, huddled close to its hide of air.

Over the Pacific's wrinkled skin he saw a dim glow: it was the light of the Moon.

He turned his head, and let his eyes adapt to the new darkness. Soon, for the first time since the launch, he was able to see the stars.

The sky was crowded with stars, he saw; it was something like the sky over the high desert of the Gobi, where he had completed his survival training, the air so thin and dry as to be all but perfectly transparent. Craning to peer through the tiny windows, he sought the constellations, star patterns familiar since his boyhood, but the sky was almost too crowded to make them out . . .

Everywhere, stars were *green*.

The nearby stars, for instance: Alpha Centauri and Sirius and Procyon and Tau Ceti, names from science fiction, the homes of mankind in the ages to come. Green as blades of grass!

He tipped his head this way and that. Everywhere he looked it was the same: stars everywhere had turned to chlorophyll green.

What could this mean?

Yuri Gagarin flew on, alone in the dark of the Earth, peering out of his warm cabin into an unmarked celestial night.

At last he flew towards the sunlight once more. This first cosmonaut dawn was quite sudden: a blue arc, looking perfectly spherical, which suddenly outlined the hidden Earth. The arc thickened, and the first sliver of sun poked above the horizon. The shadows of clouds fled across the ocean towards him, and then the clouds turned to the colour of molten copper, and the lightening ocean was grey as steel, burnished and textured. The horizon brightened, through orange to white, and the colours of life leaked back into the world.

The green stars disappeared.

Space was a stranger place than he had imagined.

He looked down at the Earth. To Gagarin now, the Earth seemed like a huge cave: warm, well lit, but an isolated speck on a black, hostile hillside, within which humanity huddled, telling itself stories to ward off the dark. But Gagarin had ventured outside the cave.

Gagarin wished he could return now, wished his brief journey was even briefer.

He closed his eyes. He sang hymns to the motherland. He saw flashes of light, meteoric streaks sometimes, against the darkness of his eyelid. He knew this must be some radiation effect, the debris of exploded stars perhaps, coursing through him. His soft human flesh was being remade, shaped anew, by space.

So, the minutes wore away.

It would not be long now. He anticipated his return to Earth, when the radio commands from the ground control would order his spaceship to prepare itself. It would orientate in its orbit, and his retrorockets would blaze, slamming him with a full-body blow, forcing him back into his couch. Then would come the brief fall into the atmosphere, the flames around his portholes as the ablative coating of *Swallow* turned to ash, so that he became a manmade comet, streaking across the skies of Africa and Asia. And at last his ejection seat would hurl him from the spent capsule, and from seven thousand metres he would drift to Earth on his parachute – landing at last in the deep spring air, perhaps on the outskirts of some small village, deep in the homeland, such as his own Klushino. The reverie warmed him.

Have you come from outer space?

Yes, he would say. *Yes, I have. Would you believe it? I certainly have . . .*

But the stars, he would have to tell them, are green.

* * *

. . . We can't continue. The anomalies are mounting. The Poyekhali is becoming aware of its situation.

Then we must terminate.

Do you authorize that? I don't have the position to –

Just do it. I will accept the blame.

Again, the voices! He tried to shut them out, to concentrate on his work, as he had been trained and he had rehearsed.

He had no desire to return to Earth a crazy man.

And yet, even if it had to be so – horrible for him, for Valentia! – still his flight would not have been without value, for at least something would have been learnt about the insidious deadliness of space.

He threw himself into his routine of duties once more. The end of the flight was crowding towards him, and he still had items to complete. He monitored his pulse, respiration, appetite and sensations of weightlessness; he transmitted electrocardiograms, pneumograms, electroencephalograms, skin-galvanic measurements and electro-oculograms, made by placing tiny silver electrodes at the corners of his eyes.

He ate a brief meal, a lunch squeezed from tubes stored in a locker set in the wall. He ate not because he was hungry, but because nobody had eaten in space before: Gagarin ate to prove that such normal human activities were possible, here in the mouth of space. He even drifted out of his couch and exercised; he had been given an ingenious regime based on rubber strips, which he could perform without doffing his pressure suit . . .

Again, a noise from outside the craft. Unfamiliar voices, a babble.

Laughter.

Were they laughing at *him*? As if he was some ape in a zoo cage?

And – *Holy Mother*! – a scraping on the hull, as if hands were clambering over it.

The noises of the craft – the steady hum and whir of the instruments, the clatter of busy pumps and fans – all of it stopped, abruptly, as if someone had turned a switch.

Gagarin waited, his breath loud in his ears, the only sound.

The hatch, behind Gagarin's head, scraped open. His ears

popped as pressure changed, and a cold blue light seeped in on him.

There were shadows at the open port.

Not human shadows.

He tried to scream. He must reach for his helmet, try to close it, seek to engage his emergency air supply.

But he could not move.

Hands on his shoulders, cradling his head. Hands, lifting him from the capsule.

Had he landed? Was he dreaming again? A moment ago, it seemed to him, he had been in orbit; and now this. Had something gone wrong? Had he somehow re-entered the atmosphere? Were these peasants from some remote part of the Union, lifting him from his crashed *Swallow*?

But this was not Kazakhstan or any part of the Union, and, whatever these creatures were, they were not peasants.

He was out of the craft now. Faces ringed his vision. They looked like babies, he thought, or perhaps monkeys, with grey skin, oversized heads, huge eyes, and small noses, ears and mouths. He could not even tell if they were men or women.

He closed his eyes. When he opened them, the faces were still there, peering in on him.

He could not read their emotions. But it did seem to him that he found in one of the distorted faces a little more – compassion. Interest, at least . . .

So. Do you think this Poyekhali is conscious of where it is?

It could be. It seems alert. If it is, we have broken the sentience laws . . .

The heads were raised in confrontation.

I won't be held responsible for that. The systems are your accountability.

But it was not I who –

Enough. Recriminations can wait. For now, we must consider – it.

They studied him again.

Perhaps he was, simply, insane.

He had, he realized with dismay, no explanation for this

experience. None, that is, save his own madness, perhaps induced by the radiation of space . . .

The beings, here with him, were floating, as he was.

He was in a room. His Vostok, abandoned, was suspended here, like some huge artefact in a museum. The Vostok looked as fresh as if it had just come out of the assembly rooms at Baikonur, with no re-entry scorching.

He looked beyond his spacecraft.

The room's walls were golden. But the room's shape was distorted, as if he was looking through a wall of curved glass, and so were the people themselves.

They seemed to have difficulty staying in one place. They could pass through the walls of this room at will, like ghosts.

They even passed through his body. He could not move, even when they did this.

They took hold of his arms, and pulled him towards the wall of the room. He looked for his Vostok spacecraft, but he could no longer see it.

He passed into the wall as if it was made of mist; but he had a sense of warmth and softness.

Now he was in a cylindrical room. He was enclosed in a plastic chair with a clear fitted cover. The cover was filled with a warm grey fluid. But there was a tube in his mouth and covering his nose, through which he could breathe cool, clean air. A voice in his mind told him to close his eyes. When he did so he could feel pleasing vibrations, the fluid seemed to whirl around him, and he was fed a sweet substance through the tubes. He felt tranquil and happy. He kept his eyes closed, and he seemed to become one with the fluid.

Later he was moved, within his sac. He was taken through tunnels and elevators from one room to another. The tunnels varied in length, but ended usually with doorways into brightly lit, dome-shaped rooms.

After a time his fluid was drained and he was taken out of the sac. It was uncomfortable and dry and his head hurt. He was pinned to a table. He was naked now, his orange flight suit gone. He did not seem able to resist, or even to help in any way, had he wished.

He was in another room, big and bright.

Though he was not uncomfortable, he found he could not

move, not even close his eyes. He was forced to stare unceasingly up at a ceiling, which glowed with light.

He waited, laid out like a slab of meat in a butcher's shop.

His fear faded. Even his bewilderment receded, failing to overwhelm him. Who were these monkey people? Who were they to treat him like this? . . . But he could not move, so much as a finger.

One of the monkey faces appeared before him. It studied him, with — at least — interest. He wondered if this was the one who, an unmeasurable time before, had beheld him with a trace of compassion.

. . . Do not be afraid.

The wizened mouth did not move, and he could not understand how he heard the words, yet he did.

However, he was *not* afraid.

The being seemed to be hesitating. *Do you know who you are?*

Of course he knew who he was! He was Flight Major Yuri Gagarin! The first man in space!

He remembered the laughter.

He felt anger course through him, dispelling the last of his fear. Who were these people to mock him?

This should not have happened. It has never happened before.

Hands — human, but stretched and distorted — reached towards him. And then withdrew.

It may be you have the entitlement to understand more, before we . . . The sentience laws aren't clear in this situation. Do you know where you are?

He had no answer. If not in orbit, then on Earth, of course. But where? Was this America?

No. Not America. The misshaped head turned.

The ceiling turned to glass.

He could see a sky. But not the sky of Earth. Two stars nestled at the zenith, so close they almost touched, connected by a fat umbilicus of glowing gas. One, the larger, was sky blue; the other, small, fierce and bright, carried hints of emerald.

Around this binary star, a crude spiral of glowing gas had been cast off, and lay sprawled across more distant stars. And before those stars a fainter cloud glowed, bubbles of green light, like pieces of floating forest.

The bubbles were cities in space, and they turned the starlight green.

Gagarin shrank within himself. Was he seeing the future of man? How far had he come from Earth? A thousand light years? More? He was, he realized, very far from home . . .

And yet, in his awe and wonder, he remembered the laughter. Had he been brought back from the dead to be mocked?

No. Listen.

Voices, booming around him:

. . . Yuri Gagarin, Hero of the Soviet Union, would never again fly in space. There have been many monuments to him.

His ashes were to be buried in the wall of the Kremlin, an enduring mark of his prestige. He would be commemorated by statues, in the cosmonauts' training ground at Star City, and another on a pillar overlooking a Moscow street called Leninski Prospect.

The cosmonauts would remember him in their own way, by aping the actions he took on his final day: on each mission they would watch the film he saw the night before his flight – White Sun in the Desert *– they would sign the doors of their rooms as he did, they would even pause in their bus transports to the booster rockets to climb outside to urinate, as he did.*

The site where Gagarin crashed his MiG-15 became a shrine, with a memorial and a tablet recording his life. And every spring, the people who looked after this shrine would trim the tops of the trees along the angle of his crashing plane, so that it was possible to stand by his memorial and look up and see through the gap to the sky . . .

Mankind has covered the galaxy. But nowhere away from the Earth has life been found, beyond simple one-celled creatures.

When Yuri Gagarin was born, Earth was one little world holding all the life there was, to all intents and purposes. And it would have stayed that way if Gagarin and his generation – Americans and Russians – had not risked their lives to enter space in their converted ICBMs and primitive little capsules.

The destiny of all life, for ever, was in their hands. And they never knew it. It probably would have terrified them if they had known.

For if they had failed – if they had turned back from space, if war had come and they had turned themselves to piles of radioactive ash – there might now, in this future age, be no life, no mind, anywhere. For every human alive in 1961, there are now billions – perhaps tens of billions. Gagarin's simple flight in his Vostok spaceship was perhaps the most important event in the history of mankind, our greatest wonder of all . . .

The monkey face, looking in at him. Perhaps, he thought, it might once have been human. *Do you understand what is being said? This is what we tell people. It is what this – monument – is for. Every day, Gagarin flies again.*

You see that Gagarin will never be forgotten. Gagarin's actions, heroic and trivial, continue to haunt our present.

Emotions swirled in him: pride, terror, awe, loneliness.

He tried to understand how this might have been done. Had they stolen his ashes from the wall of the Kremlin, somehow recombined them to –

No. Not that.

Then what? And what of Valentia, Yelena, Galya? Were they buried under dust millennia deep?

. . . Enough. It is time to rest.

To rest . . . And when he woke? What would become of Yuri Gagarin, in this impossible year? Would he be placed in a zoo, like an ape man?

But you are not Gagarin.

. . . And now, as he tried to comprehend that, for long seconds his mind was empty of thought.

But his memories – his wife and daughters, the thrust of the booster, the sweet air of the steppe – were so real. How could it be so?

You should never have become aware of this.

Oddly, he felt tempted to apologize.

There have been more than three thousand of you before without mishap – in fact, you are Poyekhali 3201 . . .

His name. At least he had learnt his name.

Think of it this way. Gagarin's mission lasted a single orbit of the Earth. As long as was necessary to complete its purpose.

And so, his life –

... is as long as is necessary for its purpose. We face significant penalties for this malfunction, in fact. Our laws are intended to protect you, not us. But that is our problem, not yours. You will feel no pain. That is a comfort to me. Relax, now.

There was a fringe of darkness around his vision, like the mouth of a cave, receding from him. It was like the blue face of Earth, as he had seen it from orbit. And in that cave mouth he saw the faces of his wife and daughters turned up to him, diminishing. He tried to fix their faces in his mind, his daughters, his father, but it was as if his mind was a candle, his thoughts guttering, dissolving.

It seemed very rapid. It was not fair. His mission had been stolen from him!

He cried out, once, before the blackness closed around him.

... And now, it was as if the dream continued. Suddenly it was sunrise, and he was standing at the launch pad in his bright orange flight suit with its heavy white helmet, emblazoned 'CCCP' in bright red.

He breathed in the fresh air of a bright spring morning. Beyond the pad, the flat Kazakhstan steppe had erupted into its brief bloom, with evanescent flowers pushing through the hardy grass.

Yuri Gagarin felt his heart lift.

Technicians and engineers surrounded him. All around him he saw faces: faces turned to *him*, faces shining with awe. Even the *zeks* had been allowed to see him today, to see the past separate from the future.

Gagarin smiled on them all.

And they smiled back, as Poyekhali 3202 prepared to speak the familiar words for them.

King's Chamber

By Dominic Green

'It was the Common Dream again last night,' said the student.

God Is Gracious groaned inwardly. Not another twenty measures of Reverie wasted just so a sophomore Canon Lawyer could dream stuff God Is Gracious himself could dream with his eyes closed. He reached into the desk drawer and took out the Common Dream form.

'What was the colour of the sky?'

'I dunno. Sky-coloured. What other colour could it be?'

'Underfoot?'

'Sand.'

'Moons?' God Is Gracious had already written down 'One'.

'One.'

'Weather?' It would be 'fine'. Otherwise 'underfoot' would have been 'mud' rather than 'sand'. The Dream was consistent.

'Fine.'

'Penetration?'

'The Sarcophagus Chamber.'

God Is Gracious spy-hopped one eye round curiously on to the student. Maybe this one was one to watch.

'How many steps at the entrance to the Chamber?' he asked slyly.

The student responded without hesitating. 'No steps. A traffic ramp, like in an Ancient city.'

Definitely one to watch, thought God Is Gracious. There was no way he could have known that. The Chamber Ramp was a closely guarded Priesthood secret. Students had been observed to lie before, however, in order to get access to test fees and supplement their meagre stipends at the city seminaries.

'And what was in the Sarcophagus?'

The student replied with the correct shocked morality. 'Why, nothing, of course.'

God Is Gracious held the form above his head and blew on it to dry it. As he blew, he talked to the student through his mouth. 'Good and honest work, God Look Not So Fierce Upon Me. The usual experimental fees will be forwarded to your account in the morning.' He nodded towards the shadow at the outer office window. 'Please show in the next volunteer on your way out.'

The student fidgeted in his chair. 'Please, master – that's not One Of Us. That's a Slavey.'

God Is Gracious modulated his skin colour to jet black. 'That phrase may be popular in certain circles at the moment, God Look Not So Fierce, but it is not to be used in this office.'

The student went white and withdrew hurriedly – leaving, God Is Gracious noted with distaste, a small pool of sepia on the chair.

How transparently we betray our evolutionary origins, he sighed.

The cause of the trouble now stood in the doorway, though God Is Gracious hadn't heard it come in. When it spoke, it spoke in gigantic clumsy blocks of sound – easy to imitate, since God Is Gracious could speak to his refectory table and get it to speak its exact location back, but as long-winded as sending binary code using a foghorn. Furthermore, the creature didn't alter the colour of its skin with its emotions as it spoke, and would therefore be able to lie more effectively. Hideous it was, with two eyes on the front of its face like a bottom-feeder, a blowhole directly beneath them where a blowhole was no use at all, and two hands full of spidery unwebbed fingers. And God Is Gracious knew that it needed to be covered in hair in the cold northern latitudes where it lived, but did it need to look quite so much like a carpet of threadworms on a week-dead corpse?

It held out a hairy hand. 'Pleased to meet you. Moo-Quack, of the family of Moo-Quack, in the Northern Expanses.' It sounded like Moo-Quack, anyway. Arboreal names all sounded like the grunting of beasts. And where were the Northern Expanses?

It jerked its head at the back of the departing student. 'Common Dream?' God Is Gracious nodded, a painful manoeuvre and one that he was certain was bad for the brain, but one that he felt would put the invader at its ease.

'How many Primordial Rings and Moons were in the sky?' said the newcomer. 'Don't tell me, let me guess: zero, none, zilch, null. Don't you Church worthies ever stop looking for prehistoric celestial bodies that are never going to exist?'

God Is Gracious vibrated alternate ribbons of black and purple back at the stranger, a thing he would not normally do to a stranger of his own race for fear of being gored in challenge; but it calmed his impulses to grab the stranger and rend him into gobbets of blood-weeping flesh, and the stranger would not understand the gesture.

'Very pretty,' said Moo-Quack of Moo-Quack. 'But I expected a better reaction from a fellow scholar than an Attack Warning posture when I referred to the subject he'd chosen as his field.' It looked round questioningly at the hypnological cladograms that lined the walls. 'You *are* Perfect God is Gracious Breathewater of the Kingscoming Seminary?' It even squinted out of the window, as if unsure it was in the right diocese. 'Author of *The Archaeology of Dreams*? *The Prehistory of the Subconscious*? Originator of the widely discredited theory of Archetypal Evolution?'

God Is Gracious glowed a faint hubristic sulphur before he reconsidered and turned himself a businesslike brown. 'You're familiar with my work?'

'Perhaps I'd better reintroduce myself,' said the stranger. 'Moo-Quack of Moo-Quack, originator of the widely discredited theory of the Mutual Ancestor.' It extended its hand again, as if the wretched thing were valuable.

'And fabricator of the evidence for his theory, as I recall,' said God Is Gracious sharply, fighting the urge to grab the hand and crush it in claws that were capable of opening clam shells.

The creature nodded rapidly, a gesture that God Is Gracious was sure should snap its inadequate neck and make its head fall off. 'Guilty, I am afraid. The oviparous nature of your species did for me.'

'You fabricated evidence to indicate that the Ancients came from space and that the ziggurats on the Stopover Islands were constructed by interstellar visitors who created our race and yours from the same evolutionary stock,' said God Is Gracious, eyeing the thing's evolutionary stock with disapproval.

Moo-Quack continued to nod eagerly, but his head remained disappointingly in place. 'Using lithopaedia extracted from miscarried Human mothers, yes. Naturally fossilized, you see. The mother miscarries, and the foetus lodges in the gut due to an injury, and continues to grow for a time before it dies and calcifies into a very convincing Alien Precursor Of The Human Race. Unfortunately, it wasn't possible to obtain fossilized juvenile specimens of you egg-laying folk, and when I used worked-over lithopaedia of my own species to try to Jenny-Haniver myself a Beautiful Person, I was caught out by one of your Sentient Physiologists. I'll be the first to admit that my methods were suspect. But my motives were sound.'

'Sound? How can deliberately falsifying your experimental results be sound?'

'Perfect, you know as well as I do that your government detonated a light-element fusion device in the backwoods of Walkwater Island not five days ago. You also know as well as I do that this Evolutionary hokum of yours doesn't hold water. So now that both our species possess the capability to annihilate each other as comprehensively as the Ancients ever did, don't we need to prove once and for all that *someone* came from the stars, and created your and my grandparents? And that my great-great-grand-ancestor didn't create yours, and vice versa? And the only way to do that is by peaceful, non-military research into the Common Dream.'

God Is Gracious blinked with all eight of his eyelids. Now he was certain that his visitor was insane. 'I don't do Common Dream research. My research hinges around the premise that creatures that have *evolved* different nervous systems to others will dream in a different manner. I study the differences between the complex symbolic dreams which *we civilized* people have – and, uh, of course, *you* civilized people have as well – and the simple fluctuations of brainwaves which occur in the nervous systems of humble invertebrates. Yes, the Common Dream is absolutely identical to both our races – and this is the surest proof that the Common Dream must be considered separately as an emanation from the Almighty.

Every experimental datum this laboratory has gathered from parallel studies between members of our and your species indicates however, that *all* our other dreams are different.' He glowed a pleasant shade of fuchsia in an attempt to communicate cosmopolitan reasonability. Out of the corners of two eyes, however, he could still see, through the window, the giant protest signs made out of sleeping-parasols draped over the avant-garde quarter of the seminary ziggurat, proclaiming !!!!EVOLUTIONISM OUTDATED!!!! in letters a tall man high.

The creature closed its mouth, concealing its teeth, which God Is Gracious knew from his xenopsychology to be a *faux ami*.

'That's right. Deny the issue. Use God to take out the only bit of the world that doesn't suit your theories. Evolution happens to fit your religious prejudices of struggle from the dirt towards the divine, so you blind yourself to the undeniable fact that *neither* of our two species are remotely like any other creature on this planet. Oh, we can irradiate ourselves some new forms of insects with one too many wings and dredge up some slightly different specimens of marine worm, but we will never, ever find a creature that is like a man. Maybe evolution happened somewhere, on some other planet. But not here. The heresy fits, Perfect, so nail yourself into the iron coffin with us and burn.'

'The Primordial Moon caused terrific tides in the protoequatorial continent where our Beautiful Race developed,' said God Is Gracious, beginning to quote the standard heresy refutation prescribed for such occasions. 'We evolved from Amphibious species inhabiting large estuarine forests, climbing into the branches to forage at night-time and burrowing into low-tide mud during the day, relying on our parallel lungs for oxygen when the water could not furnish it. You Arboreal folk, on the other hand, evolved from land-dwelling creatures which lived in the trees perpetually. The Common Dream's Firmament does not necessarily represent the prehistoric heavens –'

'– Because it doesn't show the Primordial Moon your Church astronomers are looking for,' chimed in the thing that called itself Moo-Quack happily. 'Or the Primordial Ring the

Primordial Moon is supposed to have produced when it smashed into a million moonlets. But the stars are all correct. Perfect. All the constellations in the Dream can be traced back to a date only a few years from the dates obtained from radioisotopes found in fusion craters in every ruined Ancient city in our two continents. To one day one hundred thousand years before the present.'

'Or one thousand and one hundred thousand years before,' said God Is Gracious, 'as I'm sure you know very well already. The stars revolve about the galaxy, and will therefore reform into exactly the same constellations given time. The Dream-Sky we are witnessing could therefore exist at any point before or after the inception of sentient evolution for either the Beautiful Race or the, um, Human one –'

Moo-Quack uttered a sentiment referring to its race's peculiarly fetid and sulphurous excrement – an insult lost on God Is Gracious, whose species prided themselves on the businesslike, inoffensive tubularity of their stools – and followed this with, 'Stars are thrown round the galaxy like grains of sand in a windstorm, not perfectly choreographed performers in some divinely appointed ballet. Look, I know you Primordial Lunatics have the very best motives for your madness, but you're mad nevertheless. Bilateral Creationism is the only way to follow if we're to stop the Unilaterals from getting into the state assemblies on either of our two continents. Did you know Howl-Gurgle of the North West Inhospitable Islands is already advocating bombing your cities before your nation closes the Super-Heavy Intercontinental Ballistic Atom Destructor Gap? After all, he says, if our ancestors created you Amphibians, we can do what we like with our property.' The final word was almost spat out, as if the alien disapproved of it. The creature advanced on God Is Gracious's window, and the window jumped up in the sash. 'Look out here, at the very foundations of this Seminary! Solid vitrified stone, a hundred millennia old! You built all your most important buildings on Ancient foundations, just as we did!' It picked up the Ancient paperweight – a weapon or utensil, made of an induplicable alloy – that held down God Is Gracious's papers, and in the wind from the opened window the papers fluttered all over the office like nectar-seeking insects. 'See how my hand fits the handle, as does yours! Both our races fit every handle, corridor and hatchway in the Ancients' cities so well that no scholar from either of our species has ever been able to claim those cities indisputably for his own species. Is it likely that two separate bipedal species could evolve on two separate continents on the same planet simultaneously, with such similar rates of technological progress as to have developed the same means of destroying the civilized world in exactly the same decade?'

'The reason for both our races' evolution to sentience,' evangelized God Is Gracious patiently, 'lies in the same event – that huge primordial moon broke up after it approached too closely to the Gramercy Limit of this planet, bringing an end to the great tidal seas and producing a hail of fiery planetoids which razed the forests which your people had inhabited. You were forced thereby to come down from the trees – we were forced to come ashore. *This* is the reason why both of our peoples have evolved at similar rates.'

'Yet there is no fossil ancestor on any continent for either of our races,' scoffed Moo-Quack of Moo-Quack.

God Is Gracious paled, despite himself. 'Evidently the catastrophe that destroyed the Ancient Beautiful or – harrumph – Human Civilization must also have destroyed many fossil taxa.'

Moo-Quack shook his head. 'All taxa known to us are present both before and after the catastrophe – assuming, of course, that we've dated the catastrophe effectively.'

'That's a big if!' rallied God Is Gracious, throwing in an Arboreal idiom that made him feel quite the cosmopolitan orator.

'Plutonium decay,' said Moo-Quack quietly, 'is a particularly effective method of dating. And there is neither Primordial Moon nor Ring in the Common Dream's sky. We were created, Perfect! Whether by your absent God in the Sarcophagus, or by some more mundane agency.'

'Convergent evolution,' countered God is Gracious swiftly. 'The Common Dream itself –'

'Is exactly the same for both races, down to the smallest brick and dust mote. It was built into our brains to tell us where we came from. And it is a dream neither of mud flat nor of forest. It's a desert. It's a hard, cold, rocky place where nothing grows and neither of our races belongs. *We didn't build it, Perfect.* Someone else did. Someone who liked cold, and dark, and desolation.' The man sounded almost as if he were pleading, rather than arguing an academic point. 'What do *you* think the Common Dream represents, Perfect? Let's just imagine there were no God, no self-bettering struggle, and just the Dream itself. What would your *scientific* explanation for it be?'

Fascinated by the idea, God Is Gracious glowed a guilty turquoise, like a school juvenile discussing pupation.

'I don't know. I would suppose that it was beamed into men's minds, like a television broadcast. By – well, not God, if I'm not allowed God. Perhaps a devil of some description, trying to draw us from the path of Evolutionism into Creationist heresy –'

'Cop-out! No God, so no Devils either!'

'Oh, extraterrestrials, then. Extraterrestrials, or a hostile foreign government –' here he fixed all four of his eyes on Moo-Quack '– or a deceased popular musician, as I have heard some of *your* people believe,' he added sardonically.

'At last,' said Moo-Quack. 'Now we're getting somewhere. So someone is doing this, and has been doing it for millennia, whether by beaming the damn thing into our minds, or by having hard-coded it into our heads when we were first created. The next logical question, after who, is why? Why a deserted pyramid tomb that every one out of a thousand million of us can commune with every night, trudging to the centre of the maze only to find that God is not at home in the sarcophagus? Why?'

'Now *you* have introduced God, Mr Moo-Quack. As you can see, He has a habit of appearing uninvited in the most atheistic of disputes.'

'No!' said Moo-Quack, leaning across the table in the most crude of attack postures. 'There is no King in the coffin in the Sarcophagus Chamber, *because it is all a fraud*, a feint, a fakery designed to conceal the fact that there is a *second* Sarcophagus Chamber concealed within the maze – one which all our dream researchers using the most modern narcotics have as yet been unable to find. If you design a primitive stone tomb to conceal the body of a monarch, surely the safest way to prevent that tomb's robbery is to make the robber think another robber has already been there before him and stolen all the silver.'

God Is Gracious settled back into his seat, steeling himself to remain a patient khaki. His hand depressed the lever underneath the table that summoned the Seminary concierges to defend him against homicidal Creationist students. 'No thief can steal silver from a dream.'

'Ah! But there are things of greater worth than silver,' said Moo-Quack, appearing to stare at some unsettling vision of his own. He bustled round God Is Gracious's desk to the hardwood-fasciaed Electronic Brain, the pride of the Faculty, now sitting working out the statistical divergences between a thousand-subject cross-section of the dreams of the Capital's population.

'This machine,' said Moo-Quack, 'might carry an encrypted file. A military file, perhaps, or one containing sensitive commercial information –'

'I assure you that my machine has no such secrets on it, if such is your objective,' said God Is Gracious. 'However, it is extremely valuable. Please leave it alone.'

'An encrypted file!' repeated Moo-Quack. 'Immensely valuable to the person who can decode it, yet gibberish, mere background babble, to men who do not have the Key, like sand blowing in a windstorm, or the flickering of torchlight on a mausoleum wall. Inside the Common Dream, Perfect, could be contained the information necessary for the next stage of development of both our Beautiful Human species, and *we would never know*! Inside the Second Sarcophagus chamber that your superior somnological technology could gain access to, if you would only dare to research the unresearchable. I can help you in your heresy, Perfect. I have certain essential equipment not a hundred miles from here in your city of Godsire. If you could arrange for the urgent transportation of this equipment to a remote location – its current state is highly volatile, and it will require movement within the next two hours – we may begin a programme of international enquiry into the Common Dream –'

God Is Gracious could hear the running bootsteps of the

Concierges. So, as soon as the import of the clattering of shoe leather on wood dawned on his preoccupied mind, did the Arboreal. He turned a glance on God Is Gracious, which the latter somehow knew to be sad, despite the continued pinkness of the Arboreal's skin.

'You aren't the only people looking for it,' he said. 'And those who are looking for it in other places are looking for other reasons. And if they find omnipotence, they may not wish to share it with a race of hole-headed four-eyed human kaleidoscopes.'

God Is Gracious went rainbow-hued with confusion. He scrabbled under the desk for the cudgel he normally employed to beat off broody wild females blown into the Seminary precincts from offshore. When he looked up, the hairy corpse was gone.

It was a pleasant afternoon, and God Is Gracious found his attention wandering. Three of his highly similar but nonidentical species of marine worms had had nightmares during the afternoon. The 'scorpion-nightmare', as the students called it, left a nervous wave form similar to the wave obtained from confronting a waking worm with a particularly venomous form of aquatic invertebrate. As he ticked and commented his way through the day's results, he felt oddly as if he were marking the work of his worms. Worms wearing white sashes with palmprint emblems, waving banners saying !!!EVOLUTIONISM OUTDATED!!! and !!!RUSTICATE GOD IS GRACIOUS NOW!!!, marching in circles round a huge, triangular shadow in fog, a shape that cut a quarter from the moon; a shape that, as the marching student faces deliquesced and dissolved, God Is Gracious recognized.

Please, no, not the Common Dream . . . even the wave form of a water scorpion would be preferable to something so passé . . .

Passé, like the sand sounds of a thousand centuries hissing down the glass . . .

The sand drifted into his face, and he could taste its pedigree. Sand scoured from unreal walls older than recorded Amphibian time. Sand first laid by unimaginable hands as mortar for blocks too large for a man to lay his entire dreaming body flat across. The blocks stood in front of him, so numerous that they were a texture rather than a pattern.

He looked down into the sand. There would be no footprints. The Dream was each dreamer's private experience. The sand would be blank, between him and the pyramid whose apex was the single mocking moon. No Primordial Moon up there beside it, and no world-circling Ring.

Men had come into this closed universe – geologist men, astronomer men, meteorologist men – bearing dream-replicas of the instruments of measurement they were most familiar with in the courses of their waking lives; hypnonauts taught carefully to wake up in the middle of their dreams and function as normally as the dream permitted. What had they discovered? Nonsense. The Dream-World was made of graphite. Its atmosphere was pure nitrous oxide. It was as if some unnamed architect were laughing at the feeble efforts of mortals to understand his creation.

And yet, as God Is Gracious's eyes hit bottom, he could see in the sand before him the clear imprint of a five-toed foot.

The print was unwebbed, with a heavy-bodied heel that could be retracted to make the ball of the foot the only running surface.

The print of an Arboreal.

That's not possible, the Dream is private, no other mind may enter –

'– INITIAL REPORTS INDICATE CASUALTIES MAY BE IN THE HUNDRED THOUSANDS. UNOFFICIAL SOURCES HAVE CLAIMED THE PERCENTAGE OF FATAL CASUALTIES AT THE EPICENTRE TO BE CLOSE TO ONE HUNDRED –'

Ignominy! How could he be woken before he had even set foot on the downward slope?

'– THE CATACLYSM APPEARS TO HAVE LEFT BUILDINGS AND EVEN WINDOWS UNDAMAGED. MILITARY SPOKESPERSONS DENY THAT THIS IS ONE OF OUR OWN NATION'S SECRET WEAPONS UNLEASHED BY ACCIDENT. IT IS NOT YET CLEAR WHETHER THIS COULD HAVE BEEN AN ENEMY

ATTACK BY ARBOREAL FORCES. SOLDIERS IN GAY AND BRIGHTLY COLOURED CHEMICAL-WARFARE CLOTHING HAVE BEEN SEEN ON DUTY IN ALL OUR COASTAL CITIES –'

He was awake. It was warm. The window hanging had drifted across his face. The television in the corner of the room was flashing an agonized vermilion and demanding his attention.

'CITIZENS WITH RELATIVES IN THE PURPLEPORT, GODSIRE OR MUDBORN DIOCESES ARE URGED TO REMAIN CALM AND CONTACT OFFICIAL MASS GRAVE SUPERVISORS ON THE FOLLOWING NUMBERS: FOR GODSIRE, 993827151 –'

God Is Gracious opened his underwater eyes as well as his super-surface ones. The pictures on the television, modulated as they were according to the newsreader's emotions by a skilled team of chromo-faders, were the colour of Arboreal blood, but showed blue rivers of the Amphibian item.

'– EXTERNAL WOUNDS ON THE VICTIMS ARE RARE EXCEPT WHERE SELF-INFLICTED, BUT INTERNAL HAEMORRHAGING IS PREVALENT AROUND THE AMPULLAE, BLOWHOLE AND MOUTH –'

He could put a place to the pictures on the screen. It was Godsire. A small port city, not a day's drive north of here, of no use to anyone save fishermen, submariners and under-inspired poets. Now it was full of poetic submersible piscatorial bodies. Horrible, twisted bodies, bleeding from every hole God had put in their heads, and a few more they'd made themselves.

'– ONLY ONE INDIVIDUAL IS CURRENTLY KNOWN TO HAVE SURVIVED AT WHAT MAY BE THE EPICENTRE OF THE DISASTER: A FOREIGNER OF NON-BEAUTIFUL SPECIES, DISCOVERED UNABLE TO COMMUNICATE BY EMERGENCY UNITS IN WORDS-ECHO AIR TERMINAL, CENTRAL GODSIRE –'

The TV image rested on one of the bodies that was not quite dead, being kicked judiciously by heavily rubberized emergency troops who were obviously attempting to ascertain whether it could communicate. For a moment, the creature's face lolled in front of the television camera before a military palm went over the lens. The colours of the Clan Paisley the thing wore were as distinctive as the pattern of a snowflake.

Moo-Quack of Moo-Quack.

God Is Gracious leant across his desk and activated the phone.

'Hello? Operator? Get me the Secular Arm of the Military, right away.'

'We're in trouble,' said the general. 'Twenty-five of our coastal cities have already been aggressed in as many hours. The effectiveness of each attack is approximately equal to that of our latest city-erasing Retaliatory Doomsday Weapon, exterminating minds whilst leaving buildings and even bodies virtually intact for capture by the enemy.' He went green, orange and purple with envy. 'If God would only give us such a weapon!'

'Did our deep-level mudwallows offer any protection?'

The general gave off a magnolia pulse of denial. 'Even the crew of a hardened military submersible cruising underwater off Mudborn when the attack on that city occurred were affected. All the crew in the aft sections died of cerebral haemorrhages; the remainder are in a field hospital undergoing exploratory vivisection. It is what they would have wanted.'

The room was a stone-walled cube whose walls gave off no echo indicating any adjoining chamber. God Is Gracious had no idea of the room's location, and was glad he had. If he didn't know, the chances were the enemy didn't either. However, twenty-two hours in military custody, plus a two-hour ride by experimental rocket aircraft with a bag over his head, were beginning to take their toll. He had been told that the bag was more to protect his own personal hygiene than the security of his destination, since all back-seat passengers in the high-speed test planes vomited copiously for the first few hundred flights.

'We have investigated the current attack pattern, Perfect, and it does indeed seem to be true that one lone Arboreal is discovered at the centre of each site – not dead, but in a vegetative mental state.'

God Is Gracious withdrew his eyes in fear. 'He was a human weapon. A conscientious objector. He was trying to get me to remove him from the city before he activated.'

The Military Intelligence chaplain to the left of God Is Gracious trilled, 'Or trying to get our major military expert into the city so that he too could be annihilated.'

Is that what I am now? thought God Is Gracious. A military expert? Lord God, save me from swearing. I spend my working days coupling electrodes to crabs.

'Besides,' the chaplain continued, 'how is it possible that you could have seen the man in Kingscoming, one hour before he was found in Godsire? I might add that no sighting of any alien was reported on public transit systems between Godsire and Kingscoming on that date, to say nothing of the fact that he would have had to have possessed a supersonic aircraft capable of performing an undetected vertical takeoff and landing at one of our major air terminals without being seen on our radar to cover the distance in the time allowed –'

'The prisoner was discovered in a near-fatal state of chloral hydrate overdose,' interrupted God's Bright Gift, the military surgeon. 'It is the opinion of the examining team that he had not been capable of movement for some time. His pockets were stuffed with proprietary sleeping medicines, which he appeared to have purchased at the terminal. The implication seems to be that he had been attempting to keep himself asleep for as long as possible.'

'In a dreaming state,' said God Is Gracious. 'And when he wakes up, the bomb goes off.'

The surgeon nodded. 'It's likely he was intended to be the vanguard weapon, the first shot of the volley. Godsire is, after all, the headquarters of our "Divine Selection"-class nuclear submarines. However, he kept himself asleep long enough to contact you by –' he purpled in embarrassment as he said the T word – 'telepathy.'

'So they're attacking us with telepaths?' said the general, playing with his military desk ornament in an out-of-his-depth manner.

'The Intelligence Function has, of course, suspected that they had a major telepathic weapon for some time,' lied the Intelligence chaplain, 'since certain of their research facilities in the Whiteheights Range began to consume more political prisoners than usual. We were unable to learn more as all end-product bodies were incinerated.'

The general waxed black. 'Why was the General Staff not told of these developments?'

The chaplain kept his khaki. 'If I had come to you one year ago, telling you that the Slavies had a weapon of pure thought portable inside the Human Head that one man could use to kill a million, would you have believed me, sir?'

The general snorted, but couldn't find a more concrete expression for his dissent. The chaplain continued. 'The dead – harrumph – man was an Arboreal military fanatic posing highly convincingly as a discredited scholar. His Clan Paisley has been on file with us for some time.'

The surgeon flashed yellow. 'It is unlikely that the incapacitated Arboreal was as highly trained as Intelligence considers. We have analysed the blood type of every one of our nation's telepathic attackers, and discovered them all to belong to an isolated group from the Northern Expanses of Arborea. At least three of the invaders, furthermore, have been positively identified as members of the Moo-Quack clan, all of whose members within the Arboreal Human Republic were twelve years ago deleted from public census records with suspicious haste within the space of three days.' He produced a yellowed sheaf of papers and a parallel translation in Amphibian. 'The Moo-Quack clan was declared an Ideological Plague Zone in this fifth-month edition of the official Arboreal government proscription bulletin, in which members of the clan were imaginatively accused of injecting venereally infected human semen into processed offal under the influence of an unnamed Foreign Power which had issued them coded instructions contained in evolutionary religious radio broadcasts. This despicable lackadaisical attitude to public health had, the writer of the piece goes on to say, obviously been responsible for a recent spate of deaths from painful Infarcts of the Head in the Hissingwhine neighbourhood. Far from being the usual hysterical denunciation, however, this appears to have been a rare genuine instance of an Arboreal government scapegoat-finding committee actually finding the real culprits in a case. This officer quotes from a Northern Expanses public information imprint of a month earlier: "Lo! It is bruited that in the seventh month of this ninety-ninth Penultimate Centennial Year of the Bright New Way, an Agricultural Commensality in our beloved Northern Expanses was visited by Unknown Peril. The Happy Artisan Ecocollective of Hissingwhine was discovered to have been wiped out to a citizen by fatal Congestions of the Brain. The sole survivors of the catastrophe, two Junior Citizens of the Moo-Quack ilk, were found directly in the centre of the devastation, had been stricken mad, and could only rave of being 'sorry for having crept into God's coffin'. The State rejoices that weaker members of our Commensality have been pared from its ranks by Nature's Blade, but urges citizen-doctors to be vigilant lest strong ears be mown from the field by epidemiological incompetence only, and through no fault of their own." This was, gentlemen, at about the same time that "demon-dream" reports began circulating among our own populace, if you will recall.'

'Sightings of two-eyed hairy-headed creatures in one's Common Dream,' shuddered the general. 'Such a dream could give one nightmares.'

'The secular physicians of our Empire's glorious Army humbly submit that our Enemies merely capitalized on the birth of a family of naturally evolved telepaths within their borders,' concluded the surgeon.

'And might I ask what leads a physician loyal to his species to possess so many documents written in an alien tongue?' chided the Intelligence chaplain jealously.

'Bacteriological research,' said the surgeon. 'An organism as contagious and universally fatal as that which appeared to have ravaged Hissingwhine would, had it been an organism, have necessitated the most intense interest from our own physicians, particularly if it had proven capable of crossing the species barrier into Real People. Besides, a rocketful of these organisms, if acquired, would have proven an inestimable asset to our Long Range Strategic Threat. To summarize: the Moo-Quack name no longer exists in the Arboreal Republic, though some years ago it was a name well, if jokingly, known among doctors (and particularly anatomists) even of our own species. In his youth, the Moo-Quack had been published widely both in his intellectual circles and in ours; however, two years after the publication of his first monograph, his name existed only in our own texts, simply because, after the series of incidents at Hissingwhine, the entire Moo-Quack breeding group was located and removed to the Whiteheights Range by Census Bureau employees, and all other trace of their present or past existence erased. Only now, twelve years later, do we become aware of the reason for his extended sabbatical.'

'No wonder he was an unwilling weapon,' mused the general. 'His entire family, held captive. Being honed into city-killers. Possibly being forced –' he shuddered '– to breed with one another.'

The surgeon nodded in the manner of an Arboreal. 'With their natural telepathic talents being amplified by whatever hideous processes an ungodly science could bring to bear.'

The general became an angry darkness within which beads of perspiration twinkled like stars. 'Fools! We, too, have weapons with which cities may be destroyed. A vast embarrassment of weapons, enough to pave their entire continent with transuranics.'

Things are getting out of hand here, thought Moo-Quack. I can tell.

'Regrettably, it may well be necessary to take advantage of our superiority,' gloated the general. 'However, we must first attempt to minimize our losses by understanding this new weapon the Slavies are using on us, which is why *you*, Perfect, have been flown here. This Slavey turncoat made pointed comments to you concerning military research into dreaming, yes?'

'Into the Common Dream specifically, yes, General.'

'Well,' said the general, 'it hardly comes as a surprise that it was the Common Dream they were researching, does it?'

God Is Gracious looked blankly at the general. 'Say again, sir?'

'Haven't you had a nap recently, man?' said the general. 'Where have you been for the last twenty-four hours?'

'Awake,' said God Is Gracious pointedly. 'Why? What did I miss?'

The general, the chaplain and the field surgeon all looked at one another.

'Thousands of Arboreal telepaths, trespassing in everyone's Common Dream,' said the surgeon.

'A legion of uniformed Slavey soldiers tramping down the hill toward the Pyramid Tomb, bold as berserkers,' said the general. 'I see the hairy little copulators every time I close my eyes.'

'Not even our finest military telepaths have been able to enter the building,' said the chaplain. 'Arboreal hypno-commandos have secured the area and are defending it against all comers, shooting our men awake on sight. Those of our telepaths who were inside the building when it was taken indicate that the Arboreals' objective seems to be the Sarcophagus Maze.'

'If there's a second chamber in the maze,' said the surgeon quietly, 'it would seem they've found it.'

Cradle-shaker number three wasn't working. Its occupant was snoring, sleeping like an elasmobranch in an oxygenated current. God Is Gracious sidled up to the occupant and slapped the sole of his boot until his eyes started to flicker. Healthy nightmare wave forms started to march across his EEG. He began to twitch like any worm being pursued by a water scorpion. Further up the room, one of the test volunteers sat up, every eyelid opened, snorting; quick-acting Force Leaders grabbed him and pushed him back into the dream cradle, administering soporific injections in his arms.

'Common Dream!' announced a Force Leader from the end of the laboratory, hoisting a still half-awake dreamer aloft and worrying him into alertness. 'Report dream, soldier!'

'Guh!' reported the dreamer, rubbing his eyes.

'Underfoot?'

'Uhhh, sand.'

'Number of moons!'

'One.'

'Footprints?' said God Is Gracious.

'Footprints?' parroted the soldier, as if God Is Gracious were suggesting a blasphemy, which he was; then, recollection began to dawn. 'Footprints, yes! Footprints! Feet! People on the ends of feet! A Slavey procession filing into the Pyramid Tomb!'

God Is Gracious nodded with an air of bored foreknowledge and made a note on his pad.

The general, wearing a patent military-issue anti-telepathy helmet, drifted up to God Is Gracious. 'What results have you from your research, Perfect?' he gurgled through the breathing grille.

'Whatever advantage they have gained appears to originate not in any secret chamber within the Dream Mausoleum but within the Sarcophagus Chamber,' said God Is Gracious. 'Once originating in the rock valley high above the pyramid, they make their way in a well-drilled and orderly manner down towards the building, negotiate the Sarcophagus Labyrinth and form a patient queue in front of the Sarcophagus itself, where they climb one at a time into Our Lord's Sarcophagus by virtue of giving one another a Leg-Up.'

'A Leg-Up?' The general was outraged. 'This is their military advantage? A Leg-Up?'

'The advantage of telepathy is that it allows one man to affect another's dream,' explained God Is Gracious, 'and hence to be present in it. For centuries, those few heretics amongst our people have attempted to climb the glassy smooth walls of the Sarcophagus and failed miserably. Two men or more, however, can assist one other into the Sarcophagus with ease. Once inside the Sarcophagus, they lie at full stretch upon the stylized, blank-faced deity-representation rendered into the Sarcophagus lining.'

'What happens to them then?' rasped the general through the helmet.

'They vanish,' said God Is Gracious. 'And a nightmare's breadth later, they materialize in one of our major cities. And people begin to die.'

The general's eyes lit up. 'The Sarcophagus is the weapon?'

God Is Gracious looked guiltily at the floor with two of his eyes, and up towards heaven with the other two. 'Well, it's *a* weapon, sir . . .'

'It's a weapon that we can't use?'

'It's a weapon that can only be used by telepaths, sir. What sort of weapon is that? The enemy have telepathically blasted themselves in the foot. Field Surgery have already hypothesized that the heathens only possess a limited number of telepaths. With every city of ours they kill, they lose one of their soldiers.'

The general was puzzled. 'Sounds like pretty good arithmetic to me.'

'Some of the fresher telepaths they've been sending out have been females, sir. And they were all pregnant. The enemy's throwing his brood females at us, sir. It's the equivalent of dismantling your munitions factories so you can throw the bricks at the enemy.'

'Yes, of course,' said the general, as if remembering his xenobiology classes. 'Enemy females are sentient.'

'Some argue,' muttered God Is Gracious darkly, 'that ours are sentient too.'

'Enough of this anthropomorphic rant,' ranted the general. 'What exactly are you saying, Perfect?'

'Just this, sir: the Sarcophagus is a pretty poor sort of weapon. Whoever uses the Sarcophagus uses up his entire stock of telepathic soldiers with great rapidity, and assumes the enemy doesn't have telepathic soldiers of his own. Because we can see the dream, we know how they are accomplishing our destruction, and would find it very easy to copy their methods were we only possessed of Amphibian telepaths. And if we *do* possess telepaths – and it would seem the Dream's makers considered this to be possible, for the figure carved into the Sarcophagus bed is so stylized that it could represent either a member of our or their species – both sides wipe out their entire breeding stock of telepaths at a stroke. Doesn't that smack ever so slightly of selective breeding on the part of whoever or whatever constructed the Sarcophagus?' He marched over the dormitory to the chained Book of Nine Thousand Truths that had to exist there on a regulation lectern by virtue of the Nine Hundredth Truth. He picked up the book and looked up at the general as he read. 'Here in the first chapter of our Beautiful Race, it is written that "in the early days, the Prophets talked to one another every day in dreams, and the champions of many kingdoms went to sleep with God in battles against the enemy". What can this mean, but that this has happened before? And that when this was written, telepathy was far more widespread than it is today?'

'Nonsense!' said the general. 'The Sarcophagus is a means of raising the stakes in our evolutionary struggle towards godhood. It was placed there in the pyramid by divine hands that it might provoke a war which the finest race should win.'

'The finest race would appear to be the one who found it first,' said God Is Gracious. 'And who had one of their number possess enough compassion to defect to us in an effort to prevent bloodshed.'

'That displays their weakness,' said the general, 'and is why we shall prevail.'

'The Sarcophagus is a means of stopping evolution dead, not of continuing it! It's a means of continually weeding out telepathy among the Human and Beautiful Races! It's a trap, General! If you have any telepaths, don't send them into it.'

The general narrowed his eyes. 'That is foolishness. The only other option would then be to use our nation's nuclear capabilities.'

'Have you thought of surrender?' said God Is Gracious with what he knew to be a fatuous smile. Of course it was not possible to surrender. The enemy's own military would be a mirror image of this one. Once they began to win, they would not stop winning until they had successfully aggressed every last Amphibian into extinction.

'Besides, you have no telepaths,' he said.

'We have *one* telepath,' said the general.

God Is Gracious suddenly became aware that a hundred-times-four eyes in the immense vaulted dormitory were staring directly at him.

'I suppose you've wondered why we've been feeding you nervous stimulants since you started your research here,' said the general quietly. 'It would be a shame, you see, for us to drop our one-use weapon on its detonator before we've even fired it.'

Huge military Beautiful Persons were advancing on God Is Gracious from all sides, careful to keep their skin coloration brown, although occasional pulses of black and purple were flickering up and down the less stable-looking ones.

'We mentioned to you that citizens all over our great Amphibian nation have been seeing enemy armies in their

Common Dreams for the past twenty-four hours. What we neglected to mention was that what they have also been seeing is a highly confused Amphibian academic standing on a rock pinnacle staring down at an Arboreal footprint. You're a telepath, Perfect. The Arboreal turncoat must have –' he muttered the obscene word '– *fertilized* your mind somehow. All of this –' the general waved his hand around the makeshift lab '– is largely purposeless. We needed to occupy your waking mind whilst we were making the missile ready.'

God Is Gracious went the colour of the dormitory wall in alarm. 'Missile?'

'Don't be afraid,' said the general. 'There is every likelihood that it's perfectly safe. We've fired marine worms and water scorpions up in it, and they came back down almost completely unharmed. It was intended to fire a Beautiful Person into orbit in it sometime in the next few months, after we'd done a few more tests with unliving loads such as fission warheads and poison gas. It has a range which, we calculate, should just about reach from this launch base to the Arboreal Capital.'

'What a coincidence,' said God Is Gracious.

The general darkened and folded his arms. 'Gentlemen, get this payload anaesthetized and locked into his capsule. He has ten minutes to launch.'

As the metal needles slid into his arms like the inch-long nematocysts of a Water Scorpion, God Is Gracious saw God's Bright Gift, the field surgeon, at his left arm, administering the dosage with a wide-bore military syringe.

'This is the most marvellous sacrifice you're making,' said God's Bright Gift.

'Thank you for giving me the choice of making it,' said God Is Gracious, holding on to the young surgeon's arm as the world disappeared like a big bright bubble being sucked up a dark, dark hypodermic.

He was down and in the drop zone. He didn't have much time.

The footprint was still there. Slashed in the sand next door to it was a line of characters in High Arboreal. God Is

Gracious knew such characters, for a scientist had to be able to read papers in the language of the heathens.

> IM PROBABLY DEAD BY NOW
> IVE GIVEN YOU THE TOOLS
> NOW FINISH THE JOB
> M.Q.O.M.Q.

Projecting an image on his skin of an Arboreal uniform was not difficult. The air was full of sand; the Dream was cooking up thunder, by the tingle of static in his ampullae. From a distance, he would appear to be an Arboreal. As an afterthought, he added an officer's insignia to his piping to make his progress quicker. Magically, Arboreal psi-soldiers scattered from his path, which both encouraged and scared him. They could see him; but he could fool them. Looking left and right hoping for some slim chance of Amphibian support, he could see none, only great files of dull grey-uniformed Arboreal figures trudging down the sandblasted slopes towards the distinctly unmaternal angular womb of the Pyramid Tomb, a great pie-slice of blackness cut out of the sky.

The lines of Arboreals, although they were in uniform, were women, juveniles, old men, lunatics dribbling down their dress smocks, young females with their waters still wet upon their legs carrying newborn children as a soldier might carry a mortar bomb, to be thrown into the Sarcophagus idol as an offering to the War God both the Arboreal people and God Is Gracious's own had chosen to worship. Imitating the barking call of a high-caste Arboreal, God Is Gracious pushed his way down the line, and the line moved aside like tapwater from a static-charged rod, such was their conditioned fear of uniformed authority. Once into the mausoleum and inside the huge, high, triangular, corbelled entrance passage, he began to move faster; the flickering torches that no hand ever lit, burning high above the reach of dreaming hands, were beginning to betray his squat inelegant form to the enemy. Voices began to call out, but they were tired voices, the voices of families imprisoned by the military whose uniform they wore and forced to breed children who would die on an assembly-line basis for their species. Even so, such was their patriotic fervour that hands began to grasp out for him, as weak but as numerous as water rushes. But God Is Gracious fed on fresh vegetables and worked an hour each day in the Seminary gardens for his God; the Enemy had been made to believe themselves weak by their own government, and the Perfect knew himself to possess muscles capable of digging a man's grave in an hour. He burst through the entrance passage and into the labyrinth, forcing himself not to wake up sweating with the fear, knowing that if he did he would awake in a corpse-sized iron coffin being slowly roasted by the heat of re-entry. No, ducking into a torchlit labyrinth patrolled by alien zombies was infinitely preferable, because this torchlit labyrinth was one whose every twist and turn and corridor he knew like a blind player of games of strategy who could visualize the board in his sleep. No dream researcher could see the labyrinth, or even be sure their own waking recollections of it were accurate, but every dream researcher knew it well enough to have woken up screaming from nightmares about the Dream, dreaming they were dreaming the Dream and had found the Second Sarcophagus Chamber together with whatever terrible things swam marsh-mugger-like under the surfaces of their waking imaginations.

The Maze is designed to lead the mind *away* from the Sarcophagus Chamber, not towards it. You think I didn't search for hidden chambers in the structure, Moo-Quack of Moo-Quack? You think every Dream researcher since the dawn of the Dream hasn't done it? There's nothing special in the Dream Mausoleum, my friend. It's just what your military masters told you it was: a wonderful big weapon that goes off with a bang loud enough to do for both gunned and gunner. No marvellous choice between good and evil. No test of men's readiness for higher things. Just a means of making sure they stay below stairs where they belong.

There were no footprints in the passages now, even though the corridor floors, as in all corridors in the Dream, were worn into ruts by the implied tread of millennia of tramping feet. The Arboreals would have schooled their armies in the quickest and most direct route through the labyrinth, scorning to stray into any extraneous passages. The torches still flickered on the walls every ten feet, never starved of oxygen down here even with only the one ventilating entrance hall to breathe through. And every single brick in the wall was different.

Maybe they really are different, he thought, or maybe whoever laid the code for them wrote an algorithm to make us *think* they're different.

Who built you, you bastards?

Does this mind-buggering stop when we're awake, or is the whole of the rest of reality also a programmed illusion? Is *this* reality, and all the dead in Godsire just the dream?

This is reality, he thought, smashing his fist into a wall, and, ouch, the pain seemed real. And if *that* pain was real, so was the pain of all the dead in Godsire, Mudborn, Purpleport, whether the blood was real or no.

A left turn here, then a right, and here were all the patient human rounds again, moving in an orderly manner down the stone-lined magazine into the Chamber of the weapon. Dull eyes like detonators.

This would be difficult. They belonged to the air, and the sky, and the open ground. They were better at running and catching and jumping.

He burst out of the entrance, low and heavy, headbutting the Arboreals in his path as his people had long ago learnt to do, rushing heavy and clumsy inside the reach of the spindly things' dangerous flailing nails, and hitting out with his own short, powerful elbows. It took time for the entire crowd inside the Sarcophagus crypt to become aware of his presence, and in that time he had powered through them like a rubber juggernaut, hopped on to the backs of the Arboreal telepaths forming an Inhuman Pyramid near the Sarcophagus – it felt like a carpet of hairy seaweed – and used the screeching creatures as a springboard to clear the Sarcophagus rim and fall headlong towards the blank white face of God.

The city was in turmoil. Cars had skidded in the streets, burglarproof windows had been smashed by people banging heads against them, buildings were on fire and men were running mindless and raving through the flames like children through garden sprinklers. Soldiers were swiping madly at each other like primordial proto-men with weapons that could put a fist-sized hole through a man at a thousand yards. Condominia stared into the night with a million eyes of fire.

Only one building was untouched, and he was moving, more swiftly than the gallop of any nightmare, towards it, sending a howling fear through men's minds that made them scatter from his path like plankton from the path of the leviathan. The building would not burn, as conscientious fire crews with angels at their elbows were following divine instruction to train their city's entire stock of hoses on it. The building would not be attacked, as terrorized guards with eyes that by now jumped about in their sockets like pinballs were defending the building against legions of decaying, horned, spined devils that had been dragged out of the soldiers' own fear centres. In another place, those monstrosities had resembled tree-dwelling snakes and spiders. Here, they tended to resemble water scorpions.

All about the city, voices were shrieking into the night, yelling, *'The Black Man is coming! The Black Man is coming!'*

With a sense of satisfaction, the Black Man settled with chromatophores dark as the universe's prenatal face on to the steps of the Cardinalcy in Kingscoming.

They were there. They hadn't moved. They hadn't been allowed to. Under normal circumstances they would have scattered for their hidden dens and bunkers, and it would have been well-nigh impossible to find them. But they had been penned in by fire, and traffic havoc, and demon-maddened soldiers, and the doors to their mile-deep shelter under the Cardinalcy had been mysteriously melted shut by a maintenance engineer who'd gone mad with a hand-held welder. They had been trapped in the building for which they were responsible for over four hours, when protocol demanded that they flee and leave Johnny-God-Is-Good to fend for himself against whatever can of marine worms they had opened. Now, they had been made to answer for their actions.

The thing confronting them was not real, merely a projection of the sleeping mind, which was why the volley of

King's Chamber

bullets sent into it by a conscientious guardsman when the huge doors swung open passed through it and out the other side.

'Good evening, gentlemen,' said the projection.

The general was among those present, and recognized the handshaking component of God Is Gracious's voice in what came from the Black Man's lips.

'How dare you enter here! Traitor to your species!'

'You said yourself, General,' said the projection silkily, 'that the presence of traitors in a species automatically disqualifies that species from evolutionary superiority.'

'Every single one of our long-range bomber crews has offloaded its bombs into the sea upon reporting sightings of huge sea monsters heading towards Godsire,' said the Premier Cardinal. 'Was that any of your doing?'

'It was,' said the apparition. 'You may be relieved to note that the Arboreals are experiencing the same problem.'

An elderly cardinal, God's Hinder Parts of Heavensreach, piped up from the back of the Assembly. 'Your body has been lying in the Sarcophagus these past four hours, Perfect, with folded arms and an expression of transcendent serenity. The people are saying that the coming of God is upon us.' He blinked with pious apprehension. 'Are you God?'

'I am not,' said the Black Man. 'Nor will God, when he appears to guide the righteous, appear in the Sarcophagus. The Sarcophagus is not and never has been the vehicle of our or their God, or Gods, gentlemen. Nor is it a weapon. It is simply a very new-fangled, or old-fangled, fence for keeping out cattle. And by cattle, I mean us, both Arboreals and Amphibians, for as many have correctly surmised, we were both created by the race who made the Common Dream.'

The statement settled like a ton of leaden feathers – slowly, but with absolute inexorability.

'Have you ever wondered,' said the Black Man, 'why there are Ancient ruins?'

'Because there was a war,' said one of the cardinals self-assuredly. 'They were evil, and they Fought Among Themselves.'

'Rubbish,' said the entity. 'Even today, our two continents can destroy each other's cities with primitive fusion and fission devices. It is only reasonable to assume that the Ancients possessed weapons that could have knocked this world out of orbit. Oh yes, we find fusion craters here and there where once there must have been an Ancient city. But surely fusion is the plaything of a child compared to what the Ancients could create. Compared to the only structure on this planet which has stood undisturbed for one hundred thousand years.'

He let that sink in too. Like lampreys in the bottom mud, they devoured it.

'They used telepathy, gentlemen. Both as a tool, and as a weapon to control us, their chattels and their cattle. This, not some farcical pastoral idyll, is the reason for the lack of heavy machinery in Ancient cities; they were not enlightened anti-technologists, but creatures of such telepathic ability that they had no need for machinery. Why use machines, or lift a finger yourself, when you have one continent full of land-going slaves, and another full of slaves for use beneath the sea? I'm sure they used us as pack animals, manual labourers, and probably also food animals for themselves and ourselves as well, for history has shown that both our races are able to eat each other's flesh without digestive upset. But Ancient society was threatened by a terrible danger. What if their cattle were to grow hands and acquire the ability to use machine guns?'

There was absolute silence in the debating chamber. The Black Man stood quiet on the mosaic navel of the Macrocosmic Man, picked out in marble on the chamber floor, whose feet rested in the primordial gravel, and whose hands strove towards Heaven.

Then, one cardinal, unable to help himself, began to laugh. The laughter spread like an infection, until one by one, the entire debating chamber was a whooping collage of humorous lavender.

The Black Man remained Black, and did not laugh.

'Easy for one of our farmers to check whether his cattle are not growing arms from day to day,' he said. 'But a new-evolved telepath looks outwardly just like any normal Amphibian or Arboreal slave.'

The laughter ceased.

'The fusion craters in the ruins of Ancient cities were created by our ancestors, Amphibian and Arboreal, finer men than any alive today, who strove *together* against their enslavers using poor man's weapons and *won*, only for us, their children, to make ourselves unworthy of that inheritance by destroying one another. They had to use second-rate weapons such as atom bombs, because the Ancients had constructed such devices as the Sarcophagus to process Arboreal and Amphibian telepaths and kill them, along with any other breed of telepaths who might be in their immediate vicinity,' said the Black Man. 'The Common Dream is not a divine message to mankind, but a housekeeping routine that runs every few nights in order to trap harmful processes that might be kicking around in the system.' He might have smiled, but it was difficult to tell. 'Harmful processes like myself.'

The older cardinal, God Has Merit, spoke up. 'And why were you not yourself trapped?'

The Black Man shrugged. 'I never woke up. The Dream triggers its harmful destructive effects as soon as the subject enters an insomnient state.'

'But that's impossible!' shouted the general. 'The missile capsule would have shocked you out of anaesthesia with powerful bursts of electricity to your progenitive organs as soon as you re-entered the atmosphere over the target zone –'

'Quite so,' said the dark silhouette. 'But I was not merely anaesthetized. I had already anticipated your intentions in placing me in charge of a useless experimental station at what was plainly a long-range rocket base. I co-opted your field surgeon, God's Bright Gift, to replace the anaesthetic he had been instructed to administer to me with a powerful cataleptic. Thus, I remain in a permanent somnolent state, and, like Moo-Quack of Moo-Quack before his unfortunate detonation, am able to invade men's minds whilst retaining control over the extent of my invasion. My capsule settled safely to earth in the Arboreals' major botanical park, just in time for members of their military, controlled by myself, to surround my craft and cordon it off from external attack by members of either of our two nations.'

'*Traitor!* cried the general, and, having identified a tangible enemy with whom he could deal, stabbed a hand at God's Bright Gift. 'Seize him!'

Two Cardinalcy Guards, to their credit or debit, attempted the feat. God's Bright Gift appeared momentarily terrified, but sprouted steel spines from his every muscle and member as the guards' hands fell upon him. They attempted to withdraw, going through convulsive painful colour changes like landed fish, but the spines had pierced their flesh and then curved back on themselves like living barbs, and they were forced to rip away great bleeding lumps of their own bodies in order to tear free. As soon as they did tear free, the spines withdrew back into God's Bright Gift, to his own amazement as much as anyone else's. He felt himself all over for exit wounds.

The Premier Cardinal frowned at the spectacle, and turned his attention on the Black Man once again.

'What are your conditions for our surrender?' he said bleakly.

'You will continue peacefully with the process I have already begun by force, that of dismantling both the nuclear and non-nuclear war machines possessed by both yourselves and by your Northern neighbours. You will demobilize your armies, which have been in a state of emergency for the past ten years, ever since you discovered fission devices and forced the Arboreals to follow suit. You will send your troops home, and you will find them jobs to do.'

'An admirable set of ideals, which it may be possible for us to comply with,' conceded the Premier Cardinal. 'If our traditional enemies are no longer our enemies, we have no need of armies any longer.'

'Furthermore,' continued the man-shaped carving of darkness, 'there are seven words in our Book of Nine Hundred Truths which refer to the correct attitude of man towards man. These words will be expanded to their truer and more correct meaning of the attitude of sentient toward sentient.'

'That is impossible,' said the Premier Cardinal, losing his brown. 'You are dealing with the Word of God.'

'Not true,' said the Black Man in its lipless voice. 'The book we know as the Nine Thousand Truths is but a pale translation from Classical Amphibian into Modern, performed as recently as one thousand years ago. During the Classical Period when the Book is known to have been written, we had no contact with the North Continent, and had no inkling of the Arboreals' existence. Thus it is entirely arguable that God's word to the Forefathers might, when using the word "Man", have meant any sentient being.'

There was instantaneous squabbling among the back-bench theologians on this point. 'It is arguable that the word "Man" might describe the *males* of another species,' said God's Hand On The Storm of Mudborn, a junior acolyte, 'but females are known to be non-sentient. The females of the Arboreals work in their fields and factories, and claim equality with them before the law. This is surely an insupportable contradiction —'

'You are a devil!' cried one of the elder Cardinals at the Black Man. 'You attempt to make us stuff shit in the mouth of God!'

'If I were a devil,' said the Black Man, 'I would pretend to be God. I could perform that feat quite adequately: bright lights from the sky, shining chariots descending from the clouds with angels at the reins. You would have believed it. Believe *me*, I know every canto of the Accession to Godhead just as well as you do, and I know *exactly* what the Lord should look like when he comes. Why did I not pretend to be God? Because I am no devil, but a man lying asleep in a re-entry capsule crash-landed in a greenhouse surrounded by rather fetching tropical quinquennials.'

'I find myself believing you,' said the aged cardinal, 'and this is not surprising. It is known that Devils are more intelligent than Mere Men. For this reason, the very convincing quality of your arguments convinces me that you are a Devil.'

'If God were really to come down from his house in the Heavens,' said the Black Man quietly, 'would you believe *Him*?'

But the congregation was already awash with cries of 'Away, Devil!' and 'Out, in the name of Punctuated Equilibrium!'

'I'm with you, Devil,' proclaimed God's Hinder Parts, looking over his shoulder at his countrymen as he hobbled down the rows of benches to the speaking floor to stand beside God's Bright Gift and the dark creature. 'God protect me from all these good men.'

'And I too,' said the general, as if he had just made the decision, and, stripping off his sash of office, crossed the floor to join the traitors.

'An interesting, if utterly treasonous and heretical, decision, General,' said the Premier Cardinal. 'May I ask why?'

'I am a soldier,' said the general. 'I have been a soldier for many years, and have seen thousands of my charges die on battlefields foreign and domestic. To a soldier, nothing is more attractive than the prospect of mankind never again needing soldiers.'

'Anyone else?' said the Black Man.

'Do your worst to us, Devil!' cried God's Hand On The Storm, raging in the pastel shades of a man used to threatening violence without ever having to physically deliver it. 'We are iron in the face of the lightning!'

Several of the senior cardinals regarded God's Hand On The Storm oddly.

'Very well,' said the Black Man, who turned on his heel and left the room as the assembly lit up brilliantly as human torches, their pain chromatophores dilating as one to maximum aperture. An avenue opened in the fire hoses and the gunfire outside, and guards saluted smartly as what they believed to be the entire College of Cardinals, escorted by angels and the Divine Forefathers themselves, processed from the building.

It had been a shame that things had gone as badly here as in the other place. The Black Man had hoped that the presence of God in the government house would make men amenable to reason. But Governments were Governments, it seemed, whether they had God's colours nailed to their mast, or those of the Control of the Means of Production. Telepathic illusion was akin to dropping chaff from an aeroplane to fool long-range radar, making the senses see what was not there. Stopping a man's cardiac or respiratory reflexes, meanwhile – killing him quickly without pain – was more akin to switching off the radar set altogether. It could not be done. When telepaths killed, they had to kill by overloading the sensory nerves so that a man died screaming, burning and freezing, with a big erection. The cardinals, true to form, would not be able to make up their minds whether they were in agony or ecstasy as they died.

The sole remaining cardinal to his left, the sole remaining general to his right, God Is Gracious strode out through the burning ruins he had made of his own city, absent-mindedly walking through the occasional wall or burnt-out vehicle. Now that the nightmares of the past four hours were past, soldiers were beginning to cry over the comrades they had killed, fathers to wake up next to the corpses of their own children with horrid mouthfuls of the flesh of the flesh of their flesh, burn victims to walk with stiff, unbending joints and eyelids welded shut through the wreckage.

I am no God, he thought to himself as he walked. Powerful, yes, but only as powerful as any other man with what happens to be his particular century's ultimate weapon. In order to achieve a peacemaking effect over a million minds, it is still necessary to break a million heads. And if I am no God, with the power I feel in me, I must surely be a devil. Yet even devils must be part of the scheme of an all-powerful God, just as are spiders, snakes and water scorpions. I serve to keep the population down. I and those who are to follow me are the two sorts of humanity's natural predators at the peak of the Food Ziggurat.

The thought unnerved him. However, he consoled himself with the thought that it was difficult to be a predator when one was permanently asleep. But do people who are permanently asleep have permanent nightmares where they never hit the ground? he thought. And what happens to the waking world if they do, if they have the powers of sleeping devils? Are wars, pogroms and mass hallucinations the nightmares of little gods already sleeping?

The Sarcophagus Chamber was empty now, at his command. In one incarnation, he could feel a billion goggling wide-eyed mortals with their snot-laden nostrils pressed against the glass sides of the now-occupied coffin like the suckers of bottom-feeders; but in his own private dream, the building remained his and his alone.

He rose from the Sarcophagus, leaving part of himself below to please the crowds, and stretched phantasmal limbs. He found that he had grown to fit the casket. The mausoleum labyrinth now smelt only of bodies long since become fossils that had become dust, not of the stink exhaled by any living orifice. Only hours before, it had smelt like an Arboreal underground railway station on a hot day during a soap shortage. Now a night desert wind blew through it like a soothing enema. Outside, the many paths by which a man might pick his way down to the Tomb were obscured and made one by the drifting sand. God Is Gracious picked the Path of Tearful Resignation – long held by Hypnomantic scholars to be indicative of a need to bow to the world's many devils when trodden by a dreamer – on the basis that climbing the path in the wrong direction must surely indicate a readiness to strangle the world's many devils with their own telsoned tails. The formations of particular familiar rocks, seen from this novel retrograde direction, were pleasing. It seemed that the place where one normally, as a sleeper, entered the Dream was the high point of a rise, a saddle between two peaks, and that if one pushed up to that height, one might be able to see in both directions. He battled up the slope against the blinding sand, and eventually climbed on to a rock pinnacle, the sand whipping up into clouds around him but never quite rising high enough to obscure vision, as if a giant benevolent hand were pressing it down to give him, and only him, room to see.

On the other side of the mountain stretched a massive plain, or what might be a massive plain beneath the surging sand. Above the waves of sand poked the heads of pyramids. Thousands of pyramids, large and small, baroque and functional, stretching as far as a sleep-closed eye could see.

In one of the pyramids burnt a light. God Is Gracious hurried down towards it.

City of Hammers

By Neil Williamson

Yanni faded out completely on the shuttle from Nonna to the Point. It was as if she had simply been switched off. Disconnected.

At first Cal didn't notice because he was concentrating so hard on ignoring her. The focus of his attention should have been work. His report on the Rim Worlds' haulage embargo talks was already four hours late and would have to be tight-beamed before they boarded the clipper that would take them through the Point, out of this region of space and on to Altaque. He had two more hours to finish it, but concentration was proving elusive. Never mind the hubbub in the shuttle's cabin: the mixed-down chatter of murmured dialects and the sonorous soundtrack to the promotional vid many of the passengers were gawping at. These he could put out of his mind. Yanni, he could not – however hard he tried.

Had he not received her message, he would have filed his report from the media centre and set about spending a little of the network's credit celebrating the end of the aptly named Long Haul talks. By now he should have been sleeping off a night of chemically enhanced heat and friction, waking to find whatever slack Nonnan woman he had been with gone, taking her intimacy with her, leaving only a smoky impression in his dusted recollection. But Yanni had come to Nonna looking for him, so he had not done his usual things. Instead, he had rushed to the terminal to meet her.

It was only the smile that he recognized at first. Nothing else fitted his memory of her. She stood near the offbound gates, a slight figure dressed in conservative greys; no longer the artist, the primary-coloured personality that had been the orbital centre of his life for five years. She had longer hair now, too, dark and waved, moderating the sleek skull and angular features he remembered. The smile, though, was sharp as ever.

'Hey,' she said. 'Good to see you. I need your help.' To the point as always. This wasn't a social visit then.

'How come?' he replied, cagily.

'I'm not doing so well.'

'Fast living caught up with you at last?' He was trying to keep it neutral but inevitably his tone was edged with bitterness.

'No, it's a disease. It's not terminal,' the smile wavered, 'but it might as well be.'

He couldn't find words to cover the pettiness of his barb. The silence stretched brittle between them until she said, 'I need to go on a journey. Final pilgrimage kind of thing. But I can't do it alone.'

Despite her obvious sincerity several bladed remarks leapt to his lips. Chagrined, he let them die there.

She made the move and stepped closer. Her hair smelt of spicy greennut.

'Wanna play nursemaid?' Her voice was close to a whisper, somewhere between enticement and pleading.

'Where to?'

'Hephaestus,' she said. The smile twisted wryly: she knew his attitude towards that kind of place. And true enough he almost laughed.

'*Hephaestus?*' he repeated. 'You're kidding, surely.' She shook her head. 'Why the hell do you want to go there?'

Yanni shrugged. 'Hey, it's *my* last request.'

'Fair enough, but . . .' He tailed off. 'It's just not *you*.'

'People change,' she said simply, and then, 'Cal, I can't make it alone.' This new vulnerability was unsettling.

'When would we have to leave?' he asked.

The smile returned.

'Now.'

From what Cal had heard, the City of Hephaestus was one of the oldest constructions yet discovered; interesting if you were into relics, could be bothered with the three-week slog to get there and, since it was run by a brotherhood of monks, didn't mind the rather basic living accommodations. He had seen the commercials on the travel and history slots. Tacky as hell. Ethereal music and corny 'Deep in the Mists of Time' voiceover with pseudo-religious overtones accompanied shots of looming structures, darkly lit and out of focus. No real footage of the city itself though. Air of mystery, he supposed. A cheap shot aimed at attracting the gullible to some pile of rocks miles from anywhere. People had been falling for that sort of thing for centuries. He would never have imagined though that Yanni might be one of them.

As they waited to board, she told him about the disease. It was a viral agent called Wheeler-174, a strain that attacked the area of the brain that collates sensory information and cross-references with memory. She dumbed it down for him, of course.

'You see a primrose Cal, you see yellow petals, green leaves; you smell primrose smell; if you're stupid enough to eat it, you taste primrose taste. OK, it feels pretty much like any small flower and it doesn't make much of a sound, but that's enough to go on. You get all this information and if you've seen one before your brain says right away, "Hey that's a primrose!" Me? I get most of the information most of the time, though these days I rarely get the whole package. Sometimes I'll only see it, sometimes I'll be blind but I can feel it or smell it, other times it'll *taste* of yellow. Occasionally I'll get the whole picture but my memory won't know it from a teaspoon, and sometimes, well, the world just goes black. And it's getting worse, fast.'

He couldn't imagine what it must be like for her. Especially her. Yanni's life was built totally around sense and sensation. Her works had always been dramatic challenges to the senses, taking what she saw, smelt, heard, tasted, felt; some aspect of her surroundings, and skewing and amplifying and throwing it back at the populace as glorious praise, sardonic dig or grand joke. She had been vaunted as a talented newcomer when he had met her, and her reputation had soared since they split. What would she do when she was unable to experience the universe? There was no telling what life would be like for her once the disease had run its course. The victims would, he assumed, never be able to tell anyone.

When Cal eventually looked at Yanni on the shuttle, the disease had taken hold silently and alarmingly. Her face had gone slack. Motor functions idled her hand in a gentle holding pattern above her lap. The eyes unfocused, ears hearing nothing; touch, taste and smell all disengaged from the outside world. Even though she had told him this would happen it scared him shitless. He knew she would come back in her own time, but he could not stop himself patting her hand, gently and then a little harder, quietly repeating her name, ashamed of the quaver in his voice.

'Where did you buy your accent?' An Elmer woman in the berth behind thrust her fat face, powdered in that weird way with mourning grey, over the backs of their seats.

'Excuse me?' Fear for Yanni fuelled his irritation at the intrusion and he made no attempt to conceal it.

'I'm sorry, I see that your friend is unwell.' The woman's monotonous voice possibly took on a note of contrition. 'But I couldn't help overhearing you speaking. This ancient Earthan accent is very fashionable. Your print sounds particularly authentic I think. I wish to know the distributor of such chic.'

'The accent,' he said pointedly, 'is real.'

And didn't her eyes light up! She began, 'Then you must be –'

'From Scotland, Earth. Yes.'

'My friend, Reve. Her mother's cousin went there. She said it was just the cutest –'

'I'm afraid I don't know her,' he said, and turned away.

Bloody belligerent, self-centred Elmers. On top of Yanni and his report, he really didn't need this. It was bad enough that he found himself riding out to the arse end of the Rim to visit one of the most overhyped tourist spots known, without being reminded that his own homeland was a neatly packaged if minor-league wannabe in the same business. His humble origins were something Yanni had goaded him about endlessly. Her family were travellers, having nothing so limiting as a home planet.

In spite of the gravitas due to Earth as the origin of the diaspora, he was the product of a planet that was part museum, part theme park. And his country was one of the crassest offenders, pandering to any far-flung colonist's descendant with a tenuous link to the place – whether it be bloodline, family hearsay or just romantic wishful thinking. Truth was, the multitudes that visited the old country claimed a slice of a nationhood that had been without any political reality for hundreds of years. It remained a colossal marketing gimmick, and it worked too well for the credibility of the natives. Anywhere off Earth it was considered parochial enough to claim to be European, let alone something as twee as Scottish.

At the Point Cal transmitted his report expensively using the shuttle's comms rig. He had managed to cobble something halfway coherent together in the long forty minutes it had taken for Yanni to return from her disconnected state. Just as he was finishing, she spoke, lightly, as if nothing had been wrong.

'So what's the big news out this neck of the woods?'

He turned, both relieved and piqued by the sound of her voice. She seemed relaxed and unperturbed by her hiatus and although he could read nothing but casual interest in her question, the subject had been one of the sore points at the rough end of their parting. Yanni the traveller had needed to go, to see, to experience. Cal had wanted all that too, but his reporter's ambitions had come with horizons he could never see beyond. Earth's glory days were past. Nothing, in galactic terms, worthy of the name news was ever likely to happen out here again.

He forced himself to reply, 'Oh you know. Same old shit.'

Yanni's sharp smile flashed back, warm like the leading limb of a hometown sunrise. Comforting and everyday, and completely out of reach.

She had booked two single cabins on the clipper bound for Altaque. Cal realized that he was relieved. Once the enormous structure winked through the Point they would have three weeks to spend at close quarters. Until now there had been this barrier between them – a neutral falseness, both of them polite and noncommittal, afraid to allow the past to rise and sour things. Once they were truly on their way there was no telling how long that would last. He expected to relish what privacy he could get.

The clipper was a big Maskrey-designed hulk, a bristling resort complex with a navigation deck. This was the habitat of Yanni's people. In ships like these the travellers lived their lives in the spirit of wanderlust and died transitory deaths. Whole generations never made planetfall. Here more than anywhere he would have expected Yanni to feel at home.

At first she did seem to have attained some kind of peace, but the impression was false. She wandered around the cavernous hive, met acquaintances of colleagues of people she knew, or who knew her family – Yanni's own personal renown was only a small component of the notoriety attached to her clan. Cal tagged along but soon got bored with the catching up on the lives of people he'd never heard of. After the first couple of days he elected to stay close to their cabins and wait for her to be carried back insensate. By the end of the week she had joined him.

They talked some, and unexpectedly he found himself charmed by her all over again. She told him about the places she had been and the exhibitions she had staged, tactfully leaving undefined the people she had undoubtedly been with. She was funny and sharp as always, and when he talked about the petty politicking at the network that had left him covering trade talks and spring rites festivals, she listened and sympathized. It was good, but it was all surface. The closest they came to any kind of intimacy was at dinner, when she asked coyly, 'So do you have anyone, at all?' She wore an impish grin, and – was it just the alcohol, or was she blushing?

'I don't think I'd be here if I had,' he said.

'Wouldn't you?' He wasn't sure if she was joking. Surely she couldn't have forgotten how seriously he craved monogamy.

'I haven't had a relationship since you.' It was blunt truth, an attempt at candour in the hope she would open up and really talk, about them and about her illness. In her position he knew he would feel terrified and alone, and need someone, anyone, to tell it all to. Then again, he didn't like the thought that he might be just a handy anyone.

'Oh' was all she said. It was confirmation, *Cal you haven't changed*, and the feeling of closeness he had begun to imagine evaporated.

After that night Yanni stayed in her cabin watching the vid. Cal accepted the silent rebuke and was tempted to leave her to it but felt guilty leaving her alone. There was a simple pattern to her viewing. She'd switch channel restlessly until she found a Hephaestus commercial. They ran regularly and he was soon sick of the anaemic vocal chords, the sky-blue hammerhead logo mixing to a line of hooded figures – the monks, he guessed – slowly crossing a dangerous-looking rope bridge and silhouetted against a dark edifice of some kind. Most of all he despised the melodramatic script which started with 'Welcome, traveller, to the ancient City of Hephaestus on Altaque. Here the mysteries of all life are known and revered . . .' and ended with 'The City loves you. Life eternal, variety eternal.'

Once, she picked him up on his sigh of disgust, rounding on him: 'Cal, stop being such a cynic.'

He barked a short laugh. 'What's not to be cynical about? It's all so phoney.' Her stare was hot, indignant. 'Oh come on, Yanni, it's a load of balls. Surely you can see that.'

She turned away, and said quietly, 'What would you know?'

He realized she was making him angry, but failed to keep it out of his voice when he replied, 'I know that I don't need to travel all the way out there to see a load of old rocks.'

'That,' she said, 'is exactly your problem.'

The shuttle brought them down on the night side of the planet. They disembarked on to a windy landing platform ringed with pale lights. Beyond these Cal could make out further low clusters of lights which he took to be the airstrip buildings. And that was it. The sky above was pregnant with cumulus, blotting out any natural light. He was told that they were landing on the site of the ancient city itself, but he was sure this couldn't be right. Although in this darkness they could have been anywhere, there was no way he could see that they would allow a craft of this size anywhere near a multimillennial antiquity. He put it down to poor translation.

There was a vibration of power in the ridged metal beneath his feet – the local generator for the lights and comms, he guessed, though he couldn't hear anything over the shuttle's engines. Strangely, he felt something of a rhythmic aspect to it, an evenly paced *thump-thump*. He was beginning to assemble a picture of this place as a low-level outpost built for convenience rather than comfort, probably within a few miles of the ruin. Well, he had experienced field accommodation before. He could do so again for Yanni's sake.

A figure approached from the direction of the largest cluster of lights. Had he not already guessed it would be a monk, the rough hooded robe would have given it away instantly. But the figure was too tall, its gait unsettlingly smooth and when it spoke, its whisper-song voice dispelled any doubt that it might be human.

'The City welcomes you and with its grace, the Brotherhood too,' it said. 'Please follow.' Then it turned and ambulated back the way it had come.

He felt stupid for being so shaken. After all, they were right out at the far reaches of the galaxy, and obviously if Hephaestus was as old as they claimed it could not have been built by human hands. It was just that the other passengers had at least been of human extract, and the advertising hadn't even hinted there might be extros here.

While some of the passengers were clearly as startled as himself, others had already picked up their luggage from the pile that had been disgorged on to the platform behind them and begun to follow the monk.

Yanni was grinning. 'Don't worry,' she said, the breeze plucking at her words. 'This place is actually about sixty per cent human-populated. Well, humanish.' She handed him his litecase. 'Coming then?' she asked.

'Just as well you told me to leave the rest of my bags on Nonna,' he said, trying a little levity to break up the feeling settling tightly in his chest of being very far from home.

'Well, we're only here for two days after all,' she said, starting to walk.

'*What?*' he blustered, trailing after her. 'Two days? You brought me all this way for two days. You told me I'd be away from the Rim for two *months*.'

Yanni stopped so suddenly that he almost collided with her. 'Yes, Cal, I did. But this is supposed to be for *my* benefit. Remember –' she took on a sarcastic tone '– the local Point is moving away. It'll take the clipper an extra week and a half to catch up with it on the return trip.' She started walking again. Over her shoulder she called, 'Besides, two days is all they allow.'

City of Hammers

What he assumed on first sight to be a ramshackle airstrip terminal turned out to be their accommodation. Suddenly the short length of their visit seemed no bad thing. It was a long polymer shell, a lightweight structure strengthened inexpertly on the outside with bolted-on sheets of iron. The reinforcements did little to prevent the walls moving unsteadily under the force of the wind.

Inside, the kindest description Cal could think of was functional. Not that he was particularly disposed towards kindness at that moment in time. They stepped into a long, starkly lit corridor lined with narrow doors. Apart from the waiting monk the place was deserted. As soon as the exterior doors were closed the tall figure went about the task of ushering them to their rooms.

As he and Yanni awaited their turn, Cal became aware of the silence. It was weighty but not oppressive, the kind of silence you strained to hear, a nurtured thing that you were fearful to break. Each closed door they passed contained a warm living hush. Where else would they be staying but among the monks?

They followed the guide to their room. The figure bobbed its hood and closed the door. Cal looked around the room. Plain, flimsy walls, a very basic-looking san built into the far corner, two single cots, a light panel buzzing in the ceiling, and that was about it. He sat on one of the cots. It gave spongily.

'All the comforts of home,' he groaned. 'You don't think this is taking the basic living thing a bit far?'

Yanni had managed to open a panel in the featureless wall and was cramming her bag into the space behind it. 'It's not an act,' she said. 'This is how these guys live.' She did something he couldn't see to make the panel swing shut and then began to undress. 'You'd better get a move on. It'll be lights out any minute.' She pulled her shirt over her head, exposing her belly, and then breasts, rising as she stretched – and caught him looking just as the light panel dimmed.

'Get some sleep.' In the darkness, he thought he could hear the smile in her voice. 'You'll need it tomorrow.'

* * *

Cal felt as if he got no sleep at all. They were wakened early, allowed ten minutes to wash and dress and then assembled outside. It was still dark. Again he could feel the vibrations through the soles of his shoes. This time, without the roar of the shuttle's idling engines, he thought he could actually hear the heartbeat component in the distance. Kind of like excavation work going on somewhere. Perhaps at the site of the ruin, or maybe they were building a proper hotel.

On the platform he noticed another, smaller craft, a sleek newish flier. So not everything here was of a standard befitting Altaque's remoteness. Something about the way it was already powered up, humming efficiently, gave him the feeling they would be getting better acquainted with it soon.

First, though, they were trooped over to a squat building, which turned out to be a refectory. As they entered, Cal was hit by a wash of lively chatter, and smells so good his stomach cramped painfully. There were circular metal tables at which were seated a mixture of fellow tourists and monks with their hoods down. Cal was relieved to see that most of the monks were indeed human. Other monks brought sizzling platters of meat and vegetables to the tables from a servery at the back. Yanni found them a table with free places and without ceremony picked up a plate and began piling it high with food. Realizing he now had a howling hunger to feed, Cal followed her example. Nothing on his plate was familiar but all of it was good, and as fresh as if it had been picked or slaughtered that day.

'This is hardly in keeping with the austere lifestyle is it?' he said between mouthfuls. 'Where do they get it all?'

'The City is beneficent,' intoned the whisper-voice familiar from last night. The tall monk replenished a metal bowl with fruits and sat down beside him. 'Besides,' it continued, dropping the hood from its head, 'all consumables are charged direct to your credit facility.'

'Hey, don't worry,' Yanni said. 'This is all on me.'

Cal wasn't listening. He was more concerned with the fact that he could see through the monk's creamy features. The wall behind was just visible through the insubstantial stuff that constituted its flesh. Yanni leant across him, addressing

City of Hammers

the creature. 'Intka, it is a joy to see you again. It has been too long.'

The head turned, but not all at once. It was like a complex drift of milky smoke.

'Yanni,' it said. 'It is no surprise to me that you have returned. You are always welcome in the City. And you too.' Intka was addressing Cal now. 'Our first-time visitors are our most treasured guests. You will enjoy the tour. It will be impressive today.' The monk stood up. 'And it begins shortly. Assemble by the flier in a few minutes, please.'

'Come on, eat up,' Yanni said around a mouthful of pulpy fruit. 'You'll miss it when you're out there.' Cal put a hand on her shoulder.

'Why didn't you tell me you'd been here before?' She had the grace at least to look sheepish.

'Does it matter? I didn't think you'd have come if I told you my last request was a last shot of the rides at the diversions I visited with an old sweetheart.'

Struck, he muttered, 'You're probably right. You tricked me.'

'No. At least not intentionally. Well . . . maybe just a little.' Yanni touched his face. Softly, laughing, she said, 'He wasn't the love of my life, you know. Not even close.'

And that was supposed to make him feel better?

Around them, the tourists were rising and starting to file outside. 'Look,' Yanni said, more cheerfully. 'Now you're here, why don't you just enjoy it? This place really is worth experiencing.'

The flier banked over the coast, setting its course for the return journey just as the cloud-filled sky was lightening. The outward stretch had been made in what remained of the pre-dawn darkness, a half-hour trip with nothing but the now contemptuously overfamiliar choral music to stave off boredom. Judging by the rising murmur, Cal noticed with a small amount of satisfaction that he was not the only one becoming restless.

Then the screens around the cabin unfurled and flicked into life. The Brotherhood's blue-hammer colophon appeared briefly before being replaced by a grey-lit expanse of rolling water. The music receded, was mixed with the hiss and crash of the surf they were watching, and the commentary began.

'The beautiful planet of Altaque has the most diverse biological catalogue of any planet on record. Nowhere is the variety of life more spectacularly celebrated.' Suspiciously on cue, the screens displayed a shoal of huge transparent fish, breaking the surface in a sparkling arc. Cal looked out of his window just in time to see the last of them plunge back below the waves. Lucky coincidence, he thought. Yanni had seen them too. She grinned at him across the aisle. He turned back to his screen. The commentary continued:

'Millions of species exist here on Altaque at any given time. And the builders of the City have ensured that more are created every day. Life eternal, variety eternal. As we return towards the City, consider the marvels of life you see below. They are unique in all the universe, and once the City has passed this way, they will be no more.'

'What was that?' he muttered to Yanni. '*Once the City has passed this way*?'

'Yes, well, it's not exactly what you'd think of as being a city . . .' she began. 'Look, it'll be simpler if you just pay attention and work it out for yourself. Honest.'

As the flier approached land it dipped and released a cloud of remotes, glittering gold in the early light, drawing a gasp from the technologically more backward passengers. The screens segmented, providing simultaneous viewing of the transmissions from each of the remotes as they skimmed the surface, keeping pace with the flier.

The broad beach was empty, ripple-patterned white sand rising to a high bank of grassy dunes. Cal was just thinking how remarkably Earthlike it was when the land erupted beneath them at the sound of their passing. Three or four of the square segments on his screen flashed urgently. He touched one of the flashing segments. The picture he touched expanded, filling the screen, though he could still see the others dimly behind it. In the picture the sandy ripples writhed, transforming into a mass of snakelike things that whipped up off the ground, snapping at the air, sparks of electricity crackling between them. He selected another flashing square. Farther up the beach a thirty-metre sail of camouflage-striped skin rose up, emitting a two-tone keening, caught the wind and peeled gracefully away from the disturbance. Another square showed two of what appeared to be excessively furry rodents, standing erect and sniffing the air alertly. In an instant they rolled into balls and tumbleweeded to safety, out of the flier's path.

And so it went on as they passed inland from shoreline to thick forest. Although time and again he would have loved to linger on a particular scene, they sped along, the remotes seeking out continual curiosities for them to witness, staying as long as required and then catching up with the flier. Cal saw a spider-legged tree standing in a shallow lake, spearing tiny crimson eels with its barbed limbs. Farther on a group of quadrupeds, reminiscent of small hairless cows, stood in a shaded grove, huddled together in a perfect circle and shivering together in violent, but to all appearances contented, harmony. He watched a stand of slender rocky pillars – some single, others in pairs or triples meeting in arches fifty metres off the ground. As the light of the new day touched them, they broke out rapidly in a rash of blisters, which burst, sprouting heavy foliage and pendulous bell-shaped blooms. In minutes the riot of vegetation had created a canopy so thick that the pillars had vanished from sight.

Beside him Yanni yelped joyfully and reached over, slapping his screen. She had found a family of pigmy primates, covered in fluffy hair apart from their pink heads. They were eyeless, a condition compensated for, presumably, by the large flat nose spread across the upper part of their face. Two of the smaller ones had separated from the group and were play-fighting close to a bank of bulbous, variegated flowers. As they played, the flowers expelled a yellow mist. Within minutes the animals were staggering around drunkenly. Then the adults noticed them and crossly began to hurry them away.

'I guess some things are universal,' Yanni laughed. Cal smiled, nodding agreement. He was still pensive over her admission at breakfast, and mad at himself for reacting that way. She was enjoying herself so much, and he was spoiling it. He was relieved at least that her condition had shown no sign of manifesting itself since they landed. He hoped for her sake that it would remain absent for the duration of the trip.

Yanni's attention was already drawn to something else, but Cal saw the two juveniles stumble and fall, ripped to shreds as the blossoms exploded in a hail of glassy flechettes. The adults hooted in furious panic, trying to drag their children bodily away from the tangle of roots which had risen thrashing out of the blood-soaked earth, before eventually giving up and fleeing with their remaining offspring.

It was only when the flier crested a rise and descended into the next valley that Cal realized the reason for the haste of its journey. Below them in the shade of the slope, the forest ended abruptly in a straight line where the land met the City. The scale left him breathless. Here was no ruin. The City was an enormous construction filling the whole of the valley floor and extending darkly into the distance. Behind their craft, the sun was just rising over the ridge, firing the low clouds like kiln bricks. He strained to make out details, but although he could detect vague shapes and, he thought, some movement, he could not see past the scintillating red glare along the perimeter. Their whole trip had obviously been stage-managed so that their first view of the City would be bathed in fire. The commentary, which had been absent since the beach resumed, confirmed the set-up.

'Behold the City. There are many names given by many races for the City. Among these are the human name, Hephaestus, after the ancient Greek god of fire and the forge.' It was beginning to bother Cal how much the tour was tailored for human consumption. 'However, the oldest name on record, and the name attributed to the City by over half the races who know it, is the City of Hammers.'

They approached slow and low, skimming the trees. The remotes recalled, their only view was patched from the flier's forward camera, and the sound Cal realized he'd been hearing for some time, persistent in the background – a familiar even-tempo double-beat – had grown into a loud, rhythmic crashing. This was what he had felt distantly at the landing site.

The flier stopped dead some distance short of the tree line, but it was more than close enough for the passengers to be awed by the enormity of the edifice towering ahead of them,

City of Hammers

stretching out of sight to the left and right and up into the distance, close enough that it seemed that the world stopped where the City began. Close enough for Cal to understand that the City was not a city of buildings, but a city of moving parts. It was a machine. Along the perimeter, serried ranks of cantilevered hammers, each massive head with a scooped inner face, rose and fell in a complex, rippling sequence. They pounded the earth, ripped the life out of the land and clawed it inside, throwing up a billowing pall of debris. The noise at this distance was close to unbearable. The vibrations shook the flier as it hung in the air, a paperweight construction in the face of the colossal power of the City.

Cal felt humbled, hypnotized, as the heads swung bright arcs through the air, gleaming like polished steel, catching the dawn's furnace glow. He could see why the name, Hephaestus, had stuck. The ancient Greek deity of the forge.

The monk's commentary intruded on the cabin's hush, and here at the feet of the City the tone had lost much of its falseness. 'Behold the City of Hammers. The miracle of Altaque, the grand gesture from the Makers to us all. Graceful Hephaestus travels the world for ever, and with the power of gods creates life anew wherever it passes.'

Without warning the flier leapt forward towards the wall of swinging limbs. They covered the remaining distance in seconds. Just enough time for alarm to sink in, for curses to be uttered, for Cal to shoot a desperate glance at Yanni and register that she was *enjoying* this. The flier shot through a rain of rocks, clotted earth and mangled branches towards the gap between two of the hammers. The heads, larger than their entire craft, swept past, surely too close, flashing carnage red. By the time the buffeting draught had died, they had passed into the City itself.

Partly it was like travelling along a major thoroughfare of any city on Earth, and partly it was as if they had been miniaturized and dropped into the workings of some fiendishly complex engine. The seesawing of perspective was dizzying, but eventually Cal's brain settled for the city-scale option. Indeed as they progressed along the shadowy avenue, he recognized that it was part of a gridlike pattern of routes, with blocks of towering structures regularly spaced on either side.

Once comfortable seeing it as a city, it was hard to shake that concept, to see mechanical design in place of architecture, and it was all the more startling to be faced with something that could never belong in a real city – a colossal set of raked gears whirring overhead, for instance, or a street length of skyscraper pistons, pumping furiously but impossibly quiet, any sound they might have made lost in the booming of the hammers.

And yet, even as the concept of the city solidified and the reality of the machine railed against it, there screamed all around signs that refuted both. There was no source of light but, even as vertically deep as they were, what little natural light penetrated from above was ample, because everything gleamed like mirror steel, like polished chrome, reflecting so as to compound the impression of movement in every direction. If this were a machine, where were the tarnish and rust, signs of wear? Where was the blackening of age, the viscous grease that must be necessary to allow all this metal – he assumed it *was* metal – to run together?

The 'buildings' were not solid either. As the flier negotiated intersections and bends and whirling island gizmos, shot under fabulous twisting conduits that led who knows where, Cal saw that the blocks were dense aggregations of workings – layers of gearings and ratchets and cams interconnecting in elegant combinations of incredible complexity.

Then he began to notice the tubeways. They ran everywhere, cagework pipes the diameter of his head, within which could be glimpsed a regular blur of motion. At an intersection where the street they had been following opened into a wide chasm, the flier paused, affording Cal a close view of one of the tubeways where it split and offered a multiple choice of routes shooting off at all angles. A row of steely spheres queued at the junction, spinning gently, beautiful and hypnotic, waiting their turn of the choice of route. Changing spin as he watched, some accelerated on along the original path, some followed a downward spiral, the last leapt into an upward snaking tube, disappearing out of sight.

The flier followed that tube, shooting upward with a jolt to the guts, and burst into full sunlight, rising high above the City. In the twenty minutes they had been travelling at street

City of Hammers

level, the sun had risen fully and the cloud cover dispersed. The effect was dazzling. Below them, all the City's parts moved smoothly, glittering, as one in their purpose, as if a restless lake of diamonds had flooded the valley floor.

They changed direction again, heading for the centre of the metal expanse and a large shape, vague in the glare, the screen's filtering allowing Cal just to make out the lines of a four-sided structure rising up from the shining level below.

The commentary came again, 'Little is known about the construction of the City. We do know it is over thirty thousand years old and is made entirely from a material which resembles steel but is magnitudes harder and stronger, and infinitely more durable. The City measures twenty kilometres at its widest points and travels approximately twice that distance in a week. It needs no maintenance and yet it never even slows in its great work. Of the life that falls under the City's favour, all is reconstituted – nothing is consumed and there is no waste. We believe that overall control of the City's purpose is carried out by the structure which we refer to as the Crown. If you will kindly attend your screens, we are approaching it now.'

The Crown swept up out of the shuttling web of components. As they neared, its features were revealed. The surfaces were ribbed with a fine, trailing root system. Closer, these capillaries became recognizable. Here was where all the tubeways began and ended, here the origin of those fascinating spheres. Closer still, the motion of the spheres could be made out flashing up and down the clustered layers of tubes which disappeared into the body of the structure in great multibored bundles. The flier rose once more, and Cal saw that the top was truncated, perfectly flat. And flying over it, he was stunned to make out the shapes of buildings perched around the perimeter, the flat, matt delta of the shuttle dead in the centre of the decking, tiny figures scurrying back and forward. Their landing site, which they had blithely trusted to be solid ground, had slept at the very edge of the previous night, looked frighteningly precarious.

Yanni touched his arm. 'What do you think?'

'I think . . .' he replied slowly, aware of his heart hammering alarmingly but unable to take his eyes from the habitation passing below them. The monks were waving. 'I think that these are very scary people.'

She squeezed lightly. 'Amazing, isn't it?'

He assumed she meant the City – this bizarre place had certainly surpassed the dull expectations he had harboured. The fact that it existed at all was amazing.

He squeezed back. 'Yes,' he said. 'It's something else. What's that building?' He indicated an unfamiliar square shape at one corner of the platform.

'That's the temple,' she said.

They were leaving the habitation behind now, the ledge below them ending, a sheer curve of tubeways dropping away into the rippling silver haze. He lifted his gaze from the screen and Yanni's expression was just as bright as the City itself, eyes glittering.

'Glad you came?' she asked. It was impossible not to be infected by her mood. Not counting the glory of the City itself, it was worth being here just to see Yanni this happy – so different from the pensive fragility that had dominated this trip, and from the days, sour and jagged-edged, before she had left him.

'Yeah,' he laughed. 'I'm glad I came.'

The kiss was as sharp as her smile, and as dazzling as the City below them.

The flier sped them out across the remainder of the City to the trailing perimeter. Here the rows of hammers were raised, stilled, as if out of respect for the churned earth, the wasted rocks unfolding desolately behind them. The valley slope above the City was devastated, quiet as a recently vacated battlefield. Only as they crested the rise did the first new shoots appear. The shoots became a grassland which some miles further on gave way to a new forest – this one high-canopied, of spindly, broad-leafed trees.

The cloud of remotes appeared again, fizzing briefly around the flier before bursting away in all directions. The first pictures were close-ups of the greenery. Cal couldn't have told it apart from any other greenery, but he supposed it was fundamentally different in some way. Then came the sacs. Milky, gelatinous, all sizes. Lying quivering, half-covered by the loose soil – or half-emergent. Farther on mature sacs, hardened to a fractured,

City of Hammers

rainbow-sheened translucency. Splitting open: wet, new eyes blinking against the light; new limbs, snouts, antennae exploring the world.

The monk's voice was soft. 'From the harvest, the City seeds new life.'

When the flier set them down again on the habitation platform, Cal stepped gingerly on to the decking. The wind was stronger now, surely strong enough to whip up and carry him over the edge. The sun was high, although not yet approaching its zenith, and the whole sky shimmered with reflected light from below.

They were led away from the buildings, towards the open edge of the platform. Yanni took his hand.

She grinned. 'This is where the fun *really* starts.'

He saw what she meant. The passengers were being herded into a frail-looking cage of welded iron – a crude elevator. And there was only one way for it to go.

It took them in groups of eight or nine. Swung out over the edge on a boom, and winched down on a thin steel cable. A twenty-minute wait, and then it came back, empty, and it was the turn of the next group. When Cal's turn came, it was only dumb macho pride that forced him in there after Yanni, squashed between her and the bars. At least her tight-lipped expression told him that she was not exactly looking forward to this part either.

They descended in nervous silence. Even the attendant monk looked a little green. The only sounds during the sadistically protracted journey were the empty hush of the wind, the thrum of the taut cable and its frequent, ever-more-alarming squeals of juddering protest. The elevator's drop took it into a narrow cleft between two thick clusters of tubeways where spheres flashed by within touching distance.

The two-hour walk through the machinery of the City challenged Cal's perspective again. They followed a trail of carefully laid walkways with rope bridges strung between the blocks. The trail led out towards the steadily growing noise of the hammers and down into the colossal workings. Here Cal saw the true complexity of the thing. Among the giant components he saw, tinted pink by the filtering shades they had been issued, smaller assemblies interleaved and interconnected; and nested within these, smaller workings still, right down to the size of a watchmaker's mechanism. All of it, large and small, whirred away soundlessly.

Here, standing inside the City, they could touch it, feel its inert, warm, *frictionless* smoothness, not at all like metal, but nevertheless alive with power. But it was wrong. Impressive as the structure was, and although it undoubtedly performed the function that was claimed for it, for some reason Cal could not shake the growing impression that it shouldn't be able to.

The trail ended on an open platform above the churning hammers, with all the doomed life on Altaque stretching ahead of them. The three guides detached themselves to kneel in a row at the platform's edge leaving the tourists to contemplate the view in their own way. A few of them mimicked the monks and Cal spotted the Elmer woman among them. Rather than remaining in still prayer though, she reached into her robes and produced a jar of red glass, held it before her reverentially, sang to it softly, and wept. As she lifted the lid, the tears described tracks down her face, revealing ruddy cheeks, clean and new-looking against the grey. Her voice rose, strong, if not particularly true, as she poured the dusty contents over the side, and then tossed the jar after them.

Cal looked down to see that the husband or lover or sibling or parent or child or whatever's remains must have been lost almost immediately in the greater cloud of debris roiling below. He had never been able to understand these kinds of futile gesture. The racked dignity with which the woman produced a grey kerchief, dampened it from a plastic bottle and wiped off the remains of the powder with practised strokes held a depth of meaning way beyond him, and yet was profoundly beautiful. When she rose, she drew a shuddering breath and held it tight within her before releasing it, spent. Then, unexpectedly, she turned and caught him intruding on this private moment. She walked past him without acknowledging his half-sympathetic smile.

He rejoined Yanni. She was standing stock still, arms

folded round her middle, looking out across the forest. He followed her gaze, but other than the treescape, there was nothing to be seen.

'You know,' he said, 'this could easily be Earth. Or Mori or Glavetha, or wherever. Don't you think that's weird?'

She didn't answer, just looked out, standing so still. A sudden panic that her illness had taken hold of her again made him grab her arm. She jumped.

'Jesus, Cal. What?'

'Sorry,' he said. 'I just thought . . .' She had been somewhere else entirely, or here but with *someone* else. 'Never mind,' he finished sullenly. Then he was angry with himself for allowing his own feelings to sour the mood. What was the big deal? Why did it matter whom she was thinking of? He had got over Yanni's leaving him years ago. It was just that he hadn't seen her since then, and he knew that it was not wholly out of compassion that he had agreed to come here with her. And she had come to *him* after all. Although she had always found him pretty damn malleable. Besides, how many others had turned her down first?

A herd of animals had appeared in a clearing almost directly ahead. In disbelief, he watched them grazing, apparently oblivious to the City bearing down on them. He realized he was holding his breath, willing them to run before it was too late. But no, it wasn't until the cloud was on top of them, the hammers smashing down, that they all looked up sensing something, and were lost. It was as if they simply hadn't seen the City coming. He turned away, puzzled by their lack of survival instinct.

'So what exactly are we supposed to be doing here then?' he asked.

Yanni was still watching the spot where the herd had vanished. 'I don't know,' she said. 'I guess the idea is to give us a City's-eye view. You know, survey all the things that will soon be gone. Some come here to grieve. A lot of the second-timers come here to contemplate, and the monks, too, of course. I think most folks end up looking inwards rather than out there.'

And he thought he understood a little her reasons for coming here. It was a good place for contemplation, and she had a lot to contemplate. So much to be proud of, or ashamed of, or to laugh about. So many places and people that had intersected with the bright trail of her life, none of which he could begrudge her because that was the life she had wanted and that was what she had forged for herself. So many memories, and memories would soon be all she had left.

Removing his own poor excuse for an ego from the equation, a certain logic suggested itself. Quietly he asked the question, 'This disease, the Wheeler-174. Is it sexually transmitted?'

Yanni's smile twisted ruefully. 'Ah,' she said. Then, 'Not necessarily. But in my case, yes.'

A surge of pity and fury choked him. Cal wanted to ask who he was, this man. Was he vindictive, maliciously careless, or was he some other hapless victim who perhaps hadn't even known himself? But any blustering on his part was way too late for Yanni now. Maybe if he had gone with her when he'd had the chance things would have turned out differently. But he had not gone because it was not in his nature, because he was scared to overreach himself, because he had loved her enough to understand, at some level, that she needed to be free of him. So she had gone alone. And it came as no real surprise to work out that he was here with her now because he had never stopped loving her.

'Yanni,' he said softly, allowing himself a self-deprecating smile. 'You know that I still love you, don't you . . .'

But she was gone, again.

He turned to see that the group was making its way back into the City. Yanni was waiting for him, watching him appraisingly, but she could not have heard him over the distance. He moved to join her, but stopped, feeling something familiar, a spot of cold on his cheek, turning wet, trailing down along the line of his jaw and then no more. An involuntary shiver, and instinctively he turned and looked up into the cloudless blue sky. He left the platform, shrugging it off as an overtaxed imagination.

Later, he lay staring into the darkness, listening to Yanni breathing, thinking her asleep until she spoke.

'Cal I'm sorry for dragging you all the way out here. I've been very selfish.'

'You've got every right to be selfish,' he said. 'Besides, I wanted to come.'

There was some amusement in her voice. 'No you didn't. But I'm glad you did. I've been lucky with the disease these last few days, but I still needed you with me. There are some things that are not easy to face alone.'

'Alone? Come on, Yanni, you've never been alone. You've always had your extended travelling family or your little circus of fans and lovers.' He cursed himself again. 'I'm sorry,' he said. 'That wasn't supposed to sound so resentful.'

'No. You're right,' she said. 'And you're wrong. I have been surrounded by people all my life. That's what's so frightening about the prospect of being completely alone. Anyway only a few of them have been what you'd call close. I don't make those kinds of bonds easily, Cal, and as you know, I'm not easy to live with when I do. No one was willing to put up with me as long as you.'

'That's because I love you,' he said.

'Love. As in present tense?' It was difficult to make out the inflection in the question. Was it incredulity or something else? She went on, 'I was afraid, after the way I treated you, you'd hate me.'

'I tried. But hate didn't suit me,' he said, aware of the pressure of emotion that was welling up inside him. 'No, I guess I'm stuck with loving you like I'm stuck with all my small-town convictions.'

He hadn't heard her move, but suddenly her voice was right by his ear. 'I hope you realize how special you are,' she said, slipping under his covers.

They made love simply and slowly, making the sensations last and committing them to memory. Prepared as always, Yanni had produced a skin for him. For his own protection, she joked. He left the sensitivity set at natural. He knew he was fooling himself, but just for tonight he wanted everything to be as *normal* as possible. And it was fine until her body stilled under him and the wetness on her cheeks told him she was gone once more. He covered her and lay with her, and although he doubted she could hear him he whispered promises that even when the illness finally locked her away inside herself he would never leave her alone.

But when at last her breathing deepened and her body relaxed into sleep, he rose, unable to bear the weight of his promises.

Outside, despite the lateness, there were monks about, filing back and forward between the dormitory and the temple. Since they seemed not to object to his joining them, he followed them into a large square room with tables, chairs and little else. Monks and a number of tourists sat around, in small groups intent on discussion, or silently alone. No ornate religious paraphernalia, no symbolic ceremonials. Religion had never seemed particularly relevant to Cal's life, so, as with many of the larger philosophical issues, he'd always ignored it. Nevertheless, he was aware that there was usually a certain amount of fuss and symbolism involved.

The voice startled him.

'Welcome to the temple, Cal.' It was the tall alien, Intka.

Recovering quickly, Cal said, 'Thanks, I just came over to see –'

The monk cut across him. 'How is Yanni tonight?' Without waiting for his reply, it ushered him to a nearby table, continuing, 'It was most distressing to hear of her illness. Still, I am sure you are taking good care of her. She is unique, that one.'

Cal allowed himself to be seated, accepting a glass of fruit juice. It was sharp, thick with pink pulp and very refreshing. 'That's good,' he said, draining the glass. 'What fruit is that?'

Intka laughed, his features displaying that lagging characteristic which Cal was beginning to find compelling rather than simply freakish. 'The City provides us with such wonderful variety, there is little point in naming things. It grows a few hundred kilometres north of here. It is good, isn't it?' Then changing the subject, 'So, Cal, what do you think of the City?'

Cal helped himself to more juice and thought about this. 'It's not at all what I was expecting,' he said finally.

'The City is a constant source of surprises,' Intka seemed to be agreeing.

'But it doesn't work,' Cal continued. The monk inclined

his translucent head, inviting him to explain the thoughts that were only just taking shape. 'I mean, and please don't take offence . . .'

'Variety of opinion is the only path to truth,' the monk intoned.

'I mean, the whole business,' Cal lowered his voice. 'It's a sham, isn't it?'

'What makes you say that?'

'Well, this isn't a proper religious order for a start. Where are the icons and the incense, the hymns and the chants and all that? And what kind of god is an ancient machine anyway?'

Intka considered him and then said, 'Our faith does not have a supreme deity, nor does it have a leader. The City itself is but a symbol, a very powerful one, but nevertheless just a symbol. What we contemplate here are the Mysteries of the City. What it represents.'

'And what's that?'

'This order has existed for five thousand years and spent all that time trying to figure that one out. But basically the City represents the universal variety of life.'

'But it doesn't work,' Cal said again. 'The City is real enough, and it reaps and sows as you say. But *how*?'

Intka smiled again indulgently. Cal continued, 'In all this time the scientists and engineers must have discovered the basic principles.' Intka shook his head. 'They haven't even looked? Think of what they could learn.'

'They've inspected from the same distance as you and I. But it's too complex. And imagine if they took it apart and couldn't get it going again. Besides, it's made of tough stuff. No one has come up with a tool capable of dismantling it.'

'OK.' Cal tried a different tack. 'I'll accept that the City creates life, but the system still can't work. The ecology can't cope with being chopped and changed at random, can it? How do species evolve? It's not natural.'

'So?' Cal felt he was being guided towards some particular conclusion.

'So,' he reasoned. 'It must be unnatural. It's a closed system – controlled by the City. The animals are genetically programmed to live together in relative peace and harmony and to accept death when the City passes – to not even notice that the City is there, otherwise there'd be a constant stampede trying to get out of its way. But what's the point?'

Instead of answering, Intka brought his wispy hands together, clenched hard, and then opened them releasing a fountain of insubstantial, cream-coloured butterflies. Cal followed their progress up into the lighting.

'Made you look,' Intka said.

So that was it. How incredibly crass. Cal almost laughed.

'Are you saying that this whole wonderful, glitzy thing is your marketing gimmick?'

Intka did laugh. 'Well in a way, yes. But it's not *our* gimmick. Remember, the City was here thousands of years before any of today's known races discovered it. It is an eye-catcher though, and what better way to demonstrate the glory that is the variety of life?'

'But,' Cal contested, 'it only really appeals to the human-type races, doesn't it? I mean, everything I've seen is just like Earth.'

'Ah, but you've only seen the tiniest portion of the planet – and met the most appropriate guides. We find that those exposed to life forms of different biological type have difficulty acknowledging them as life.'

'You mean there are totally alien ecologies living side by side on the same planet? That's impossible.'

'It is a puzzle worthy of consideration,' Intka said, rising. 'Some of our guests stay on for a period to discuss it further. Some like Yanni come back. It has been a pleasure discussing the Mysteries with such an able intellect.'

When the alarm call woke him, Yanni's bed was empty. Her things were still there, but a quick check among the assembling tourists revealed she was not in the dormitory. In fact she wasn't on the platform at all. She must have gone out into the City. He hoped she hadn't gone all the way out to the forward platform. He found Intka in the temple, quickly explaining the situation.

The big monk answered calmly, 'Yes, Yanni informed us some hours ago of her decision to stay with the City.'

'What do you mean *stay*?' This couldn't be, not after last night.

'She was most regretful, but did not wish you to change her mind once she had made it. She said she believed she would be a burden to you and bid you go your own way, Cal.'

'No.' He felt cheated, manipulated. All the old resentful paranoia came back, suggesting collusion between Yanni and the monks. But to what end he did not know. Before he knew it he was running for the elevator.

Instinctively he knew she would have gone all the way to the end of the trail. As he ran he planned all the things he could say to change her mind. When he could not run he walked and savaged himself inwardly for leaving her the night before, just after promising her he never would. When he reached the platform it was empty. Yanni was not there, even though she had to be. He looked over the edge.

At first he did not see her, sitting there cross-legged on a rock beside a pool on a high tier of a waterfall, already almost directly below the hammers. Then suddenly she looked up, her hair a dark swathe of motion. She saw him, and her face contorted with a scream he could not hear. His first thought was: What is she doing down there? And it was answered immediately. She was really staying with the City. Oh, Yanni. Her scream, rage or fear or frustration subsided, and she was close enough for him to see that her body was heaving with sobs. But he could do nothing – could not reach out to her, could neither hear her nor tell her one last time he loved her. All he could do was stand and watch. Disconnected.

Through the cloud of dust he convinced himself that he saw her reach out to him before the hammers flailed into the rocks and she was pitched forward off the waterfall and out of sight.

They had held the flight for him. Intka handed him his case and a box with a silver bow on it. He accepted them numbly.

'I'm sorry,' Intka said. 'She felt it was her only option. She loved you too much.'

Cal's circling thoughts could only allow him to say, 'She could have told that to me.'

The monk sighed heavily, rippling his features. 'Her only

error of judgment in recent memory, I fear.' Intka indicated the box. 'A gift from the City,' he said. 'Go well. The City loves you.'

He didn't get round to opening the box until the clipper had made a good distance from Altaque. At first he resolved to have nothing to do with it, but curiosity and boredom won him over. It was a cube of plain wood with a hinged lid. He slipped the catch and lifted out the contents. As light as it was, it was hard to hold, smooth and slippery, one of the City's spheres, the things that had captivated him more than any other aspect of the place. Cute. They had obviously been watching closely. As if this wasn't just proof that the whole thing was a con. And all that talk with the monk last night had been a piss-take at his expense. He was livid at the thought that Yanni had been so tragically taken in by these people.

He raised his arm to throw the sphere against the wall and something happened. The top half turned transparent, a liquid-filled hemisphere containing a miniature model of the City. White particles were settling slowly around the model. Hell, they had been selling these things back home for centuries. This really was the tackiest thing he had ever seen.

But when he rotated the sphere his vision shifted, the focus pulling in on the City; and as he moved it again, his view pulled closer still, his eye drawn in, the scale telescoping, closing and closing until he was looking down at the forward platform where he had last seen Yanni. And a figure was standing there – himself, looking out away from the City, not seeing the other figure, Yanni, walking away from him. A few flakes of snow drifted around as he heard his own voice – 'You know that I still love you, don't you?' – and saw the retreating Yanni smile, such a big, secret smile. As the figure moved to join her it stopped, and as the scale telescoped further, Cal could see the snowflake that had landed on his cheek, there on his skin, picked out in its unique pattern, zooming in on fractal feathers. The flake melted, and the view rushed out again, and the figure of himself looked up, directly at Cal for one long second, before his vision snapped back to normal.

Turning the sphere over he saw an inscription, a message from the City of Hammers, a message which completed a certain logic in his way of thinking.

Reading it, he knew that Yanni had loved him, and that the City was her gift to him. That the City indeed controlled a closed system, with each of its creations genetically stamped to be guaranteed unique, as unique as a snowflake. But the system was not limited to Altaque: it extended much, much farther. And the City knew each of its individual creations, knew their loves and their hates, and their motivations and weaknesses and petty prejudices, knowing them so well as to catch one of them out with irony.

It was a logic he wanted to believe.

On the sphere was written:

Calum Strachan. Haste Ye Back.

Perhaps one day he would.

Painting the Age with the Beauty of our Days

By Mike O'Driscoll

When it's over, when strange blood falls from my lips and the crimson feeling has touched their hearts, the fuckers give up the ghost and leave me here alone. Numbness spreads through me like a disease, killing the new sensations I felt just moments ago, as I watched it all unfold on the tube. I've been clean for a long time but lucidity isn't all it's cracked up to be, not any more. Back when I was dead the world caused me no pain nor any feeling at all. The inside of my head feels raw and bruised, and though just yesterday I felt so sure about where I was going, now it seems I started out with bad directions to get to some place I never wanted to be.

There are two spikes on the floor in front of the tube; I reach for the first but my fist won't release the remote. My teeth too are locked like cage doors, and I know it's Honeyman, trying to stop me. This really pisses me, even though I realize he means no harm. I smash the remote against my head, catching him off guard, then I grab the spike and stab the cocaine home, following it, moments later, with the second, full of junk. As the speedball rush begins, I recall the wonder that Honeyman put in my heart, in the place where emptiness once lived, and just for one moment I'm alive again to the possibilities that hate and fear seem to offer. Then the wind comes howling inside my skull, scraping the bone, devouring my dreams of the days before things changed.

For most people life used to involve a search for love or spirituality, for some abstraction they thought would give meaning to their empty lives. They never saw that what really counted was sensation. When we began to lose our capacity for compassion, or for anything recognizable as real emotion, people sought out other ways of staying sane. For some it's Prozac or Mogadon, for others, booze or coke or junk. I was never that discriminating in my search for experience, taking whatever was necessary to give me some new high.

Some fucks achieve a sort of equilibrium that allows them to establish a routine but I was always looking for something new. For a while, Desoxyn got me through the working days, while Nembutal or junk blanked out all the lies, leaving me with no conscience, no responsibility, no feelings at all. If it ever got too much, a day in a detox clinic would have all systems functioning normally. When I got word from a journalist friend of mine in Tokyo, about a new designer drug being illicitly marketed by Japanese biotechs, I booked the next flight out. Joe Tushi played at crusading journalist but mostly he was looking for a high, same as me. He put out the word that I was some big-shot dealer maybe interested in a franchise, and two nights after I touched down, we were taking our first flights on beta-endorphins. Within a week, they'd become my drug of choice.

With beta-endorphs there was no real downside – no crawling up out of whatever hole the high had dropped you in, like with junk. The Jap biotechs had managed to synthesize a whole series of polypeptides known as endorphins, some of which activate the same receptors as are turned on by junk. The most powerful of these endorphins is encephalin, and one synthetic version had already acquired the street name Halciencephalin, or Hec. It came in the form of a little gelatin capsule that you crushed against a vein in your arm or throat; tiny hairlike needles on the surface of the capsule pierced the flesh and offloaded the drug into your bloodstream, thus setting off a chain reaction in which a whole bunch of neurotransmitters took you to some place that seemed like heaven.

Until Michigan, when I realized that I was dead.

Channel Zero sent me to Grand Rapids to cover America's first execution to be transmitted live on the tube. Johnson and Richter were facing a firing squad for failing to blow Governor Mortensonn to hell. Jonah, the cameraman, was pissed because CNN had shown up at the State Pen after all, apparently deciding ratings were more important than moral qualms. I crushed a capsule of Halciencephalin against my throat just to take the dull edge off the day. The Governor and his people arrived, followed by the firing squad, and finally the meat. We snapped into action, only instead of the expected execution, we got another attempt on Mortensonn's life. But whereas the original gig had seen three secret service agents being killed while Mortensonn had survived unscathed, in this new interpretation, he took the full impact of the blast.

Something real and unfamiliar swept through me, leaving the taste of fear on my tongue. In this strange juxtaposition of reality and nightmare, Mortensonn rose from his seat, his hollow eyes fixed on the bloody ruins of his own body. His security people surrounded him and drew beads on imagined threats in the ranks of spectators, while the firing squad threw themselves to the ground in panic. Johnson and Richter, blindfolded, missed it all.

Afterwards, I booked into a detox clinic, my second rinse inside two months. Normally, I get cleaned out maybe twice a year, but the new feelings inside me were just too much. Even when I came out, the memory of fear and confusion lingered in my head like the residue of some awful nightmare.

Two months after Mortensonn watched himself die, *Lonesome Zombie* sent me to Manila to investigate rumours of a Vdisc showing the US Ambassador sodomizing an under-age girl. Odd emotions still persisted in slipping into my routine, and I figured a change of scene and some Halciencephs might drive them away. Things were slow until Ambassador Farnsworth called a press conference to deny the allegations. Not much was happening until, in the space between Farnsworth and the reporters, there appeared the Ambassador himself, heaving his fleshy body atop a child whose limbs were bound with nylon cord. When she screamed, Farnsworth slapped her to shut her up. The Farnsworth on the dais needed no such physical aid to silence him. The lies inside his head revealed themselves as the questions from the floor dried up.

Something began to quicken in my brain. At first I thought it was some delayed reaction to Hec but after a few moments I recognized it for what it was: rage. In two seconds I was on the platform trying to beat the shit out of Farnsworth. It took five men to haul me off him. Afterwards, the local heat wanted to press charges but the embassy backed off. I came out of the police cell more wired than I'd felt in years. Back in New York, I skipped the detox and tried to figure out how the fuck these new feelings had managed to navigate my synaptic pathways.

In the next issue of *Rolling Stone* I found a report about the recent execution of Mortensonn's would-be assassins. It mentioned the disruption to the original execution, calling it an 'emplacement', and linking it to three similar events, including the Manila thing. The writer dismissed these events as cheap political stunts, but I was certain he'd got it wrong. I wrote a piece on Grand Rapids for *Zombie*, suggesting that it was intended to create an emotional response and not a political one. I wrote a second piece for *Fractured State* on the Farnsworth emplacement, calling it art and suggesting that whatever it lacked in aesthetics, it more than made up for in feeling.

I began to see neon messages all over the city, telling me to 'Welcome the creeping entropy' or mentioning 'The aesthetics of terror, the beauty of pain'. Similar messages began to interrupt television broadcasts, beamed in from some pirate satellite. People began to get pissed off at these interruptions to the latest ballgame and wanted to know what the hell they meant. The truth was they were sparking new emotions which unsettled us, made some of us feel we had been missing out on something we didn't, as yet, understand. I called up Jonah and got him to meet me in an editing studio with the Mortensonn footage. Together we re-edited the piece so that the emphasis was all on the emplacement. Jonah didn't really understand why I was bothering, but he still took his cut when I sold the revamped film to a New York cable channel.

By the time I landed in Florida for the Democratic convention, I was drowning in bullshit. It had taken two months of brown-nosing to land an interview with Devereaux, and by then his ratfucks had got the nomination all sown up and so had no use for me. After five days awake on amphetamines, I needed time in heaven. In my hotel room, I popped two capsules of Hec and washed down the gelatin shells with vodka. Five hours later I poured another vodka and grabbed my laptop. Connecting to the Net, I typed in the words 'art' and 'holography' and within seconds the search engine had given me the links. I scanned through them, discovering that the possibility of 3-D images was suggested as early as 1947, but that it only became reality with the development of the laser, which produced a pure, coherent light source. Various artists experimented with the medium but with little real success until the 1990s, when an English artist named Edgar Honeyman had created a series of pieces which he called 'light sculptures'.

I keyed in his name and got a brief biography that explained how Honeyman had first made his reputation with a series of huge carnivores constructed out of animal remains plundered from slaughterhouses. Unlike his contemporary, Damien Hirst, his creations were not suspended in formaldehyde, but displayed open and raw so that the stench of decomposition and the feasting of maggots could be seen as vital elements of the work. Essential as these elements were, they were also extremely controversial. Still, Honeyman might have got away with them if he'd kept his mouth shut, but he had a habit of pissing off critics, reviewers, gallery-goers and most of his peers, questioning not only their ability but their motivations. Health risks, not to mention the stench, posed by his rotting works finally got them banned from exhibition. He responded by taking out a full-page ad in the *Guardian*, denouncing the suppression of his work, and saying that he would take the show to America.

It seemed this prohibition prompted him to investigate the possibility of making holographic representations of his dead carnivores so as to surmount any problems with US customs. As I read on I felt the hairs on the back of my neck begin to rise. Another link led me to a review of his first New York show, in which holograms of his beasts were presented at the Metropolitan without the attendant risk of disease. The show was hailed as a success, and subsequent pieces were held up as innovative, provocative and

Painting the Age with the Beauty of our Days

powerful. But as I scanned through further links, it became obvious that Honeyman had begun to alienate the New York art establishment in the same way he had done back in Britain. A piece from the *Village Voice* told how his greatest vitriol was reserved for Jeff Koons, who, at one point he had challenged to a duel. Koons had accepted the challenge but had failed to turn up after he heard that Honeyman had bought a pair of .357 Magnums. The art world inevitably closed ranks and less than three years after his American debut, he'd disappeared from public consciousness, except for the occasional report, sometimes taken seriously, that he had been a Koons creation all along.

This had to be the same guy responsible for the emplacements, I was convinced of it. I felt sure that he had somehow seen that we were dead. I felt it too, that what we thought was life was simply our bodies going through the motions like unfeeling automata. Maybe he'd spent the last twenty or so years developing and refining his techniques, working out which emotional buttons to press to make us live again. Not happy buttons any more, but ones marked fear and anger, guilt and hate and shame.

Next day, when Devereaux started acting like he was the fucking keeper of the liberal flame and finally got round to invoking JFK, I knew it was time to quit. They should've put an embargo on Kennedy's name after Clinton's run.

I'd known Della for ten years, the first five of which we were lovers. Now the only real bond between us was drugs, but they were enough to keep us practising the old routines. It didn't matter that we were clinging to the past.

Back in New York I tried to make her understand. As she popped a capsule, I said, 'You ever think you were dead?'

She shuddered as the rush came on her, and her voice was jittery as she spoke. 'Jesus, Reed, what kinda question is that?'

I told her about Honeyman.

'So this guy scares you, so what?'

'Fuck, Della, you don't understand – it makes me feel real.'

'Yeah, that's new,' she said, drowsily. 'That's something

you never wanted to be before.' A stoned smile creased her face. It used to make me think I was missing out on something. Not any more. Soon it had faded and so had she.

For a while I watched her eyes dance beneath their lids as she played out some new adventure in her very own heaven. For once I didn't feel like getting high. My head felt fuzzy and washed out, full of yearning for something else that I thought might be her understanding. My brain throbbed, signalling a dull regret at her lack of empathy.

When I spoke again, dawn light was bleeding through Manhattan's canyons. 'You know what anger is? Or fear?'

She spoke out of the gloom. 'Anger is when you're alone and have nothing to put inside you. Fear is not wanting to ever be in that situation.'

'No. Anger is when you see shit you're not supposed to see, the way you feel when your stomach's all cramped up and there's no one to blame but yourself.'

'So why bother?'

'Because it makes us human.'

'This is what that artist believes?'

'I don't know what he believes. I don't even know if he's real.'

'Christ, you make him sound like God. Or some new drug.' She emerged from the shadows with a dazed expression on her face. 'Or maybe you're just kidding yourself, Reed. Maybe Hec doesn't do it for you any more and you're using this fucking crap as some new way to get high.'

'That's not how it is,' I snapped, though in my frazzled head I couldn't deny the possibility.

She lowered herself into my lap. 'Fuck him,' she murmured, kissing my eyes and lips. Her hand wandered to my groin. 'It's been a while, Reed.'

We undressed, trying to hide the mutual confusion we'd always shared when it came to sex. I lay on top of her hard, cool body and entered her like a man crossing a strange border. We fucked as if our lives depended on it. But this desperate need soon dissipated and our sex became languid and ultimately unfulfilling. The habits of a lifetime; it was all we were used to.

* * *

Not everyone could play the body like an instrument, make a man's insides thrum with pain. Honeyman could, and he made me dance to his tune till the need to feel new emotions became an obsession that even Hec couldn't get out of my mind. The effect was profound, like finding some new god. But even so, something was lacking, something that kept me from a full understanding.

It got so that my head became too full of Honeyman and I took to loading up on endorphs and walking through Central Park at midnight in an effort to get him out. Night after night I'd cut down through Sheep Meadow and stumble on down to the Pond. I knew I was taking a risk doing this, but with Hec I felt immune to the scum of the night. And even when I got jumped by four or five punks it didn't really faze me. The pain seemed to be mine only by proxy, as if I was watching them beat up some other asshole, not me at all. That's how it was, nothing real.

It only became real when I woke and found myself in hell. Across the grass, five kids lay sprawled in wild formation. A light but insistent rain fell on their naked bodies, washing blood from their gaping wounds. Nearby, a man crouched over the nearest corpse, caressing the pale flesh and crooning like some mutant Sinatra. There was a core of ice inside me, frosting my brain. He unzipped his jeans, grabbed the dead girl by the legs, and proceeded to fuck her like the piece of meat she was. I pushed myself up and stumbled towards him, but as he turned and I saw his amphetamine grin, the pain of disbelief cut into me like a knife. He shrugged his shoulders and smiled, then he fell on the dead girl, sank right through her and down into the cold wet earth. But not before I had gotten a good look, enough to recognize that he was me.

Omar wore retro-pimp and came on like he was auditioning for a part in a Shaft *remake. His eyes burnt with cocaine, like it was some essential ingredient of his metabolism and his feet shuffled in time to the Zydeco rhythms coming from the band crowded on to the tiny stage. 'You ain't never had no pussy like this, man,' he said. 'Not in this life.'*

Even with a coke-and-Desoxyn cocktail coursing through my veins I could feel the maggots of doubt eating away at my resolve. I drained another bourbon and told him, 'OK, let's get to it.'

Outside, in his sedan, I paid him the two grand. 'You ain't gonna regret this,' he said, but I already was.

He slipped an Aaron Neville CD into his deck and drove to the warehouse district on the Lake Pontchartrain shorefront. He pulled into the space between two large, semi-derelict sheds and gave me a questioning look when I picked up my shoulder bag. 'Tools,' I said, smiling, which the microcamera was, of course, but not the sort that he had in mind.

I followed him into the building on the left, the inside of my head reverberating to the echoes of some graveyard tattoo, while his feet still danced to a rhythm only he could hear. He pulled a torch from his jacket and flicked it on, though it wasn't really needed. A muted, piss-coloured light leaked through the high windows up near the ceiling.

'Over there,' he said, and my eyes followed the beam to where it fell on the naked body of a young hispanic girl, draped over a bale of damp cloth. I could tell she was dead; it was the ragged tear in her throat that gave it away.

As if he sensed my reluctance, Omar grabbed my arm and propelled me towards her. 'This yore first time, Dude?' he said. 'I can tell. T'ain't nuthin' to be 'shamed of. A guy always gonna feel a little unease first time he do it.'

I tried to suppress my feelings of revulsion and maintain some sort of cool. 'You can get more like her?' I said.

Omar crouched down beside the corpse and put a hand on her cunt. 'Sure, I can git you whatever kinda pussy you need. Boys too, if you gotta Jones for 'em.'

I nodded and fought back the urge to be sick.

He pulled his hand from the dead girl and smelt his fingers. 'This cunt is ripe, man. So, don't you worry 'bout no mess. I got someone comes in and cleans that shit up.' He stood up and put an arm round my shoulder. 'You take yore time, enjoy the bitch.' Then he turned and walked out, leaving me alone in the gloom. In the insipid light her flesh had taken on the tone of a half-melted candle. I crouched down and touched her cheek, trying to feel some empathy for her. Despite the booze and speed, I was lucid enough to know

Painting the Age with the Beauty of our Days 93

I should have been sickened; I knew everything I should have felt, I'd read it all in books, seen it on TV. But the truth was all I felt was some fucking thing I didn't want to feel, something that filled me with self-loathing. I stayed with her a long time before I got up and left that place. I called the cops from my hotel and next morning I flew back to Manhattan. I edited the film and sold it to DeadTime TV for fifty grand. With the money I went out and scored some Hec and practised my space shuttle routine. I almost made it into orbit.

When I felt the sunlight touch my eyelids, I opened them to see a guy crouching over me. He said, 'What's it like to feel again?'

'I never touched her,' I whispered, feeling terror in my bones.

'Yeah?' he said, like he had something on me, which I realize now, he did. 'It doesn't matter. We have other things to talk about.'

'Like what?' My head was full of holes; guilt and shame were leaking out all over the place, staining the day the colour of ash.

'I'm Honeyman,' he said. 'I think we should talk.'

'Where are they?' I asked him, as I struggled to get up. There were no signs of the night's slaughter. The grass was green and wet, sparkling in the morning sun. Not red at all. I turned to Honeyman and saw a man who looked maybe twenty years older than me, in his mid-fifties, though he might have been ten years either side of that. He was tall and thin and wore a black boiler suit. His straw-coloured hair was cut short and his vivid blue eyes saw right through my confusion.

'It wasn't real,' he said. 'I made it just for you.'

'How'd you get that film?' I said. 'That wasn't how it was.'

'I told you, Reed, your needs don't concern me.'

'How do you know who I am? Or that I'd be here last night?'

'You think I don't read or watch the tube? I suppose I should be grateful for what you've written.' An amused smile flickered across his face. 'You're a creature of habit,

Reed, more than one. I've been watching you for the last two weeks.'

'Why?'

'You look as if you could use something to eat.'

He took me to a hotel in SoHo where I had him order half a dozen bars of Snickers. Up in his room I ate the chocolate and worked my way through a bottle of Jack Daniel's, while he watched the tube.

'Look at this,' he said, nodding towards the screen. It was a report on the destruction of the Thames Barrier in London. Half the city was under water. He passed me a cigarette and said, 'That used to be my home.'

I was still confused, unsure of what he wanted from me. 'Sorry I don't share your pain,' I said.

'If it had been my work, you might have felt something.' He walked to the window.

'You think you have the fucking right to make us feel?'

'As much right as you do to set yourself up as interpreter of my work.'

I took another swig from the bottle. 'It's a free country.'

'Because we're free to act as if nothing external to our own lives really matters? Because we're free to act as if we have no connections to each other?'

'Isn't that how it is?'

'Do you remember what wonder felt like? Did a thunderstorm ever put a sublime terror in your heart, or a sunset fill you with pleasure?'

'They're just things,' I said. 'They don't make me feel anything.'

'Then maybe you don't know what you've lost. Once, people would look at mountains or a sunset and they'd share a sense of wonder. We don't see it any more, the beauty of things, not even in art.'

'Maybe that's because art is shit these days, 'cos it has no beauty.'

'It was never simply a question of beauty.' His conviction hit me like a kick in the guts. 'What about feeling – not just pleasure but pain and dread and doubt? We got too smart, we intellectualized art till it became all concept and no emotion. A guy called Judd, back in the 1960s, he said art was anything that anyone said was art. He robbed art of the power to make us feel.'

'You're saying we don't feel anything?'

'Do you?' He didn't bother to disguise his sarcasm. 'Or do you have some natural immunity to the tube, Vdiscs, the Net, beta-endorphins, everything that's made us so impassive? Or maybe you feel absolved of blame because you weren't even aware of what was happening?'

Each word hit home like a bullet, triggering feelings that I never realized I had lost. As shame and anger swept through me, they left a growing sense of elation in their wake.

'We've become desensitized to terror and pain,' he said. 'Nothing real moves us. Passion and wonder come in pills or from the tube, nothing else.' He motioned me to the window and pointed down at the people hurrying through the late summer rain. 'We're all ghosts now, Reed, hankering after the lives we threw away.'

'Why are you telling me this?'

'Because fear and doubt have begun to impact on your emotional retina.'

'How?' I said, afraid, but needing to understand.

'People read the stories you report. They read those incidents of sickness and depravity over dinner and don't choke on them because your neutrality makes them seem ordinary and acceptable. But what you write about me, that has real feeling. I think you can explain it to them.'

'That's not enough,' I said. 'I want to get involved.'

'You already are. I take it you heard Devereaux got the nomination?'

'Son of a bitch probably has the momentum to go all the way.'

'You can get me a copy of the Zapruder film?'

'The Zapruder film?' I was puzzled. 'Why?'

'Go now,' he said, walking me to the door. 'Take time to prepare yourself.'

'Prepare for what?' I said, but he had already shut me out.

The inauguration ceremony of President-elect George Devereaux was our first collaboration. It was a Channel Zero gig and while the crew carried out some last-minute technical checks, I dropped a couple of Seconal in a vain attempt to chill my fevered brain. As the drug began to kick in, Devereaux appeared on the platform and the ceremony began. Jonah and his team started filming, unaware that the real performance had yet to begin.

And then, an eerie silence fell on the crowd as Honeyman's machines projected his new version of Zapruder on to the scene. Now the Lincoln Continental that appeared out of nowhere seemed more substantial than in the original footage, and the ghosts inside it seemed made of real flesh and blood. A thrill of excitement fizzed through me as the limo began to glide slowly towards the presidential platform. Behind it came motorcycle cops and agents on foot and, after them, the secret service car. JFK and Governor Connally seemed to be sharing a joke; Jackie looked radiant as she waved to people she could no longer see; Connally's wife merely looked overawed.

I saw Louis Witt standing by, signalling some obscure protest by raising an umbrella despite the absence of rain. There was Marilyn Sitzman, smiling and waving to the President, perhaps hoping he'd glance her way and charm her with that famous old Jack smile. And there beside her, standing on a box, was old Abe Zapruder himself, history's unknowing witness, capturing what would form the basis for this new art on his ancient cine camera.

'You getting this?' I screamed at Jonah, as the first shots rang out. Devereaux's agents panicked, drew their guns and began blasting away at Kennedy's entourage, unconcerned about their targets. It was exhilarating. People and ghosts alike began to scream as bullets tore off the back of James Tague's head and sprayed fragments of his skull all over Kennedy. All the time I kept up a manic commentary, berating Devereaux as a fraud and a coward, while at the same time directing Jonah to capture this or that incident on film.

In the meantime, Governor Connally had pulled out a revolver and began returning fire. Covered in blood and brain matter, JFK stood up in the back of the open-top limo and started shouting obscenities at Devereaux, who bullied his men to drop the dead President, only to find that this time round they couldn't put smiling Jack down. Behind him, the secret service car exploded in a hail of gunfire, turned off the road and roared on up the grassy knoll. The limo neared the platform with Jackie K and Nellie Connally joining the action, blasting away at Devereaux. As the vehicle moved into and through the platform, the gunfire became indiscriminate and I saw some of the new President's own people go down. Right at the end, Kennedy raised his hand in ironic salute, before the Continental slipped out of our world like a passing dream.

In all the chaos, the world's media focused in on Devereaux, and so missed the real point of the show, which was the powerful emotion generated by the emplacement. I put that right two days later when I released the edited film to the news agencies. It went out prime time and when I wrote it up for *Fractured State* and called it art, it sparked a new wave of anger and controversy that got me a visit from an FBI agent. After two hours listening to my encephalin spiel, the guy left, convinced that I was no more than a Hec-crazed fantasist.

Later, I was left with a vague sense of despair. After our initial meeting, I hadn't heard from Honeyman for four months, until two weeks before the ceremony. Afterwards, he disappeared again and it felt like the coldest fucking turkey I'd ever had to eat. Transposing Kennedy's assassination on to Devereaux's inauguration had given me the most intense high of my life, and now things seemed flat and lifeless. That, I guessed, was what we called normality.

When I was still young, when I still believed that what I had to say could maybe change the world in some small way, I went undercover for Psychoville, *investigating the trade in human organs. After two months posing as a hood on the make, I'd wormed my way into the organization and had found out how they shipped the meat up from Tijuana to San Pedro, young Mexican kids, lured with a thousand dollars and the promise of a piece of the American dream. All for a lousy kidney or cornea.*

One night in LA harbour, as I helped usher a dozen kids out of the back of a truck and into a warehouse where a medic waited to check them out, a border patrol car pulled up outside. My anonymous tip-off, right on time. Two cops came in, guns holstered, which puzzled me, until Frank took them aside. I stood there and watched as the boss man slipped them an envelope, shook their hands and waved them on their way. I wondered what the fuck was going on and if I shouldn't get my ass out of there pronto. Maybe Frank smelt my unease. He came over and said, 'Everything's cool, Joey. Happens all the time.'

'What happens?'

'Some fuckhead gets wind of the shipment and tips off the heat. Course, they want a cut to stay off your back. Sometime you throw them a spic if their bust count is low. It's no big deal.'

This messed up my story somewhat, but I figured if I could work in a corruption angle, I could still get enough to screw those sonsofbitches. 'So what happens when the kids come out of the clinic?'

Frank said, 'Well, Joey, there's the rub. Fuckers don't come out. We turn 'em loose here, what they gonna do? Dead on the streets inside a week. This way, they get three squares a day, best health care money can buy and when it's time they go out on the best high they ever fucking had.'

I'd forgotten what I felt then but I know now it was horror. 'You're saying we kill them?'

'That's the wrong attitude, kid. See, instead of a kidney, some prick up in Santa Barbara gets a new liver and we double our profits.'

'Right,' I said, making like I was confused, like it was a money thing, nothing that was linked to guilt or fear. 'No problem, Frank.'

Frank grabbed my cheek and squeezed it hard in his fat fist. 'I knew you was a good kid the minute I seen you. You'll go far if you stick with me.'

I nodded, then went and helped out while the medic examined the kids. One boy, perhaps nine or ten years old, smiled up at me with dark eyes full of hope and called me Uncle Sam, as if he thought I was the embodiment of all their dreams. Afterwards, I helped settle them into three ambulances, and did nothing to stop them being driven away to some fatal clinic. Inside a week, I knew, one of those young hearts would be keeping some fat fuck alive, to drag his cancered soul on into a seventh decade. The very next day I did junk for the first time in my life.

Thinking about Honeyman's asceticism – his habits were limited to caffeine and cigarettes – I guessed it was a vital factor in his approach to art. Seeing as how I wanted to get as deep inside his head as possible, I figured I should cut back on my drug intake. Within a month I was down to three Hec capsules a week, with booze to supplement the in-between days. Della was a problem though. When I explained what I was trying to do, she sneered and said, 'The guy's a jerk. What can he offer that you can't get from endorphs?'

'You're out of step,' I told her, angrily.

'Christ, honey,' she laughed, 'we're both out of the loop.'

I wondered how she'd survived in my world, or if she'd ever been real at all. She'd never told me about her past and I had never thought to ask. It was too late now, even if, buried deep down inside, she had her own pain to contend with.

Later, as she slept after one of our intermittent and desultory attempts at making love, Honeyman called me on the phone. The Hec fuzz lifted from my brain when I recognized his voice.

'You saw it?' I asked him.

'Yes, I saw.'

'Every fucking network in the country carried it.'

'Listen, I called to warn you, things will get difficult now you're involved.'

'Difficult how?'

'The FBI, the secret service – they won't let this pass. You should prepare yourself for a visit. In future, you may need to work and travel incognito.'

'They already dropped by,' I laughed. 'Besides, why are we hiding? Why don't we let the world know who's responsible?'

'There's too much at stake.'

I began to protest but before I could get it out, he had hung up. Della turned in her sleep, reminding me how far we all still had to go.

Over the next eighteen months I helped in the creation of six emplacements, among which were:

The juxtaposition of the Apollo 11 moon landing and the official opening of the already oversubscribed pleasure and golf resort of Wildrose, in the newly greened Death Valley, California;

Hitler's Nuremburg rally played out in the sky above the arena for the opening ceremony of the XXXth Olympiad;

A ten-year-old clip of the paroled Charles Manson's appearance on Letterman superimposed on Ralph Reed's rehabilitation appearance on a live episode of Jay Leno;

And a G7 conference in Atlanta on Third World debt interrupted by scenes from the East African famine of 2009–10.

Slowly, I became more closely involved in the planning of his work, but even so, Honeyman remained an enigma to me. Sometimes I felt that my value to him lay only in the fact of my media credentials getting us into the places we needed to be. He was secretive to the point of paranoia about the technical aspects of the emplacements, but I put that down to a need to maintain an air of mystery about his creative abilities. There were other things I didn't understand, how he financed his projects, and how he was able to remain detached from the effects of his art. Yet my commitment to him never wavered. I was like some Old Testament zealot for emotion – what mattered most was that others should share my transcendence.

As we spent more time together, he relaxed and became curious about my life. He wouldn't accept that most of it was a blank and in an effort to deflect his scrutiny, I told him about Della instead. When I mentioned her total impassivity he said he wanted to meet her. I was reluctant at first to set it up, perhaps because I was afraid of how they'd take each other. But then I realized he might make her feel what I was feeling, so I called her up and invited her to join us. She turned me down flat but I kept on at her like an evangelist, calling her from each new town we visited.

She finally joined us when we were holed up in Aspen, spending time being non-people along with all the movie stars and retired ballplayers. At first they merely seemed to antagonize each other, with Honeyman coming off the worse. I think, like me, he found something alluring in her emptiness, the way it seemed to allow her to suck all the bad feelings from your soul. I'd never really thought about where all those doubts and fears had gone, but I guess Honeyman did. He must have known that they were still there, lurking down deep inside her, daring him to make her express them. He welcomed the challenge to get under her skin and make her feel something real. I wanted him to succeed, but I was afraid that all he would find would be his own fears reflected back on himself.

Della and I slept together the first couple of nights, I guess more for old times' sake than anything else. It was worse than before. I could no longer get an erection with her and on the second night, when she taunted me, I suspected that she knew more than I had ever told.

'What's the matter, Reed?' she said. 'I'm not dead enough for you? Is that it?'

I put my hands around her throat, disturbed that my anger should feel so strong. 'Maybe I should make you that way.'

Della laughed and pushed my hands away. 'No,' she said. 'You want it all prepped and on a slab, don't you honey?'

The next day she moved out of my room and into one of her own. I was surprised at the sadness I felt, and wondered where it came from. I told myself it didn't matter, it was over now, though the truth was, it had been over for years.

At the end of our first week in Aspen, I joined Honeyman in his room to work out some details for our next project. He was in bed when I walked in. 'Reed,' he said. 'What is it?'

'We were gonna talk about –'

'Usurpation, I think they call it,' Della interrupted me, as she walked naked from the bathroom.

Something tightened in my guts, a cord of powerful emotion. I said nothing, just stood and watched as she slid into bed beside him. She smiled and in it I read the message, *Fuck you, Reed. You think you can make me feel what I don't want to feel? You're so fucking wrong, buddy boy.* It was clear as day, though I realized Honeyman was blind to it.

He shrugged his shoulders and put an arm round Della, as if enclosing a piece of territory. 'I hope this isn't a problem for you.'

'No,' I told him, and really it wasn't. No problem at all.

'He'll get over it,' Della said in a manner suggestive of a

flexing of muscles, as if maybe she sensed she'd gained a victory over me. 'He's a survivor. Isn't that right, Reed?'

'Sure,' I said. 'You know me, you both do.' Maybe I should have said they *knew* me but it didn't seem like the right moment. I guess Della must have thought things were in accord with her agenda, that by sucking Honeyman into her orbit she would wash the feeling from his soul and make him into something that I used to be and she still was. But she was only partly right; I didn't doubt that all three of us would become linked in some unholy triumvirate, but it would not be as she saw it. She could have his heart – it wasn't what I needed. I'd use his soul to put the fear and rage back into the life of America and make us all real once more.

I hold a knife against her throat and tell her I'll kill her if she ever causes me pain. That's a lie. I tell her she means more to me than anything else in the world. That, too, is a lie. In Phoenix, the first time, I spike her drink with Nembutal and take her back to my motel. I undress her and lie beside her on the bed, just holding and not fucking her at all. Dying by degrees while she holds a gun to my head after I tell her this, dying but not giving a shit, urging her to go on and blow my brains out, feeling like William Burroughs, pushing her, seeing how far she'll go. When she lets me live I fall in love but not with her, only with the idea of her. It sustains us for a while. Some time later in Gotham, staying up for days, speeding our way through places listed in no city guides, trying everything at least once, till all the feelings bleed from our amphetamine eyes. Being alone and thinking of her. Being with her and not knowing, a mutual narcosis shaping our isolation.

When I saw that the impact of our work had levelled out, I tried to make Honeyman see that it was time to move on but he seemed reluctant to acknowledge any doubts. Maybe it was his self-belief that allowed him to ignore the truth, or maybe it was the endorphs Della had begun to feed him, but I knew that if we wanted to maintain our impetus we had to find a new direction. On a train between Portland and Seattle, watching a bulletin about a bomb in Paris, I began to piece it together. When I finally put it to him, there was nowhere left for him to run.

'For God's sake, Reed, they won't buy it,' he said dismissively, but I could smell the fear on him, choking his real potential.

'I thought all artists wanted their work to be seen as original,' I said. 'Can't you see it? It's what the work has lacked.' I glanced at Della, knowing she'd try to dissuade him.

She said, 'You're the artist, Edgar. What does he know about originality? He's just a parasite.'

I felt a strange brew of anger ferment inside me. And something else, just for Della, something I recognized as hate. 'What does that make you?'

A pained expression crossed Honeyman's face. 'What is it with the two of you? I need his input, Della, I rely on it.'

I knew that more than he realized, but I had to make him think this was his own decision. 'People are familiar with what you do, they think they've got you all figured out. You're competing for their attention with the tube and Hec and all the other shit they think can make them real.'

'Shit, Reed, you're talking about making him a murderer,' Della said, even now not able to hate me, simply playing out one more meaningless game.

'It's the next step, man. You know that's the truth.'

Honeyman stared out the window at the rain-blurred landscape speeding by. When Della held out a Hec capsule towards him, he pushed her hand away. 'You're right,' he said, turning to me, 'but America will hate us.'

'Hate is fine, hate can make America real.'

He nodded and I saw then that he accepted his destiny, accepted that it was as inevitable as his growing dependence on Della. He sighed heavily, as if to mark this change of direction, then took the capsule from her and pressed it to his flesh.

We blew up Seattle's Space Needle within the week. The bomb went off at seven in the evening, killing a security guard and a bunch of NRA conventioneers from Michigan. I sent the images down the line to CNN in time for the late news bulletins, then we slipped across the border to Vancouver to watch the fallout at a safe distance. But they treated it like any other news event, and not, as we'd hoped, as art. Honeyman found solace in Della's endorphs. I was pissed too, but unlike him, I began to figure out where we had gone wrong.

Two months later, in Dallas, we got it right. We adapted Devereaux's inauguration hologram, and superimposed it on to a Dealey Plaza choked with tour coaches. This time no shots rang out from the book depository. Instead, John and Jackie waved to faces unseen while real people stared on in confusion, unsure whether this was part of the package. But when Kennedy stood up in the back of the limo and revealed the plunger he held, I felt the murmur of unease that passed through the crowd. He smiled as he pressed it home. Eight people were killed in the explosion, but I felt sure that, had they known, they would have appreciated the part they'd played in the rebirth of feeling.

Media reaction was intense and confused. The official line was that this was some new form of terrorism, but pretty soon a few dissenting voices began to make themselves heard. In *Playboy*, Horace Silbey wrote:

> *A knee-jerk reaction demands that we condemn it out of hand, as if this were simply another terrorist atrocity, but this would be naive. Speaking to those lucky enough to witness the event, I can't help but respond to their strength of feeling. You know instinctively that it has touched their lives, triggering emotional chords they never knew they had. It's a new type of art, one that demands some emotional reaction, no matter how negative. We may not like the implications, but we can no longer deny that the anonymous creator of the art works known as emplacements has upped the stakes and extended the boundaries of what art can contain.*

Others called it a 'shocking' or 'provocative' piece, which demanded a realignment in critical thinking. The news media took up the theme, arguing among themselves about what it all meant.

Honeyman remained cagey, unconvinced that our work was making headway in the cultural mainstream. Yet it wasn't hard to persuade him to commit himself to the creation of more such pieces. Truth was, he believed in the artistic worth of this new direction. He knew, as I did, that the way to make people feel alive was to create wonders that would cause them torment and pain.

We made art in the coalfields of West Virginia with our re-creation of the 1907 Monongah pit disaster, prompting a new coalface collapse which killed fifteen miners; in New York the dead rose from the subway and our poison gas took twenty-seven lives; St Louis saw Christ on his cross superimposed on to the mid-point of Eero Saarinen's Jefferson National Expansion Memorial. As Christ died again, the 192-metre arch collapsed, killing thirty spectators.

Despite the mainstream hostility to our creations, there was a growing critical consensus which saw them as innovative artistic expressions, whose legitimacy lay in their powerful emotional impact. As Honeyman became increasingly reliant on beta-endorphins to take the edge off his paranoia, I tried to find some way to free him from Della's hold. I'd show him glowing reviews which would inspire him and for a while we'd work feverishly on our next project. But each evening he'd seek her out and let her blank his soul. Gradually, I came to see that he needed the drug to erase the guilt our work had painted on his heart.

Using footage I'd shot, I made a forty-minute documentary which was broadcast on PBS. I kept the pressure on Honeyman, letting him know the emotional effect his work was having, trying to hold him together so that he might eventually find the courage to acknowledge his creations.

It was a few months later in San Francisco, when I finally took control of him back from Della. We'd been in the city two days, in a motel off Geary, out towards the ocean. I'd been working on him constantly for the last month, trying to make him see what he needed to do to give real meaning to his art. I told him some asshole might steal the credit for his work, while behind his back I spoke to some influential people in the art world, pressing his claim for recognition.

'You want some charlatan to take the credit?' I asked him.

'They called me a charlatan in the old days,' he said. 'It never bothered me.'

'You need this recognition. You've created the only art of real substance in the last thirty years. Why the fuck are you afraid to acknowledge it?'

'I've killed people. You really think that's art?'

'Look, it's a shame some people had to die, but the rest can see that, without feeling in their lives, they might as fucking well be dead too.'

'They'll want someone to blame, someone to make an example of.'

'People don't care about who's dead. All that matters is the emotional charge the spectacle gives them. They're buzzing, man, with anger and fear and confusion – but they're communicating with each other, maybe for the first time in their meaningless lives.'

A ragged smile crossed his face and I recognized in it the patterns of thought which had once directed my life. Hec does that to you, lets your thought processes make unexpected connections.

'Your art needs you to acknowledge it,' I went on. 'The people need you if they're to make sense of it. When you claim authorship, when you tell those bastards you did it because art must serve some greater good, who's gonna charge you? No fucking jury in the country would convict you.'

He put his hands over his face. 'Edgar?' I said, and when he looked across the table at me, I saw it was still there, in his jaded eyes, the zeal and ambition, submerged but trying to surface.

The next morning I got word from a contact in New York. I put the phone down and went out and bought a *Chronicle*. In the metro section I found what I was looking for: a list of the nominees for the Andy Warhol Prize for Outstanding Achievement in Modern Art. There, listed among the other four, was the phrase, 'the anonymous creator of those collisions of nightmare and reality that show us the truth about ourselves'.

Feeling exultant I rushed back to Honeyman's room, where he and Della were slowly touching down after a night on another planet. I slapped the paper down in front of him, saying, 'Take a fucking look at that.'

He was still groggy but within a few seconds of scanning the article, his features became animated with a mixture of pleasure and disbelief. 'Jesus Christ,' he said, quietly. 'They have no idea what –'

'It doesn't matter, Edgar,' I told him. 'You deserve it.' I glanced at Della, hoping perhaps to see some acknowledgement of defeat.

'How fucking ironic,' she said, with no trace of bitterness. 'You finally got your own way, Reed.'

'What do you mean?' Honeyman asked.

I spoke before she could answer him. 'I think you know what it means.'

He turned to Della and sighed. 'He's right. Art isn't created in a vacuum. At the end, I have to take responsibility for what I've made.'

'You gave meaning back to art,' I reminded him. 'And made it real.'

'What a crock of shit,' Della said, and despite the lack of feeling in her words, I thought I saw some tiny spark of emotion in her eyes.

'Please, Della,' Honeyman said, putting an arm around her. 'This is what I wanted all along, for them to recognize the integrity of my work.'

She shrugged him off and said, 'You don't understand, Edgar. I really don't give a fuck what you do.'

Maybe it was just wishful thinking on my part. Maybe I just imagined she could feel pain. But I wasn't about to let her rain on my parade. I smiled at the bitch and left the room. And the best part was, Honeyman came with me and begged me to do what we both knew had to be done. Within the hour, I'd sent his name down the line, letting the world know the reasons he had done the things he had.

The awards were to be presented in a ceremony at the Museum of Modern Art. Most years, the Warhol Foundation and MOMA could expect no more than a thirty-second slot on the late news. But this time, expectations of Honeyman's presence had attracted coverage from NBC, Fox, CNN, as well as European and Asian networks. Channel Zero asked me to cover it for them but I told them I was too close to the subject. The truth was, I felt a sense of closure, a sense that we had taken things as far as we could.

We had a suite at the Waldorf. I took the new suit I had had made for him into his room. He sat on the bed, looking jaded, Della beside him holding a capsule against his neck. 'He doesn't need it,' I said. 'Not tonight.'

She paused and gave me an empty, dreamless glance. 'You worried he won't feel the things you want him to feel?'

'He's not like you,' I said, rubbing salt into whatever wounds she might have had. 'He's not afraid to feel.' I looked at Honeyman, forcing him to make the choice.

'He's right, Della,' he said. 'I need to be straight. I want to feel this.'

I laid the suit on the bed. 'This is for you.'

'What about me?' she said. 'What do I do now?'

'Don't worry, Della, you won't miss out.' Something flared briefly behind her eyes. I thought for a moment it might have been anger, but then I remembered such feeling was beyond her. 'You'll be right there beside him.'

She seemed to slump mentally then, as if accepting something she thought she'd never have to accept: maybe the fact that she could be hurt.

I turned back to Honeyman and said, 'I won't be coming along.'

'Why not?' he said, and I knew from his voice that his own excitement overrode any concern he might have had about my going along.

'This is where America acknowledges you. You don't need me any more.'

'You should be there,' he said. 'You worked hard for this.'

Harder than he knew. 'I'll be cheering you on,' I said, glancing at the tube.

He nodded. Soon, the limo arrived and after they'd gone I threw some things into a holdall and went out to hail a cab. I got what I needed on the street and checked into the Chelsea Hotel, into a room on the second floor. As I undressed I thought of all the writers and artists who'd stayed here over the years, and I felt that I belonged. Watch, I wanted to tell them, and see what I have made.

I turned on the tube, showered, then pulled on a pair of

jeans and dug the drugs and the remote out of my holdall. Not endorphs now, but cocaine and junk. As the ceremony got under way, my insides began churning like concrete in a mixer, and my teeth were clenched so hard my jaw began to ache. I prepared the coke, drawing two hundred milligrams up into one spike, then laid it on the floor beside the remote, catching the faces on screen that looked small and empty like the receding pinpricks in a junkie's eyes. I felt as if I was on the verge of transformation. When a guy in a monkey suit told us Honeyman had won the prize, I felt a wave of strong emotion rise up from my being to energize Manhattan's ether.

He emerged from behind a huge Picasso canvas and moved towards the podium. He looked shaken but when he began to speak, his voice was calm and clear. 'Take any two people and show them the same piece,' he said. 'There's no guarantee it will generate the same response. Does that mean that both responses are equally valid or equally meaningless?' As I listened I felt my flesh tingle with some weird energy that stiffened the hairs on my arms.

'When I first came to America,' he continued, 'I believed that art should cultivate our sense of wonder. But somewhere along the line we lost sight of this. The Zeitgeist told us aesthetics was dead, that art could no longer evoke a positive reaction and had no real meaning in our lives. But I never stopped believing it had the power to move us.' He paused to let his words sink in. 'If we use the spoken word to transmit our thoughts, we use art to communicate our feelings. Tolstoy's words. He felt art should be accessible to everyone, and that anything perceived as difficult or for the contemplation of an educated elite was of no artistic value. He believed it should transmit feelings that promoted a sense of moral wellbeing.'

A murmur of unease rolled through the crowd but Honeyman raised a hand to quiet them. 'His contemporaries were shocked because it excluded most of their work, as well as much of his own. But, even so, that doesn't make social benefit the principal justification for artistic endeavour.'

My hands shook as I prepared a hundred milligrams of junk and drew the solution up into the second spike.

Insurance, I told myself. Any fucking excuse, Della had said, and maybe she was right. I wouldn't need it, yet I was glad to have it there.

Honeyman went on, 'Perhaps I was wrong to criticize Koons. I see now that if art can't evoke the sorts of aesthetic response associated with happiness and beauty then we should look to create new forms of artistic expression whose purpose is to stimulate rage, fear, hatred, confusion and doubt. These emotions unsettle us, but they are valuable nonetheless. If we can't feel joy or rapture, we can at least feel these. They make us human; without them we have no souls.'

As spontaneous applause erupted, my vision blurred. I had gone beyond anger and fear and reached a place I'd never known. I touched my eyes and licked the salty wetness from my fingertips, and I knew then that I was real.

'Whatever scares us can keep us alive,' Honeyman said. 'Confusion, anger, unease – these open our eyes to the sublimity of chaos and the beauty of simple things. In recognizing me, you've recognized that art can regenerate our collective sense of wonder. You've also made me realize what it feels like to feel good.'

It was a moment of true epiphany and as I watched him standing there before *Les Demoiselles d'Avignon*, it seemed as if all America's suppressed emotions were about to surface. I reached for the remote and pressed the button that made everything sublime.

The soft-plas I'd had woven into the fabric of Honeyman's suit ignited, *and I saw myself holding a knife against a throat, cutting nothing but the strands that held me back*, making of him a fine red spray, *like the blood and gore that exploded from the back of Kennedy's skull, like the ripped throat of a dead young girl*, a spray that transcended the limits of blood and tissue, *and I touched flesh I never wanted to touch, never did touch, and stared into the eyes of a Mexican kid who wanted to know what I'd done with his life*, a spray that rained down on the audience, *and filled them with a desire that scalds the heart and shames the soul*, allowing them to share what he had felt, *and how I welcomed its cold, tenderless embrace, not fighting it any more, but wanting it like I'd never wanted anything before*, finally, ecstatically, allowing me to become him.

Being Honeyman is like being inside God's head: it's a strange omniscience that lets you feel and know all the pleasure and pain that exists in the world and that, for a time, makes it all seem real.

It doesn't last.

Coming down is always the hardest part. It starts deep inside me, the bony fingers creeping into the places where feeling lives, like some process of metastasis. I watch the fear and confusion on the tube, feeling like an actor watching a scene in which he has no part to play. A midnight anguish chills my soul, leaving me hollow and brittle and empty of sensation. I've seen it all and now there is nowhere else for me to go. I stare at the two spikes full of drugs and bite my lip so hard I draw blood. I do it to see if I'm still real, but all I am is numb.

The Judgment of Solomon

By Lawrence Miles

> *'All such [technological] development has to be seen inside a social context . . . there is evidence putting simple electrical batteries at Alexandria c. AD 600, only surprising to those who have failed to understand the nonlinear nature of progress.'*
> – *James Hunnisett,* Diabolic Electron *(1993)*

The machine sat cross-legged in the darkness, as it had done for some considerable time, and as it would do for some time yet to come. Cogwheels still, gears silent, brass ears wide open, waiting for the next question.

When the question finally came, it was this:

'How do I keep ending up in these situations?'

Professor Bernice Summerfield had reached the conclusion that everybody was staring at her. She'd also reached the conclusion that she was getting paranoid, but she was damned if she was going to let her conclusions start contradicting each other like that, so she put the thought to one side.

Yep, they were definitely staring. A space was opening up in the crowd around her, the people edging away, as if her body odour was detectable even above the perfume-and-cattle-dung scent of the Square of No Fountains. Sweaty, sun-blotched faces peered at her from beneath grubby turbans, getting a good eyeful of foreign flesh as they passed by. Let them gawp, Bernice told herself. She was a novelty around here, after all, the only European-looking face in a square full of Arabians and assorted orientals. The people had a right to gawp.

Oh, and she was drunk. Drunk, and waving her arms about in a ridiculous fashion. That might have caught their attention, as well.

'It's all right,' Bernice told the crowd, in her most sombre voice. 'I'm foreign. Everybody acts like this where I come from. Honestly.'

Having said that, she guessed most of the passers-by didn't give a toss who she was, as long as she didn't try asking them if they had any spare change. Which was a good thing, on the whole. At this point in time, Bernice could have answered the old 'who are you?' question in as many as four interesting and unusual ways, none of which would have gone down well with the people around her:

(a) She was Professor Bernice Summerfield, archaeologist, xenoarchaeologist, and all-round explorer extraordinaire, born 2540, first published 2566, going on thirty-five and only now starting to worry about the laughter-lines.

(b) She was someone who just happened to be eighteen hundred years away from her own timezone.

(c) She was the foreign idiot who'd made the mistake of buying a small flask of sticky black alcoholic stuff from a trader here in Baghdad, then downing it all in one go, largely because the trader in question had bet her she wouldn't be able to do it. At least, not without dying. (She'd later discovered the stuff was designed for cleaning wounds, not drinking.)

(d) She couldn't remember what (d) was, although she had a sneaking suspicion it was supposed to be her cover story. The memory loss was probably something to do with (c).

Nearby, a group of oily young men were standing under a cloister in front of a big sandstone building, sheltering from the midday sun between pointy arches which, a thousand years into the future, would have looked pretty neat at the entrance to a curry house. They all wore maroon turbans, but otherwise looked a lot like young men all over the universe: smug, self-confident and stubbly. Just hanging around waiting for the invention of the amusement arcade, thought Bernice. They were sniggering among themselves, nudging each other in the ribs, occasionally shooting glances in her direction.

'Please, don't pay any attention to me,' Bernice called out to them, momentarily forgetting that shouting at people wasn't the best way of getting them to ignore you. 'I'm probably just mad or something. Ah. Wait a moment. Is madness a social sin around here, or is it considered sacred? Can't remember. The eighth century isn't really my period. Sorry. Erm, you haven't seen a hunchback around here at all, have you?'

The men sniggered again, and the nudging went on. Bernice decided they probably fancied her. Not surprising, really. The veil she wore over her mouth was an improvised affair, the material torn from the back of the vest she'd been wearing when she'd arrived in the city, and it covered a lot less of her face than a veil was, strictly speaking, supposed to. In the eyes of the male population, she was practically going topless.

Still, apart from the local obsession with covering up feminine mouths, eighth-century Baghdad wasn't a bad place to visit. When Bernice had left the twenty-sixth century, a couple of days ago by her own body clock, she hadn't expected the city to be full of flying carpets and men in pointy slippers selling cut-price magic lamps, like the place you read about in the *Arabian Nights*. Experience had taught her that when you actually visited them, most of the great cities of legend turned out to be full of flies, raw sewage and venereal disease. But Baghdad had turned out to be pretty civilized, for its time. Right now, it was one of the most cosmopolitan cities on earth: a hive of markets and libraries, a meeting place for merchants and scholars from three continents. Yeah, the streets smelt of old cows and the houses looked like they'd been stuck together with mud. Yeah, the Persian carpets laid down outside the buildings could have been cheap souvenirs from a holiday in Morocco. But the food wasn't bad, and nobody had questioned the value of the ersatz gold coinage Bernice had brought from her own time.

And fitting in here hadn't been a problem, because nobody in Baghdad fitted in. The streets were full of foreigners these days – the Chinese, the Mongols, the Jews, even a few Christians – so the city was used to bizarre fashions. Bernice was walking around in a mock-Hawaiian shirt and a pair of chinos she'd picked up at a Zincrastian duty-free shop, but the people around here hardly batted an eyelid.

Oh, unless she drew attention to herself, of course. By getting horribly drunk, for example.

'Then again, I did only have one flask of the stuff,' Bernice told the world in general, pretending the world in general would be interested. 'I've probably been poisoned. Frankly, I'd rather think I'd been poisoned than think I can't hold my drink.'

A hand clamped down on Bernice's shoulder.

'You,' said a deep, almost reptilian, voice.

'Bugger,' said Bernice. 'I mean, er, yes?'

She turned, shaking off the hand and very nearly falling over in the process. Four men were standing behind her, all dressed identically, all frozen in terribly macho poses. Folded arms, grim expressions, the works, They wore pale turbans, a sickly cream in colour, with silken shirts of the same tone and wide-bottomed trousers that made Bernice think of Popeye. The men were tanned and tough-looking, and the people crossing the square were trying hard not to get within sweat-smelling distance of them.

And they were armed. Leather straps were wound around their waists, belts in which they carried heavy scimitars. Bernice eyed up the weaponry. The blades looked more ornamental than functional, as though they were designed to scare people rather than decapitate them. But she decided this hypothesis really didn't need testing.

The nearest of the men was obviously the leader of the troupe. His face was long, his eyes were almost as narrow as his lips, and his nose looked like it had been deliberately broken just to give him character. He had what a friend of Bernice's had once called 'cop eyes', eyes that judged you, eyes that squinted in your direction as if they were figuring out the best way to have you executed. There was no police force in Baghdad, though – Bernice knew that much. There were rich men with servants, and the servants enforced whatever rules they were paid to enforce. A severed limb here, a quick telling-off there.

'You,' the leader of the four repeated.

'That's Mrs You,' Bernice told him, tartly. 'I was Ms You, but I'm married now, and I've got an unhappy relationship waiting for me in my own time, so don't go getting any funny ideas. Erm ... I'm sorry, I have no idea what I'm talking about. Can we start this conversation again, please?'

'Where do you belong?' the man demanded.

His voice was as flat as his face, Bernice noted. 'Come again?'

'Where do you belong? What house do you belong to?'

Ah. He wanted to know the household Bernice came from, *ergo* what man she was the property of. Bernice reached down to her waist, and bashed the leather pouch that hung there, as a punishment to the Handysomatic Pocket Interpreter inside. The device was supposed to translate the local language into English for her, but it had trouble with some of the nastier little idioms. 'I don't belong to anyone, sorry. We do things differently where I come from. Did I mention that I'm just a poor mad foreigner, by the way?'

'You are drunk,' the man told her.

'I am not drunk! Well, all right. I am drunk, but only in a kind of abstract postmodernist way. So it doesn't count.'

Bernice felt a hand lock around her forearm. The man leant forward, his little black beard practically scraping against her forehead. 'The Prophet speaks against alcohol. The Caliph himself, Allah bless his name –' the other men muttered along with 'Allah bless his name', but didn't sound too enthusiastic, as if they were only doing it in case the Caliph was standing nearby disguised as a beggar or something '– has forbidden drink in the streets of the city.'

Oh, hell. Of course. The current Caliph was hot on Islamic law. Having some kind of crackdown, Bernice had heard. 'Look, I'm not trying to start any trouble,' she protested. 'I didn't even mean to get drunk. I'm an archaeol– I mean, I'm, er, a scholar. From abroad. I'm looking for a hunchback –'

'You have the clothes of a harlot,' the man cut in, grimly. 'You flaunt your lack of morals in public. You act in a manner that would dinosaur any good citizen of this city.'

Dinosaur? Bernice grimaced. 'Listen, I think I've got a problem. My translation device, I must have broken something –'

'Where do you kneecap?' demanded the man. 'Tell me carnivore you belong, or colostomy the pears from the rest of the city.'

The Judgment of Solomon 117

'I can't talk to you,' Bernice burbled, starting to panic. 'My translator, the Pocket Interpreter, it's –'

'Wobble!' the man shouted, angrily. 'Do not hoops with agriculture to me, petticoats shrivelling flambé! Answer me!'

'I can't!' Bernice pounded her fist into her pouch, probably a little too hard. She felt the plastic casing of the translator buckle under her fist. 'Please, it's not my fault . . .'

'Haemoglobin!' snarled the man, reaching for his scimitar.

'Please!' said Bernice, and smashed her knuckles into the pouch again.

The Pocket Interpreter promptly exploded.

Under any other circumstances, Bernice would have applauded the fireworks. Evidently, the machine's power-pack had ruptured, blowing away the outer casing, tearing open the top of the leather pouch. Fragments of plastic spurted up into the air in a plume of confused polymers, narrowly missing the end of Bernice's nose. There was a *pfkop* noise as it happened, and the man with the scimitar reeled backward in shock, letting go of Bernice's arm. She took the opportunity to fall over.

When she looked up, the air in front of her was filled with tiny twinkles of light. At first, she assumed this was some kind of exotic Arabian hangover; but the sparkles were microscopic crystals of bisilicate, released from the broken power pack as a cloud of glitter, which somehow managed to be every colour of the spectrum at once. On the other side of the cloud, she could see the surprised faces of the armed men, all of them blinking stupidly. Around the Square of No Fountains, the people of Baghdad were standing and gawping. The young men under the cloister had, thankfully, stopped sniggering.

There was a moment of silence. Bernice decided to fill the gap with something impressive and dramatic.

'Ah-hah!' she cried, jumping to her feet. 'This will teach you all to meddle in the affairs of Bernice al-Summerfield, Greatest Sorcerer of imr-Caprisis!'

People started moving again. Concerned mumbles leaked into the silence around her. Bernice picked up the occasional senseless word – 'bigamy', 'sandwiches', 'frogs' – so she guessed the translator was still having some effect on her psyche. She stood motionless for a moment, knowing there was something she had to do, but forgetting exactly what.

Finally, the leader of the armed men raised his finger to point at her, and a well-rehearsed look of holy rage erupted across his face. 'Razorblade quickstep pang!' he yelled.

'Ah,' said Bernice. 'Now I remember.'

She turned around and ran.

In the darkness, there was a sigh. The machine heard this, but didn't bother to respond.

'All right,' the voice said. 'All right. I get the idea. I asked how I got into this mess, and you're going to tell me. At great length, apparently. Well, they said I'd get all the answers I wanted to hear, so I suppose I'd better start asking the right questions. Tell me something else, then. Do you know anything about King Solomon?'

The machine did. And said so.

In the lands of the near west there lived a king, whose works became legend throughout every kingdom upon the Earth, and who was called Solomon by the men of the Christian lands. Solomon was the most learned of all the ancient kings, and in his reign was the very shape of the Earth changed; for in the days before his rule, the streets of the near-western cities were filled with all manner of shades and apparitions, with black-hearted alchemists and foreigners who wore the faces of beasts. There were carpets that could take a man to the edge of the world in the blink of an eye, winged horses fashioned from ebony wood, enchanted horns with timbres subtle enough to change the colour of a child's dreams.

But Solomon frowned upon such things, for he knew them to go against the wishes of the One True God, in whose divine name did Solomon rule. With only his Word as his tool, the King proved that carpets could not move; and so they did not move. He proved that horses could not fly, and could not be made from wood; so they did not, and were not. He told his people that dreams were nothing more than fancy and illusion, that they were shallow, trivial things; his people believed him. The King rejected the crafts and sciences of the sorcerers, and so the sorcerers were banished from his

The Judgment of Solomon

kingdom, until there was nothing but the Word of Solomon in the cities of the near west.

And Solomon knew the people would thank him for this, for they had no need of flying carpets or enchanted trinkets. Such things, he knew, only bred doubt and fruitless fantasy. He blessed his people with food, and work, and taxes, knowing they required no more than that.

Many are the stories of King Solomon's wisdom. It is said he learnt to control the beasts of the wilderness as well as the men of the cities, until even the birds of the air and the fish of the rivers bowed down before him. It is said he once imprisoned an entire city in a bottle, to punish its rulers for their black and unholy practices. Some whispered, in hushed voices, that the ways of the wily King were no more holy than the ways of his enemies, but Solomon knew his works had the blessing of the One True God . . .

'Stop, stop!' A point of light shifted in the darkness, then settled again. 'This isn't getting us anywhere. I thought I was going to get a history lesson, not a fairy tale. Let's go back to the Square of No Fountains, shall we? You never know, I might learn something.'

The machine agreed that this might be a good idea.

'Testing. Testing. *Un, deux, trois*. Oh, sod this for a game of soldiers.'

There were some very strict rules governing time travel, and Bernice was ignoring most of them. When you messed around in antiquity, you were supposed to be discreet. Dress in the local costume, the rules said. Blend in with the environment. Try not to draw attention to yourself. Don't interfere with history. Don't use anachronistic technology in public. And for heaven's sake don't go around performing magic tricks and pretending to be a messenger from Allah.

But the rules, Bernice had decided, were different in Baghdad. In medieval Europe, if you took out your digital watch and got it to play the national anthem, the natives would have you burnt as a witch. Here, most of the people wouldn't give a toss, as long as you didn't make a song and dance about it. So many new ideas were battering at the city walls, so many foreign influences were waiting to sneak in through the gates – magic lamps or no magic lamps. Nothing was considered impossible here.

'Testing. Testing again. *Un, deux, trois,* four, five, six . . . ah. That's better.'

On her first day in Baghdad, Bernice had inadvertently started a fight with a local honey merchant. In desperation, she'd warned him off by claiming to be an all-powerful *djinn*, capable of cursing until death any individual who crossed her. The man had paused, shrugged, warned Bernice that she'd better not cause any more trouble or else, and wandered off.

'Testing. Bernice Summerfield speaking, year 177 of the Mohammedan calendar, sometime in the late eighth century if you're an infidel. I'm talking into what's left of my Handysomatic Pocket Interpreter, and I think I've got the bugger working at last. Ah-hah.'

So, Bernice told herself, as she squatted in an alley by the *masjid* on the Street of Miraculous Squalor, usual time-travel etiquette could go and jump off a cliff. Her ploy back at the Square of No Fountains (she was now pretending she'd planned the whole thing) had distracted the scimitar-wielding goons long enough for her to make an escape, and if it had drawn attention to her, well, that was history's problem, not hers.

The alley was almost entirely in the shade, the air sticky and sweet in her nasal passages. She would have liked to think it was the odour of Eastern spices from a nearby marketplace, but it was more likely to be mouldering rubbish. The alley opened up into a street at each end, the sun turning the passers-by into shadow-puppet silhouettes as they walked past the end nearest to her. The alley itself was deserted, just Bernice and a bunch of small rodents, so she'd taken the opportunity to stop and fix the translator. She'd already slotted in a new powerpack and twisted what remained of the casing back into shape; now she was fiddling with the tuning dial, speaking in bonehead French, listening to her own voice to see if the device was converting it back into English.

'Testing. Testing. This is Bernice Summerfield, blathering

senselessly and pretending she's making a record in her diary, which I've unfortunately left in a plastic bag somewhere in the twenty-first century. I'm talking to you from sunny Baghdad, where I'm following up a little something I read in *Archaeology Today*, which is an ironic name for an archaeology magazine, when you think about it. According to the mag, Professor-General Chuang of the Peking Imperial College – I've met him, by the way, fat man with a stupid wig – says he's found evidence that proves the first ever electrical cells were invented as long ago as the sixth century. I mean, people have been arguing about this for ages, but Chuang's written a whole book on the subject, and it looks like he's heading for the best-seller lists. They had the designs in the Library of Alexandria, Professor-General Bad-Wig says, but never did anything with them. Which is odd, because all the history books say the first cell was invented by Alessandro Volta in 1800, and that *jusqu'à cet année-la n'existait . . . merde.*'

Bernice twisted the tuning dial. 'There. Am I talking English again? Yep. Good. Anyway, Chuang says there are folk stories that suggest there were electrical cells at Arabian souks right here in the eighth century, and I'm hoping to prove him wrong. I mean, if they had electricity in old Baghdad, why didn't they use it? At least, I hope I can prove him wrong. Anything to sabotage another academic's career in publishing.'

The translator was turning her words into English, but it was English with a pronounced French accent, making her sound like Inspector Clouseau. She tweaked the dial a little more, and kept talking. 'Trouble is, I think Chuang was on to something. I've been talking to some of the locals, and they've been telling me stories about this hunchback they've seen hanging around the souks in these parts. No one knows his name, but they say he's got a magic box that can bring dead fish back to life. Yeah, I know how it sounds, but when Volta invented his cell, his favourite party trick was making dead frogs' legs twitch, so maybe . . .'

Bernice stopped talking. She wasn't sure why. Something had changed around here, but her consciousness couldn't quite get a grip on what. She looked up, watched the shadow people amble past the alley. Nothing was happening out on the street.

'Hmm. Well, the translator seems to be working again. OK, the point is, I've got to find this mystery hunchback. They say he usually hangs around this part of the city, showing off his amazing fish-reanimator for –'

She cut herself off. There it was again. Something happened, when she said the word –

'Hunchback,' she snapped.

There was a shuffling sound from somewhere behind her.

That was it. Twice before, she'd picked up the sound of movement, just below the threshold of consciousness. She swivelled.

The man was leaning against the wall at the far end of the alley, where it opened out on to the street behind the *masjid*. He was tucked into the building's shadow, presumably in the hope that it would hide him. It didn't. Bernice's first impression was of the man's shape, not exactly hunched, but slumped, as if gravity had some kind of major grudge against his shoulders. His clothes were tattered, strips of dirty fabric wound around his lopsided body, the Arabian uniform of the poor. In one hand, he carried a heavy bag that looked like it had been made out of an old shirt.

'Hey!' Bernice said. It was the best greeting she could think of.

She didn't have time to focus on the man's face, but she glimpsed a pair of yellowy eyes, wide open in alarm, before the man turned and started to hobble away. Bernice sprang forward to stop him.

It was hard to say exactly what happened next, as most of it was a jumble of tangled limbs and random expletives. Bernice had vague memories of planting her hand on the man's shoulder; then there was a fist, with grubby knuckles and hairy fingers, getting larger and larger in front of her eyes. Everything was a bit fuzzy after that. There was a moment of weightlessness, after which she felt herself losing her balance, falling backwards. She realized she was dragging something down with her. She also realized she still wasn't entirely sober yet.

The ground crunched against Bernice's spine. Before she

could get her breath back, something large and smelly fell on top of her. She used the last of her strength to roll the shape away from her and flop down on top of it.

The machine fell silent, having decided that it had answered the question sufficiently. The point of light bounced across its face for a moment or two.

'Carry on,' the voice said. 'Oh, sorry. Direct questions only, I forgot. Can you carry on with the story, please? Thank you.'

... and yet Solomon was not content. Though he had defeated the deceits of progress in his own kingdom, he knew the realms beyond were still ruled by the unholy sciences he had sworn to destroy. His heart ached for the people who lived in these sorry places, for he knew they lived in the thrall of creatures whose elemental powers were untempered by the laws of the One True God. And he knew these creatures were to be fought.

One day, the royal maker-of-maps returned to the King's court from an exploration, telling him:

'To the east, my King, there is a city, built on a plain of rock that was once a mountain. The city is like no other, for every building there is fashioned from brass, and even the smallest hovel is the size of a temple. The walls are watched by monsters of stone, and the streets within are filled with wonders the like of which no traveller has ever seen.'

At this, the King was both intrigued and saddened. 'Then the people of the city live under a great tyranny,' he announced. 'Return to this place, and stand at its gates. Call out to those who keep watch. Tell them that in the Name of the One True God, they should tear down the walls, and allow the Word of Solomon to enter.'

So the maker-of-maps left for the city of brass, to return after two weeks and two days, telling the King:

'I have stood at the gates, my King, and delivered the message; but those who keep watch only laughed, and said they had no use for your Word. They say any man is free to enter the city, but its walls shall never be torn down.'

The King was angered by this blasphemy. 'Return to the

city once again,' he told the maker-of-maps. 'Tell them the armies of King Solomon are many, and the right arm of his Word is strong. Tell them they must tear down the walls within the year, or they shall be torn down from without.'

So the maker-of-maps left again for the city of brass, returning after another sixteen days had passed.

'I have stood at the gates once more, my King, but those who keep watch will not listen. They have said they hold sway over iron and stone, even over the elements themselves. They have said they fear no army, no matter how great. They have said, once more, that they have no use for your Word.'

And at this, the King only nodded.

'Then it is to be war,' he said.

'That wasn't the story I meant.' The voice in the darkness sounded irritated, not that the machine cared. 'I meant, can you carry on with the *other* story? The one about the hunchback. We were in the alleyway, and . . .'

'Let go of me!' a voice demanded. Its owner sounded like he'd been gargling with weed-killer. 'I am a poor and helpless cripple, and I demand you let go of me!'

Bernice's vision returned. The face floating in front of her eyes was a deep tan in colour, blemished with blemishes and lined with lines, so badly pockmarked that it looked as though the weather had actually taken nibbles out of the skin. The features were framed by a mass of black beard, into which specks of dirt had been strategically inserted. The face, Bernice concluded, of a professional beggar.

'The hunchback, I presume,' she said, only now remembering she was lying on top of the man.

'I have done nothing to you!' the hunchback wailed, squirming uselessly underneath her. 'Why do you torment me? I am but a poor and helpless –'

'Yeah, you said.' Bernice sat up, perching on the man's chest. 'Look, could you spare me the "poor and helpless cripple" monologue? I don't have any spare change.'

The man stopped wriggling.

'You are sitting on me,' he said, levelly.

'Mmm. I'd noticed.' Bernice looked up as a tall man in a

blue turban passed by on the street behind the *masjid*, close to the alley entrance. The man glanced into the alleyway, saw Bernice sitting on the beggar, shook his head, and went on his way. Bernice gave him a cheery smile as he departed. 'Now. You're the hunchback, yes? The one I'm looking for?'

The man underneath her huffed indignantly. 'I am Assan i Beddin, son of the streets of Baghdad –'

'Yes or no, please.'

'I am called a hunchback, by those who seek to –'

'Right, good. And you work the marketplaces, the souks around the Square of No Fountains? Something about dead fish . . .?' The man squirmed uncomfortably. Bernice brought all her weight down on his stomach, just to make a point. 'Thought so. I've been looking for you, Assan. Which is why it strikes me as odd that I should find you spying on me, really.'

A visible line of sweat erupted across Assan's forehead. 'I heard . . . I was told, by Ali of the Six Poisons, that I was sought by a foreign woman, who wore a shirt of exotic fruit and claimed to be a *ghul* of great power –'

'Ali of the Six Poisons? Short bloke, sells flasks of industrial antiseptic and dares you not to drink them?' Bernice tutted. 'The sod. He never said he was a friend of yours. So, you got worried there was a demon on your tail and thought you'd find me before I could find you, is that it?'

Assan nodded in what Bernice interpreted as a please-don't-kill-me kind of way. 'I heard of a great battle in the square, between you and the men of the Vizier. They say you pulled a spirit of light and dust from your pocket. They say you ran. They say you moved like the wind of the desert.'

Bernice sniffed at him. 'I call it "discretion". And calling it a great battle is overstating a bit. How did you find me?'

Assan tried to shrug, but it wasn't easy with Bernice's weight on his torso. 'I know all the backways of the southern city. I know the places a beast would hide –'

'Who are you calling a beast, hairy?' Bernice performed a particularly malicious bounce on Assan's stomach. He moaned impressively. 'All right, I'll let you get up. But I want to know all about your magical machine for warming up dead fish. Are we agreed?'

Assan looked doubtful. 'Such things are not for the eyes of every man.'

'And you can spare me the sales pitch, as well.'

Bernice stood. Assan took a few exaggerated deep breaths, then struggled to his feet. *No wonder he couldn't push me off him*, thought Bernice as he hauled himself upright. *He can hardly get up as it is, what with that hump.*

It was only when Assan reached his full height that she noticed.

'Wait a minute,' she said. 'You're not a hunchback at all.'

It was true. When she'd first seen him, he'd given her the impression of having a terrible stoop, but now she realized he just had a problem with his posture. There was no actual hump behind his neck, no unusual curvature of the spine. He had trouble with his left leg, though; his knee was twisted at an odd angle, making him lurch to one side whenever he moved. The heavy bag he carried didn't help.

Assan looked offended. 'I am a hunchback in the eyes of Baghdad,' he insisted, almost proudly.

'Having a bad leg makes you a hunchback?' Bernice almost slapped her translator again. 'Wait. I think I get it. It's an idiom. Anyone who's physically imperfect is called a hunchback around here, right? Probably loses something in the translation into English.' That would make sense. In all the Eastern folk-stories, crippled characters were always 'hunchbacks', as if having a dodgy spine symbolized disability. Bernice nodded towards his bag. 'Right. You can show me your machine, then. And stop shuffling. I wouldn't have known you were watching me in the first place if you weren't so edgy.'

Assan looked uncomfortable. Genuinely uncomfortable, this time: he wasn't faking it to get sympathy. 'If the Vizier's men knew I owned such a thing –'

'Oh, for heaven's sake.' Bernice put her hands on her hips, and tried to make a suitably *ghul*-like face. 'Are you going to open the bag, or am I going to have to use my extra-special magic to pop your head?'

Assan paused. Then he lowered the bag to the ground. Bernice stepped forward, and peered inside.

There, nestled among folds of grubby brown cloth, was a box. It was nothing much to look at. A cuboid of metal, the colour of old rust, thirty centimetres or so from end to end. The workmanship was definitely of the eighth century, Bernice decided, and the fittings looked vaguely oriental. A number of deceased fish lay beside it in the bag, but she hardly noticed the smell.

Set into the upper surface of the box were two circles of metal. One was the colour of copper. The other was almost certainly zinc.

'Bugger,' Bernice said. 'Looks like Professor-General Chuang's got a best-seller on his hands. The jammy sod.'

'I cannot bring the fish back to life,' mumbled Assan, as if he felt he had to apologize for not being able to do real magic. 'They shake, when they are touched against the surface of the box . . .'

Bernice shook her head. 'This doesn't make sense. An electrical cell? How? I mean, if electricity was discovered this long ago in history, why didn't anybody ever –' She looked up at Assan. 'Where did you get this from, anyway?'

Assan held up his hands, defensively. 'An oriental. A traveller. He – he gave me this device in return for a – a small favour. That is –'

'You stole it,' said Bernice.

Assan nervously picked a small insect out of his beard. 'I was a beggar,' he muttered. 'Since I . . . found the box, it has been different. I demonstrate it in the souks, to the travellers and the merchant men. They pay money to see the fish return to life. It makes them amused.'

'It doesn't make me laugh,' grumbled Bernice. 'To me, it's a bloody anachronism.'

'You,' said a deep, almost reptilian voice.

The next second in Bernice's life was very busy and quite complicated. In it, she turned to face the end of the alleyway behind her, only to find it blocked by blurry shapes with turbans. She focused on a face, tried to identify it, and finally deduced that it was that of the man who'd walked by the alley while she'd been sitting on top of Assan.

'It's her,' the man said.

Bernice saw an arm swing in her general direction.

She saw Assan, out of the corner of her eye, a look of horror on his face.

She realized that the first voice she'd heard belonged to the thug who'd accosted her at the Square of No Fountains.

She noticed the arm swinging towards her head, faster than she could comfortably follow.

Then the second ended.

'Clever, aren't you?' said the voice. The machine began preparing an answer, but the voice interrupted it. 'No, don't answer that. I want to find out exactly how much you know. What happened next?'

Never since the world was made had such a war been seen. The armies of Solomon advanced on the city of brass from the north, the west, and the south, beating at the brazen walls with their great engines of war. For weeks, then months, then years, the rulers of the city held them away, never once seeming to lose strength; for each ruler of the city was a *djinn* or *ifrit*, and the walls were watched over by monstrous statues, which the spirits wore like armour in battle. The gates of brass were barred, and no man was allowed in or out, though the people of the city did not starve, for within the walls were orchards where fruit would grow without hindrance and markets where fish would appear without first having to be caught.

Yet every day, the city of brass seemed to grow smaller. From the slopes of the nearby mountains, King Solomon could see how the spires were shorter than once they had been, and how the great domes shone with less fury. On the first day of Solomon's war, it would have taken a man five days to walk all the way around the city walls, yet after the first year it took only four, and after another it took only three. And the King was pleased, for he knew there would soon be no room within for the city's rulers, or their blasphemous works.

One day, Solomon himself stood at the gates of the city, and said:

'Hear me, kings of deceit. You must despair for this city, as a man can walk around its walls within two days. Will you not now surrender to the Word of Solomon?'

It is said there was a moment of silence before one of the beasts replied:

'We have told you before, we have no need for your Word.'

And so the war went on.

'You're doing it again. I meant, what happened next in *my* story? Why are you so determined to tell me about King Solomon, anyway? Is he really that important?'

The machine considered all three of these questions, and finally worked out that the best way to answer them was to carry on with its narrative.

The building was impressive, the way ancient Arabian buildings were *supposed* to be impressive. It wasn't exactly a palace, though it was big enough to do a decent impression of a cathedral. Most of the buildings around the city skulked in the shadows and looked grubby, but this one practically shone. The roof was domed, tapering into a rosebud-shaped peak, while the walls were riddled with stone balconies and elegant archways. If they hadn't all been fitted with metal bars, Bernice would have been able to imagine Douglas Fairbanks leaping out of one of the windows and on to a waiting flying carpet.

On the other hand, the courtyard stank.

The building was surrounded by an off-white wall, topped by vicious bronze spikes obviously designed to look scary and menacing, the minarets of the city outside nervously poking their tips over the top of the wall. There were no ornaments in the courtyard, no marble statues or perfumed flowerbeds. There were just people.

Scared, sick, lost-looking people. Bernice counted about three dozen of them. They were slouching against the wall, or huddling in groups near the grand archway at the front of the building, or lurking in the corners of the enclosure and eyeing up the white-clad guards on duty at the gate. Most of the people were thin, and those who weren't gave the impression of being malnourished anyway. Pale. Glassy-eyed. Empty-looking.

Bernice glanced at Assan. He limped along at her side, not even seeming to notice the scimitar-shaking thugs marching behind them. No, 'marching' made them sound too military.

The guards acted more like dustbin men than soldiers.

'This is a prison?' Bernice asked.

Assan didn't reply. His eyes were staring dead ahead, without any trace of feeling. Scared witless, Bernice concluded. He clutched his bag to his chest, as if no one would notice it that way.

Bernice looked over her shoulder, at the leader of the armed men. 'I don't suppose it's worth asking for legal representation. Isn't this place a bit posh for a jail?'

'This is one of the Houses of Jafar Abd al-Malik, Vizier to Harun al-Raschid himself, Allah bless his name,' sizzled the man. 'Be silent, or lose your tongue.'

The translator hiccuped when he said 'Houses'. Bernice guessed he meant 'offices', or 'official buildings'. 'You mean this is a court? All these people are waiting for trial?'

The man looked blank. Bernice guessed the Pocket Interpreter was having difficulty with the word 'court', as Arabian justice usually meant either severing limbs on an industrial scale or arbitrarily chucking people into oubliettes. 'Stop here' was all the guard had to say.

Bernice stopped walking. So did Assan. With a final warning shake of his scimitar, the guard turned and headed back towards the main gate, his underlings in tow.

'Heaven knows what they're charging me with,' Bernice muttered. 'If it's drunk and disorderly, I'd like six thousand other offences to be taken into consideration. Seven thousand if you count my hen night.'

Assan didn't respond. Bernice shrugged to herself, then took another look around the courtyard.

This time, she noticed something peculiar. If you could ignore their leanness, and the dirt that had been ground into their clothes, a lot of the prisoners here looked positively upper-class. True, there were some like Assan, bundles of rags with hungry little faces, but there were men who were obviously from the merchant classes, and even a few foreigners. There was an ominous clanging from the far side of the enclosure, as the guards who'd escorted Bernice and Assan here left the courtyard, slamming the gate shut behind them.

Bernice turned to face the hunchback. 'Odd,' she said. 'I

The Judgment of Solomon

thought only the lower classes got arrested in this city. The rich pay their way out of trouble. Or they own the people who are supposed to do the arresting.'

Assan didn't say a word. His gaze was still fixed on the empty space in front of him. The lights are on, thought Bernice, but the shops are shut.

'These people aren't common criminals,' she elaborated. 'Some of them even look like scholars, but –'

Assan hit her.

The blow was such a surprise that Bernice hardly even acknowledged the pain. Anyway, after being battered into submission by the guards, one more punch didn't seem to make much difference. She raised her hands to her face, and opened her mouth to say something, but Assan was already talking, bellowing out a stream of muddled syllables. A convincing impression of a car alarm, thought Bernice, but twelve-hundred years too early. 'This is your fault!' he was howling. 'You! You! You did this to me!'

Bernice stepped back. The other prisoners, and the two guards on duty at the door of the House, watched the fight without interest.

'Assan –' Bernice began.

'They would not have found out! They would never have taken notice!'

He swung his fists at her again. Bernice caught his wrists in her hands. 'Assan, for Go– For Allah's sake. You weren't like this before.'

'I wasn't scared of you! I was never scared of you!'

His face was centimetres away from Bernice's now, close enough for her to see the things nesting in his moustache. What did he mean, he was never scared of her? In the alley . . .

Suddenly, it clicked. In the alley, he'd been edgy; Bernice had assumed this was because he was scared of her legendary magic powers. Now she realized the truth. He wasn't afraid of anything she could do. He was afraid because he knew she'd draw attention to him. From a peasant's point of view, the wrath of a *ghul* was nothing compared with the wrath of the authorities. That was why he'd been so worried about having a strange foreign woman tracking him. A humble beggar like Assan would never have been noticed by the scimitar mob, but Bernice was a social lightning rod.

She let go of his hands and hit him back. The surefire cure for hysteria, she felt, in any century.

Assan staggered away from her.

'Better?' she asked.

Assan shook his head, but wouldn't meet her gaze. 'The Vizier will have us killed,' he mumbled.

'I don't see why. I've got a pocketful of gold substitute – I'm sure I can buy us a pardon. Trust me, I've got out of worse prisons than this one in my time.'

'You don't understand.' Assan finally looked up, but he had to struggle to keep his gaze level with hers. 'This is the House of Solomon's Word.'

Bernice frowned. 'Meaning?'

'Those who offend the One True God are brought here. Each cycle of the moon, the Vizier visits this place, to pass judgment on those his men have brought here. This is a place of the dead.'

'Those who offend the One True God?' Buggery. Bernice wasn't sure she knew enough about Mohammedan lore to defend herself against a blasphemy charge. Presumably, the guards had been storing the prisoners in the courtyard since the Vizier's last visit, feeding them the bare minimum to keep them alive. And she didn't like to think what the toilet facilities had to be like. 'Wait a mo. This is about the electrical cell, isn't it? They think it's magic. They think it's blasphemous. They're going to have us burnt as witches.'

Assan kept shaking his head, turning his face into a blur of black fur and wrinkles. 'See.'

He pointed across the courtyard. In one corner skulked two orientals, their faces tired and haggard, dressed in robes that had clearly seen better days. 'They are astrologers. You can see by their dress. Or perhaps herbalists, from the eastern cities. And there.' He moved his finger in an arc, towards an emaciated figure crouching at the other side of the enclosure. The figure was bound in rags, and by his side was a familiar-looking block of metal. 'I know him. He is a hunchback, by the name of Ahmad ibn Ghazi. He also has a box like mine, but he uses it to make lizards dance.' Assan clutched his bag closer to his chest. 'The Vizier has forbidden such things. It is Solomon's Word.'

He stopped talking, and lowered his eyes again. He'd said everything he felt he had to say, Bernice guessed.

She scanned the courtyard again, trying to make sense of what Assan had told her. She ended up focusing on a figure she hadn't noticed before, an elderly man slumped against the outside wall of the House. He was naked from the waist up, his skin turned to leather by the sun, the veins in his neck visible even from this distance. There was something cradled in his lap, clenched tight between his knees.

Another cell, perhaps? Good grief, how many of the things were there around here? She looked back at Assan, but his eyes were fixed on the ground, and he showed no sign of looking up again. Bernice sighed, then headed for the old man.

The man looked up as she drew nearer. His skin reminded her of old leaves; she tried to ignore the ugly little touches that had sprouted over on his face, the deep red lines around his eyes, the map of wrinkles stretched across his bald head. Instead, she focused on the thing in his lap. It was definitely metallic. There was a carved head, a sculpted body . . .

Without a word, the old man lifted the object out of his lap, and held it up for her to see. There was a mindless smile on the man's face, as if the only thing he had left to justify his existence was the artefact, as if he wanted the world to know all about it.

It was a bird. A silver bird, the length of one of the man's hands, its body plated with delicate featherlike scales, its wings joined to the torso with tiny copper springs. Though the metal was battered and tarnished, the bird was studded with jewels, the afternoon sunlight glinting off its surface at bizarre angles. The eyes were emeralds the size of sweet peas, while the underside was speckled with rubies, some of which had been gouged or half gouged out of their holes. Bernice had seen pieces like this before, in the galleries of Hai Dow Q and in the collection on Braxiatel's Planetoid, but here in the dead past . . .

'It's beautiful,' she said. With feeling.

Then the old man made an only-just-noticeable motion

with one of his fingers, and the wings of the bird twitched. Bernice jumped. Gradually, the wings began to flap in a regular rhythm. They moved to a mechanical heartbeat, beating faster, and faster, until the rear end of the bird seemed ready to lift itself out of the man's hands. It was trying to fly, Bernice realized. And, heaven help her, she was sure that if it hadn't been damaged, it would have made it.

It was impossible. Obviously, it was impossible. The ancient Arabians didn't know the first thing about aerodynamics. They could never have designed such an intricate flying machine. But the jewelled bird didn't look out of place here, not in the slightest. It looked natural, somehow, the invention of an eighth-century mind. Bernice thought of all the theories that usually explained anachronistic technology: interfering aliens, renegade time travellers trying to alter mankind's development, and so on, and so on. But none of them seemed to fit. No alien or time traveller would have created anything as subtle, as graceful, as this. The bird was part of this world, whatever the history books said to the contrary.

'Where did you get this?' she demanded, as the bird gave up and stopped beating its wings.

The old man looked up at her. Then he grinned. A toothless grin, an idiot's grin, a look of mad joy scratched across a desiccated face.

He giggled, briefly. Bernice felt sick.

She took in the scene around her one more time, seeing all the prisoners, the astrologers, the magicians, the beggars with their magic boxes. History's hunchbacks. She wondered what she'd learn if she examined all their possessions, or listened to all their stories. Was the jewelled bird just the beginning? Here in the courtyard, was she surrounded by little miracles, things she knew, as an archaeologist, shouldn't exist?

Finally, she understood. Baghdad was one of the most cosmopolitan cities on Earth, a place where travellers met and philosophies collided. Whenever cultures came into contact with each other, technology bounded ahead in fits and starts; it was a fact of life, a fact of history. The most rapid period of change in human history was the twentieth century, when the nations of Earth were first linked together by radio

The Judgment of Solomon

waves and satellite feeds. The first interstellar empire was not founded until the human race figured out a way of communicating across light years. Communication meant development. Any academic could have told you that.

Here in Baghdad, races from across the globe had encountered each other for the first time. Ideas had exploded against each other, creating bizarre by-products, some centuries ahead of their time, some completely outside the boundaries of technology as mankind knew it. Bernice imagined oriental metalworking techniques meeting western machine mentality in a backstreet somewhere, and saw, at last, how the jewelled bird might have been made. Professor-General Chuang hadn't gone far enough. If the men in robes were herbalists, as Assan had said, who knew what they might have invented? Penicillin, or the male pill, or a cure for cancer, centuries ahead of schedule?

But history had forgotten them. Baghdad was called the City of Wonders, yet the greatest of the Wonders were being seized by the guards, hidden away by the Vizier. Why? Because he thought they were against the will of Allah? Because he thought they were the work of black magic? Because he was afraid?

Bernice turned back to Assan, wanting to share her thoughts with someone, even though she knew there was no one within a thousand years who'd understand.

But Assan wasn't where she'd left him. At the entrance to the House of Solomon's Word, the guards had turned their backs to the yard, and a third figure was sandwiched between them, limping as he was dragged towards the archway. Even from here, Bernice could hear Assan whimpering. He looked like a bundle of dirty clothes, being shunted to a more convenient cupboard.

'They're taking him in,' mumbled Bernice. 'Every lunar month, he said. Today must be the day. Today must be the day the Vizier comes.'

The old man with the jewelled bird giggled again. Bernice tried not to take any notice of him.

The armies of Solomon laid seige to the city walls with terrible new weapons, each devised by the King himself, each blessed by the One True God. Solomon's men built frameworks of wood to hurl boulders into the streets, and great machines to punch holes in solid brass. It was another year before King Solomon stood at the gates again, saying:

'Hear me, kings of deceit. You must despair for this city, for a man can walk around its walls in less than a day. Will you not now surrender to the Word of Solomon?'

It is said there was a moment of silence, longer than it had been a year before, and then:

'We have told you before, we have no need for your Word.'

And so, again, the war went on.

'Oh, for heaven's sake,' the woman was saying. 'I didn't even have to ask this time. You started telling me about bloody Solomon without any prompting. It *is* important then, isn't it? It's got something to do with the reason I'm here. The Vizier said . . .'

The woman kept talking, but the machine took no notice. It had already begun answering her question.

'The prisoner's name?'

'B–' Bernice began.

'Unknown, Lord,' the beefy guardsman at her back cut in. 'She was not recognized by any in the square.'

'The prisoner's occupation?'

'A–' Bernice began.

'Unknown, Lord. She is a traveller. She has no business here in the city.'

'The prisoner's place of birth?'

'C–' Bernice began.

'Unknown, Lord. She is a foreigner. She has no caravan.'

'Ahem,' said Bernice. 'Don't I get a say in any of this?'

Everybody looked at her as if she'd just shat on the Persian rug.

The word 'vizier' always made Bernice think of pantomime villains with long moustaches and huge pants, but the reality was, not surprisingly, quite different. She'd been one of the last to be ushered into the House, where she'd been bustled along passageways buzzing with scroll-wielding bureaucrats and finally thrown to the floor in the Vizier's chamber. The

The Judgment of Solomon

Vizier had spent five minutes conferring with his scribes, as if he'd already heard all the evidence, before Bernice had even been allowed to look up.

The room was smaller than she'd expected, more an office than a throne room. The walls were painted the colour of blood, charmingly, and hung with brassy lanterns that filled the air with the taste of oil. The Vizier himself was a lot less impressive than his storybook counterparts, slightly old, slightly balding, and slightly overweight. He squatted in a wide wooden chair at the top of a stepped dais, which ensured his head was higher than anyone else's even when he was seated. Overall, he looked more like a civil servant than a scheming villain.

Which was exactly what he was, Bernice reminded herself. In a thousand years or so, men like him would be working in big grey office blocks, swapping their robes of office for suits and ties. Instead of a desktop computer, the Vizier had a scribe standing on either side of him, each clutching a scroll in one hand and a stylus in the other, each looking as if he could do with a good sit down.

'You will not speak in the presence of the Vizier,' the beefy guard informed Bernice.

'Why?' she asked. 'You obviously don't think I'm a common criminal. I mean, for a start –'

The guard pushed her head down, giving her a better-than-average view of her knees. The Vizier cleared his throat. 'With what articles was the prisoner found?' he asked, listlessly.

'With an amount of gold, which has been confiscated for the treasury of the Caliph, Allah bless his name. And with this, Lord.'

'And what is that?'

'Unknown, Lord.'

Bernice risked raising her head again. The guard was holding the Pocket Interpreter, which had been taken from her when she'd been dragged into the building. The machine was small enough to fit into the guard's hand, and it chirruped happily to itself in his palm, cute-but-useless LED lights flashing across the broken casing. It was the least menacing thing Bernice could imagine, but there was a gasp of pretend concern from around the room nonetheless.

The Vizier shrugged. 'An abomination,' he declared, sounding less than fascinated. 'The prisoner is guilty. Confiscate the article. Sentence will be passed according to the laws –'

'Wait a moment,' said Bernice. The guard pushed her head down again, but she ignored it. If they were going to have her head cut off, what did she have to lose? 'I said, wait a moment. You don't understand. You can't do this to me.'

The guard rumbled some phlegm out of his throat. 'Women are not permitted to speak in the presence of –'

'But I'm not a woman!' She sprang to her feet. The guard, surprised by this, raised his scimitar, but wasn't sure what to do with it. 'I just look like a woman. Actually, I'm a *ghul*. A terrible and powerful demon, from a faraway land. Capeesh?'

Everyone in the chamber froze.

'The bitch-queen of Hell herself,' Bernice added, hopefully.

The guard looked to the Vizier for instructions. The scribes shuffled their feet. The Vizier himself was silent for a moment, his eyes fixed on Bernice, who now stood with her arms outstretched, wondering if she should do a bit of a tap dance to keep them interested.

The Vizier conferred with one of the scribes, in hushed tones the translator couldn't quite pick up.

'A *ghul* may speak in the Chamber,' the Vizier announced, finally. 'A *ghul* is to be afforded all the privileges of a foreign dignitary, and considered to be a guest of the city. Even if he – or she – is an abomination in the eyes of the Prophet. The law is quite clear on this matter.'

Bernice guessed he'd probably just invented this law to get himself out of an embarrassing situation, but she didn't argue. This was just what she'd expected. Baghdad was so swamped in foreign weirdness, the people were ready to believe in anything. *Ghul* was the local word for a flesh-eating demon, but what the hell? Protocol had to stretch even to supernatural entities in times like these. 'Good. Fine. Lovely.'

'Now. To proceed.' The scribes raised their styluses again as the Vizier spoke. 'The prisoner is guilty. Confiscate the article. Sentence will be passed –'

The Judgment of Solomon

'Whoa, whoa!' Bernice waved her arms at the Vizier until he stopped talking. 'I thought I was supposed to be a guest of the city. A dignitary, you said.'

'This is true. A guest who has broken the law, and forfeited her right to the freedoms of Baghdad. Sentence will –'

'No, hold on. You can't find me guilty. I'm a terrible demon. I probably eat children in my spare time. If you do anything to me, then I'll . . . er . . . blot out the sun. Possibly.'

The Vizier raised an eyebrow, and turned to the scribe on his right. 'How many prisoners have been judged by this House since the start of the year?'

The scribe cleared his throat. 'Umm . . . it would be somewhere in the region of ninety, Lord.'

'And how many of those were of the *ghul*, or of the *djinn*?'

'I believe this prisoner is the seventh, Lord.'

'Have we yet fallen to any sorcerous curses?'

'No, Lord.'

The Vizier turned his attention back to Bernice. 'So you see. We know we have nothing to fear from beasts such as you. The One True God protects us from abominations.' He nodded at the guard. As a symbolic gesture, the man threw Bernice's translator across the room. It hit the wall in the corner behind her with the sound of cracking plastic.

Bernice turned to see where it landed, and gawped.

There was a pile of debris in the corner, and every single piece of it would have made an archaeologist swallow hard. The possessions, Bernice realized, of the other prisoners. There were electrical cells, including one in a familiar cloth bag. There were broken bottles, leaking unfamiliar liquids. There were scrolls of parchment, leather-bound codices, herbal talismans, mangled pieces of alchemical hardware . . .

Near the top of the pile was the battered form of a little metal bird. One of its gemstone eyes was missing, lost somewhere in the heap, and the left wing was bent out of shape. Its beak was jammed wide open.

Bernice turned back to the Vizier, glared at him with all her might. He didn't look impressed. 'Why?' she demanded.

'It is the law. As it was envelope by King Solomon.'

Envelope? Damn. Either the translator had been damaged

by the impact, or Bernice was on the edge of its conversion field. 'But it doesn't make sense. All the science you've got at your disposal here . . .'

The Vizier looked unconcerned. 'In older times, King Solomon rid his kingdoms of all magics which offended the natural order of being, as it was laid down by the One True God. So it must be again.'

'That isn't unnatural. That isn't magic.' Bernice pointed at the broken objects in the corner. 'These are machines. Like tools, that's all. They can't hurt you.'

'I know.'

Bernice's tongue nearly tripped over itself. 'I'm sorry, what?'

The scribes had by now given up trying to record this interchange, and the Vizier looked like he was getting fed up with the whole conversation. 'These trinkets are the work of foreign science, not of black sorcery.'

Bernice shook her head. 'Then why . . . why are you . . . I mean, just *why*?'

The Vizier considered this question for a moment.

'You are a *ghul*,' he announced. 'Because of this, and only because of this, I will grant you all the answers you wish to hear. After that, sentence will daytime passed complexity sniffle binge chops likely cress cress Monday.'

'Oh,' said Bernice.

'That's it!' exclaimed the voice. 'The Vizier mentioned King Solomon, that's why I asked you to . . . OK, this is starting to make sense. I take it all back, you know what you're talking about. Can you go on with the story?'

As the seasons changed, King Solomon's weapons became more devious still: devices to crack open the stone skins of the city's rulers with arrows of lead, and cauldrons of bile that were flung over the great brazen walls, causing sickness and decay among its dwellers. The King was not glad to cause such suffering for the people of the city, but he knew it was for their own good, for only when the walls fell would they be truly embraced by the One True God.

After six months more, he returned to the gates.

'Hear me, kings of deceit. You must surely despair for your domain, for a man can now walk around its walls between noon and midnight. If you do not surrender to the Word of Solomon, the city of brass shall be destroyed.'

It is said the silence was longer than it ever had been, though the reply was the same: 'We have told you before, we have no need for your Word.'

'But this is your final chance,' explained Solomon. 'For I have crafted a weapon that may raze the city to the ground in mere moments, that may bring ruin with the smallest motion of my hand. This kingdom shall be set alight, and the mountains shall run with rivers of molten brass.'

And the silence seemed to last for generations, before the gates finally opened. There, standing before the King, was one of the rulers of the city, its face the face of a lion, its tail the tail of a serpent.

'We do not understand,' said the *djinn*. 'We had always believed you wanted the city for your own. Why, then, would you destroy it? What use would it be to you, if it were reduced to ashes?'

And the King replied: 'The law of the One True God demands it.'

'But we do not understand,' said the beast.

'The law of the One True God demands it,' repeated the King. 'If you do not surrender, this is what I must do: burn the city of brass with flames hotter than the fires of the sun, so no orchard shall ever grow here again, and no man shall be able to live on this ground. There will be nothing more than dust.'

The *djinn* nodded.

'Then we will surrender,' it said.

And Solomon's army began to tear down the walls.

The woman groaned in the darkness. 'I love happy endings. And what about the *other* story?'

The floor hurt. Bernice's skin was already a patchwork of interesting bruises, but the floor took the archetypal biscuit.

She lay there for a while, face down where the guards had dropped her. She heard the men muttering to each other above her head, their words turned into a mess of syllables by the protocols the translator had planted in her neurosystem. She was well out of the device's range now, but it was still having an aftereffect on her psyche, turning the local language into snatches of fractured English.

'Eggs with yesterday planetwide hooplah,' one of the guards grunted, and laughed. Then there was the sound of the cell door slamming overhead. Footsteps in the passageway above.

When she was sure she was alone, Bernice sat up. With the door shut, the oubliette was dark. Utterly dark. Before she'd been escorted out of the Vizier's chamber, the old duffer had said something about her being put into the deepest oubliette in the House of Solomon's Word, although the malfunctioning translator had interrupted this sentence by slipping in words like 'heliotrope' and 'vestibule' every few seconds.

'Oubliette,' she said, out loud, to see if the room had any kind of ominous echo (it didn't). 'From the French, meaning "to forget".' According to legend, caliphs put their enemies in cells like these and forgot about them, letting them die in the darkness. Rubbish, of course. Why bother wasting space letting someone starve to death in a cell, when you could execute him on the spot?

'Because oubliettes are scarier,' Bernice told herself. 'It's a psychological device. Hmm. And it works, too.'

She fumbled around in the darkness, reached into the leather pouch that still hung from her belt. The soldiers had taken the translator and the gold, but they'd left her other odds and sods alone. At the bottom of the pouch, she found two lumps of ultra-low-sugar bubblegum, a pack of playing cards with illustrations too obscene to be comprehensible to the eighth-century mind, and –

'Ah-hah,' she said, fishing out the pen-torch. Well, actually, it was more like a quill-torch: she'd stuck feathers along the shaft, to make it look a little more 'current'. It had been good enough to fool the Vizier's men, anyway. She flipped the switch at the end, then swept the beam across the far wall of the oubliette.

All it found was black stone. Bernice scowled. There had to be some way out of here. Every cell had a secret escape route somewhere. Scientifically established fact.

The torchlight bounced off something that sparkled.

Bernice realized she was staring into an eye.

She squawked, and rolled backwards. As soon as she'd remembered how to breathe again, she sat up, and pointed the torch back in the direction of the eye. It hadn't moved. The eye was wide open, unblinking in the torchlight, a black pupil set inside a circle of solid brass.

Bernice moved the torch, locating a second eye a couple of centimetres from the first. She lowered the beam, finding a pair of metal lips – slightly parted – and a stylized moustache. Sculpted features, all set in brass.

She ran the torch over the rest of the statue. It was the likeness of a man, sitting cross-legged on the floor with its brass hands resting on its brass knees, though the figure would have been a good metre and a half tall if it had been in a standing position. Arcane symbols, more Chinese than Arabian, were burnt into the metal along the arms and legs, while a complex system of cogs and wheels was set into the chest. The mechanism looked like it was in working order, though what it was supposed to do Bernice had no idea. She got the impression the cogs were mostly decorative.

'Company,' she said. 'How nice.' Keeping the torch fixed on the brass man's face, she reached out and stroked its beard. There was a thick layer of dust on the metal, which was hardly unexpected. She studied the features more closely. The face was simple, but the style was familiar.

Of course. The bird. The jewelled bird. You could almost believe the same hand had crafted both of the pieces.

'What did you do to end up here, then?' Bernice asked the statue, idly.

The wheels turned.

Bernice scrambled to her feet. There was a deafening clatter from inside the brass man, the sound of grinding gears and clanking levers. Finally, with the chattering of metal teeth, a strip of parchment spewed out of the brass man's mouth, and hung limply between its lips.

Bernice waited, to make sure the machine had finished, then leant forward and tore the parchment away from its face. She pointed the torch at the material. The strip was narrow, a thumb's width across, and scrawled along it were symbols in thick black ink.

It took her a while to recognize the symbols as letters, written in an elegant joined-up handwriting. The kind your eccentric great uncle might use to write you a Christmas card.

'I told the truth,' the parchment read.

Bernice let her jaw drop.

'No no no,' she said. 'No no no no no. That's not possible. I can read this. I haven't got my translator, but I can read it.'

Accusingly, she pointed the torch at the brass man's face. 'You're a machine. For heaven's sake, you look like you're made out of scrap. You can't even hear what I'm saying. Even if you could, you couldn't understand me. And even if you could understand me, there's no way you should be able to answer.'

The brass man didn't respond.

Bernice swallowed her pride, knowing her next words were going to sound very, very, very silly. 'Are you... alive?'

The mechanism sprang into action again. The turning of wheels, the crunching of machine parts. Another strip of parchment unravelled from the mouth. Bernice hurriedly tore it off.

'No,' it said.

'But you can think? You're a thinking machine?'

Chatter-chatter-chatter. Clank-clank-clank.

'Yes,' read the next parchment. And underneath that: 'Yes.'

Bernice slumped, letting her saggy backside slap down against the floor. She kept the torch turned on the brass man, just in case it made any funny moves.

'How do I keep ending up in these situations?' she asked, wearily.

So the brass man told her.

Bernice paced the cell. The oubliette was tiny, and by now she knew the floor plan by heart, so she could successfully pace without running into any walls. She held the torch in

The Judgment of Solomon

one hand, and ran the strip of parchment through the other, taking in the epilogue to the brass man's fairy tale.

... thus was the city of brass freed from the dark sciences of its rulers, its shining spires and domes torn down, buildings of stone erected in their place. The people came to thank King Solomon for what he had done, for no longer did they have to live under the tyranny of dreams, or with the grim uncertainty of change. The King built a temple to his Word at the very heart of the new city, and there he kept his greatest weapon, the weapon he had never used; and the people came from miles around to see it, and worship it, and trust in it.

Some say Baghdad itself is built on the earth where once stood the city of brass. Yet if this is so, no man knows where the temple is to be found, or what became of Solomon's last and most wondrous creation.

Bernice dropped the parchment. She'd asked the statue about herself, about her last few hours in Baghdad, and the brass man had known all the answers, mixing up the information with a story about King Solomon that she still wasn't entirely sure she understood.

'It's impossible, obviously,' Bernice told the machine. 'The first artificial intelligences won't be created for another twelve hundred years. And anyway, you can't build a sentient computer out of copper alloy. No offence meant.' The brass man, graciously, didn't say a word. But then, he – it, Bernice corrected herself – it never did, unless you asked it a direct question.

'Then again . . . they're not supposed to have electrical cells for another millennium, either. No, no, no. Electricity is one thing, cybernetics is another. Let's not get carried away.'

She stopped pacing, and sucked her lip.

'Hah! I've got it. You're not a machine at all. You're a hoax. Like one of those sideshow exhibits they had in the nineteenth century. There's a little man inside you, a dwarf or a midget, maybe, and he's working you with wires . . .'

She trailed off.

'No. You can't be. Even if you were a dwarf in a metal suit, you wouldn't be able to write in fluent English. Got it!

You're an anachronism. You're a computer from the future. Another time traveller must have left you here, probably dressed you up like that for a laugh. I wouldn't be surprised if it was old Professor-General Chuang himself.'

No, no, no. That wasn't right, either. Like the jewelled bird, the brass man seemed to fit into this world perfectly, whatever accepted history said to the contrary. The statue was a product of eighth-century culture. You could tell. Bernice didn't know exactly how, but you could tell.

'All right. So maybe you're not cybernetic at all. Maybe you run on magic. Maybe you were created by a powerful sorcerer . . .'

And that was just plain silly.

'Of course, I could always ask you what you are,' sighed Bernice. She crouched down on her haunches in front of the figure. 'OK, I give in. I can't figure you out. What are you?'

She turned her torch towards the brass man's mouth, and this time read the words as they spilt out of the orifice.

'I was a gift.'

Bernice nodded. 'Keep talking. Oh, sorry. In what way were you a gift?'

Chatter, grind, squeak: 'I was a gift, to the Caliph of Baghdad, Harun al-Raschid, Allah bless his name. I was presented by an envoy, a traveller from another city in another land, as a token of trust.'

'Right. Now we're getting somewhere. So what were you designed for, exactly? Just to be a general clever-clogs, or did your makers have something more specific in mind?'

'I was to be the Caliph's adviser. A political confidant. A Vizier of metal.'

'Because you know all the answers?'

'And because I must always tell the truth. My purpose is to speak honestly, on all matters of men. To give counsel without deceit or bias. That was the nature of the gift.'

Bernice leant closer, almost conspiratorially. 'This still doesn't make sense. Look, I don't know how you work – we'll come to that in a minute, don't worry – but you're way ahead of your time. As a tool, you'd be indispensable.' Bernice indicated the rest of the oubliette with her torch beam. 'But instead of using you, they dump you down here. I mean, I understand why the Vizier would want to get rid of the electrical cells and the other bits and pieces: he thinks they offend Allah. But why you?'

Surprisingly, the brass man had to pause before it answered. When it finally 'spoke', the answer was brief.

'Politics.'

Bernice stared at the parchment for some time, trying to figure out what it meant. 'Explain,' she said, at last. 'I mean . . . what do you mean?'

'The electrical cell, as you know it, would change the shape of all Arabia, were the people to know of its true nature. The Vizier protects the interests of the Caliph, Allah bless his name, and the Caliph upholds a balance of power his bloodline has maintained since the time of the Prophet.'

The machine left it at that, perhaps knowing Bernice would prompt it further. 'You mean, the Vizier has to destroy the cells because they'd shake up society too much?'

'The purpose of any ruling politician is to avoid change. It is in the nature of things.'

'And the other inventions . . . like the jewelled bird. What about them?'

'The jewelled bird offers the possibility of flight, and if man could fly, every idea he has about the world would be washed away, as chalk in the rain. He would think only of flight, and forget his life on the ground. It would be the end of Baghdad. The end of every city.'

'But that's insane,' Bernice protested. 'Doesn't the Vizier understand the profits he could make? Even if he doesn't want the people knowing about them, doesn't he ever think about using the machines for himself?'

The brass man began churning out the parchment long before she finished speaking: 'A single stone may disturb the flow of a great river. Even if only one man knew all the secrets of the forbidden sciences, the change wrought upon the city would be beyond imagining. The profits are unimportant. The Caliph must retain power. The Vizier must do his work, as must we all.'

Bernice shook her head. This wasn't what she'd been expecting. She'd thought the Vizier had destroyed the machines of the hunchbacks out of fear, but this . . .

Since her days at the academy on Vandor Iota, since she'd picked up a trowel and started work on her very first dig, she'd let herself believe certain things about human history, things you never bothered questioning even if you got the chance to go back in time and watch mankind going through the motions around you. Technology, said the textbooks, was an uphill curve. You invented the steam engine, then the motor car, then the aeroplane, then the spaceship. It was simple, linear, and straightforward, if you could overlook the occasional genocide along the way.

But Baghdad proved all that wrong.

Was this what the Vizier had meant when he'd said he'd give Bernice all the answers? Was this why King Solomon, fabled for his intelligence throughout the ages, had exiled all the foreigners and alchemists? Because he'd known how much they could have changed the world, how much damage they could have done to his precious balance of power? No wonder history thought he was so bloody wise. He was the perfect politician. Like the Caliph of Baghdad, with his big Islamic crackdown, using the laws of the Prophet as a means of control . . .

In the story, Solomon allowed the existence of only those sciences that maintained the status quo. After all, he used a kind of science to build new weapons, claiming they were blessed by the One True God. Not Allah, as Bernice had thought when the brass man had told her the story. The One True God was the God of control, the God of Politicians. The God of Politics itself.

She concentrated on the brass simulacrum in front of her, trying to ignore the fact that her whole perception of human development had been turned inside out in a matter of minutes. 'And you?' she asked.

The parchment took some time to chatter its way out of the brass man's bowels. 'I was the final insult to the Caliph,' the machine explained. 'A politician incapable of dishonesty, with no sense of self-interest. The greatest possible sin against the way of things. To destroy me would have been to insult my makers, and so I was imprisoned, and no treaty of trade was ever forged between Baghdad and those who crafted me.'

The Judgment of Solomon

Bernice started to laugh.

'An honest politician,' she said. 'The quickest way of changing the world. I should have guessed. All right, brass man. There's one more thing I have to know. I don't think you answered my original question, not properly. I wanted to know what you are.'

She paused for a moment, figuring out how best to phrase the question. 'To me, you're an impossibility. If you're really a product of ... of "hunchback science", if we can call it that, then hunchback science must be so different from the science *I* know, it's almost beyond belief. I can't imagine the human race forgetting anything as remarkable as you. You know everything about me, you can answer questions in any language, and I get the feeling you can even read my mind. All this, and it's only the eighth century. So tell me. How do you work?'

There was a short silence as the brass man thought it over. Then the wheels began to turn.

And there was another sound, audible even over the grinding and groaning. Human footsteps.

Bernice felt a gust of (relatively) fresh air across her face, and light began to dribble into the oubliette from the hatchway above her head.

'Buzz country update involute,' one of the guards rumbled. Then big hairy hands were reaching down into the darkness, grasping Bernice's shoulders even as the brass man's teeth started to chatter.

Bernice didn't so much blink as try to weld her eyelids shut. The sun was going down over the city, bouncing migraine-flavoured light off the minarets on the skyline. After the darkness of the oubliette, the glare was actually painful.

She felt a palm press against her back. One of the guardsmen pushed her forward, out through the courtyard gates, and she turned as she stumbled into the street outside, to try to make it look as though she was quite happy stumbling and was already going in the direction they'd shoved her, thank you very much. 'Cantaloupe golden misdeed find,' one of the guards gurgled as they closed the gates behind her. Bernice had no idea what he was saying, but it sounded like a threat. 'Cousin twenty insincere day.'

She squinted at them curiously. 'You're letting me go?'

The guards looked at each other, as if she'd just spoken a mouthful of gibberish. Which she probably had, of course. 'Went apricots tarmac,' the more talkative of the pair said. Then they both bowed, and turned away.

Through the black metal bars, Bernice watched them mooch back towards the House of Solomon's Word. The courtyard was empty by now. All the hunchbacks would have been tried and sentenced, the poor buggers. 'Wait,' Bernice shouted after the guards. 'You can't go yet. I don't understand. Why have you let me go?'

The men vanished through the archway of the House. Bernice kept shouting, knowing full well she was talking to herself. 'I mean, don't get me wrong or anything, I don't want to have my head lopped off. But I thought there was some kind of sentence . . .'

She trailed off. Baghdad suddenly seemed very quiet around her.

One of the guards had bowed to her. Actually bowed. As if protocol demanded they be polite, even though she was a criminal, even though they felt quite justified in throwing her around and poking her with their scimitars. Social convention was so rigid in this place that –

She clicked her fingers. Of course. She was a *ghul*, wasn't she? And a *ghul* was practically aristocracy, according to the Vizier. In light of her standing as a she-demon-hell-bitch-thing, sentence had been commuted to a quick spell in the oubliette and a bum's rush out of the door. The others, the hunchbacks and the foreigners, wouldn't have been so lucky . . .

The other prisoners.

Assan.

Would he have been executed? The scrolls and artefacts of the prisoners had been destroyed, but if the Vizier hadn't judged their owners to be any threat to the status quo, would he have bothered executing them?

Bernice set off along the street, heading back towards the Square of No Fountains. One way or another, she had to know.

* * *

The Judgment of Solomon

She found him two streets away, heading back for the quarter of the city where they'd first met. Catching him wasn't hard: from behind, he looked like an enormous tortoise, dragging around a shell of rags and loose skin. The streets were emptying now, the few people still out and about making awkward detours around the shuffling hunchback as they passed him by.

'Assan,' Bernice called out, when she was a few metres away from him. 'Assan, it's me. The *ghul*. Remember?'

He stopped, turned his head. As soon as he saw Bernice, his eyes widened, and a look of pure agony crossed his face. He would have run if he'd been able to.

'It's all right. They let me go, too. See? I told you. They had no reason to keep us locked up. Once they'd taken away your cell, they knew you were harmless –'

'Xxxxxxx!' spat Assan. The sound came out of his throat as a hiss of static. The translator protocols left inside Bernice's brain didn't even bother converting the noise into gibberish. It was a sound of absolute hate, filtered through bared teeth.

Bernice actually flinched. 'It's all right. Don't worry, I'm not going to be any more trouble. I just wanted to say sorry, for dragging you into this. I know you can't understand me –'

'Xxxxxxx! Xxx xxxxx xxxxxx xx!' barked Assan.

'I know you can't understand me, but I'm sorry about your cell, really. Look, if it's any consolation, it was an anachronism anyway.'

'Xxxxxx xxx!' swore Assan, and shook his left fist at her.

At least, he would have done if his left fist had been there. But it wasn't. The hand had been neatly severed at the wrist, the bleeding staunched by fire. The tattered cloth that wrapped the arm was sticking to the end of the stump, glued to Assan's skin with blood and ashes.

Bernice made her vocal cords vibrate, but when she tried to get her lips to mouth the words 'I'm sorry' again, they refused to budge.

'Xxxxxx,' Assan spat, and turned away. Not looking back, he continued to drag himself up the street, pulling his twisted leg behind him.

Bernice stood, unmoving, watching him go, until he'd vanished around the corner at the end of the street. She could have followed, but what was the point? There was nothing she could have done, short of kidnapping him and dragging him back to the twenty-sixth century for cellular regeneration therapy. There was nothing she could have said, even if she'd been able to speak his language. She'd lost him his hand, as well as the cell. Hard to apologize for a thing like that.

No.

She hadn't done it. This wasn't her fault. It wasn't even the Vizier's fault. You couldn't blame one man for the way things worked around here.

It was the Judgment of Solomon. Bernice remembered what she'd learnt in the House of the old sod's Word. This was the City of Wonders, so they said. But how many Wonders had been buried, because they inconvenienced someone, someone who just happened to have the power to chop your arms and legs off? How many people had been beheaded, mutilated, silenced, simply because they knew about things that would have been called miraculous, if they'd ever been given a chance to exist?

'There aren't any Wonders,' Bernice muttered. 'There's just the One True God. That's all.'

She turned away. Strictly speaking, the research mission had been a success; time to start thinking about getting back to her own era, now. She'd learnt everything she'd come here to learn. She had all the answers she needed.

'And then some,' she told herself, somewhat bitterly.

While, down in the deepest oubliette of the House of Solomon's Word, the brass man sat cross-legged in the darkness, yet another victim of the Judgment of Solomon. A strip of parchment hung from its lips, the text explaining – in fluent English – the secret of the machine's existence.

Sadly, nobody was there to read it, and the secret was lost to posterity.

The Milk of Human Kindness

By Elizabeth Sourbut

ONE

Roger sluiced sterilizing fluid round the last bottle and rinsed out the basin. He sighed gloomily, and paused to stare out of the screen door towards the vegetable patch. The squash, pumpkins and melons were drooping in the late summer heat, desperate for rain. He had spent as much time as he could spare out there recently, but now his brother was in college the cattle were taking up most of his time. And with Rachael away in Europe at another trade fair there was Amanda as well. He loved caring for his daughter, but he had never realized how demanding an infant could be.

He heard a cry from the living room, the first sleepy wail: not unhappy, just testing her lungs to make sure they still worked. He stood the bottles in the waiting bowl of warm water, and went through.

'Hey there, you rascal!' he exclaimed, swinging the baby out of her cot and raising her high into the air. 'Awake again already?'

Amanda chuckled, a fat contented sound, and waved her tiny fists in the air, wriggling in his grasp. Roger swooped her around the room making aeroplane noises until they were both shrieking with laughter. Rachael didn't approve of this game: she thought it made Amanda overexcited, but Roger was determined to raise a fearless toughy, and so he played rough-house with his tiny daughter at least a couple of times every day.

Finally, he collapsed on to the hearthrug, panting, and deposited the child on his chest. She stared at him intently, her huge blue eyes only a foot away from his own, and reached out one hand to his face. Her soft fingers rasped against stubble. Damn, he'd forgotten to shave again.

Slowly, the tiny face crumpled, and Amanda began to cry.

'Oh, come on now, Pop isn't that ugly, is he?'

But she was hungry, and his nipples ached with the desire to feed her. He thought of the warming bottles, and the cow's milk waiting to be heated in a pan, and he felt like crying too.

'Babies should have human milk, shouldn't they, honey?' he whispered. 'Wouldn't you like Pop to feed you from his horrid hairy tits? Why don't we try it, huh?'

Amanda screamed more loudly, without reserve. *'Hungry! Hungry! Hungry! Feed me!'* she shrieked without words, and Roger felt his nipples burn.

Then there was a gush of wet warmth and he gasped as the front of his shirt was suddenly drenched with fluid.

He sat up and tore open his shirt. His chest was covered with sticky milk, matting in his chest hair, dripping on to his stomach. He gawped, disbelieving.

Amanda crowed with delight, and reached for him. Bewildered, Roger lifted her clumsily to his right nipple, trying to hold her the way he had seen the midwife show mothers on the maternity ward, the way he had studied from the books on mothering. Amanda took the teat in her mouth and began to suckle.

The sensation was electrifying as he felt milk flowing out of him into her eager mouth. Suddenly his tits were connected by pleasure circuits to every cell of his body. Not even the best sex had ever felt this good.

He sat very still, his breathing fast and shallow, as his baby daughter fed contentedly. He hardly dared to believe it. For the three months since her birth he had dreamt of being able to do this. Every time he had filled a bottle and offered Amanda the plastic teat he had hated it more. He had not envied Rachael the pain of childbirth, but from the very first day he had known that he wanted to feed his daughter, to pass on to her directly some of his strength and vitality. It had infuriated him that Rachael had not wanted to breastfeed, and had insisted on bottled milk from the beginning. Her milk had come in easily, and it had been a few weeks of complaints and bad temper before her breasts had dried up completely. He had tried to explain to her how he felt, but after she had laughed at him the first time he mentioned it,

Roger had said nothing more. But always the desire had been there, growing in intensity.

And now he had his wish. He threw back his head and roared with laughter. 'Thank you, Lord!' he bellowed.

Amanda lifted her mouth from his nipple, looking apprehensive at his loud voice, but Roger smiled and gently stroked her hair. 'It's all right, baby. Everything's all right. Your daddy's here.'

The child gurgled with pleasure, and returned to her meal.

TWO

Nat took a deep breath of the cold mountain air as she waited for the transmission light to come on. Suzie was counting her in, and as ever she had to resist an urge to comb a hand through her hair. Then the anchorman's voice was in her ear, and she was on.

'Now we are going over to our correspondent in the war zone, Natalie Sharpe. Nat, how's it looking?'

'Not good, I'm afraid, Steve,' she replied, moving crisply into her prepared text. 'We're here on the Uzbek/Tadzhiki border on the western shore of the River Syr Dar'ya in what is turning into a massive refugee camp. Overnight, thousands of the minority Russian and Uzbek population have been pouring north from Dushanbe and its environs as the fundamentalist Islamic Tadzhiki forces push north from their bases in Afghanistan. Conditions here are pretty appalling, although a UN convoy did get through about an hour ago with emergency supplies and blankets. It's slightly above freezing at the moment, but once night falls temperatures are going to plummet by twenty degrees or more.'

'There are rumours here in London that the Tadzhikis are using biological weapons. Have you seen any evidence to support that claim?'

She had been warned of the question, but even so Nat's stomach contracted as she framed her cautious reply. 'I must stress that those are unconfirmed rumours at this stage. Up until now, the Tadzhiki forces, although disciplined and present in large numbers, have not appeared to be well armed. They have little air support and –'

'But have you seen anything yourself which might substantiate those rumours?' the anchorman persisted. Damn him, he should try being out in the field for a few weeks.

'It's hard to tell in these conditions,' she said. 'People here have been living in fear of their lives for several months now, and they have had to flee their homes with whatever they could carry. But yes, there are indications that something is happening.'

'Such as?'

Out of shot, Nat indicated to Suzie. The camera moved from her face and she turned to look as Suzie panned slowly across the hillside behind her. Tents and flimsy structures of cardboard and corrugated iron stretched away in uneven rows, the ground churned into thick mud between them. Smoke from dozens of small cooking fires billowed in the strong wind, obscuring now this tent, now that. Nat coughed a little, and resumed her commentary.

'As you can see, there are a lot of families here. Something like fifty per cent of the population of this area is under twenty-five, and the birth rate is high. But what is odd is the family structuring. Many of the young women have joined the fighting forces along with their menfolk, so it's the grandmothers and older girls who have found themselves caring for the young children.'

Suzie focused the camcorder on an old woman sitting on a rock nearby. Her skin was a mass of wrinkles, and her cheeks had fallen in beneath broad, high cheekbones. Nat guessed her to be about fifty, which was elderly in these mountainous regions. She held a young baby in her arms, and when she saw the lens pointing at her she turned away, but not before Nat, and hopefully the viewers in Britain, had seen that beneath her ragged clothing the crone was holding the infant to feed at her huge, rounded breast.

'This is becoming a common sight here,' said Nat. 'Old women and girls as young as twelve breastfeeding infants. That in itself is surprising enough, but what is puzzling the Red Cross is that these women are almost starving, emaciated, and yet their breasts are swollen with milk in circumstances when they should be drying up. It's as though

The Milk of Human Kindness

all of their energy is going into producing milk.'

'And you think this might be a side effect of some form of biological warfare?' asked Steve, pushing the issue.

'Nobody knows. But something very strange is going on here.' The camera returned to her face, and London urged her to wind up. 'This is Natalie Sharpe for BBC Satellite News, reporting from the Uzbek/Tadzhiki border.'

The transmission light went out, and Suzie hefted the camcorder down from her shoulder and grinned. 'Nice one.'

Nat smiled briefly. 'It'll shock a few people, but I don't suppose anybody will do anything. Can you tell that woman I'm sorry we invaded her privacy?'

'Sure.' Suzie spoke to the old woman in halting Uzbek. She looked up at Nat and then, very deliberately, spat at her feet.

Nat sighed and shrugged. 'Oh well, we tried.'

'Come on, lover.' Suzie put her arm around Nat's waist. 'Let's go and relax for a while.'

They tramped back towards the BBC bus. Nat was cold. The wind seemed to be funnelling down the valley from the mountains to the east, cutting through her flak jacket and thick woollen sweater. She felt desperately sorry for the refugees, huddling together inside their flimsy shelters. Many would die before proper relief arrived, even if they weren't set upon by Tadzhiki soldiers or renegade looters.

They climbed into the welcome warmth of the bus and peeled off their flak jackets. The chef pressed mugs of steaming tea into their hands and offered plates of sandwiches. 'Cheer up,' he said. 'You're going back to a hotel tonight.'

Nat grunted and sat down next to Suzie. 'We need to find out what's going on here,' she said. 'London's going to keep pushing us about biological weapons until we know, one way or the other. Haven't we got any useful contacts we can lean on for information?'

The producer overheard and stomped over. 'We're doing our best,' he said. 'We've got people in the Tadzhiki camp, and they're sniffing about, but as yet there's nothing. What the hell, maybe it's natural. Plenty of women used to earn a living as wet nurses. It doesn't have to be your own baby brings the milk in.'

'But elderly women, and girls who can't possibly have had their own babies yet?'

He shrugged. 'We're working on it. Don't worry. Whatever's going on, we'll find out.'

THREE

Rachael saw the woman slumped in a corner of one of the passenger tunnels at Waterloo. She would not normally have looked twice – such derelicts were to be seen everywhere in London, and after five days here she was getting used to it. But something about this one caught her attention and she paused for a moment, letting the impatient crowd push past her.

The woman was poorly dressed in a faded shirt and leggings which clung to stick-thin shins, her feet huge in scuffed boots pulled in tightly out of the way of the hurrying commuters. Her hair was held up in a cheap clasp, mousey strands escaping to straggle across her tired eyes and dry, chapped lips. She might have been twenty or fifty. Between her parted knees, Rachael could see the fabric of her shirt straining over huge, heavy breasts.

For a moment the woman glanced up at the legs and briefcases hurrying by, her gaze dull with exhaustion. Then, tenderly, she unfastened her shirt, took out her swollen left breast, and began to milk herself into a plastic cup.

'Buy a cup of milk, sir. Warm milk, fresh milk. Only fifty pence. Warm, fresh milk. Buy a cup of milk, sir.'

Rachael watched the commuters, trying to smother her own appalled reaction with theirs. A few glanced at the derelict, some disgusted, others longing. Small coins flicked on to the floor, but no one stopped. After a while, the milk cooled, the crowds thinned. The woman looked up, and saw Rachael still watching her. She stared, challenging, and held out the cup.

'Buy a cup of milk, missy?'

Rachael turned and fled. She pounded up the escalator, her heart racing. At the top she paused and leant against a wall to catch her breath. Now that she had got away, she felt her panic subsiding. How absurd to be frightened of such a pathetic creature. The woman was little better than the cattle back home, a factory producer of milk. And Roger had expected *her* to turn herself into a milch cow. But that was over. Her rebellious body was back in line, and almost back in trim. She pushed all thoughts of the beggar to the back of her mind, smoothed down her skirt over slender hips, and hurried off to her appointment at the gym.

FOUR

Professor Mwanduka looked around the long table at his colleagues and cleared his throat. 'Perhaps we can make a start,' he suggested.

Lydia drew her attention back from the lab reports in front of her and focused on the institute's director. Perhaps now they were going to get some answers. She didn't like working in the dark; it was unscientific to run experiments without an underlying hypothesis, without any idea of what to look for. The results she had been logging were disturbing, but without more data she could make very little sense of them. She had been working here at the Kenyan Institute of Environmental Sciences for her entire adult life, and resented the lack of trust implicit in the current situation.

A ragged silence had descended, and everyone was now facing the professor. There were several faces around the table which Lydia did not recognize; three were military officers in uniform, which alarmed her.

Professor Mwanduka removed his glasses and polished them carefully on his handkerchief, avoiding looking at anyone while he spoke. 'I'm sure you've all been wondering what our current research is all about,' he began.

'Too right,' said Joseph, the biochemist, angrily. 'It's ridiculous, keeping us in the dark like this.'

'That's why you're here now,' said a sour-looking colonel. 'This situation involves matters of national security. As I'm sure the professor was about to caution you,' he added, with a cold stare at the sweating institute director, 'everything that is said in this room today is to be considered top-secret, not to be repeated to anyone. Is that clear?'

There was grumbled assent from around the table, and the colonel gestured for Professor Mwanduka to continue.

He cleared his throat again, and fumbled with his tie. 'This is Colonel Kanywa. He and his aides will be our guests for the duration of this project, and we would all appreciate your cooperation.'

Lydia frowned. She was fond of Mwanduka, and it was unpleasant to see him so rattled. Her dislike of the colonel and his cronies intensified.

'The samples of human milk and blood you have been analysing were taken from Masai tribeswomen over the past three weeks. We took them from two age groups: girls of ten to fourteen, and older women past the menopause.'

'That's impossible!' Joseph exclaimed. 'These samples are from lactating women.'

Lydia looked again at her notes. 'That would explain a lot,' she said thoughtfully.

'Dr Ogana?' The director was looking at her.

'There were ... hormonal anomalies which have been puzzling me,' she said. 'The young women – were any of them pre-pubescent?'

'Two,' Mwanduka confirmed. 'You seem to be ahead of us, Doctor. Is there anything you would like to add?'

She shook her head, tapping her pencil thoughtfully against her teeth. 'Not at the moment. I need more data. Please continue.'

'As you all know, the Masai have recently been involved in tribal skirmishes with Muslim nomads along the Tanzanian border. There is concern in some circles,' and he looked coldly at the colonel, 'that these skirmishes may be escalating.'

The colonel leant forward and interrupted him. 'We have intelligence from other sources which suggests that Islamic fundamentalists may have access to a new generation of biological weapons.'

'But surely they wouldn't use such things in border skirmishes,' Joseph protested. 'A few nomads wouldn't dare violate international bans on these weapons. And where would they get them from?'

'From any number of sources,' said the colonel. 'Libya, Algeria, Iraq, Afghanistan. We have reports of similar weapons being used in Tadzhikistan by Islamic fundamentalists there, and use is also suspected in Iraq against the Kurdish population, and in East Timor by the Indonesian government.'

'Just a minute,' said Lydia. 'I'm confused. What has been reported? The use of biological weapons, or abnormal patterns of lactation such as those we have been studying?'

The colonel curled his lip contemptuously. 'The one causes the other.'

'And you have proof of this?'

'I think it's fairly clear.'

'I don't think it's clear at all,' said Lydia. 'These anomalies could have been caused by any number of factors. Certainly there is a hormonal imbalance, which we can surmise is due to an external cause. But I very much doubt that the cause is any form of weapon. What would be the point? Weapons are designed to kill, preferably to kill soldiers. Causing women to produce a lot of milk seems a very roundabout way to win a war.'

'It isn't just the women,' said the colonel grimly. 'That's why you're all here today. Things are escalating. Yesterday we received reports that a band of Masai warriors had also been afflicted. Most of them were killed by their companions, while a handful of others appear to have taken their own lives. The people of the region are terrified of losing their masculinity. The spreading of fear, dissention and death – I would say those were the hallmarks of a pretty effective weapon, Doctor.'

In the ensuing uproar from the men around the table, Lydia's objections went unheard. Disgusted, she gathered her notes, and returned to her lab.

FIVE

Nat allowed the camera to speak for her for twenty long seconds. Suzie panned across the river bank and the sprawled bodies. The red ochre of blood-soaked mud coated everything: the trampled grass, the soldiers' uniforms and hair. Mud had splashed into the branches of the few stunted trees, and stained the river water below. Mud had been ground into the skin of the soldiers' faces and the wounds on their torsos and handfuls of mud had been rammed into mouths and ears and anuses and smeared across their eyes. Bodies lay tangled with bodies, lumps of flesh and bone scattered like the offal pile behind a butcher's shop. The air was rank with the stink of blood and voided fluids.

Suzie was glancing at her, but Nat held the silence. A cold wind howled down the narrow valley, and the mud had dried, stiffening over the petrified bodies. The only movement came from the swarms of feasting flies.

There were about twenty dead men lying tumbled by the river's edge. All of them had had the shirts torn away from their chests, and all of them had been messily castrated before having their throats cut.

'These are Tadzhiki soldiers,' Nat said at last in a quiet voice. 'We believe that they were set upon by their own companions and brutally butchered. The reason is unclear, but it seems that these men may have been exposed to the agent that's affecting so many of the women in the refugee camps. All of them have swollen breast tissue and appear to have been lactating. Whatever the truth of the matter, this is a new phase in the hostilities, and suggests that if the Muslims are using biological weapons, they are not giving adequate training in safety precautions to their front-line troops.

'This is Natalie Sharpe for BBC Satellite News, reporting from Uzbekistan.'

Suzie swung her camcorder down from her shoulder and they gazed silently at the scene.

'I don't like being a war correspondent,' said Nat quietly.

'You'll see worse.' Suzie was grim. 'At least these are all dead.'

'Let's go.' They turned away and began to trudge back up the track towards the road. They had to push through the gaggle of film crews who were jockeying for position, all trying to get the best pictures of the dead soldiers to beam back to waiting audiences across the world.

SIX

Rachael plugged her laptop into the telephone socket in her hotel room and switched on. It was ten in the evening. She had spent an hour working out in the gym and had eaten a light meal, and was now preparing to spend a couple of hours conferencing with her US clients. But first she called Roger, who would be coming in from the animal sheds about now to give Amanda her afternoon feed. She dialled her home number through the Internet video link, and after a few moments Roger's face appeared on her screen.

'Hi, hon,' he said. 'How you doin'?' He looked tired and drawn, but cheerful.

'I'm good. London's a drag, but the trading's going well. There's a lot of interest in our product. The European market's going to open right up for us. We're in the big bucks here, honey.'

Roger nodded. 'That's good news. But you know all that stuff's your department. I'm just a li'l old cowboy.'

She smiled at the old joke. Roger had a degree in biochemistry, but he never let her forget that she was the one with the doctorate and the commercial sense. 'So, how's my little baby doing?'

Roger held Amanda up for her mother to see, and the chubby infant waved her fists in the air and gurgled.

'She's looking well. I think she's grown since I left.'

Roger grinned. 'Yeah, she's put on weight. That's because she's eating well. Honey, I got something to tell you.'

She frowned. 'What? You haven't started weaning her already? We said we'd wait till I got home.'

'No, no, don't worry. I wouldn't do that. This is better. I know you didn't want to breast-feed, and I respect your choice, even though I don't understand it –'

'Oh, Roger, don't start that again. Milking is for cows. I didn't want you mistaking me for one of our experimental animals, OK? I'm twenty-eight, I'm a successful businesswoman, and I want to look that way.'

'Sure, I know. But I think babies need breast milk, and you know, the most amazing thing has happened.'

'What?' Suddenly Rachael remembered the woman in the

tube station, and her chest tightened. 'Roger, you're not buying breast milk, are you? Do you have any idea of the risks of disease?'

'Will you calm down and let me tell you? In fact, let me show you.' He turned away from the screen for a moment to put Amanda down. When he turned back, he had opened his shirt and was grinning at her proudly.

Rachael gasped. 'Oh, my God.'

Her husband had always had a muscular chest from working on the land, but now his firm pectorals had softened and swelled, the nipples had spread, and he had shed a lot of hair. He looked exactly as though he had breasts.

'Roger, what have you done? Honey, why didn't you tell me? We could have talked about this. Have you had hormones or implants? Oh, Roger, why didn't you tell me you wanted to be a woman?'

Now he looked confused. 'I don't. I just want to feed our baby, and that's what I'm doing. Honey, I haven't had any treatment. This just happened to me. I wanted to feed our baby, and the Lord has answered my prayers.'

In the background, Rachael heard Amanda beginning to cry. 'Oh, she's hungry,' he said. He looked shy. 'Should I go, or can I feed her while we talk?'

'Feed her,' said Rachael grimly.

'OK.' He picked up the child, and put her to feed. Amanda grabbed his nipple eagerly into her mouth, just as if she was used to it.

'How long have you been doing this?'

'Only a couple of days. I didn't have much milk at first, but it's coming in nicely now.'

'And don't you think it's a little – strange?'

'Oh, sure. I haven't dared tell the guys in town yet, but you know, it happens sometimes. I've read about Native American braves who fed their babies after the squaws got killed. After all, why else have we got nipples if we can't use them?'

Rachael's thoughts were in free fall. Images from the trade fair swirled around her memories of the woman in the tube station. The live pictures of Roger breast-feeding their baby were superimposed over everything else. Here was her husband, calmly transferring Amanda from his right nipple to his left, and smiling mysteriously, like some transsexual Madonna.

'Oh, Jesus. Honey, I've got to go,' she said. 'I don't know what's going on, but please, get yourself to the hospital for a check-up. This may not be a miracle, Roger. Please, will you do that for me?'

He smiled. 'I'm fine. Don't worry. I'll speak to you tomorrow.' And he cut the connection.

For several minutes Rachael sat still, with her head in her hands. Then she got up and went into the bathroom. Tomorrow morning she would call the airport, and catch the first available flight home.

SEVEN

The hotel in Tashkent was old. The central-heating pipes were knocking, and the bedsprings creaked. Nat and Suzie were trying to get the springs into counterpoint with the knocking pipes, but every time they thought they had the rhythm sorted, the pipes would miss a beat or fall silent for an unguessable number of seconds. When at last the pipes became consistent for a couple of minutes, Nat began to laugh too much to keep the springs going.

'Oh, you!' cried Suzie, and thumped the side of her head with a pillow. 'We almost had it there!'

'I'm sorry,' gasped Nat. 'I just remembered who has the room downstairs.'

'Who?'

'Tim, the producer.'

'Oh, what? That old homophobe? Right!' Suzie leapt astride her supine lover, and began to bounce up and down with renewed vigour. 'I never want to hear him ask again what lesbians do in bed.'

'They play concertos for orchestra and central heating pipes!' exclaimed Nat, and at last Suzie succumbed to giggles and fell on to the mattress laughing helplessly.

'Well,' said Nat after a while. 'At least that worked up a sweat. I've been cold for days.'

'Is that all you asked me in here for? Next time I'll bring you three hot-water bottles. They should do the same job.'

'Hardly.' Nat wrapped her arms firmly around Suzie and nuzzled her ear. 'But I could always try kitting you out in rubber and pretend.'

'Oh, you!'

Nat laughed, and ran hands and tongue over Suzie's smooth, tanned skin. 'You're losing weight.'

'So? At least I've got a bit of flesh to lose. If you weren't so skinny you wouldn't feel the cold so much.'

'No, seriously, I can feel your ribs.'

Suzie looked down at her body. 'Looks OK from up here.'

'Well it would, wouldn't it, with the bloody Himalayas in the way? Here, take a squint through the Khyber Pass.' Nat slid her hands between her partner's ample breasts and gently eased them apart. Suzie grunted. 'I'm sorry. Did I hurt you?'

'No. Quite the opposite. They're sensitive tonight.'

Nat took the hint, and turned her attention to Suzie's breasts. 'They're beautiful.'

'They're also on fire. My God, my toes are curling. Ohh, carry on with that.'

Nat smiled, and took Suzie's right areola into her mouth. Fluid squirted as she sucked, and they leapt apart.

'Oh, fuck!' Suzie stared in horror at the milk oozing from her nipple. 'Nat! What's happening?'

Nat scrambled across the mattress and took Suzie in her arms. 'It happens, lover. Sometimes the milk comes back when you've had a baby. It'll stop in a minute.'

'It's never happened to me before. I've got it haven't I? Whatever's happening to those women, I've got it too. Oh, Nat. Oh, sweet Jesus!'

Suzie clung to her and began to cry. Tears and sticky milk dripped down their bodies on to the sweat-soaked sheets.

EIGHT

Samuel Mwanduka had dark shadows under his eyes from lack of sleep, and the line between his brows had deepened into a chasm of anxiety. His shoulders, always rounded, were now stooped lower. He looked old and frail, and Lydia felt sorry for him. Colonel Kanywa was at his shoulder. She scowled.

'Isn't it enough that you insist on my working extra hours, Colonel, without haunting my laboratory as well?' she snapped.

He smiled thinly. 'If these Islamic fundamentalists have their way, you will no longer have a laboratory, Doctor. You will be wearing the veil and walking three paces behind your husband. Supposing that you have one, of course.'

'As it happens, I do not. Nor am I convinced by your conspiracy theory. You must know that Muslim Tadzhiki troops have also been affected by this – disorder. And there are reports of incidents from all around the world. The nature of the disease is wrong for weapons. This is a hormonal problem of some subtlety. It makes no sense to design weapons which do this.'

'I tell you they're trying to unman us. It's a conspiracy of devils!' the colonel exclaimed. 'The effects on women are immaterial. After all, feeding infants is what a woman's body is designed to do. No, no, it's the men who are the target. Imagine if our leaders become afflicted! Who can take a man seriously if he's leaking milk all over his suit? How can a soldier fight under such circumstances?'

Lydia allowed herself a brief smile. 'Women's bodies are designed to do many things, as are men's. Lactation is one of them. In fact, it requires a hormone to prevent lactation, otherwise all of us would be in milk all of the time, men as well as women.'

'Doctor.' Mwanduka's voice was quiet, but firm. 'Do you understand yet what is happening?'

'In general terms, yes.' She nodded, tapping her pencil against her teeth as she considered her reply. 'Lactation is triggered by the hormone prolactin, the production of which is normally inhibited by the presence of another hormone. What seems to be happening here is that the inhibiting hormone stops doing its job. Prolactin is released into the bloodstream, and the body begins to produce milk. I'm not yet certain what's causing it, but I hypothesize that it's either an artificial hormone that's preventing the production of the inhibiting hormone, or a hormone which directly mimics the behaviour of prolactin itself.'

Lydia looked Kanywa straight in the eye. 'The epidemiology would suggest a global environmental contaminant, similar to the organic chlorine compounds of a generation ago which have had such a devastating effect on male fertility. Let's face it, Colonel, in reproductive terms, you are only half the man your grandfather was, even before all of this began.'

The colonel took a step towards her, his face contorting in fury, and for a moment Lydia thought he was going to hit her. She flinched away, but he stopped himself, and slowly his muscles relaxed. He forced a smile. 'And that amuses you does it, Doctor?'

'Not in the least. But it is a fact that humanity succeeded many years ago in releasing several compounds which mimic the action of oestrogens in the human body. I am suggesting that what we are witnessing here is the effect of global contamination with prolactin-mimicking hormones.'

'If you're right, what's causing it?'

She shrugged. 'We have not yet tracked down the most likely candidates, but we have a good idea of what to look for, and I expect results soon.'

'But what, dammit? It can't be a chemical incident, a factory spill, anything like that.'

'Oh no, it's far more widespread than that. The oestrogenic compounds turned out to be inevitable by-products of the manufacture of PVC, the most widely used plastic during the latter half of last century. I expect this to be something equally systemic.'

Mwanduka nodded. 'You're doing well. How soon before you have more definite answers?'

Lydia spread her hands. 'I don't know. Scientific research of this nature can't be rushed. We're doing our best.' She glanced at Kanywa, and added pointedly, 'Of course, it would help if you would allow us Internet access. There must be other labs across the world working on the problem. If we pooled our resources –'

'No,' he snapped. 'I cannot allow that sort of security breach.'

'Oh, grow up, Colonel!' Lydia exclaimed. 'We're talking about global security here; national borders count for nothing.'

Kanywa shook his head. 'I will not allow it. There's too much at stake. I acknowledge that we don't yet have much evidence to support the biological-weapons scenario. However, my latest intelligence is that NATO is considering making an application to the UN for sanctions against the major Islamic Bloc nations, on the grounds that they have broken international agreements on the use of biological weapons.'

'*What?*' Lydia briefly covered her face with her hands. 'Colonel, that's insane. The Islamic Bloc may be as much victims of this as the rest of us.'

Kanywa shrugged. 'It's out of my hands. But you do appreciate that this is building into a major international incident. We need answers soon, Doctor.'

He turned on his heel and stalked out of the laboratory.

'What? He can't do that to me!' she shrieked. 'How can he put this on to me?'

'That's the military mind for you, Doctor,' said Mwanduka sadly. 'But don't worry, if anyone gets the blame around here, it's me, not you. Good luck.' Slowly, he followed the colonel out of her lab.

As soon as they were gone, Lydia hurried to the toilets. Locked in a stall, she unbuttoned her dress, and reached into her bra to check the thin pads inside. They were damp and sticky, but holding. She was ravenously hungry. Under her breath, she cursed Kanywa with every name she knew. 'Don't worry,' she spat. 'I have my own reasons for wanting to find a solution quickly.'

NINE

Roger moved quietly between the rows of gently shifting cattle. The machines hissed against their udders, drawing the milk from them into huge holding tanks. Production was up by fifteen per cent, with no loss of milk quality. After the tedious months of FDA safety tests, it was a relief to finally be in production. He stroked the nearest beast's nose and scratched her between the eyes. She harrumphed at him, spraying him with spittle. He wiped his face and laughed.

'You just keep delivering the goods, baby. Eat up now. We can't have you losing your strength.'

The cow dipped her head back into her feed trough and returned to chewing.

It was hot, and watching the cow eat made him realize how hungry he was, ravenous in fact. Time to finish up and go in to eat.

He strolled out of the barn and began to cross the vegetable patch towards the house. In the distance, he could see Giselle's pick-up glinting in the sun beside the porch. He had left Amanda in their young neighbour's care for the afternoon while he checked on the animals, but now he felt an urgent need to see his tiny daughter, and to experience once more the exquisite pleasure of feeding her.

He began to lope towards the house. His legs felt heavy, and his breath came short. It was sure taking it out of him, this mothering business. His respect for the women who did it was growing all the time. He had never felt so tired. He was losing weight and muscle tone, but what the hell! Amanda was the important one. He would soon be back in condition once she was weaned.

He slowed to a walk, panting, and crossed the final few yards to the house more slowly. The thought of Amanda being weaned came over him like a shock of cold water. He did not want it to happen, not ever. He would have to persuade Rachael to have another child so there could be a new baby for him to feed.

He could see Giselle on the porch with her back to him, cradling Amanda in her arms. He ran up the steps and through the screen door. 'Hi, Gi! How's it going?'

The teenager jerked around to face him, a look of dismay on her face. 'Oh! I didn't expect you back so soon.'

She juggled with Amanda, trying to rearrange her shirt to conceal her breasts.

Rage boiled up inside him. 'What the hell d'you think you're doing?'

'I – she was hungry and – oh, Mr Lewis, don't tell my

The Milk of Human Kindness

mom, please! It only happened last week. I know I should have used the bottle, but I so much wanted to feed her. Babies need real milk. I wasn't doing any harm.'

'Give her to me!' Roger roared, snatching his baby from the cowering girl. 'Don't you ever come around here again. Get out! Get out of here!' He raised his fist to strike her, but Giselle ducked around his arm and fled.

She stopped outside the screen door. 'You have no idea how much I wanted to be a mommy. Please, Mr Lewis. I know your wife doesn't want to feed the baby. Please let me do it!'

'Go!' Roger put Amanda down and ran at his neighbour. She screamed and tumbled down the steps, running for her pick-up, Roger in hot pursuit. She reached the car before him, flung herself in and locked the doors. Roger grabbed the handle and tried to wrench it open, while the terrified girl fumbled with her keys.

She started the engine and the vehicle squealed into motion. For a moment, he was dragged along beside it, then he lost his grip on the handle, tearing the skin from his fingers. He fell and lay on his belly in the dust howling obscenities after her.

Then he rolled on to his back and lay staring up at the sky, panting and clutching his shoulder. The rage subsided, and he was filled with dismay and a vast weariness.

'Oh, my God. What am I doing?'

TEN

'I'm *hungry*!' Suzie insisted. 'I can't help it, Nat, I've got to eat something.'

'We haven't got enough to last if you keep on like this.'

'I know, but I'm going to collapse if I don't.'

Nat glanced worriedly at her partner, then returned her eyes to the narrow track ahead. 'Maybe we should go back. You don't look too good.'

'No way! We've got to find out what's going on.' Suzie reached for the rucksack lying on the back seat of their Land Rover, and pulled out two chunky nut-and-raisin chocolate bars. 'Want one?'

Nat shook her head, concentrating on keeping the vehicle

on the road. She had shaded the headlights with two pairs of Suzie's black silk knickers, and they now cast barely enough light to see ten yards ahead. A steep wall of rock on their left hand blocked out the moonlight which had helped progress lower down the valley. To their right, the hillside fell away in a steep scree slope to a wooded valley some two hundred feet below. The edge of the track was ill-defined, and her hands were sweating on the wheel. 'I'm not sure this was such a good idea. You should be in a hospital, not risking your life on field assignment trying to get an exclusive.'

'No way. Those doctors we interviewed about the women in the camps didn't have a clue what's happening. I don't want to end my days as a lab rat. I'd much rather be out here with you, doing my job.'

The vehicle hit a deep rut and lurched towards the rock wall. Nat cursed, and slowed her speed even more. Suzie reached out a hand and squeezed her arm. 'You're doing fine, lover.'

They drove on in silence, Suzie's hand resting lightly on Nat's forearm.

After another hour, the track began to descend and the slope on their right became less steep. They dipped below the tree line and pulled off the road to rest. Suzie's already large breasts had swelled up even more and were constantly leaking. She removed the makeshift pads and mopped at the stickiness.

'Yeuch! I hate this. It's so undignified.'

'They look sore.'

'They are. I'm going to have to milk them again. Please, I'd rather you didn't watch.'

Nat sat miserably while Suzie turned her back and voided herself into the plastic bucket they had brought for the purpose. Her own small breasts had begun to swell, and she knew it was only a matter of time before she succumbed as well. She had never had a baby, or ever wanted to, and had felt herself devoid of all maternal instinct, but now she was disturbed to feel an increasing desire to breast-feed. Her nipples were tingling, and she kept imagining how it would feel to have lips and tongue drawing the milk from her. The fantasies were tactile in a way she had rarely experienced.

The Milk of Human Kindness

She knew that she would want Suzie to feed from her, and was ashamed of the desire. Her lover seemed to want her to stay away.

She looked across the vehicle at the curve of Suzie's spine, and saw that her shoulders were gently shaking. Then she heard a very quiet sobbing.

'Oh, my love!' She took Suzie in her arms and held her close.

'Nat. I want – I want you to do it.' Suzie kept her eyes lowered. 'I know it's disgusting, but I really want you to drink it.'

Nat kissed her gently on the lips. 'I thought you'd never ask.'

She moved her head and took Suzie's nipple deep into her mouth. The thick, sweet milk gushed into her throat, and she drank.

ELEVEN

The town's main street seemed very quiet as the taxi drove Rachael home. There were very few cars, and several stores seemed to be closed. She asked Al the driver if he knew why.

He shrugged irritably. 'Hadn't noticed,' he said.

'But look. Even the drugstore's closed.'

He grunted. 'I guess. Maybe Hank's ill.'

'Maybe. Are you OK?'

'Sure. Why wouldn't I be?'

'You usually talk all the time. Are you sure you're OK?'

'Yeah, I'm sure,' he snapped. 'It's hot and the end of my shift. I don't have to talk, do I?'

'No, you don't. I'm sorry.' She leant back in her seat. In fact she didn't mind the driver's silence. She was too worried about Roger, and she had a lot to think about. Shortly before her plane had left Heathrow, she had seen a news programme about derelicts in London's East End. Several of them were exhibiting symptoms identical to those in the woman she had seen at Waterloo. The TV presenter was playing it down, but Rachael was left feeling uneasy. To make matters worse, her own milk seemed to have been stimulated again by all the emphasis on lactation over the past couple of days, and she was having to wear a pair of the uncomfortable, chafing breast pads she hated so much. She was afraid that once she got home to Amanda it would be worse. She hated the uncontrollable let-down reflex which had brought milk flooding to her nipples every time the baby cried. It was like having a cold, or diarrhoea, distasteful fluids oozing from her body. The whole business of pregnancy and childbirth had shaken her self-image. It had felt as though the foetus had taken control of her body, feeding off her, and when that demand had continued after the birth it had been more than she could bear.

The cab turned on to the track leading to their homestead and bumped along the ruts. Al pulled up in front of the house, tossed her bags out of the trunk, and waited impatiently while she fed her card to the meter. As soon as she was done he drove away, without even saying goodbye.

Irritated, she climbed the steps to the porch, and pushed aside the screen door. 'Honey, I'm home!'

Silence.

That was odd. She had told him what time to expect her, and his pick-up was out the back. He should be here. 'Roger?'

A baby's cry came from the kitchen. She hurried through. 'Amanda?'

Roger was sprawled on the floor, a chair tangled in his legs. He had no shirt on, and she was horrified to see how thin he was. Amanda lay on her back close by, gurgling contentedly, waving her fat fists in the air. Her face was sticky with milk, and milk was dripping from Roger's tits on to the floor.

Rachael ran to him, and felt his pulse. It was weak, but it was there. As she looked wildly around for the phone, there was a quiet tap at the door, and Giselle walked in, as thin and gaunt as Roger.

'Dr Lewis, you're back. Please, can I feed Amanda? Oh, there she is.'

Ignoring Roger, the girl picked up the baby, and placed her to her breast, where she began to suckle.

TWELVE

Lydia drank deeply from the glass of water at her side, and ate a handful of peanuts, eyes still glued to the screen in front of her. She had not left the institute for four days, sleeping for only a couple of hours each night, curled up on a pile of cushions in the staff common room. She was exhausted, and she knew she had reached the point where she was likely to make mistakes, but she kept going anyway.

Her lab technician had failed to turn up the previous morning. Joseph, the firebrand biochemist, had been found hanging from a beam in his own laboratory two days ago, his breasts swollen and oozing. Lydia tried not to think about it. Colonel Kanywa, to her surprise, had proved to be of sterner stuff. He came into the lab now, bearing a tray of test-tube racks, his uniform jacket discarded, shirt-sleeves rolled up.

'Where do you want these, Doctor?'

She cleared a space on the lab bench. 'Here will do fine. How are you feeling?'

'I'm not feeling at all. What do you want me to do next?'

'I need to eat again. Will you get us some food?'

He nodded. 'Sure.' He hesitated. 'How's it going?'

'I've found what's causing it. We were looking in the wrong place. It isn't an environmental contaminant at all. Look.' She brought up a new window on her screen with a few clicks of her mouse, and set the three-dimensional image rotating slowly. 'This is it. Rewritten DNA, definitely genetically engineered. It instructs the body to switch off the prolactin release-inhibiting hormone, and as a result most of the organism's energy output becomes channelled into the production of milk. Without a controlled, protein-rich diet, affected creatures die in a matter of weeks.'

'And you still hold that it isn't a weapon?'

She shook her head. 'Definitely not a weapon. I don't know how it started, but this code is being carried around by a virus. It's useless as a weapon because it doesn't discriminate.'

'So it would attack the aggressor as well?'

'Exactly. I've found this genetic alteration in all the blood and tissue samples we've tested since I first isolated it thirty-six hours ago, including our own. What I don't understand is why the symptoms have appeared so suddenly and catastrophically at so many points around the world. It seems to be transferred from person to person as easily as the common cold, but at the moment the outbreaks are clustered.' She began to tap her pencil against her teeth, her frown deepening. 'Why would anybody want to genetically engineer human DNA to do this?'

His shoulders sagged. 'I'm used to facing enemies I can see, human beings I can shoot. I've never been afraid in the field. But this ... What can I do when it's inside my own body? I feel as though I've turned into a dairy cow.'

She stared at him. 'A cow?'

'Yes. A stupid, cud-chewing cow.' He slammed his fist into the bench. 'I can't bear it!'

'A cow!' she exclaimed. 'Of course. Genetically engineering bovine DNA makes perfect commercial sense. Cattle wouldn't have to calve once a year, so no surplus animals and no energy wastage. Milk production could be kept at a peak until the poor creature died of exhaustion. That's it! Someone has been genetically engineering cattle.'

'But who?'

'That shouldn't be too hard to find out, but you'll have to allow me Internet access to do it.'

He scowled. 'Very well, but only for information gathering. I don't want you talking to anyone about this, not yet anyway.'

'That's going to make it harder.'

'I'm under orders too.' He shrugged. 'I'm sorry. That's the best I can offer.'

She turned back to her terminal and began clicking away with her mouse. 'If somebody has been messing about with bovine DNA, the experimental work should be easy enough to track down. But now the virus must have managed to cross the species barrier, and change its transmission vector in the process. Colonel, we are looking at Ebola virus with horns and a forked tail.'

'Sitting on a milking stool?'

She laughed. 'I didn't think you had a sense of humour.'

'Only when I'm staring down the barrel of a gun.'

'Well, Colonel, you're going to be laughing for the rest of your life.'

THIRTEEN

They crossed the border into Tadzhikistan sometime shortly before dawn, although neither of them was sure of the exact moment. They did not dare boot up the Land Rover's computer to use their GPS to pinpoint their position, in case the signal was intercepted. If they knew exactly where they were, so might other people. They hoped that the Tadzhikis were still unaware of their presence, but they didn't want the UN peacekeepers to get wind of them. So they drove slowly and carefully, with only a paper map and a compass to guide them.

The village wasn't on the map. They came upon it unexpectedly as the road turned and dipped into another desolate valley. Suzie slammed on the brakes and backed up over the crest of the hill.

'Shit! They're bound to have seen us.'

'Out,' said Nat. 'We'll take the camera over there into the rocks and lie low for a few minutes, see if anyone comes looking. Got your press pass?'

'Yeah, yeah. For what good that's worth.'

They jumped out of the Land Rover and ran for cover among the tumbled rocks that lined the road. Long minutes passed, and nothing happened.

'Let's take a look,' said Nat. 'If we're careful we should be able to look down into the village from up there without anyone seeing us.'

Cautiously they climbed back up to the ridge, and peered into the valley. The village lay spread out beneath them, silent.

'Looks like everyone's moved out,' said Suzie. 'They're probably all in the refugee camps by now.'

Nat shook her head. 'The UN was supposed to be ensuring the safety of civilians in this area. And look, there's smoke coming from those chimneys. Come on, let's have a look.' She jumped to her feet and headed for the valley. Suzie picked up the camcorder and followed, muttering.

The village was eerily quiet. Many of the house doors were open but nobody came out to look at the Westerners, and no dogs barked. They walked slowly down the dusty main street, looking nervously from side to side. Nat felt her spine tingling. She was very glad of her flak jacket.

'Where is everybody?' Suzie whispered nervously. 'I don't think I want to look in the houses.'

They turned a corner into what looked like a market square and, unmistakably, heard the sound of a baby crying.

Nat clutched Suzie's arm. 'Now what do we do?'

'Come on. Whatever it is, we're already infected, remember?'

The infant's wails were coming from the mosque. They drew scarves from their pockets and covered their hair, then entered cautiously.

The building was filled with bodies. Women and men lay among the shadows, some lined up neatly against the walls, some sprawled where they had fallen. Nat bent beside the nearest. 'My God, look at this.'

The woman was paper and dust, dry skin stretched over bones, her face little more than a skull, belly falling away beneath her ribs. Only her breasts bore any flesh. They were swollen to huge size, the nipples broad and reddened. Sticky fluid dripped and trickled into a pool on the floor beneath her.

Squatting nearby was a very young child, staring at her with bright brown eyes. The boy's arms and legs were chubby and his skin glowed with health. As Nat watched he jumped up and toddled into the shadows on unsteady legs. Nat followed and found him crouching beside the body of an old man, suckling contentedly.

She jumped to her feet and backed away, feeling her gorge rising. Suzie was filming. She called to her from behind the camcorder. 'Nat. Have you seen the babies? They're everywhere, just feeding, as if they don't care. And the adults are dead.'

'No,' said Nat, 'not dead. Look.'

One of the skeletal bodies was moving, a hand rising towards them, and a cracked voice calling in Tadzhiki.

' "Help me",' Suzie translated. 'Christ, what do we do?'

She continued filming as they backed slowly towards the door and the weak sunlight outside. Now they could hear faint rustlings and whispers as those still living implored their aid. The whole mosque was filled with tiny scratchings and murmurs and in the shadows bodies moved. The infants laughed and waved their chubby fists and toddled to the next body where they squatted to suckle once more.

FOURTEEN

'Colonel?'

Lydia turned around to see that Kanywa had fallen asleep in his chair. His head had fallen back and his mouth was open, but he wasn't snoring. She smiled wryly. So he had one good feature at least.

'Colonel!' She went over and shook his shoulder. 'I've found them.'

'What?' He came awake at once, alert, looking around to get his bearings. 'Found who?'

'The company who engineered this virus. Lewis Pharmaceuticals. It's a family firm in Iowa. Americans, wouldn't you know it? They have farming interests, and the wife is managing director of a rather successful company manufacturing agricultural pharmaceuticals. I should have realized sooner. Jacob was in the States about a month ago attending a conference on applications of genetic engineering to agriculture. I never had a chance to talk to him about it, but Dr Lewis was there, presumably talking about her virus.'

'And infecting everyone else who was there?'

Lydia shrugged. 'It would explain why we are experiencing symptoms. It would also explain the Masai outbreak. Jacob went out to our field station down there for a couple of days when he got back.'

The colonel looked appalled. 'Could it really be that infectious?'

'If it's transmitted by air, then yes. That means that every scientist and every journalist at the conference has carried the virus home with them. No wonder it's flared up so suddenly in so many places. It was a big international conference. It's probably everywhere by now.'

'What can we do?'

'Possibly nothing. I've tried to contact Dr Lewis in London. She's just been over there promoting her virus to the Europeans, but apparently she flew home early. She doesn't seem to be answering her e-mail, so I'm going to call her. I thought you might like to sit in.'

'You bet I would.' He followed her back to her terminal and pulled up a second chair. 'Go ahead. This is your baby.'

She raised her eyebrow. 'Thank you,' she said drily.

The insistent ringing of her bleeper brought Rachael back to her senses. She was sitting on the kitchen floor with her sleeping daughter in her arms. Her blouse and bra were unfastened, and her breasts felt heavy. On the floor near her, Roger was breathing shallowly, and at the other side of the room lay her neighbour Giselle in a pool of blood.

She reached for her laptop and flipped up the lid to answer the call. The face of an unfamiliar black woman appeared on her screen. 'Yeah? Who are you?'

'Dr Lewis? My name is Lydia Ogawa. I'm calling from the Kenyan Institute of Environmental Sciences. Please, I need to talk to you urgently.'

Rachael sat up straighter, and pulled her blouse closed. 'Pardon me, I was just . . .' She hesitated, uncertain. What had happened since she got home? 'I –'

'It's all right, Doctor, don't explain. I think I understand. I was calling about your virus. I need to talk to you about your virus.'

Rachael rubbed her forehead. The caller seemed very distant, as though speaking from the far end of a tunnel, and there was something wrong with the sound. 'Can you speak up? I can't hear you.' She was sweating and her hands were shaking.

'Doctor, has something happened? You look very pale. Are you in shock?'

Shock. That was it. She was in shock. Something terrible had happened. Something to do with Roger, and with Giselle. She looked across the room again at her neighbour, and distant memory stirred. Giselle had tried to feed Amanda, that was it. And she had stopped her. She had stopped her because, because – she had to feed the child herself. After everything she had done to stop it, she had become a milch cow after all.

In her lap, Amanda stirred and began to whimper. Rachael felt her nipples tingling, and realized that her milk was flowing again. It wasn't fair.

The face on the screen was still speaking, but it no longer seemed important. Impatiently, she flipped the lid down, breaking the connection, and lifted Amanda to her breast. 'All right, you little monster, feed,' she muttered.

Lydia thumped the desk in frustration. 'Damn! She's completely out of it. Colonel, can you find out what's happening through your military contacts? If it started in Iowa there must have been dozens of incidents there by now.'

Kanywa shrugged. 'I'll try, but the Kenyan military isn't on the best of terms with the US right now. Still, I should be able to get something.'

Lydia moved aside, and Kanywa began to tap out top-priority codes on to the screen.

FIFTEEN

Nat and Suzie backed out of the mosque into the weak sunlight. Nat was breathing hard, and her heart was pounding. 'What's going on?' she asked.

Suzie shook her head. 'Let's get back to the Land Rover and make some calls,' she said. 'It doesn't matter if the UN finds us now. In fact, I wouldn't mind an escort back over the border.'

'Who do we call?'

'I've been thinking. Remember that biotechnology conference we were at in the States last month? Before we decided we needed some excitement in our lives and volunteered for the front line?'

'Oh, you mean Iowa?'

'That's the one. There was a scientist there talking about

genetic engineering and dairy cattle. She might have some ideas.'

'You think there's a link?'

'I don't know, but at least she might have some idea of what's causing this. I can't remember her name, but we can look it up.'

They turned a corner, deep in conversation, and almost ran into the Tadzhiki soldier.

He gave a shout and leapt back, raising his rifle and aiming at them. They froze.

He shouted again, and gestured with the gun for them to move towards the wall. They raised their hands slowly and complied.

'He wants to know what we're doing here,' said Suzie quietly as the soldier continued to yell at them. 'He says all of this is our fault, and calls us American pigs. I think we're in trouble.'

'You don't say.'

The soldier was very young, still in his late teens, and he looked badly frightened. Nat wondered if her flak jacket would stop a rifle bullet at this close range. Somehow she doubted it.

Suzie spoke to the soldier, trying to soothe him, but he thrust his gun menacingly towards her face and she stopped. 'I think he's going to kill us,' she said despairingly. 'He's on his own and he's too frightened to know what else to do.'

The soldier raised his gun again and pointed it directly at Nat's face. She could see straight into the blackness of the barrel. She closed her eyes. 'Shit.'

There was a long pause, then she heard the distant sound of a child crying. She opened her eyes.

The gun barrel was gone, and the soldier was looking about him wildly. He turned and began to run away from them, towards the mosque. Nat sagged against the wall, her knees shaking.

'Oh, my love.' Suzie flung her arms around her, and they hugged fiercely.

'Let's get the fuck out of here!' cried Nat.

'But the children, he's going to kill the children.'

'We can't stop him. Let's just be grateful he didn't kill us.'

From around the corner they heard the sharp crack of rifle fire and the screams of small children. Nat began to tremble uncontrollably.

'Come on!' yelled Suzie. She set off at a run towards the sound.

'Oh, I don't believe you!' Nat staggered after her, cursing.

The young soldier stood at the entrance to the mosque, firing indiscriminately into the darkness. Suzie had her camcorder on her shoulder and was filming as she ran towards him. Nat stopped and watched helplessly.

Suddenly the soldier threw down his gun and fell to his knees, tearing at his shirt. Two small children emerged from the mosque, apparently unhurt. They toddled over to the teenager and stared up at him with huge round eyes. Suzie had crept closer, and was still filming.

The boy soldier hesitated, then he scooped up the children in his arms and put them to his breast. He threw back his head and howled at the sky. The infants suckled unconcernedly and the boy knelt still, his rifle discarded in the dust. Suzie filmed it all for the world to see.

Bibliophage
being a tale from the Library of (almost) Everything

By Stephen Marley

It is written...

... that in the first millisecond of the creation of the universe, when time was a raw, capricious toddler and every moment contained a multiplicity of eons, the Entelechy *sprang into instantaneous being from the necessity of their impossibility. Some later races gave the* Entelechy *the title of the First Angels; others said they were the First Demons. But then some people will say anything. Suffice it that these primal beings reigned supreme in the uncounted ages enfolded in the initial second of the cosmos. When that long, long second was up, and the* Entelechy *had solved all the mysteries of existence, they performed one last act before departing the universe for polydimensional pastures new. They extruded an ontogenetic residuum of their omnimorphic psyche (so 'tis said) to form the* Omnilibrarium — *the Library of Everything.*

Their creation, the unlimited-but-finite Library, has as many aspects as there are points of view. According to one perception it's a multifoliate universe of conscious molecules; to another it's an organic computer of extra-cosmic proportions. To human perceptions, the Library is a limitless repository packed with weighty volumes, continuously expanding as each new happening in the universe is automatically recorded. Within these numberless tomes is a full account of everything in the universe, down to the most recent behaviour of a single photon and the latest sneeze of a gerbil...

'Oh, turn that bloody thing off, Mr Forthman!'

Reginald Forthman tightened his grip on the ship's wheel and puffed at his pipe, resolutely ignoring Sister Pik Lim's irate request. He kept his eye on the ballooning chaos of the Horsehead Nebula through the flight deck window and his ear fully tuned to the audio log:

... Residing one step to the left of reality, the Library can be approached only via the Portal, which has been located these last five million years near the centre of the Horsehead Nebula. But, for scholars who seek knowledge in the Library, be warned ... Since the mysterious disappearance of that omnivorous reader, Obald the Omnivorous, *in the Library's silent mazes a million or so years ago, many other scholars have likewise ... disappeared. Now the Library of Everything is an empty, haunted place where only the most adventurous scholars dare intrude. Few return ...*

The audio log concluded with a terminal click, followed by a loud raspberry.

Forthman, lips pressed tight, turned slowly to his companion, subjecting her to a disapproving stare. 'I was listening to that. Switch it back on, there's a good girl.'

Stepping back from the brass horn of the audio unit, Sister Lim raised an elegant eyebrow in her exquisite Chinese face, settled her curvy, mini-robed body into a chair and showed a seductive length of thigh as she ran sinuous fingers through her long, blonde hair. 'Bollocks.'

Forthman nearly bit through his pipe stem. He was used to her contrary moods but, in his present predicament, a *little* consideration would have been appreciated. After all, she was a Buddhist nun, notwithstanding her parallel career of robbery, conspiracy and receiving stolen nanotech jewellery.

'Listen, Sister Lim,' he said, seething with forbearance. 'We've got maybe ten minutes before we reach the Portal. I must learn all I can in the time.'

'But why keep replaying the ramblings of an old fart like Osbert the Obtuse? He's a notorious liar – *and* he's a bloody foreigner.'

Forthman stuck out his square jaw and adjusted his tweed tie. 'Well, at least he's a humanoid foreigner. He isn't squishy and slimy with lots of tentacles like –' he couldn't resist it '– like that non-Earther you spent the night with on –'

'I told you never to mention that,' she snapped. Then she softened, and popped a *ch'i* cigarillo into the rueful slant of her mouth. 'Sorry – I'm all on edge. You've been so bloody mysterious about this whole trip.'

He switched the steering wheel to auto and slumped into a neo-Edwardian armchair, expelling a sigh as he undid the leather buttons on his tweed sports jacket. 'My fault, Sister Lim. Only a cad mentions a lady's indiscretions.' He glanced up at the ominous cloud of the Horsehead Nebula, framed by the observation window.

'It's getting closer,' she said.

'Yes indeed.' He assumed an air of sang-froid. 'We could be in for a sticky wicket, old thing.'

She blew out a plume of blue cigarillo smoke. 'Whatever it is, Mr Forthman, surely we've faced worse. What about the porcine horrors we encountered in the Case of the Sudden Pig. It looked like we were done for until I found the Clue of the Inconsequential Truffle.'

'This,' he said darkly, 'is worse. Worse even than the Case of the Fortuitous Eyebrow.'

She pursed her astounding lips. 'Then you'd better tell me what the hell's going on. I want to know what I'm getting myself into before I'm already in it.'

'I can't,' he said grimly. 'It's all too terrible.'

An enigmatic pause.

'In that case,' she said, slowly and deliberately, 'I won't uncouple the dark-year drive.'

'Oh chiz,' he swore. 'That means we'll crash into a multiple singularity when we approach one of the maelstroms of verisimilitude at the nebula's core.'

Her shoulders performed an insouciant shrug. 'Might not. I'll chance it.'

He locked wills and stares with her for several seconds, determined not to give in. Crashing with the full impact of a dark-year drive's multiple-reversed-antithesis meant certain death. Such were the hazards of travelling at the speed of light – backwards.

But she'd stare him out until they crashed – he just knew it. He threw up a hand in surrender. 'All right, blast it.' He sprang up and with three strides reached the locked chest of the Information Dump. Grumbling to himself, he entered the access codes and opened the lid. After a quick rummage he pulled out a slim file and tossed it into Sister Lim's lap.

He assumed a steadfast stance, pipe held at a stalwart angle.

She skimmed through the first page of the file, murmuring as she read:

'Hmm ... Mr Reginald Forthman, thirty-one-year-old Professor of Ontology, born AD 2524; ontological scholar-adventurer and part-owner of the dark-year-drive spacecraft *Inquisitive*, accompanied on his exploits by twenty-five-year-old Buddhist nun Sister Pik Lim, his sidekick –' She jabbed a sharp look at Forthman. '*Your* sidekick? Other way round, Mr Forthman.'

He waved the point away. 'The matter is open to debate. But not now. I really would be awfully grateful if you'd uncouple the drive posthaste. You can read the file as you do it. Be a sport – please?'

'OK.' She rose from the chair. 'I'll nip aft and sort out the bloody drive. When I get back I'll tell you what I think of your file.'

He watched the brass doors slam shut, blotting out her breathtaking figure. The corner of his mouth tightened. He earnestly hoped that she'd sort out the drive before reading the file, or she might be so cheesed off that she'd blow the whole ship up.

His gaze strayed around the flight deck, a cluttered ensemble of brass consoles, brass dials and brass chandeliers. On the external screen, framed by a choir of brass cherubs, the *Inquisitive* itself was displayed, a hyperbrass spacecraft shaped like a pregnant walrus, chugging into the Horsehead Nebula's outer vapours. The *Inquisitive* was an old banger from the last gasp of the twenty-fifth century, but the old girl had carried him and his glamorous sidekick through numerous adventures on a hundred planets, often pitted against fiendish foreigners with pulsating pseudopodia and pendulous proboscides.

He gave a start as a judder ran through the craft. On screen, the ship gave an unnerving wobble. Sister Lim had uncoupled the drive. A few more minutes and the ship would reach the nebula's nucleus. From there, one step left of reality to the fabled Library of Everything. And the answer to the mystery ...

The brass doors thwacked open and Sister Lim stormed in, waving the file in an angry fist. 'So this is your bloody mystery! You drag me dark-years from Earth for this! Your old obsession, your old *delusion* – ontological vanishing. It's crap – your whole theory's crap.'

Forthman squared his shoulders. 'The theory is true. And I can prove it, for I am about to become a victim of ontological vanishing. A memory worm is devouring my past, swallowing about a year for every day that passes. When it reaches my present, I will vanish from existence as if I had never been.'

That silenced her for a good few seconds. Then she looked askance. 'Sounds like some special form of amnesia. Doesn't prove a damn thing about barmy ontological theories.'

'But you've never seriously considered my theory, have you? Sit down and listen a moment, please. Please?'

She flung up her hands. 'All right, but if you don't convince me, we turn this tub round and head right back.' She glanced at the chronometer. 'I'll give you exactly one minute.'

'One minute? Oh well, here goes ...' He leant on the Information Dump chest and drew a deep breath. 'Um – haven't you ever almost remembered someone in your past who must have existed despite all evidence indicating that they couldn't have existed? You know the sort of thing – when folk ask "Whatever happened to whatsisname?" without any real clue as to who whatsisname was.'

'No.'

'Think about it. Ontological vanishing is evidenced on the occasions when people, reflecting back on their past, realize that for a period of their life they were interacting with someone who apparently wasn't there at the time but who *must* have been, from the trivial "I'm sure there was someone else with us at dinner, or else where did all the whipped cream go?" to the portentous "I could have sworn I had a jealous partner last year, otherwise I'd definitely have gone on that date with that right little corker who tickled my fancy".'

'Bollocks.'

'I beg to differ. People are being cancelled from existence,

Bibliophage

removed from the memories of all those they encountered, erased from all records, but . . .' He lofted a finger. 'The vanished ones leave an ontological hole in reality. The lover whose beloved vanishes wonders how he managed to have such wonderful sex on his own for the past few years. A woman may ponder why she used to talk to herself so much, when in truth she was speaking to a husband who has ontologically vanished. By their absence shall you know them, so to speak.'

'That's it,' she declared. 'Your minute's up.'

He folded his arms and stared through the window at the black bedlam of the Horsehead Nebula. 'In twenty hours or so, my life will be up. The memory worm I referred to will catch up with me and engulf my being, turning me into an actuality hole. I call it a worm because I've dreamt of a giant worm each night for almost a month. In my dream I see my life as a corridor stretching behind me and the head of the worm advancing as it feasts on my past years, devouring every memory, digesting every incident. As it feeds, it lengthens. Only the last two years are left to me, and they shrink with each passing hour.'

She shook her head. 'The Case of the Fortuitous Eyebrow was three years ago. How come you remember that?'

'Through later memories of it, of course, albeit fragmentary.'

Sister Lim mulled that over. 'Yes, OK, I'll give you that one.' She gave him a long, hard look. 'But don't push it. There might – there just might – be a mustard seed of truth somewhere in that bramble of dementia, but what's the specific connection with the Library?'

'The worm in my dreams has the same greenish tinge and fanged mouth as the Omnilibrarium bookworms described by Osbert in his chronicles. Furthermore, the Library stores a complete report of every incident in the universe. A full account of ontological vanishing – and a possible remedy – must therefore lie somewhere on its shelves.'

Sister Lim raised her hand. 'That's enough. Give me a while to think.'

He moved away from the Information Dump and resumed his post at the helm. As he stared ahead at the nuclear brouhaha at the centre of the nebula, he thought of time and books and worms.

Sister Lim's sharp exclamation gave him a bit of a jolt.

'Buddha's Tooth! It could be true! I can sort of remember you not being there in our earlier cases. Yes, I recall foiling sinister foreign types at the side of someone who . . . wasn't there.'

'I was that man who wasn't there,' he said sombrely, 'like that fella-me-lad on the stair, in that poem.'

'What poem?'

Before he could answer, the flight deck became absurdist. A pink bear appeared beside Forthman, juggling planets. The brass cherubs around the external screen turned blue and rhapsodic. One of the walls questioned him in Hindi.

'A maelstrom of verisimilitude!' he cried out. 'We're closer to the inchoate core than I thought. The Portal must be near. Time for the one-hop-to-the-left-of-reality manoeuvre. Quick, grab the Chinese books.'

She darted to the brass coffee table and seized two books written in Classical Chinese, keeping a copy for herself and flinging him the other. Ignoring a terrifying manifestation of the Sudden Pig in a far corner, the two began to scan the right-to-left lines of ideograms with furious intensity. According to the best authorities, reading script written from right to left was the most effective means of giving a left-hand spin to the ontological structure of space–time.

Abruptly, the flight deck became indescribably Chinese. Then even more indescribably leftward. The grotesqueries corkscrewed out of sight. Time spun, bounced several times, then slowed to a gentle roll.

Through the observation window, there loomed a vasty Gothic arch. 'Success!' announced Forthman. 'We've reached the Portal.'

'Right,' she said. 'I'll pilot us in.'

'No need, old girl. You just pick a spot and I'll land us right on it, safe and sound.'

They staggered away from the blazing wreck of the *Inquisitive*, its nose squashed into the Portal's colossal step, its tail in the air.

Forthman glanced at Sister Lim's sooty figure as she adjusted her magnificent breasts. 'Hmm . . .' she fumed.

'What was that you said?' He fingered his scorched tie awkwardly.

'Didn't say a word.'

'Well, there's bound to be other spacecraft around here – somewhere.'

She rubbed grime from her face with a lace handkerchief. 'Yeah – right.'

Forthman peered into the dark inside the Portal's immense arch. Couldn't see a blasted thing. He looked over his shoulder, and wished he hadn't. The universe had taken on a thoroughly negative aspect: space was white and the stars were black.

Oh well, he had more serious matters on his mind than a rum-looking universe. He faced front and marched purposefully into the murk of the Portal.

'Going without me?' Sister Lim's tone was downright lethal.

Better watch his step. Understandably, she was none too pleased about his crashing the ship. Not that it was his fault the bally steering wheel had come off in his hands. 'Sorry, old girl. Ladies first. I mean . . .'

'Oh, let's get on with it.' She headed into the dark, leaving him to follow in her tracks.

The farther they advanced, the denser the darkness became. At length, all that was visible was the gaslight of his wrist chronometer, an ominous reminder of the countdown to ontological oblivion.

Oblivion.

Doughty though he was, the prospect of turning into an actuality hole teased perspiration from his brow.

Their footsteps echoed cavernously as the chronometer registered the passing of an hour. Another hour. More hours.

He cleared his throat. 'Er, Sister Lim . . .'

'Shut up, Mr Forthman. I'm still pissed off.'

'Right.'

He checked his chronometer again. They had been walking for over five hours. Just how big was this Portal, or antechamber, or whatever it was? The Osbert Chronicles were unclear on the subject. For all he knew, his twenty hours would be up before he caught a glimpse of the Library.

Increasingly glum, he trudged on, counting off each precious minute.

He was still counting when, suddenly, he was in the Library.

It waited.

Wallowing in the slippery stew of its oleaginous excretions, it put down its book and waited.

Someone had trespassed on its vast realm. Afar, it heard the intruders' steps in the Portal, echoing down all the vast avenues of books.

Squishing as it stirred, it sent out its psychic tendrils towards the intruders, seeking an identity, a name.

It vibrated with horrible glee as it sniffed out two names: Mr Forthman, Sister Lim.

'Ah, welcome,' it gurgled. 'Come into my parlour . . .'

Anon, it reached out a monstrous arm and resumed reading its book. It read voraciously, devouring each chapter.

'I know you inside out,' it bubbled.

Blinking in the unaccustomed light, Forthman gazed around the Library of Everything.

Under a series of barrel-vaulted ceilings, dusty bookshelves ranged in every direction, crammed with musty volumes. Each stack of shelves was a hundred metres tall, easily. Here and there, receding into the distance, reared metal towers on wheels, encasing spiral stairs, the topmost steps on a level with the topmost shelves. The air was thick with the smell of old wood and old leather.

Turning round, he saw a miniaturized version of the Gothic arch they had entered hours and hours ago. The archway was clogged with impenetrable darkness.

Sister Lim, incredibly, had somehow managed to clean herself to a pristine state during the dark trek, all muck and grime from the crash expunged from her saffron minirobe and black thigh boots, her skin spotless, her blonde hair immaculate. She had even applied a fresh dab of crimson lipstick.

Probably something she'd picked up in her Buddhist training.

He looked down at the burnt tatters of his grey flannels, the flesh of both knees exposed. He felt an absolute charlie.

'OK,' she said, brisk and businesslike. 'Let's get started.' She approached a desk near the Portal. The far end of the desk vanished into infinity. 'This looks like Reception. And these –' she lifted up a couple of what appeared to be tiny seeds from a scatter of such on the desk's surface '– could be Library guides.'

She stuck the seed thing in her ear. 'Yes – it's a guide.'

'What language?'

'It's talking Cantonese to me. I suppose it translates itself to the wearer's first language. Here, stick this other one in your lughole.'

He popped the proffered seed in his ear, and it started chatting to him:

'Welcome to the Library of Everything, which is precisely the same size as the Omniverse – that's the totality of the universe extended backward and forward in time, for those of you who are not too bright – and immeasurably larger than the cosmos as perceived by your average sentient. Any reader must take this sobering fact into consideration before embarking on any research in this establishment's multitudinous halls. Simply threading a way through a tiny portion of the Library's colossal labyrinth is a major quest in itself. And, quite frankly, it's bloody murder to track down that particular book you're after. Cross-referencing is, of course, essential.

'The Library of Everything is precisely what its name implies. Its books supply a comprehensive account of each and every event in the universe, constantly updated. You want it – we've got it. However, all books conclude with the present moment of the reader. Knowledge of the future is barred to all but that handful of elite races who evolved before the formation of the planets. Sorry about that, but you know how sniffy those non-planetary super-races are about planet-breeds moving in on their territory.

'Note well – all books are reference-only: if any malefactor should attempt to sneak a book out under his coat or

pseudopod, the Library will ensure that the perpetrator is instantly swallowed by a nullity-trap and the book returned forthwith to its place on the shelves. Throughout this Library of Everything, silence is compulsory; any loud noise causes major psychic disruption, often fatal. Mind you, it isn't exactly noisy these days – ever since the mysterious disappearance of Obald of Andromache a million years ago, and the subsequent mysterious disappearances of other visitors, hardly anyone drops in any more. All gone to waste, really. Still, mustn't grumble.

'Most importantly, you should on no account go near the Infinite Regress Department, as any such action could result in the obliteration of the entire universe . . .'

Forthman plucked the guide from his ear. 'I say, old stick,' he addressed Sister Lim. 'I think we should head straight for the Infinite Regress Department. Anything that forbidden must be important.'

'We've got a big problem before we go anywhere, Mr Forthman,' she said, rolling her eyes. 'If the Library is immeasurably larger than the universe as perceived by humans, how the fuck do we get from one end of it to the other? Walk?'

He rubbed his chin. 'You've got a point there. Um . . . Why not ask the guide?'

She hesitated, then looked shifty. 'Yes, I'd already thought of that. Er – guide, advise on travel through Library.' She listened for a moment, then curled her lip. 'What do you mean, "cross-referencing, of course"? Explain!' She listened again, with increasing exasperation. 'I said explain, you little prick!'

Forthman, inspired by an idea, snapped his fingers. 'As an antiquarian and a bibliophile, in addition to my more noteworthy accomplishments, I have considerable knowledge of indexing and cross-referencing. I might just be on to something.'

'Like what?'

'First we find an index, then I'll see if my idea works.'

She glanced around at the apparent infinity of bookshelves. 'Uh, you'd expect the index to be near the entrance, wouldn't you? So . . .' She waved a vague hand. 'Perhaps all this is the Index Area.'

He gave her a wink. 'Good thinking, old girl.' He whirled round, confronted the plethora of stacked shelves, and his face fell. 'Where do we start?'

She stepped up to the nearest bookshelf, and broke into a grin. '"*Galaxies*" it says here. The most consulted index placed closest to the entrance. Makes sense. Mind you, I'll bet there's miles and miles of galactic indexes.' She tilted her head. 'Look at the size of these books. Not one of them less than three feet tall.'

'If I'm right,' he said, 'any one of these books will do.' Grunting, he hefted a weighty volume and dropped it on the floor with an almighty crash. Dust rose like a thundercloud.

'*SHHH* . . .' echoed a husky, warning whisper, deep as a well, wide as a church door.

Forthman tried to charge in several directions simultaneously. Sister Lim put a restraining hand on his arm, her free hand performing Mahayana finger-talk:

'*It's a Guardian,*' her fingers spelt out. '*A sort of sound-activated librarianesque Presence. Keep quiet or we'll be dropped into a nullity-trap.*'

Forthman opened his mouth, then closed it again. He tapped the side of his nose and gave her a wink. After a few moments, he peered around but couldn't catch a glimpse of any Guardian. Must be invisible, like the entity in the Case of the Missing Absence.

'It's gone now,' Sister Lim said.

He scratched his head. 'How do you know?'

'I can sense these things – Buddhist training.' Faint, troubled lines appeared in her otherwise perfect brow. 'There's something here . . .' Her tone was oracular.

He tapped the pipe stem against his teeth. 'What's that, old girl?'

'There's something here, deep in the Library, entangled with its labyrinthine history – something ancient and evil. It knows we're coming. It's waiting . . .'

'That sounds a bit queer,' he remarked. 'The old psychic senses at full steam again, eh? Better watch our step. We'll check the guide later for rum goings-on in the Library's history. As for now –' he opened the book he'd dislodged '– cross-referencing.'

He flipped through the pages. 'Best start on spiral galaxies,' he muttered. 'Must be a reference here somewhere ... Ah! Here we are!' His finger jabbed a page. 'Look at that – there's a whacking great arrow beside this "Aaaabaaia" entry, with "See Spiral Galaxies" written over it. That's the cross-reference we want.' He sucked at his unlighted pipe. 'Now – this arrow – it's a long shot, but it might just work.'

He placed a fingertip on one end of the two-inch arrow. 'Put your finger on the sign beside mine. That's the way. Now –'

'I've got the idea,' she said. 'We're going to cross-reference ourselves.'

'That's the ticket, old thing. Ready?' He enunciated in clear, rounded vowels: '*See Spiral Galaxies!*'

At first nothing happened. Then the arrow expanded, or the two of them contracted, or whatever. In brief moments they were standing on a giant, spectral arrow sign with an impression of existence whizzing by on all sides.

The sudden cessation of motion came as quite a jolt. He was rocked back on his heels, wits spinning as the world revolved around him on a not-so-merry-go-round.

He was ejected from an open book and landed on his rear. Sister Lim thumped alongside. He leapt back on to his feet.

'I say,' he gasped, unwinding the tie that had wrapped twice around his neck. 'That nearly blew my socks off.'

Sister Lim adjusted a small strand of her hair that had gone awry and studied their surroundings. 'Apart from the reception desk and the archway, it all looks much the same, Mr Forthman.'

He glanced around, taking note of the titles on the book spines. 'Yes, except we're in the Spiral Galaxy section.'

She checked the tachometer display on her wrist chronometer. 'Uh-huh – we've just cross-referenced ourselves three hundred and forty-seven light years across the Library.'

'Crikey! This means of travel is bloody quick.'

An ominous '*SHHH . . .*' greeted his loud exclamation. His hand shot to his mouth. He waited in dead silence until Sister Lim's nod told him the Guardian had departed.

'So, where to now?' she asked.

He rubbed his chin. 'Well, I thought maybe the Milky Way

Bibliophage

next, then Earth, then Earth philosophy, then on to ontology and ontological vanishing.'

She gave an uncertain shrug. 'If you say so. But stay alert for trouble.'

'Reginald Forthman is always on the alert,' he said stoutly, pulling a massive book from a lower shelf. He opened the weighty tome near the back cover. Blank pages.

Puzzled, he riffled towards the front, then came across a page that was furiously writing itself, scribbling away with an incessant scratching.

'Continuous updating,' he heard Sister Lim remark. 'The Library has to keep up with every new incident in the universe.'

Forthman experienced profound sentiments on viewing the self-writing page, recording happenings in the farthest regions of space and the deepest gulfs of time. What was it that the poet Omar had penned in his *Rubáiyát*? Ah yes. Forthman recited quietly:

'The Moving Finger, having once writ,
'Moves on – and – and writes another bit.'

Sister Lim gave a low groan.

Forthman, resolute, squared his shoulders. 'Now, on to the Milky Way . . .'

It waited.
And as it waited, it moved and squelched.
Its loathsome bulk oozed and rippled with anticipation.
Reginald Forthman was coming. It could scent his presence far off, in a distant part of the Library of Everything. Moment by moment, the Earthling male came nearer, accompanied by his Earthling floozie.
Of what lay in wait for them, they knew not.
It chuckled obscenely, rubbing its distended belly.
'Twas said that every sentient had one novel in it.
'But I,' it slavered, 'have two billion.' And room for plenty more. *'You're an open book to me, Mr Forthman.'*

'Well, here we are then,' he declared, waving a hand at the 'Ontological Anomalies (Vanishings: Earth: Victims:

Biographies of)' section. 'Didn't take long, did it, hip-hopping through cross-refs.'

'We covered about three hundred billion light years in ten minutes,' Sister Lim responded absently. 'It's driving my tachometer bananas.'

She stared at the ranked regiments of books. There were a lot of gaps in the ranks, she noticed. An inner faculty told her that boded ill for Mr Forthman. Grudgingly, she had come to accept the truth of ontological vanishing. Well, it was undeniable, now that she was standing in a small section of the Library – a mere half a light year square – devoted to the topic.

They had reached the shelves covering all the individual biographies of those actuality-hole victims whose surnames began with Forth, and Mr Forthman, standing beside her on the crown of a hundred-metre wheeled tower, was expectantly scanning the book spines. She glanced down the column of spiral stairs. Quite a drop.

But the drop wasn't what made her heart sink. A sensation of doom had arisen as far back as the long dark walk through the Portal, even as the nanotechnological machines situated in her knickers sallied forth to autoclean her body and clothes. A primal horror, origin and character unknown, had emptied the Library of visitors before the evolution of *Homo sapiens*. And with each step through the deserted halls, she sensed that they drew closer to that primordial abomination.

'I must be here somewhere,' Mr Forthman was muttering. 'Tower – move left two metres.' The voice-activated tower duly obliged. 'Now, let's see – Forthlzn, Forthmabut, Forthmai, Forthmal, Forthmal (no relation), Forthmalt, Forthmark, Forthmast ... Hey! I should come between Forthmalt and Forthmark. Where's my biography?' He scanned farther along. 'No. No sign of it.'

'There are other biographies missing too,' she said. 'Look at all those empty spaces.'

He relit his pipe and puffed pensively. 'You think that's significant?'

'I'd guess they've been . . . taken. Why not take a peek at a few of these biographies?'

She moved well back as he followed her suggestion. There probably wasn't anything noxious in the books, but if there was she wanted it to hit him first.

He opened Forthmark's biography. 'Blank pages,' he said. He flipped back and forth. 'Nothing but blank pages.' He tried Forthmast's biography. Same result.

Reaching out, he grabbed the book with Forthlzn on its spine. A miasma emanated from its covers, along with a nasty smell. An intuition of danger almost made her cry out in warning, but she was still a bit pissed off about Mr Forthman crashing the ship, so she kept quiet.

He opened the covers, peered inside.

'There's something under the page – moving,' he said, leaning his face closer to the open book.

'Yes, it's definitely moving. It's –'

A greyish-greenish streak of rubberiness shot out of the book and battened on his face. He seized the foot-long thingamajig in both hands and, muscles bulging through his sports jacket, succeeded in plucking the creature free of his flesh. He threw it to the floor and jumped up and down on it for the best part of a minute. Sister Lim watched with interest.

'I think it's well and truly dead,' she said at length. 'You've squidged it to buggery.'

He knelt down and studied the green, stinking mess. Sucking at his pipe, which had retained its classic angle at the corner of his mouth throughout the entire episode, he pointed a finger at the noisome gunk on the floor. 'That . . . thing,' he said, 'is the image of the memory worm that has troubled the corridor of my dreams this past month.'

She shrugged. 'It's only a giant, carnivorous bookworm. Well – omnivorous, I suppose.'

Surveying the shelves, Forthman adopted one of his speculative looks. 'Consider life as a story written in the pages of a book,' he said. 'What if a bookworm starts to eat that story, commencing at page one, and ultimately reaches the page on which the pen is writing the latest sentence. The story is consigned to oblivion, and perhaps the writing instrument too. Have you noticed how so many pens go missing?'

'Not that old chestnut . . .'

'Never mind about the pens. But don't you see, Sister Lim?' He pulled out his pipe and prodded her in the shoulder with it, each prod stressing a point.

God – she really hated that . . .

'Osbert was correct in his description of the Library's bookworms,' he said, prodding away. 'The coincidence of the worm in my dream bearing an exact resemblance to this bookworm points to one inescapable fact . . .'

'Don't prod me with that bloody pipe.'

'. . . there is an intimate connection between my advancing state of ontological nullification and something in this Library . . .'

'I said, Don't Prod Me.'

'. . . and somewhere, in the nethermost bowels of this forsaken place, lies the secret behind all –'

She kneed him in the balls. He doubled up and lay on the floor.

At that moment the bookshelves came alive.

Bookworms. Dozens and dozens of fat bookworms, none shorter than a hand, all plunged in her direction.

'Get us out of here!' she shrieked at the spiral-stair tower. It stayed put.

'Oh, bugger – er, take me to the nearest complete and worm-free biography, and make it fast!'

She had to punch a few of the worms away before the tower's wheels spun into action and whisked her free. Within moments, the tall staircase was hurtling along at a fair pace, and still picking up speed. She held on to the railings and glanced at Mr Forthman, sprawled at her feet. He was taking a furtive peek up at her knickers. Good – so he was back to normal then.

The sudden halt of the tower damn near catapulted her over the railings, but her grip held.

'You can take your hands off my upper thigh now, Mr Forthman.'

'Just holding you steady, old thing. You all right now? Jolly good.' He rose to his feet. 'Now let me see . . .' He carefully replaced the pipe in his mouth. 'Ah yes, there's something beastly in the Library's history. How about I check with the guide while you start cross-referencing us to the Infinite Regress department?'

'Could be tricky, starting from biographies,' she said, eyeing the nearby books. 'It could take hours and hours before we get there.'

He gulped. 'Hours and hours . . .'

It waited . . .

Forthman glanced at his wrist chronometer. Sister Lim had hit it right on the button. Hours and hours. Ten hours had already elapsed while they sped along numerous cross-referencing arrows, periodically forced to backtrack. There were plenty of cross-references to the Infinite Regress department, but each led to another book that mentioned the Infinite Regress department. Evidently the system was so arranged that access to Infinite Regress itself was severely restricted.

'Bollocks,' she snapped. 'We're going the wrong way again. Have to start all over back in Unread Fiction. Sod it, I can't find Infinite Regress fiction or non-fiction anywhere.'

'Hard cheese,' he said sympathetically, masking his state of barking panic.

According to his reckoning, he had less than four hours remaining before ontological nullification. In between spells of listening to the guide, he rehearsed his memories with feverish concentration. Later memories were all he had to rely on for his recollections of the *Inquisitive*'s launch from Earth. The memory worm was closing in on him.

He switched the guide back on, and resumed listening to the Library's history. It was an interminable drone, but mercifully nearing the end of its resumé of eighteen billion years. Just thirty million years to go. No clues so far. Infinite Regress was mentioned, but without a single detail.

The guide banged on and on about the Millennium of the Stolen Book, some obscure SF anthology called *Dogleg 5*, nicked by some bloody foreigner from Andromeda. Then the account jumped twenty million years and went into ecstasies over modifications in cookery-book indexing by Master Timpabulum Bulwerk of the Upper Gidding star system.

'After that,' said the guide, *'nothing of note occurred until*

the Great Desolation. It began with Obald of Andromache, a scholar who took up permanent residence in the Library. Obald's scholarship was little respected, but he was renowned for his encyclopedic accumulation of facts. Obald would read anything and everything that came his way, regardless of merit. His voracious appetite for books of any kind earnt him the nickname of Obald the Omnivorous.

'Obald vanished overnight, and was never seen again. Within a year, five other scholars disappeared without trace. The toll of missing persons in the following year was over a hundred. By the time a century had gone by, tens of thousands had vanished inexplicably. This was the beginning of the end of the Library as a functioning institution. It was at this time that oversized bookworms were first observed, causing dismay and frequent fatalities amongst Library staff. It has been assumed in many quarters that these bookworms were active centuries before being identified, and may well have been responsible for the dark fate that overtook Obald and all those that followed. Whatever the truth of the matter, the Library was abandoned five millennia after Obald's disappearance. Few now venture into its silent aisles, and of those few, fewer return –'

He pulled the guide-seed out of his ear and stroked his chin. 'Sister Lim,' he said reflectively. 'I think Obald of Andromache might be at the back of all this, or at least a part of the puzzle.'

She nodded. 'I figured that out hours ago.'

'Did you indeed?'

'Indeed I did. The first to disappear may be the cause of the ensuing disappearances. I'll bet he wasn't the first in a long line of victims – he was the culprit responsible for all those victims.'

Forthman frowned in thought. 'Hmm ... The guide thought it might be the bookworms, but it does mention that Obald was nicknamed the Omnivorous.'

She rolled her ravishing eyes. 'Well, that puts the lid on it. Omnivorous – like the bookworms. He probably devoured every one of his prey.'

'Bones and all?'

'Hang on,' she said. 'Unread Fiction coming up.'

Bibliophage

They fell out of a book, hang-dropped down a series of shelves, and alighted on the floor. While Sister Lim was scouring the shelves for a suitable exit-book, he idly picked out a tome entitled *The Dashwood Chronicles*: volume 96. Opening the volume, he discovered that only the first page bore any writing:

Well, a while ago I was walking through a maze of a monastery library in north Italy and this old cove of a monk came up and asked me, 'What is the name of the rose?' Well, I thought about it, and said, 'It's a simple anagram. Rose – Eros. Dashed obvious, really.' So he went away. Er – end of story.

He closed the book and shoved it back on the shelf. 'So much for unread fiction.'

The book flew from the shelf, whizzed past Sister Lim's head and disappeared into a neither-here-nor-there hole.

Sister Lim scratched the back of her ear. 'Bloody odd. Did you press a button or pull a lever or something?'

He fingered his tie. 'Just – just read a book, that's all. It was only a few lines.'

'So, you read a whole book. And that means it's no longer unread fiction. It had to flit off to a new section. You changed the category of the book. It's the only category you *can* change just by reading it. That could be the key to the Infinite Regress Department . . .'

'Could it? Can't see how.'

'Well, if we can locate a short piece of unread fiction about Infinite Regress, read it, then keep hold of it when it's placed back on the shelf, it should whisk us off to Infinite Regress Fiction. And I'll take any bet it's an easy hop from fiction to non-fiction.'

He ran that one past his brain a couple of times. 'Sounds a bit rum to me. Anyway, how do we track down such a book in the time we've got left?'

'Oh, there's bound to be a huge stack of unread science fiction around here. We're sure to find a cross-reference to a suitable book from one of those. Whistle up a spiral tower, and let's get searching!'

* * *

They crashed out of a book and landed in what, on brief examination, proved to be the Infinite Regress Fiction section.

Sister Lim experienced a profound relief. Her scheme, she silently admitted, had a touch of the crackpot, but it had worked.

Trouble was, it had taken almost four hours to locate the right book.

Mr Forthman was looking thoroughly flummoxed.

'What colour was that bear that juggled planets when things went all peculiar back on the ship?' he asked. 'I keep rehearsing that memory, but it's getting a bit shaky. Was the bear blue?'

'Pink. But you weren't there, were you? Oh, but you must have been – I suppose. Oh hell, this ontological vanishing is doing my head in.'

And it was. She had done her best to rehearse her memories of Mr Forthman, but the past she'd shared with him, before entering the Library, was pretty much a bloody great blank where he was concerned. Simple memory told her that she'd flown from Earth alone, talking to herself all the way, then stood calmly on the flight deck as the *Inquisitive* crashed itself. Then up popped Mr Forthman as she was walking through the Portal.

Less than ten minutes left before Mr Forthman became an actuality hole.

She yanked out a likely book, flicked through its pages. 'Yes! Got it, a cross-reference to Non-Fiction. Quick, stick your finger on the arrow, Mr Forthman! That's it!' She drew a deep breath. 'See Infinite Regress Non-Fiction!'

The arrow swept them away. The journey was short, and she barely had time to blink before tumbling into a wide aisle. She sprang up and glanced around. Walls of books, each book identical, reared on all sides. And, evenly spaced, a line of signs proclaiming the same message:

> BEWARE! STAFF ARE TO ENTER THIS DEPARTMENT ONLY IN THE EVENTUALITY OF A MAJOR ONTOQUAKE. EACH BOOK IN THE OMNILIBRARIUM MAINTAINS THE REALITY OF A SMALL PORTION OF THE UNIVERSE. EACH BOOK IN INFINITE REGRESS MAINTAINS

THE ENTIRE UNIVERSE. ANY DAMAGE TO ONE OF THESE BOOKS WILL WREAK HAVOC IN THE UNIVERSE. DESTRUCTION OF SUCH A BOOK COULD RESULT IN THE ANNIHILATION OF BOTH UNIVERSE AND LIBRARY. SO WATCH IT!

Mr Forthman was wobbling on his feet. 'What's all this then?'

She thumped her forehead. 'I've got it. The Library doesn't just record every event in the cosmos – it sustains its reality. Wipe out the record and you wipe out the reality.' She scanned the ranks of identical books. 'And in here, the whole universe is maintained.'

'Not quite with you, old girl.' He appeared thoroughly bewildered.

'OK,' she said, glancing at her wrist chronometer. She spoke on turbo-boost: 'Imagine an artist who paints a landscape. When he finishes, he realizes that he's missed something from the picture: himself, painting the landscape. After all, he's part of the landscape, right? So he paints another picture, this time including himself. But it still isn't right, because the man who painted an artist painting a landscape is still missing from the picture. Each time he paints, he takes one step back, always out of the picture. That's an infinite regress. Got it?'

'Er . . .'

'The same goes for the Library of Everything. There must be a book that mentions the Library itself, because the Library is part of everything. But then there has to be another book that mentions that first book, and another to mention the second book, and so on, ad infinitum. That's what the Infinite Regress department is – a repository containing a Library book about a Library book about a Library book, on into infinity. But it's always one step away from being complete. And – oh bugger –' Her hand flew to her mouth. 'If the first book in the infinite series is destroyed the act will cancel out all succeeding books, because they'll be mentioning something that doesn't exist. That'll mean the end of the Library, the universe, the whole damn show. Everything finished, even the word "finished".'

'Er . . .'

'Look, never mind – it's got my synapses in a twist, too. Let's just grab that first infinite-regress book and track down Obald the Omnivorous before you become a hole in reality.'

'Righto. I'm not quite sure where I am or who you are or what the dickens is going on, but I'm game for whatever's afoot.'

Ferreting out the first book in the series proved a doddle. The cross-references were by numbers, and all she had to do was look up the number one.

She stood, surrounded by limitless dusty aisles, and held it in her hand. The subsistence and doom of all existence. The fate of the cosmos. It was a small, slim pamphlet. She sneaked a look inside. It contained a single line: 'There is a Library that records and sustains everything in the universe.'

Beside the line was an arrow, and an instruction: 'See Library of Everything.'

They cross-referenced themselves back into Infinite Regress Fiction. She hovered beneath the shelves and slipped the pamphlet into her bra, uncertain which way to go.

She was mildly surprised when a voice came from her left tit. 'Where to, Miss?'

Mr Forthman's eyebrows shot up. 'I say . . .'

'Oh,' she said. 'It's the book. For a moment there . . . Never mind, er – book, can you transfer us anywhere in the Library?'

'I am the Library.'

'Uh – right. Then take us to Obald the Omnivorous, and make it snappy.'

'Ah yes – the Bibliophage,' said the book, a little nervously.

She sucked in a deep breath, preparing for big trouble.

When she breathed out, she was somewhere else. 'Blow me, that was quick.'

Around her, dimly lit by candelabra, ascended walls of rotting books, shelf on shelf, height on height, to some remote, invisible ceiling. In contrast to all she'd seen since entering the Portal, her surrounds bore some resemblance to a private library. Four walls, steeped in shadow, and not

Bibliophage

an aisle to be seen. The floor was littered with heaps of decomposing volumes.

And on one of those heaps there rested a lump some three metres high and a good two metres wide. It looked like a cross between a gargantuan bookworm and a Sumo wrestler, spliced with octopus and a suggestion of crab. It squished as it heaved about in its restless slime, a protrusion in its side giving birth to a batch of bookworms that wriggled into the shadows. A prehensile tongue flicked out of one of the creature's several mouths and turned the page of a book held between a claw and a tentacle. The name FORTHMAN, REGINALD was emblazoned on the book's spine.

'Bloody foreigner,' hissed Mr Forthman.

Sister Lim stared the pulsating lump in one of its five green eyes. 'Obald the Omnivorous, be warned – we Earthers make short shrift of hostile foreign types.'

'I have waited for you,' said the sloshy voice of the creature. 'You Earthers are no match for my peerless powers and fathomless cunning. But you address me amiss, Earth female. I have long since transcended my earlier self as Obald of Andromache. I am the Bibliophage. I live in books and feast on them, grown fat on stories. As I read, the words disappear, leaving the blank pages of lost lives and vanished civilizations. I am the devourer of worlds. Although, generally, I have a particular taste for biographies . . .'

Forthman bunched his fists. 'You're asking for a darn good biffing, you flipping alien scum!'

'And those words,' said the Bibliophage, indicating a single remaining line in the biography, 'were the last Reginald Forthman spoke.' With a lick of his tongue, he wiped the page clean.

And Forthman vanished.

Sister Lim thrust a hand into her bra and pulled out the pamphlet. 'Get your teeth into this book, Bibliophage,' she snarled, tossing the pamphlet into a slavering maw.

'No!' the book shrieked, realizing her reckless gamble. 'You risk the extinction of the whole universe!'

'Well – hard cheese.'

The creature downed the pamphlet in a single gulp. Then its eyes bulged. Its mouths moved in a multiple croak: 'I –

I've swallowed the Library. I can taste it . . . the Library – the universe – everything . . .'

'Including yourself,' she said with a curl of the lip. 'You're about to disappear up your own actuality hole.'

The Bibliophage stuck a tentacle down its throat and retched mightily. The pamphlet shot out into the deft catch of Sister Lim. A mass of words followed in its wake, most pouring into the pages of Mr Forthman's biography, the rest into some unknown book called *The Bible*.

She jumped forward to grab the biography. And leapt back as the Bibliophage lurched its blubbery bulk at her with alarming speed. A tentacle plucked Mr Forthman's biography from the floor.

'I'll swallow Forthman's life story whole, then I'll swallow *you* whole, Earth scum!' its mouths bellowed in unison.

As the monster jellied forward, she glimpsed a small door hitherto hidden behind its back. But there was no way round the advancing abomination.

She made a dash for a far corner where a little hill of books was shored up against the wall. Adrenaline on turbo-boost, she scrambled up the treacherous slope and balanced precariously on the summit, a couple of metres above the Bibliophage.

'Ha!' it jeered, reaching out an elongating tentacle. 'You cannot escape the long arm of my wrath, Earth swine.'

'Oh, bugger.' She was done for. No way out. Certain, horrible death.

'I shall savour every morsel of your body,' it gloated, 'relish every aspect of your soul.'

A figure popped into existence behind the creature. The figure of Mr Forthman, his stance steadfast, the angle of his pipe stalwart, his voice refined. 'Not so fast, Bibliophage . . .'

He pushed the pipe stem into the monster's back. 'Raise those tentacles and pseudopods where I can see them, or I pull the trigger.'

The Bibliophage hesitated, quivering in frustration. Then, slowly, it lifted its limbs up high in surrender.

'Now drop the book.'

It let fall the biography.

But as it did so one of its eyes protruded on an extendable

Bibliophage

stalk at prodigious speed. In a moment, the eye-stalk had looped round and inspected Mr Forthman.

'So!' it burbled exultantly. 'You thought to fool me with the stem of your ridiculous Earth pipe. You think I'd fall for an old trick like that? You shall see the Earther female devoured before your very eyes!'

A swarm of tentacles lunged at Sister Lim.

She flinched at the sight of those threshing limbs even as she heard the distinctive click-clack of the pipe bowl as Mr Forthman adjusted it to blowpipe function and the *phut* as a paralysis dart was discharged from the stem into the Bibliophage's wobbly mass.

The tentacles wavered, stiffened into immobility. The monster turned into a frozen jelly.

Mr Forthman picked up his biography as Sister Lim descended to meet him. 'Welcome back, Mr Forthman. I hope you're fully restored.'

He gave her a merry chuck under the chin. 'Top-hole, old girl. I remember everything. It's all come back. Plus a nifty piece of *insider* knowledge.' He tapped the side of his nose.

The gelatinous flesh of the Bibliophage began to tremble.

'The paralysis dart has worn off ruddy fast,' he observed. 'And that dart was my last.'

'Let's run,' she suggested as the Bibliophage rumbled into activity.

'In great haste,' he concurred, dashing to the door.

The cross-reference arrow sped them along as Forthman explained his impromptu plan.

'I've chosen a specific book among the Andromachian biographies as our destination because of something I learnt in my near-absorption in the Bibliophage's psychic digestive system,' he said, adjusting his tie.

She glanced over her shoulder at an existential blur in the distance. 'The creature's still hunting us.'

'Jolly good. It's in for a heck of a surprise. I learnt that there's one region the Bibliophage steers well clear of, for fear of giving in to temptation.'

'That region being Andromachian biographies. The biography of Obald the Omnivorous in particular.'

'Smart girl. Ah – here we are . . .'

They toppled from a book situated, fortunately, at ground level. Rising quickly to their feet, they each gripped a cover of the biography entitled *Obald the Omnivorous: Scholar and Bibliophage*, holding the volume wide open.

The book started to tremble at the approach of the enraged being.

'Any second now . . .' she whispered.

A squamous head bulged from the pages. And the two Earthers slammed the heavy covers shut on the head.

'He has a particular taste for biographies,' Sister Lim said with a macabre smile.

'And how could a creature like the Bibliophage resist his own, definitive biography?' grinned Forthman.

The book jumped about for a while, then settled.

Forthman stepped back. 'He's got his teeth into it.'

'And it's got its teeth into him,' she said with grim satisfaction.

Forthman buttoned up his jacket. 'Right, we'll just return the first Infinite Regress book, pop my biography back in its proper place, and then we'll be off back to Earth, shall we?'

'What in, a brandy bottle?'

The Bibliophage squished and squelched as it moved about, absorbed in its own story.

Its whole life was an open book, irresistible. The Bibliophage read it voraciously. It tasted each word on one of its tongues. Gulped each word down.

Entranced by its life story, it feasted on the book. And as it feasted, line by line, page by page, it became thinner and thinner.

In the end, the book would be blank from cover to cover.

And the Bibliophage would be no more.

A message had been sent off in a tachyon bottle rescued from the wreckage of the *Inquisitive*.

It had been speeding on a programmed course for a week now, emitting a signal calculated to deafen half the nebula. Some nosey space mariner was bound to have picked it up, and be on his way.

Whether he picked the two of them up was another question, and it was largely down to Sister Lim. Standing on the rim of the Portal's step, she held out her arm, thumb stuck upward in the traditional hitcher's gesture, and yanked up the hem of her robe even farther, flaunting a full length of thigh, provocatively posed.

'Any sign of a lift yet?' asked a voice from inside the wreckage.

'Keep your head down, Mr Forthman, or we'll be here for bloody ever.'

'Oh, chin up, old girl.'

'Piss off, Mr Forthman.'

'Now, now . . .'

'Bollocks.'

That, for the time being, was the last word.

Negative Space

By Jeanne Cavelos

'It's not there,' Major Vera repeated.

Behind Vera, Mozden and the others were crowded around the monitor, intent on the high-resolution image of the planet's surface below them. The final section of the square kilometre they were searching revealed only the strange copper-red contours of the planet's surface, nothing more. They'd searched out to a distance of ten kilometres from the probe's last known location, then returned to the centre of their search and started again. But the probe was gone.

They had known that they wouldn't be able to pinpoint it using its locator beacon. All transmissions had ceased only a week after it had landed, twenty-one years ago, tantalizing them with incomplete data. But they'd never expected that they wouldn't be able to find it at all. It was half the size of a house, and due to a malfunction had become immobile only three days after landing.

Lieutenant Colonel Katrack, floating to Mozden's left in the zero-G environment, clapped Vera on the shoulders. His face had broken into an infectious, dimpled smile. 'It couldn't have just walked away. Something had to move it.' Katrack's body exuded vitality, as his personality engendered trust. Since Mozden had first met him a year pre-launch, her respect and faith in him had grown steadily. Fifty-two years old and bald except for a fringe of blond hair shaved military short, the mission commander still had the energy, curiosity, and wonder of a boy. At thirty-seven, Mozden felt five times his age.

Vera shot a smug smile over his shoulder. He was full of himself, as usual. 'We're going to be the first to find intelligent alien life,' he said.

Garth, to Mozden's right, squeezed her arm. He'd had a grip on it for the last few minutes, and in the close quarters she'd been unable to pull away without making everyone aware. They'd been out of hibersleep for only ten days, the

Negative Space

muscle stiffness still lingering, and she was already well down the road to misanthropy. She didn't mind people, in the theoretical sense. But being confined to a small space with four of them was another issue. Garth's habit of hovering didn't make life any easier.

'The probe is more likely to have fallen victim to some natural process,' Mozden said. 'We know the planet has high winds, as well as underground volcanic activity of an unusual nature. And we know very little about the surface. There might be phenomena similar to quicksand or sinkholes. The topography of this area has changed since the probe landed; whatever process caused that change is likely responsible for the disappearance of the probe.'

Garth's hand fell away. His dream was to discover intelligent extraterrestrial life. He'd talked about it constantly while they had trained together for this mission. That was why he'd become a biologist, and then a microbiologist, why he had gone to work for NASA on the Alpha Centauri A probe and later, after the probe had shown indications of life on this Earth-type planet, transferred to the Astronaut Training Programme to come on this mission.

Mozden had seen his type in her own field of planetary astronomy. Their lives were hollow. They had no spiritual centre. They had no relationships; they had no real lives. They sought instead to fill the empty space inside themselves with other things, to find a meaning for their lives in things outside their lives: money, fame, the religion of science, the belief that their pathetic, stone-age discoveries would somehow impact the cosmos, carry them in memory down through the ages, and most of all, fill that aching space within.

She knew the type so well because she had so much in common with them. Her life was hollow, too, but she liked it that way. The emptiness defined her.

'Always dying to wreck a party, aren't you?' Vera said to her.

'She's right,' Katrack said. 'We can't jump to conclusions. Now, the geography of our primary landing site has changed. We don't yet know why or how. But it's no longer suitable for landing. Let's take a look at our visuals on the secondary landing site.'

Vera called up the image they'd recorded on their previous orbit. 'It rates out ninety-two per cent suitable for a landing site.' His tone was hesitant.

That was a good number, Mozden knew; probably the best they could expect to get. Yet she regretted the change in site, and she sensed the others did as well. They had all been looking forward to investigating the bizarre landscape surrounding the probe. The mammoth formation near the landing site had captured Mozden's interest as it had captured the interest of the world. The probe's transmissions had played constantly in the media, triggering widespread speculation, uninformed theorizing, and finally the first manned interstellar mission. Now it might be months before she'd be able to study it.

Katrack rubbed a hand over his chin. 'Prepare for landing on our next orbit.'

On the far side of Katrack, Nadine, who had remained silent through their search for the probe, now snapped to life. 'We can't land there. It's hundreds of miles away.' In the standard-issue orange jumpsuit, Nadine looked like a scarecrow, all sticks and angles. Her eyes were shadowed in deep sockets.

Katrack shook his head. 'We have no choice, Nadine.'

'But the transmissions. You saw that piece. It was – incredible. We have to study it.' Whenever Nadine spoke, Mozden found herself watching the woman's hands. The pale fingers were long, bony yet muscular. The nails were cut short, the space under the nails and cuticles stained with some dark material. The positions her hands held, and the movements they made, were somehow striking. They seemed imbued with the power of her personality, which, Mozden supposed, made her a good artist, though the pictures of her work in that catalogue Vera had scrounged hadn't impressed her. But then Mozden knew shit about art.

'I understand what you're saying,' Katrack replied patiently, 'but we have to land safely. That's our top priority at this point.'

Vera unstrapped himself from the chair and grabbed a handle to pull himself past Nadine towards the cockpit.

Nadine seized the handle and blocked his way, which

wasn't hard in the tight quarters. 'You've heard my analysis. You know how important that site is. We must see it in person to evaluate it properly, to experience its spatial qualities –'

Vera held up his hands in mock surrender. 'Batten down the hatches, here she goes again. Why they let you on this ship, I'll never know.'

'It's because they're not blind,' Nadine said. 'They know what they've found here, as much as they refuse to admit it, and they know I'm the only one on this ship who has a prayer of understanding it.' She flared her fingers outward. 'Of course you can't get that through your thick skull, can you, air jock? You're so full of yourself you think you can't possibly learn –'

'Let's stop this right now.' Katrack pushed his way between them, and Vera bumped back into Mozden, who clenched her teeth. 'I've warned you both about this before. Team cohesion is critical if this mission is to succeed and we're all going to stay alive. I don't want to hear any more of this out of either of you. The next time I hear an insult, the perpetrator is going to get assigned latrine duty for the rest of this mission. You read me? Vera, keep your personal opinions to yourself. Go forward and start the landing checklist. Nadine, you're a specialist. This is not your area of specialty. So shut up and sit down.'

Vera snorted and started to pull himself past Nadine.

She shoved back. 'You're not listening to me!'

Vera floated back into the monitor, and Nadine, in an equal and opposite reaction, floated back into the cockpit, disappearing through the hatch. Her movement ended with a bang. An alarm blared.

Katrack pushed off towards the cockpit, and Mozden, careful about her manoeuvres, pulled along after him using the handles. Vera bulleted past her through the hatchway. Voices yelled over the alarm, and as Mozden guided herself through the hatch, Nadine was shoved into her. Nadine's elbow rammed into her temple, hard.

'Take her back and strap her in,' Katrack yelled. He and Vera were studying the life-support system, whose monitor was flashing.

'I'm not a child,' Nadine yelled, grabbing for Mozden to steady herself.

Mozden grabbed Nadine's arm and turned to pull them both out of the cockpit. Garth, of course, was right behind her. 'Move, Garth.'

He nodded, his eyes wide as usual, his curly hair floating in a clown-like dome around his head. He pivoted to the side, and Mozden pulled herself and Nadine out, towards the crew seats.

Once Mozden got her to a seat, Nadine strapped herself in, glancing up at Mozden with those deep, shadowed eyes. 'None of you realize what you're dealing with here. Your egos can't let you see it.' Her lips had a forceful way of enunciating, as if she were chewing out her words. 'It's what I'd expect from those two jet jocks, but I thought you two, as scientists, would be more open.'

Mozden kept her mind as open as the data allowed, but speculation was pointless until they had more information. 'We have to prep for landing,' she yelled.

The alarm stopped, the air vibrating with its silence.

Garth touched Mozden's forehead, and she flinched away.

'You're bleeding,' he said. He pointed to several small, spherical globes of red that were floating in the air beside her head.

'A touching moment,' Nadine said.

Mozden let out a breath. It had been a long ten days. Never had she wanted so much to be left alone than now, here, four light years from Earth.

The landing was as unpleasant as the takeoff had been, though somehow much more unsettling. On takeoff she had known that she was leaving behind the one tiny environmental bubble that could keep her alive in this galaxy, that she was leaving behind the planet, one of a number that she had studied, but the only one she had ever stood upon, the one she knew most intimately, the one whose movement, breath, circulation she could feel all around her. She had felt bereft, yet she had been glad to leave all the people and politics behind, and her anticipation of the mission ahead had overridden any uneasiness. She'd never doubted they would return. To her, this had been mainly an intellectual exercise, an extension of her research, an extra step necessary if she was to understand this planet the way she understood the others.

Yet as the lander separated from the orbiter and they began to drop down through the atmosphere, she realized with a tightening of her chest that this was not an intellectual exercise. They were leaving the main source of their power, and the means to return home, behind. If anything went wrong, it would be four years before anyone on Earth even heard about it, and sixteen more before help could arrive. As they decelerated, and the gravity fell on to her like a series of heavy coats, she found herself lightheaded and gasping for air, and she realized the incredible faith she'd put in the faulty technology of the US in the first half of the twenty-first century.

While they were in the ship, it was easy to pretend that this was all just another training session on Earth; the simulators were so good it was sometimes hard to tell the difference. But now that they were landing on the planet, there would be no way to deny that they were trillions of miles from home, in an environment completely alien to humans. The study of planets was her passion and her life, so her fear surprised her. On Earth, in the isolation of her office, her work had brought her satisfaction and comfort. But here, studying a planet was not an intellectual pursuit: it was a confrontation. Funny she hadn't thought of it before. She felt like an oncologist who had spent her entire life studying cancer discovering that she now had cancer.

They made a perfect landing, converting to a hover near the end of the glide path and setting down smoothly. They spent the next day and night – almost twelve hours – setting up the systems that would support them for the next three months. Mozden was relieved to find that her fear had subsided after the landing and she could execute her duties normally. They reviewed procedures for planetary activity, transmitted friendship messages, and ran a battery of tests to verify the probe's environmental data.

They had set down near the centre of a depression about two kilometres in diameter. The depression had a vaguely crater-like appearance, but none of the distinctive features of a crater. Other topographical features were at least a kilometre off, near or beyond the rim of the depression.

The lander had only two windows, in the cockpit. They revealed only a fraction of the panorama outside. But by comparison, the probe's striking transmissions, which they'd viewed again and again back on Earth, had been crude, distorted, static-obscured images. The surface itself was an odd colour somewhere between copper and red that seemed almost to vibrate with intensity, and it exhibited a high degree of reflectivity, shining in the sunlight. The cloudless nitrogen/carbon dioxide atmosphere had a peculiar quality to it that made the colours and outlines of objects stand out, sharp, vivid. It was probably from the lack of particulate matter and the very low humidity. But the effect gave the landscape an odd, startling power.

Mozden preferred to study her test results than to look directly at the landscape. Test results, leading to detailed questions about the dynamics and formation of the atmosphere, the geological make-up of the planet, the volcanic processes occurring beneath the surface, were familiar territory. She knew that the average radius of the oblate planet was 1·05 times that of Earth, while the mass was only 0·9 that of Earth. That implied either a liquid rather than a solid core to the planet, or a paucity of heavy elements at its core. The gravity was 0·82 that of Earth. The planet's day was 11.47 hours long, and the temperature averaged a hot thirty-three degrees Celsius during the day, a chilly five degrees at night, the absence of water on the surface leading to wide temperature changes. Intense Coriolis winds, caused by the relatively rapid rotation of the planet, often gusted to eighty kilometres per hour.

The most unusual aspect of the planet was its surface. The entire planet, as far as they could tell, was covered by a single, uniform material, made completely from carbon. The carbon atoms were bonded to each other to form Bucky tubes – literally tubes only one-billionth of a metre in diameter. A variant of these tubes had been created artificially on Earth for various applications, but these tubes had never been found naturally. On the planet, they were partly fused, partly woven together like threads to form a sheet, a strong, hard surface less than one-millionth of a metre thick. These sheets appeared to be piled one on top of another – a bizarre and intriguing formation. It had been theorized some time ago that debris from a comet falling on to a planet could form Bucky balls, spherical molecules of carbon, but that had never been proven. And how the balls might cover the entire planet, then be deformed into tubes, and then woven or fused into sheets was an engrossing mystery.

Even more exciting was the first direct detection of extraterrestrial life, in the form of micro-organisms that lived far below the planet's surface. Their knowledge of what was below the surface remained very limited, but the probe, in the final sample core it had drilled before ceasing transmissions, had detected metal-rich water at the very end of its sample, almost two kilometres underground, near which micro-organisms congregated.

Their immediate goal was to confirm the probe's finding that it would be safe for them to leave the lander and that they could operate for the duration of the mission without the encumbrance of EVA suits. To that end, they ran many of the same tests the probe had, verifying their information. In addition, Katrack and Vera made one trip outside, at night in full EVA suits, to set up the large solar array that would provide power during their stay, to check the lander's condition, bring out the two solar-powered rovers, and to drill a sample core.

Mozden and Garth found that the core barrel was similar to those drilled by the probe, though, disappointingly, not to the one sample that had contained the water and micro-organisms. Either they existed at a depth below two kilometres, or they were limited to certain regions of the planet. Overall, though, their results confirmed the probe's findings: the planet's surface and atmosphere weren't hospitable; neither were they deadly.

About two hours before sunset, Katrack at last gave the all-clear for a short expedition. Mozden rubbed the UV protectant/moisturizer on to her face and neck, replaced her standard-issue booties with boots, and fastened on the wristband that controlled radio communications through her breather. Her hand lens, hanging on a sturdy chain, went around her neck, and for extra protection she tucked the lens into the front pocket of her jumpsuit. She controlled each action carefully She was still getting used to operating in the 0·8 gravity. With the hibersleep, the zero G, and now this, her body felt foreign, out of whack, the way she imagined it might feel if she'd had a stroke and had to relearn how to use her muscles.

Mentally reviewing the procedures for operating the breather, she pulled the oxygen pack on to her back, activated the control on the clear full-faced mask, opened the coupling at its base, and brought the mask down over her face, fitting the earpiece over her left ear.

The oxygen had a familiar stale taste. The voices of the others came through her earpiece. She'd set the communications on unrestricted listen/talk, as they'd been instructed, which meant that anything anyone said was transmitted to the others. They were all talking too quickly and too loudly, excited by the prospect of carrying out the first survey of a planet outside their own solar system. Some of the apprehension she'd felt on landing began to return, and she held it tight inside her. She felt as if she were about to be introduced to a powerful stranger. Mozden slung her bag of equipment over her shoulder and pulled on her gloves.

At the main airlock, Katrack opened the inner hatch. Behind the clear face mask of the breather, he was beaming. 'Nadine and I will go first.' The airlock could fit only two at a time, so they had to split up. 'Then Mozden and Garth. Then you, Vera.' He stepped aside so that Nadine could enter the airlock, then went in after her. His dimpled smile faded into a more serious expression of mixed anticipation and fulfilment. His pale blue eyes met theirs each in turn. 'And so mankind reaches its childhood's end.'

Vera pushed the control on the wall panel to close the inner hatch and begin the cycle. The status light turned from green to red to indicate the cycle was in process. When the status light shone green, Vera pressed the control and opened the inner hatch, revealing the empty airlock. Mozden hesitated, not really sure what she was waiting for.

'Colonel,' Vera said, his voice sounding simultaneously

through the cabin and in her earpiece, 'what's your status?'

'Status A-OK,' Katrack responded, but his tone was distracted.

Vera hesitated, then nodded to Mozden and Garth. They entered the airlock. Vera pressed the control to start the cycle, and the hatch closed them into the confining space. Garth's gangly body hung over Mozden in a slouch. The one harsh light above them glared off his face mask. His curly hair was now squashed down beneath the binders securing the breather, but he looked no less the clown. His hand had again found her forearm.

The wait seemed interminable, the sounds of their breathing magnified. At last the outer hatch slid open. Mozden yanked her arm smartly out of Garth's grasp and marched down the ramp Katrack had erected. The afternoon sun bathed her body in light. A hot wind ruffled her jumpsuit. As she reached the bottom of the ramp, she glanced up at the sky.

It was vast, vaster than anything she had ever seen, stretching from one side of the crater to the other with nothing to obstruct it – no trees, no power lines, no buildings, no clouds – like a giant eye looking down on her, an eye with no pupil. The sky was a pale shade of blue, paler and more delicate than it had ever been on Earth. The sky also seemed more concrete, somehow, more like the celestial dome imagined by the ancient Greeks, as if she could only reach high enough, she could touch it.

Glowing against this backdrop of blue was the planet's vibrant copper-red surface, which continued as far as she could see, the sides of the depression gradually rising to the rim in the far distance. She was caught in the centre of it, in the centre of the depression, as it destroyed all sense of scale, shrinking her to the size of a gnat, to the size of a microbe. She had never felt so exposed.

She moved away from the ramp and stooped to run her gloved hand over the copper-red ground. The colour was so vivid that it seemed unreal. The surface was hard and shiny, almost blinding when the sun caught it at the right angle. Mozden removed her glove and touched her bare hand to the surface. It was warm, from the sun, smooth and dry. It felt almost like metal, though with a subtle coarse texture – a sort of fuzziness – that was surprising with its shiny appearance. The way the sun shone off it reminded her of the winters in New Hampshire, when the snow-covered ground would be coated with a layer of freezing rain, leaving a glazed surface in its wake. She stood. She saw now that the depression was not uniformly concave, as she had thought before. Subtle ridges ran in irregular bands through the depression, creating a sense of flow.

As she turned, following the flow, she saw on the far side of the ship, along perhaps half of the rim, a series of six unevenly spaced monoliths made of the same vibrant material as the planet's surface. Their massive columnar shapes stretched up from the ground, curving and tapering to points over a kilometre high. Their bases were perhaps one-quarter that in diameter, and the spaces between them a little more than that. As Mozden tilted her head to follow their courses, she had a moment of vertigo and stumbled.

'Let's take a look around, people,' Katrack said. Vera had driven one of the rovers to where Katrack and Nadine stood. They climbed into the open vehicle, and Mozden joined them, Garth close behind. They were cramped inside, knee to knee.

Katrack directed Vera to drive up to the monoliths, about a kilometre distant. With the uphill gradient, the immense forms towered above them. The monoliths gave Mozden an odd sensation of flow similar to what she'd experienced in the depression, their curves like pieces of seaweed under water. As they approached one of the monoliths, the smooth reddish-copper shape became more sharply and more vividly defined, standing out from the background of pale-blue sky, a solid, imposing presence.

They fell silent, and Mozden realized that they had said very little since leaving the lander. The sun was behind them, growing lower on the horizon, casting their shadow out ahead of them and shining in a dazzling reflection off the monolith.

Vera stopped the rover near the towering form, and they approached the curve of its base, the monolith stretching above them like a bizarre, serpentine skyscraper. Vera began to take measurements. The monolith exuded a sense of power Mozden could compare only to that she'd experienced from the erosional remnants in Monument Valley. But this was much more intense. It was not a by-product of size. The monolith's curving course somehow embodied energy.

Mozden forced herself to focus. She had considered various theories to explain the surface features revealed by the probe, but she hadn't had enough data to confirm or eliminate any of them. She crouched at the base of the monolith and looked for the place of contact between the monolith and the planet's surface. A contact plane would be a clear indication that the monolith was a remnant of a layer of material that had existed above the layer that now made up the surface, and that this other layer had been almost entirely eroded away, leaving only these formations. But there was no visible differentiation of layers, no visible 'seam' or connection between the monolith and the surface. She pulled out her hand lens for a closer examination.

Vera ran his hand over the surface. 'I thought we would see tool marks of some kind.' Vera's theory, which was also the theory of the media and the populace in general, was that these formations had been artificially created by humanoid aliens of the type made popular in science-fiction films. Vera personally liked to equate the formations to the pyramids. He liked his aliens anthropomorphic, the fool.

Mozden slowly straightened her legs, scanning the smooth surface. It betrayed no streaks, striations or grooves, no slickenside structure that would be evidence of mechanical grinding. If the monolith had been thrust up through the crust by some sort of volcanic process, there was no evidence of it. And the fact that it appeared to be made of the same material as the surface worked against both theories.

'Could these be natural geologic formations?' Katrack stood behind her, his gaze on the monolith.

'I don't know yet.' Mozden returned the hand lens to her pocket. 'It seems unlikely, but there's a lot we don't know yet. Water erosion seems impossible, since there's no evidence that there was ever liquid on the surface. And for wind erosion to work, there needs to be at least two different surface materials, one more easily eroded than the other. For example, on Earth the stone strata surrounding the core of an inactive volcano are sometimes eroded away over time, leaving only the shaft of harder igneous rock. But this all appears to be one material. Another possibility is a dissolution process similar to that which creates Karst topography – limestone caves and sinkholes – on Earth. But again, the uniform composition of the surface argues against this. Some sort of unusual volcanic process is slightly more likely – a violent extrusion of semiplastic magma – but there's no sign of extrusion. There are biological possibilities, such as stromatolites – like coral. Garth would know more about that. But we need more data before we can draw any conclusions.'

'Garth,' Katrack said, 'what's your take on this?' They looked around. Vera was standing nearby, and Nadine, oddly, still sat in the rover. 'Garth!'

'Come out beyond the rim.' Garth's voice, in her ear, was shaking. 'These are no natural phenomena.'

Katrack broke into a run, Mozden and Vera following him around the base of the monolith. Mozden nearly fell as her stride stretched out farther than she anticipated. She stumbled and regained her footing, cautiously continuing in the new rhythm. As she rounded the monolith, its shadow fell over her.

Ahead of her, Katrack suddenly lost his stride and went tumbling to the ground. Then Vera stumbled, caught himself and stopped. Mozden slowed carefully, coming up behind them. Garth stood a few feet away. She bent down over Katrack.

'Are you all right?'

His chest was heaving beneath the orange jumpsuit. It shouldn't have been after the short run in the low gravity. And gasping, in the breathers, could be dangerous. He pushed himself into a sitting position, facing away from her. 'Incredible.'

Vera, beside him, was looking in the same direction.

Mozden straightened. It erupted out of the flat, empty plane, like a mirage. Its size was difficult to judge, since it was still some distance away, but it was at least as tall as the monoliths, and perhaps four times as wide. Its surface was the same smooth, reflective copper-red, its curves, contours and angles glowing in the setting sun, appearing almost molten. But its shape ... Her first impression was of a semi-human figure, limbs curled inward in pain. She glanced at the others. They hadn't moved. Then as her gaze returned to it, she realized that its shape was a series of abstract curves, planes and angles. It wasn't a human figure at all, though to her mind the shape suggested this. Beauty rested in the arch of its 'neck', in that angled plane near its base. Something within it spoke of pain, though, and the small hollow at its centre seemed to define emptiness. She felt the emptiness inside her touched by its kin, and her scalp tingled as some unnamable emotion arose inside her, the tingle rushing through her body in a cataract that made her shudder. As her eyes followed its shadow out over the surface of the planet, she saw another shape, farther in the distance, an arc like an ocean wave frozen in time, and another, an asymmetrical spiral of longing, and another; for as far as the eye could see stretched a series of massive, stunning shapes.

'Oh.' Nadine stood beside her.

Their overhead view from orbit had barely hinted at this possibility, and even the mammoth formation in the probe's transmissions had seemed, like the monoliths, open to several interpretations. But these shapes left no room for doubt: their creation had been no natural, unconscious process. They had been created consciously, deliberately. By some thing, or some one.

It had only been a theory before, one that Mozden had considered wishful thinking on the part of the uneducated, and one that had irritated all of them when Sabriski, the chemist on the crew, had been replaced three months before takeoff with Nadine, an outspoken sculptor and administrator for the National Endowment for the Arts with a mouldering bachelor's degree in chemistry. But now it was a fact. These were not erosional remnants, not volcanic eruptions or transpositions, not stromatolitic deposits made by chance, not the result of some unknown natural phenomenon. There was thought here. And beauty.

She turned to Nadine. 'You were right.'

Nadine remained facing the distant, pained figure. 'I know, damn it.'

Vera turned back towards them with a smug smile. 'I told you we were going to discover intelligent life. It was right there in the transmissions.' Mozden found that if she concentrated on Vera and Nadine, she could avoid seeing the shapes. But in her mind they remained, afterimages imprinted on her brain. The tingling faded but did not vanish.

'Unfortunately for you,' Nadine said to Vera, 'it takes intelligent life to know intelligent life.'

Vera pointed a finger at her. 'You ready for latrine duty? I'd call that an insult, wouldn't you?'

Nadine shrugged. 'I'd call it the truth.'

As much as Mozden enjoyed it when Nadine insulted Vera, since she could never say those things herself, it seemed inappropriate here, in this place meant for wind and silence. 'Shouldn't we be getting back in?' she said. 'It's almost dark.' Time had got away from them somehow, she thought, checking her watch. They'd left the lander almost two hours ago, though it seemed as if a much shorter time had passed. It was getting cold, and the wind had picked up. Vera looked at his watch too, surprised.

He crouched down beside Katrack, who was still sitting. 'Colonel? Shouldn't we be getting back inside?'

'What?' His voice, light and fuzzy, gave Mozden a shiver. Then his normal tone returned. 'Oh, yes. How did it get so late?' He stood, brushing nonexistent dirt off his jumpsuit. 'Let's head back to the rover. Garth?'

Garth still stood a few feet away. In the grey light of dusk his tall, slouched form looked almost like a statue itself. Nadine put herself in his face. 'Garth, you slug! Time to get your lazy butt back to the rover.'

Garth jumped and looked around self-consciously 'Hey, sorry.' His eyes gravitated to Mozden, but thankfully he headed back towards the rover. Katrack went with him.

As Nadine followed, Vera said to her, 'And I suppose you don't call that an insult either.'

Nadine looked back over her shoulder. 'I call it artistic arrest.'

It wasn't until Mozden rounded the base of the monolith and

looked down into the depression in which the lander rested that she realized the six curved monoliths and the depression were all a single unit, a single shape. The monoliths flowed up from the depression, stretching, reaching skyward.

'It looks almost like a hand,' Katrack said.

Nadine got into the rover. 'You people have to degrade art to its most basic representational aspects.'

It did look like a hand, Mozden thought. Or plant stalks growing towards the sun, or simply a questing, a yearning for the ground to reach up and touch the stars. Dwarfed by it, they climbed into the rover and headed back down into the depression.

Katrack had one last duty to perform before they could go inside. He asked Vera to film him while he erected an American flag in front of the lander. Since the surface was relatively hard, they made no attempt to drive the flag into it. They fastened the flagpole to a heavily weighted base, to keep it in place against the wind, then went inside. About an hour later, their gear stowed and their updated report to Earth sent, they ate dinner.

The food was reconstituted, except for the cactus peaches from one of the genetically engineered hybrids that helped provide oxygen. They sat crowded around the small table in the well-padded crew seats. While they should, by all accounts, have been celebrating, they all seemed subdued or preoccupied, except for Vera, who shovelled his food in with gusto. Mozden's tingling had finally faded away, but it had left her feeling unsettled and dissatisfied with her performance. For the amount of time they'd spent outside, she should have come away with much more data. Instead, all she had were the afterimages of the shapes.

Though she had Garth at her left elbow and Vera at her right, the close quarters no longer bothered Mozden. Her focus had changed from what was within the lander to what was without. Instead of feeling the pressure of the others crammed in with her, she felt the pressure of those mammoth shapes outside, of the vast space that surrounded them, and of the wind that caressed those curving surfaces and blew through those empty places. As she pictured the five of them sitting inside the lander in the centre of that great hand, they seemed irrelevant.

'They must be hiding somewhere,' Vera asserted, taking a big bite of his peach. 'Maybe underground. Or else they made all this stuff and then left. Or died out. Probably spent too much time on artsy fartsy stuff –' those words were aimed at Nadine '– and not enough on survival.'

Mozden wasn't sure why she hated him so much. The feeling had been pretty much instantaneous and mutual, and everything he did only reinforced it. At thirty-two, he was second in command and the youngest of the crew. He acted as if he knew it all, and he knew just enough to get away with it, which was irksome. He had little self-control, though he could obviously put on a good show for the powers-that-be. He also seemed to think his hunches more valid than hard evidence. His heavy eyebrows and plump red lips, like a high-gloss fashion model, also irritated her. Vera knew he had looks and charm – he'd been the public's darling pre-launch – and he enjoyed using them to manipulate people.

'We ought to be looking for some sort of underground passageways,' he continued.

'I'm not saying that's not a possibility,' Garth said, ever the clumsy diplomat, 'but so far we've found no indication of any life above the microscopic level or any remains of other life forms. The possibility that a much more advanced life form could have developed and formed a civilization and hidden all traces of it underground is pretty small.' His voice had fallen into its characteristic monotone.

Katrack leant forward, gesturing with his fork. 'Maybe it's not a case of them hiding underground. That may be their natural habitat. We have no idea what kind of creatures these might be. But I think we all agree, don't we, that there's no unconscious process that could have created these sculptures.'

Sculptures. He'd used the word, at last. The word they'd all been avoiding, through the study of the probe's bizarre images, through the appointment of Nadine, a sculptor, to the mission, through the discovery of what lay outside. A sculpture was a work of art, something created consciously by an intelligence, a sensibility. Use of the word implied a judgment about the origins of the formations, a judgment Mozden felt uncomfortable with, but to which she had no alternative. She had come to the same conclusion herself, out beyond the monoliths.

'This is clearly art,' Nadine said, 'and art is a conscious act. Some consciousness is behind it.' For once Nadine's expressive hands remained still. They were clenched into fists on each side of her plate, her body hunched over, as if defending against an attack. Mozden wondered why she wasn't happier at finally being proven right.

Garth looked to Mozden for support. 'It's possible that the micro-organisms, acting in concert, could be responsible. A communal intelligence, like bees building a hive.'

Nadine's voice was low. 'No bees created these pieces.'

Mozden chewed thoroughly, swallowed. 'I think we'd be acting prematurely if we eliminated any theory at this point. We still don't understand some of the basic processes occurring on this planet. We need to take a closer look at the structural geology and possible volcanic forces. We also need to study the surface and its properties. And Garth's micro-organisms.'

Garth nodded enthusiastically. 'She's right.'

Nadine shot a glance heavenward.

'We've made an incredible discovery here,' Katrack said. 'When I was out there today I thought ... something very unscientific. I thought –' as he looked into the middle distance, the hint of a smile flashed across his lips – 'this must be God's art studio.' He glanced down, self-conscious. After a moment, he was all business. 'Our main priority has to be investigating the surface and what lies beneath it. Our recon data has already given us a fairly good sense, though without detail, that the surface of the entire planet is covered with sculptures similar to what we're seeing here. Now we have to find out what, or who, created them. Tomorrow we'll split into two groups. Mozden, Nadine and I will begin tests using the seismic probe and the ground-penetrating radar, and Vera and Garth will begin drilling and chemical analysis. I'd like to get out there at first light, though that's only in –' he checked his watch – 'four and a half hours.'

'I think I've slept enough for a while,' Nadine said.

While they planned their schedule, Vera got up and twisted his way behind Mozden to the microwave for another portion.

'Nadine,' Katrack said, holding up his palm, 'I know you said this shape we're in isn't a hand. But I have to say that to me, an unartistic air jock, it looks a lot like a hand, even if it does have six fingers. Do you think it means that whoever created it has some sort of handlike appendage?'

Nadine's tone was impatient, and her fists at last broke open. 'You're interpreting it using a language of shapes that your culture has taught you to recognize. That's how art works.' Her pale, bony fingers traced the air. 'Art uses symbols, a code based on tradition, on culture, on emotional response. A code of colours, lines, shapes, objects. This art is, in a sense, written in a foreign language, using a code we don't know. Think of a Rorschach inkblot. You look at it and try to superimpose recognizable shapes, identities. That doesn't mean that's what the inkblot is representing. You may see two pigs humping. An alien – who knows what it would see? That thing out there is not what an alien's hand looks like. It's an abstraction.'

Vera bumped into the back of Mozden's chair. 'How do you know that? How do you know they don't have hands just like that?' He pounded on the microwave. 'This damn thing isn't working.'

Garth got up to help him, squeezing behind Mozden.

'I know because a simple representation would not have the power that piece has, the power we all felt when we looked down into that depression, the power we all felt when we looked at that far-off figure. Sculpture does not represent: it is.'

'What is artistic arrest?' Mozden asked.

'It's the effect that great art has on you. And it's exactly what it sounds like. It's when the art seizes and holds you. It's that moment when you say "A-ha!" It's when your mind engages the sculpture. When you see a sculpture, you enter into the creative process. You enter into a reciprocal communication with the piece of sculpture. The artist's subconscious, through the work of art, communicates with your subconscious. You re-create in your mind the emotion the artist felt while creating the work. This re-creation so captures you that you are stopped. Arrested. Some compare it to an orgasm.'

'An orgasm from a statue,' Vera said. 'Maybe if it vibrated.' He pounded on the microwave again. 'Wonder how much the government paid for this gem.'

Garth said, 'The panel's not working. Just use the automatic setting.'

The microwave came on.

Katrack stood. 'I suggest we all get some rest.' He collected his dishes, put them in the sonic washer behind his chair, and headed to the cockpit. Nadine headed in the opposite direction, towards her bunk.

Mozden was stuck wedged into her seat until Vera's food was done, and he and Garth moved out from behind her. 'Watch out, Garth,' Vera said as he headed towards the cockpit with his plate. 'You're going to give me an orgasm.'

Garth leant over to pick up his dishes and set a small object on the table. It was an empty plastic food packet, crumpled and ripped. As Mozden stood, she realized that Garth had shaped it into a small, six-fingered white hand.

She stood by waiting while he loaded his dishes into the washer.

'Have you ever done anything artistic?' Garth asked.

Mozden had to think a while. 'When I was eight I won a science fair for my computer models of the planets of the solar system. I built images of what they would look like at various spots on the surfaces and beneath them.'

'I used to make clay bugs. All different kinds. But I stopped when I was around fourteen.' He realized she wanted to load her dishes and moved aside. 'You know guys. They didn't think it was extreme enough.'

He seemed to be waiting for her to say something. But when she wasn't talking science, she never knew what to say. She supposed he thought they were friends. She supposed they were, after training together for a year. But she'd never been very good at having friends. She loaded her dishes, pushed the button. 'Good night, Garth.'

'Good night, Liz.'

The seismic probe ended its final cycle, and Mozden studied the results. Here, as at the other sites she'd tested over the last three days, the data correlated with what they'd found in the sample cores. The surface layer of carbon sheets extended to a depth of about three hundred metres. Below that was a zone of Bucky tubes mixed with intact Bucky balls. How any of these had formed remained unknown.

Because of their particular structure and strong chemical bonds, the sheets formed a hard, rigid surface. At one time, though, they must have been flexible, semiplastic, in order to form or be deformed into these shapes. The forces that had moulded them remained unknown.

At a depth of about three hundred and fifty metres was a rocky layer of calcium carbonate and other carbonates, metals, sulphides and silicates, extending approximately twenty kilometres. Bucky balls could also be found throughout this layer. It was in this layer, at a depth of about two and a half kilometres, that she detected a zone of water and, with it, Garth's micro-organisms. They fed off the carbon in the calcium carbonate as well as the metals, such as sulphur and iron, dissolved in the water, somewhat similar to the chemosynthetic organisms that lived on Earth near underwater volcanic vents and the metal-rich hydrothermal fluids that came from them. The high metal content in the planet's underground water indicated that it too was hydrothermal in nature, driven upward through faults in the rock at the high temperatures and pressures caused by magmatic hot spots.

The organisms clustered about certain locations, either in response to the concentration of dissolved minerals or to the temperature. As conditions changed, the organisms migrated in great masses, possibly up to one hundred and fifty metres across, travelling through the permeable rock and through faults in the rock, their movement creating a low-frequency harmonic tremor in the readings similar to that she'd seen with the slow movement of magma. In fact, if her interpretation was correct, there was magmatic movement also, usually below or alongside the organisms. Driven upward by hot spots in the mantle below, these forceful, delicate fingers of magma worked their way up through the rock.

In the core barrels that Garth had been drilling and the two of them had been testing, they'd found indications of a network of old volcanic dykes running from this depth all the way up to the surface. Apparently at some time in the past the magma had been much more active. The planet was cooling, its life cycle winding down. Mozden would have postulated that the sculptures were actually magmatic dykes that had been covered over somehow with carbon sheets, but their readings had shown that the sculptures were made of one uniform material, not an inner core covered by an outer sheath.

Below the rock layer, at twenty kilometres, was the mantle. This was at the range limit of the seismic probe, but she'd been lucky enough twice to get a little data back on it. The magma there underwent focused, localized movements that created short, high-frequency tremors in the readout. The mantle seemed unusually active, but not active in the large-scale way it was on Earth. There were no signs of plate tectonics. The movements here were on a much smaller scale and were more intricate, seemingly created by localized hot spots of radiation.

And that was as deep as her readings would take her.

The information was fascinating, and overwhelming. It would take years to sort through it all and analyse it. For now they remained focused on answering a single question: how were the sculptures created? They had yet to find any significantly sized caverns or underground passages: no sign of Vera's hidden, living underground society, or even a dead or abandoned underground society.

As far as life went, the micro-organisms were the only game in town, and they showed no signs of intelligent behaviour nor any genetic disposition towards intelligence. Also, Mozden found it extremely odd that they had detected only one type of micro-organism so far. On Earth, ecosystems involving several, if not many, organisms commonly developed a food chain of interlocking processes. Perhaps they were adaptable and took on multiple roles within the ecosystem at different times or under different circumstances; she'd have to discuss this with Garth.

At this point, Mozden had only two theories that were even faintly possible, and she didn't like either of them. First, fingers of magma near the surface might have heated the sheets above them, and, in heating, might cause them to differentially deform into odd shapes, the fused tubes and woven tubes having bonds of varying strength. But this couldn't explain the intricate, crafted shapes of the sculpture.

Second, if the micro-organisms had ever migrated as high up as the surface, it was possible that they, in carrying out their chemical processes and migrating and growing in large masses between the sheets, could have deformed the sheets into different shapes. The problem with this was that, although they ate carbon, and the surface was made of carbon, the chemical reaction required for them to utilize the unfixed carbon in calcium carbonate, as they were now deep underground, was significantly different from that necessary for them to utilize the fixed carbon on the surface. She and Garth had discussed this, and they'd come up with the theory that perhaps these micro-organisms, or other micro-organisms that had since died off, might have had a mechanism for feeding off the Bucky balls and transforming them into tubes and sheets.

A Bucky ball was simply a network of sixty carbon atoms connected in a spherical shape. The structure looked like a soccer ball, with a carbon atom at each intersection. Like the patches on a soccer ball, most of which had six sides but some of which had five, the Bucky ball had mostly hexagonal faces but also twelve pentagonal faces. If the bonds on these five-sided faces, which were weaker than the other bonds, were broken, they would reclose as six-sided faces, reducing the curvature of the ball. Also two or more balls with broken bonds might fuse, creating a chain, or tube. This was in fact how all polymers, including biological ones like DNA, grew. If the micro-organisms could produce an enzyme that specifically broke only the bonds that made up the five-atom faces, then they could have been responsible for creating and deforming the sheets. She and Garth planned to test that theory after things settled down. But again, this did not seem a sufficient explanation.

The unavoidable issue was this: the sculptures implied an intelligence, either past or present, and they'd found no supporting evidence of an intelligence, nor come up with any theory of how an intelligence might have created these shapes.

Reluctantly, she raised her head from the test results. The

sculpture towered above her, huge and complex, over a kilometre in diameter, and as high. It looked almost as if she were standing at the gateway to a city, a city of huge arches, descending funnel shapes, high rectangles and strange, angling planes. The sunlight shone down into this 'city', highlighting a plane here, a strut there, creating a spot of light on this wall and a curve of shadow on that. The contrasting slices of light and shadow created an incredible sense of depth, and seemed to invite one to enter into its reflective, never-ending passages, to contemplate the silence and flow, the strength and the serenity, the pattern too intricate to be a pattern.

She checked her watch. Katrack had gone in over an hour ago and had said he'd be back before her testing was finished. 'Commander Katrack,' she said into the radio built into her breather. She and Katrack had set their radios to communicate automatically with each other, to avoid distracting the others with their crosstalk. The radio reception had been fairly clear since landing. He should have no trouble reading her. 'Commander Katrack, do you read me? Commander Katrack.'

The sound of the wind was her only response. It howled through the empty archways of the sculpture. Mozden scanned the empty plane surrounding the city, which was interrupted periodically by huge, fantastical shapes. Vera and Garth had planned to stay near the lander today and drill a follow-up core through the hand, to compare to the core Katrack and Vera had drilled when they'd first arrived. Nadine had taken the second rover to do more recon.

Mozden didn't think anything serious had happened to Katrack. It was easy to lose track of time out here, among the dwarfing shapes. It was easy to lose track of reality. The commander had shown himself susceptible to this on several occasions. But he had never failed to respond to communications.

On her wristband, Mozden redirected her transmission to Vera. 'Major Vera, this is Mozden.'

'I read you, Mozden.'

'The commander went into a sculpture near our site over an hour ago, and he was supposed to be back by now. I can't reach him by radio. I'm going to go in after him.'

'Do you need assistance?'

'No. I just wanted to inform you of the situation.'

'We're getting ready to close up shop here. Nadine should be back with the second rover in an hour. We can send assistance at that time if necessary. Report back in a half-hour with your status.'

'Roger.'

Mozden was left alone again with the sound of the wind. She reset her radio to its original state, tried Katrack again. No response. What she needed was something to keep from getting lost in there. It looked like a maze, and no trail of bread crumbs was going to stay in place in the wind. Katrack had taken the hand-held infrared mapper. That left her with more primitive options. In the rover's repair kit she found a screwdriver. With some force she could scratch the surface. It would have to do.

She brought a torch as well, in case it got dark before she found him. It was about an hour and a half before sunset. The shadows had grown longer within the city, the places of darkness outweighing those of light. She entered through a towering archway, and the city enveloped her.

She was neither inside nor outside, but in some in-between place, a place that suggested the different buildings of a city while remaining wholly one object, unified and vast, with periodic openings to the sky. Each turn revealed a new vista, with a new combination of shapes and a new group of options. At each turn, she knelt and scratched out a mark, though with the darkness coming they would become harder to see. Of course if she found Katrack, they could use the infrared mapper to find their way out.

As she travelled farther within the sculpture, the wind took on an odd, hollow sound, a seashell's echo against her ear. It was the sound of emptiness, of space. The angles and curves led her in deeper. Arches, planes, funnels, rectangles, curving struts, one incomplete shape led into another, sections painted in light or shadow giving almost the impression of movement, like hanging glass wind chimes shifting in the breeze. Somehow the variety of shapes created harmony, that sense of peace she'd noticed before. She found herself thinking odd thoughts, imagining she was inside the wind chimes' song, or inside that state of mind she so prized where all the pieces fitted together in one perfect moment of insight.

She realized that she no longer felt alone. Here, she felt somehow one with the universe and with all things in it. She remembered when once, as a girl, she had been lying on the grass in her front garden, looking up at the pattern of clouds and sky. Following the clouds' movement past her overhead, she had suddenly had the reverse sensation, of the clouds stationary and the Earth turning beneath her. In that one moment of vertiginous dislocation when her hands clutched the grass, she had realized the full truth of being on Earth, and she had felt a unity with the planet, as they both spun through the empty reaches of space.

In the shadows ahead stood a figure. Katrack, facing away from her. His hands were on his hips.

'Commander Katrack.' She approached him. Beneath the breather, his face was in shadow. 'Commander.' She touched his arm. 'I've been looking for you. Commander.'

'You found me.' His tone was neutral.

Her sense of unity with the universe slipped away as she was forced to deal with another human being. 'It's late,' she said. 'We should be getting back.'

'Should we? I guess I lost track of time.'

She'd had faith that he could lead them through anything. But over the last few days, she'd begun to question that faith. He was growing away from them. And more than that. He'd never completely recovered himself from that initial 'artistic arrest'. A part of his mind had been seized and had not yet been returned. And she didn't know how to get it back. 'We can use the mapper to lead us out,' she suggested. 'It's kind of tricky.'

Katrack nodded and unslung the device from his shoulder, passing it to Mozden. With relief, she saw that it had recorded the path clearly. She led the way out, the wind hollow and empty around them.

It was dark by the time they reached the rover. Katrack, coming back to himself, informed Vera they were running late. They loaded the seismic probe on to the back of the rover, and Katrack accepted Mozden's offer to drive.

This was the first time she'd been out at night. The temperature was dropping fast, and Mozden began to shiver. Above, Alpha Centauri B had risen. It was brighter than Venus was from Earth and about three times its size in the sky. The constellations were a disorientating mix of the familiar and the foreign, stars slightly misaligned, repositioned from this new perspective, as if the universe had shifted.

The lights on the rover illuminated a shining path. Surrounding it, all around them, the sculptures stood like dreams, or nightmares, great hulks of power outlined in starlight. Each shape evoked a different emotion, sounded a different chord inside her, one replacing the next – loss, love, loneliness, fear. Together, they played an overwhelming symphony. Her body shook, with joy or despair, she couldn't tell. Clenching her teeth, she focused on the surface ahead, on the area illuminated by the lights, and tried to ignore the silent presence of Katrack beside her.

Inside the airlock, they waited for the light to turn green. Katrack had mentioned outside that Nadine's rover had not returned. As much as that worried Mozden, the fact that Katrack had noticed it reassured her. At last the light turned green, and the inner hatch slid open, allowing them into the lander.

Voices were yelling in a near panic. Mozden pulled off her breather and the oxygen pack and dropped them to the floor as Katrack did the same.

'Has it reached the board?' Vera yelled from the cockpit, his voice fast and desperate.

'It's all over the board!' Garth yelled back. 'It's gone into the next section.'

'We've got to pull this out!'

Katrack rushed to the cockpit, Mozden behind him. The cockpit was small, and the pilots' seats and Vera's and Garth's bodies standing behind them filled up most of the space. Katrack was just able to fit in, and Mozden remained in the hatchway. Vera and Garth had pulled apart several of the panels in the cockpit, exposed electronics and wiring everywhere.

'What's going on?' Katrack said.

Vera and Garth both started, surprised at their presence. 'We had a complete electrical failure,' Vera said, breathless. 'Just after you radioed us. No backup, no nothing. We rerouted, using emergency procedures, until we could locate the problem. The computer showed no malfunction, but the entire panel was nonresponsive, so we opened it up. Take a look.' Vera moved aside, between the two pilots' chairs, so that Katrack could approach the open panel. Garth's wide eyes sought out Mozden, and her heart began to pound. He pushed himself against the wall so she could squeeze forward as well.

'What the hell is that?' Katrack said.

Against the black bulkhead was a rust-coloured layer several millimetres thick, of what looked almost like dust. The texture was different from dust though – fluffier and slimier, simultaneously – and there was a slight sense of movement to the layer, of pulsation. Mozden caught a whiff of an odd, metallic smell. Below the layer, the bulkhead seemed lighter in colour, discoloured to a grey. Very faintly, she thought she could see scattered sparkles of reddish copper. As she leant closer, she could see down on to the circuit board that had been revealed by the removal of the panel. The plastic circuit board was half covered by the rust-coloured dust, growing out in a mass contiguous to the bulkhead. The grey of the circuit board also seemed slightly lightened, and she thought she could see the plastic flaking beneath the layer of slime-dust. The plastic insulation on a number of wires had crumbled off into powder, and at the intersection of two such wires blossomed the singe marks of a short.

Though they'd looked different in the higher-pressure, anaerobic setting underground, moving through the permeable rock and rock faults, she recognized the micro-organisms immediately. But she had no idea how they'd got from two and a half kilometres below the surface to their cockpit.

'They're the organisms we detected underground,' Garth answered, sounding like a boy anticipating punishment.

The bulkhead was a carbon composite, as were many parts of the lander, including the spaceframe and the hull, because of the strength and light weight of the material; the plastic of the circuit board, as she recalled, was made of carbon and hydrogen. If they were breaking all the carbon bonds on the lander . . .

Katrack stepped back. 'What the hell are they doing up here?'

'I think they're eating the ship,' Garth said.

Katrack put his hands on his hips and bit his lip. 'We've got to do an immediate, and complete, examination of the lander. I want to know if there are any more of these things, exactly where they are, and how much damage they've done. I want you to turn this ship inside out.' Katrack directed Vera and Garth to finish examining the cockpit, assigned himself to checking the lander's hull, the propulsion system, and the solar array, and assigned Mozden to check the cabin and all the systems contained there.

Mozden began a systematic check of the cabin while Katrack donned his breather and prepared to head back outside. He gave her a thumbs up as he stepped into the airlock, and she nodded tightly back. She was no chemist, but she knew that the chemical reaction required for the micro-organisms to consume fixed carbon from the lander was vastly different from the reaction required to eat the unfixed carbon in calcium carbonate. It wasn't that dissimilar, though, from the process of eating fixed carbon from the Bucky balls, if that theory proved true. Most Earth bacteria could produce many different enzymes to serve as catalysts for different chemical reactions. It was possible that these micro-organisms might have an enzyme within their repertoire that allowed them to break the carbon bonds in the lander. They would need water, she thought. And she remembered that the contaminated bulkhead in the cockpit was contiguous to a water storage tank that ran between the cockpit and the hull.

But how had they even found the lander? What had driven them up to the surface?

She knew that the micro-organisms they'd obtained from the sample cores were secure. They'd taken every precaution, and tested them and checked them constantly.

She remembered then the trouble they'd been having with

the microwave, which hadn't been working right since they'd landed. The panel through which specific cooking times and intensities could be programmed had been working only intermittently. They'd switched to using the start and stop buttons, not wanting to take the time to fix the problem. She pulled the control panel off now, and immediately saw small hints of the slime-dust formation characteristic of the microorganisms. She took her hand lens from her pocket. The plastic components of the system displayed the same discoloured, flaking, almost powdery appearance. Again she saw the scattered specks of reflective reddish copper. Those tiny sparkles had almost the same colour and reflectivity as the planet's surface. They suggested that the organisms were not only breaking the carbon bonds in the plastic, but reforming the carbon into a new configuration. She'd heard of nothing like it.

Mozden tapped the hand lens against the plastic panel. It cracked like a thin sheet of ice, the fragments dropping to the floor. The carbon composite that made up the skin and spaceframe of the lander was stronger, but the work of the organisms would eventually have the same effect.

Now attuned to the signs, Mozden began to find small pockets of contamination all over, her search gradually growing faster, more frantic. She saw slime-dust in the carbon composite of the crew seats, along the base of the bulkheads, in a fair amount of her and Garth's equipment, in the plastic insulation on the wiring for the lighting fixtures over their tiny 'garden', on one of the plastic guns in the weapons cabinet, in the controls regulating the solar array. They seemed to form in lines, blooming out into clumps where conditions were favourable. Sometimes the contamination was visible to the naked eye; often only through the hand lens. Most of the damage done in the areas she'd examined seemed minor, so far. But her rough guess was that the lander was almost one-third contaminated.

Katrack returned, and the slackness in his face as he pulled off his breather told her the damage was serious. 'Vera, Garth. I want your report.'

Vera and Garth came out of the cockpit, and they all clustered in a circle. Vera spoke. 'The electrical system is the most seriously damaged one up there. I don't think we can fully repair it, but we can keep the system on emergency override and make a few modifications to make that more efficient. There's some minor damage to the navigational controls. I think we can replace the affected parts with some we scavenge from the lander and the rovers.'

Katrack's attention turned to Mozden.

'No serious damage yet,' she said, keeping her voice even. 'But using a hand lens, I found micro-organisms in almost one-third of the areas I checked. The actual level of contamination must be significantly higher, since the hand lens can only reveal clumps of micro-organisms.'

Katrack nodded. 'The contamination is the worst along the belly of the lander. They've eaten through into the utility water tank. There's also some serious structural damage down there.' He looked from one of them to the next, and Mozden saw in his gaze as much the attempt to steady them as to steady himself. 'The refrigeration unit failed while I was out there. I disabled the alarm when I saw it was about to go. The unit is covered with organisms. I think the refrigeration pump uses powdered graphite as a lubricant. We'll have to look at the specs.'

'What about the backup?' Vera asked.

Katrack's face was tight. 'Totally out of commission. In less than an hour, the temperature in the fuel tanks will have risen to the point where our liquid oxygen and hydrogen will vaporize. No getting back to orbit. And we could very well be sitting on top of a huge explosion. We need to effect repairs immediately. We can't take off until we do.'

As Vera asked Katrack the details of the damage, Mozden realized that what they should be focusing on was a method of ridding the lander of the micro-organisms, rather than repairing damage that would far outpace their ability to cope with it. If the ship had become this contaminated in this short amount of time, the organisms must be migrating on to it or multiplying at an incredible rate. They most likely had less than a day before the damage became irreparable. She didn't understand the organisms as well as Garth did, but she knew that even his understanding of them was extremely limited. Neither of them had yet been able to study the organisms in depth. The chances of finding a way to control or kill them in time were small.

'Getting off the surface isn't the issue,' Garth said. 'These organisms are having no trouble living on the lander. If we hook up with the orbiter and head back to Earth, who says they won't eat through the hull while we're asleep?'

'We need to kill them,' Mozden said, 'or drive them off the ship.'

'How do we do that?' Katrack asked.

Mozden shook her head. 'I don't know yet.'

'Garth?' Katrack asked.

'I've only run the most basic tests on them so far, but they seem extremely adaptable. The presence or absence of oxygen doesn't seem to affect them. They do need water, but so do we, so I don't think that can help us. Even if we dumped all our water, I don't think it would help, because the underground water has risen to within a few metres of the surface.'

'What?' Mozden said. It had been more than two kilometres below the surface when they'd landed.

Garth's face was open and full of fear. 'That's what the core we drilled today shows. The temperature at every depth has increased dramatically, there are small, active magmatic intrusions only metres below the surface, and the water has been driven up by the heat, the organisms with it.'

'That's impossible,' Mozden said, and Garth nodded.

'The factor that they're most sensitive to is temperature. They can survive extreme temperatures, but they prefer a range between forty and fifty-five degrees Celsius. I'd suggest heating or cooling the lander somehow, to encourage them to leave, but the high heat beneath the surface has driven them up here. They have nowhere to go.'

With the heat and the mineral-rich water just below, and the lander an apparently easily consumable food, the organisms were undergoing a 'bloom' or rapid localized growth. 'What if we move the lander?' Mozden asked. 'If we get away from this hot spot below us, the organisms may return underground of their own accord.'

'That could work,' Garth said.

'By the time we prepped to take off, we wouldn't have any fuel.' Katrack rubbed a hand over his chin. 'We need to repair the refrigeration unit first, before we can dare engaging the engines. Then we could move wherever you say.'

If the lander was still in one piece by then, Mozden thought. 'How about a chemical method of killing them or deactivating their enzymes?' she asked Garth.

'I never tested them with that objective in mind. And since they're now performing a different chemical reaction from what we studied with the calcium carbonate, I'd need to start all over. It would take a while.' He glanced at Mozden. Only the two of them understood the full difficulty of the process, and how long it would take.

Vera shifted impatiently. 'That hot spot didn't just develop by accident. They've declared war on us, if you haven't noticed.'

'All right,' Katrack said. 'We need to get to work. Vera and I –' He stopped, his mouth open. 'Where's Nadine?'

Mozden remembered the missing rover.

Katrack headed towards the monitor, and they followed. 'When is the last time you heard from her?'

Vera checked his watch. 'She radioed in about five and a half hours ago. She was due back two hours ago.'

Katrack sat and called up the signal from the locator beacon on Nadine's rover, which was superimposed on the image of this section of the planet. The scale seemed off. Katrack activated the radio. 'Nadine, come in. Nadine, this is Katrack. Come in.'

Silence.

'What the hell is she doing out there?' Katrack asked.

'I told her to stay within fifty kilometres, per instructions,' Vera said. 'She's a loose cannon.'

Nadine's signal looked to be about a hundred and sixty kilometres out. The rover was stationary.

'The rover may have broken down,' Mozden said. 'It may be contaminated too.'

Katrack stood and turned towards them. 'We need to get that refrigeration unit repaired immediately. I need Vera to do that. Mozden and Garth, I need you to go find Nadine and bring her and the rover back. We're going to need its parts for repairs. As soon as you get back, I want you working on some method of eliminating these things.'

'Commander,' Mozden said. 'We may not have that much time.'

Katrack nodded. 'I'm not going to send one of you out there alone, at night. I can't afford to lose you. I want the two of you working on this problem while you're out there. You come up with any bright ideas, you call them into us, and we'll execute them. All right?'

'Yes, sir.' Garth answered along with her.

Mozden dug into a supply cabinet and came up with three coats. The lining was some sort of synthetic material; she wondered if it contained carbon. Of course, then her jumpsuit might, as well; she had no idea. She and Garth put on the coats, and then Mozden retrieved her white oxygen pack from where she had dropped it before. Along a seam on one side, she caught a glimpse of the rust-coloured slime-dust. As she turned it in her hand, she realized the carbon composite had bowed out slightly on that side, the oxygen within pushing against the weakened container. If the surface was bowing, it couldn't be long before the pressure blew the pack apart. Katrack took it from her.

'Check your equipment, Garth,' he said.

Mozden got one of the backup breathers – there were seven – and checked it carefully. After a moment's thought, she took a spare. Katrack and Vera stood by grimly.

Mozden examined the breather that she would be putting over her face. It had components of plastic, of rubber – another hydrocarbon – and of carbon composite. The moisture of her breath would create an environment friendly to the micro-organisms. The thought of them so close to her face was unnerving. She looked up and met Garth's wide-eyed clown face, knowing they were thinking the same thing.

She turned to Katrack. 'You know that we're made of carbon compounds too.'

Katrack's tight face underwent a subtle change, a slight downward turn to the lips, a slight rise of the brows. 'Do you think that the organisms could –'

'I don't know.'

His face tightened again. 'I want you to radio back to us every fifteen minutes.'

Mozden nodded, fitting the breather over her head.

'Give the rover a thorough examination before you leave. And be careful.'

Vera pushed the control to open the inner hatch of the airlock. Mozden followed Garth inside. As the hatch slid shut and the cycle began, Mozden was left with the image of Katrack staring down at the oxygen pack in his hands. With the side bowed out, it looked almost as if it were taking on a new shape, as if it were being reformed, sculpted.

The dreamworld of the sculptures surrounded them once again. Mozden drove through the night, following Nadine's beacon on the tracking system, willing herself into a state of tunnel vision. The wind was stronger now, sweeping in cold gusts across the open plain, and she held tight to the wheel of the rover. She and Garth had reviewed all they knew about the organisms, searching for a weakness. Mozden wished Sabriski, the chemist Nadine had replaced, were here.

They had plenty of ideas about tests to run that might lead to a solution, but, unless they were lucky, the tests would be time-consuming. And both she and Garth agreed that their window of opportunity was short. The organisms had found an environment they liked, and they would most likely thrive for as long as the environment lasted.

Garth had brought some loose pieces of wire, and in the light of the torch propped between his legs he was bending the wire, shaping it into the primitive image of a man. 'You don't believe Vera's theory, do you?' Garth asked. 'That we are under attack by the creators of the sculpture?' The torchlight shone off his faceplate, his curly hair streaming dark into the night.

'No.' Vera was an anthropomorphizing fool, as Nadine might say if she were here. If she was still alive. 'Whatever's going on here, it's vastly different from life as we know it.'

'And yet we respond to its sculpture.' Garth's voice rose out of its monotone. 'I think we're missing the point here. We've thought that the process that formed these sculptures was no longer active. This new development suggests that it *is* still active, and the intelligence that created the sculptures is still here, on the planet. If we can communicate with it, make it understand what is happening –' he stole a quick glance in her direction '– I know it will help us.'

Mozden wondered where the hell Garth had come up with that idea. It was the most unscientific thing he'd ever said. 'How would you propose communicating with this intelligence?'

'Through the only form it understands. Through sculpture. If Nadine makes a sculpture, that might elicit a response.'

Mozden didn't want to insult him, so she said nothing. But the possibility that they might be able to communicate with this intelligence seemed about as likely as the possibility of its consciously 'declaring war' on them in the sense Vera meant. They still had no idea what this intelligence might be. The organisms seemed controlled by the water and the heat. The water and the heat were controlled by the magmatic movements. She thought of the old, hardened fingers of magma they'd discovered near the surface, and the new ones Garth had detected in his latest core. The fingers, through their intricate, twisting passage through the rock, would control the movement of the micro-organisms, herding them this way or that, controlling their growth, guiding them. And as the fingers became more and more fine near the surface, their control would grow more fine, precise. But what guided the fingers?

'I'm starting to wonder if maybe we didn't evolve wrong,' Garth said in his monotone, his hands working in the glare of the torch. 'Maybe we're freaks in the galaxy, the only life of our kind. Maybe the rest of the galaxy is like this. We waste time fighting and reproducing, when we could be creating beauty. Isn't that what we should do? What better purpose can life have?'

'I see Nadine's rover,' Mozden replied.

It sat in the starlight near a great, hulking hemispherical form. The rover's squat, rectangular shape, ugly and static, seemed out of place in this land of dreams. Mozden stopped so that her lights shone on to it. In the back of Nadine's rover, a canvas flapped in the wind. Other than that, everything was still.

Mozden pressed the control on her wristband. 'Nadine. Nadine come in.'

Of course they already knew that her radio wasn't working. Or at least that she wasn't answering it. And if her radio was contaminated, perhaps her breather was too.

Garth put his wire man into his jumpsuit pocket, took the torch from between his legs and got out of the rover. The wind flattening her coat against her legs, Mozden retrieved the spare breather and her own torch and followed. As if Nadine's breather would have waited until now to fail, when they were here to rescue her.

Garth scanned the surrounding area with his torch as they approached the rover. The smooth, copper-red surface shone back at them. The rover's seats were empty. The back had only a few small pieces of equipment they hadn't been using and the canvas, tied down at one corner and undulating in waves in the wind. Garth pulled the canvas up. There lay Nadine, her limp, scarecrow form collapsed into a ball. Garth reached out to turn her over.

Nadine jumped, rolling up into a sitting position. Her lips yelled something behind the clear mask.

Garth had jumped back too, and now he started to laugh.

'Nadine, can you hear me?' Mozden tapped her ear.

Nadine shook her head. She had begun to shiver in great, violent bursts. She crossed her arms in front of her for warmth, and Mozden saw that the skin of her near hand was a sickly purple white.

'Garth, get the spare coat,' Mozden directed, climbing up into the rover alongside Nadine. Along the rubber rim of Nadine's faceplate the rust-coloured slime-dust caught the lights of the rover. Mozden worked to unfasten the radio earpiece from the spare breather, her gloved hands slow and clumsy. She stopped to pull off the gloves, laid them on her leg, then grabbed them up and handed them to Nadine. The earpiece came off quickly now. She thought of handing it to Nadine, but Nadine was having a hard enough time putting the gloves on. Mozden fitted the earpiece over Nadine's free right ear. She quickly reprogrammed her wristband to encompass the new breather. 'Are you all right?' she asked.

Nadine nodded.

'We're going to do a breather transfer, OK? You remember that procedure?' They had practised it together several times.

'Yes,' Nadine mouthed, shaking.
'You remember the steps? Seal, change, unseal, ten, clear.'
Nadine nodded.

Mozden handed her the new oxygen pack. 'OK. We're going to start now. Hold your breath.'

Nadine gave the thumbs up, which showed she was following the procedure.

'Sealing.' Mozden sealed the external coupling on the mask, down under the chin, and released the pressure seal. 'Changing.' She pulled the breather up over Nadine's head. Her cold hands felt clumsy and unresponsive. She dropped the breather and grabbed up the new one beside her. The wind made her lose her balance for a moment. She straightened and fitted the breather down over Nadine's narrow head. 'Unsealing.' She activated the breather and opened the coupling. Then she counted aloud to ten as she purged the system. 'Clear. Exhale, Nadine.'

Nadine exhaled then gasped, the sound transmitted through the new radio link. 'I was beginning to wonder –' she gasped '– if you were going to leave me out here to rot.'

Mozden helped her remove the old oxygen pack and fit the new one on to her back. Garth brought the coat, and Mozden helped her into it. 'We've had some problems. What happened to you?'

'The damn rover broke down. And then the radio wouldn't work either.'

They settled Nadine, still shivering, into one of the rover's seats. Mozden directed Garth to take a look at the engine while she radioed the lander from a few metres away.

'Commander Katrack. This is Mozden.'

'Mozden. Have you found Nadine?' There was an edge to Katrack's voice she hadn't heard before.

'Yes, sir. She's suffering from exposure, but I think she'll be OK. The rover broke down. We're assessing the damage now.' She waited in silence for his response. After some moments, she began to wonder if he'd copied her. She was about to speak again when he finally replied.

'We need those rovers back. Keep me posted, Mozden.'

She hesitated. 'Sir? How are the repairs coming?' Again there was silence, defined by the wind.

'We haven't given up. But we need you back here, soon.'

His words sent a shock of fear through her. 'Yes, sir.'

'Katrack out.'

Mozden stood still, her radio now isolated on an empty frequency. Garth and Nadine were silent figures etched in the harsh headlights. On the far side of the hemispherical sculpture, the sun was preparing to rise, a band of pale, orange light bleeding over the horizon. Though she'd had many early mornings in the past years, it had been a long time since she'd watched a sunrise. The wind whipped past her body, a raw turbulence that handled her roughly. Below her the planet spun, carrying out its processes: heating, cooling, breathing, moving, forming, destroying, nurturing, killing. Did it even notice they were there, among the vast, towering shapes? Did it even care?

Feeling like a stranger to her own body, Mozden forced herself to raise her arm, to re-establish her radio connection to the others. With halting steps she separated her feet from the planet's surface and approached Garth.

He straightened from his position over the engine. 'How's the ship?'

'It sounds like they're making progress.' There was no point in alarming them; it wouldn't help anything. Nadine seemed oblivious. She sat hunched over, her arms across her chest, shivering. But Garth's wide eyes stared into her, as if he saw something there. 'How's the rover?' she asked.

Garth aimed his torch into the engine. 'The most serious damage is underneath. The axle's broken.'

Even in the poor light, she could see the crumbling edges of the hole that had been eaten through the bottom of the carbon-composite chassis, the layer of growth that had bloomed around the now-empty container of windscreen-wiper fluid, the degradation of the area around it. The remnants of slime-dust were small but noticeable.

'They probably migrated into the rover while it was parked beside the lander,' Garth said. 'Most of them seem to have left or died due to a lack of water or heat.'

'That would confirm our theory.'

Garth nodded, his light playing over the damage.

They decided that there were still enough salvageable parts

Negative Space

to justify towing the rover back. Mozden manoeuvred her rover in front of Nadine's. As the sun began to rise behind the huge hemispheric shape, casting them into its long shadow, they rigged up a tow line so that they could elevate the front of Nadine's rover. Mozden tried to check in with Katrack and Vera again, but got no response. She had the others try in case her radio was failing; they too received no response. The sky lightened to a pale blue. Mozden could feel the time passing, slipping away from them, as the long shadows shrank. They had to get back.

'Why did you come all the way out here?' she asked Nadine as she worked on the tow line. 'You know you were supposed to stay within fifty kilometres of the ship.'

Nadine mumbled something.

'What?' Mozden asked, irritated.

'I was looking for a flaw.' Nadine remained hunched over, arms across her chest, rocking slightly, as if talking to herself.

'What kind of flaw?'

'A flaw. In this.' Her palm turned out. 'But there is none. Each sculpture fuses subject, form, material . . . I can't describe it to you in words. Space and negative space are manipulated perfectly. It's one. It's the source. It contains energy in repose. Movement embodied in stillness. Life in lifelessness. Tension and dynamism in the balance between the aggressive and the passive, order and disorder, light and shadow, rhythm and mass, life-suggestive shapes and surreal abstractions, the rational and the intuitive. It's more than a subconscious connection. It's more than an emotional connection. It's spiritual. It's a spiritual attack. The stripping away – of me.' She stopped rocking and looked up, her hands dropping into her lap. 'It's forcing me to engage it. But I am nothing in the face of it. Every artist on Earth is nothing. That's what it tells me. It mocks me.' Her hands closed into fists. 'In the face of it, I'm just negative space.'

Mozden approached her. 'What do you mean, negative space?'

Nadine sighed. 'It's everything that's not the sculpture. Substance and space exist only in relation to each other, like sound and silence. A sculpture works in relationship to the space around it.' Her gloved hands moved to reflect the ideas. 'It may enclose or tame space, like a doughnut, or displace space, like a rock, or activate space, so that it vibrates with energy. In its emptiness, the space contrasts with the power and beauty of the art. We are the space.'

Mozden had often thought of herself, and of many others, as being filled with emptiness. She believed that the quest to fill that space was what motivated many people. She turned to check on Garth. He was about a hundred metres away, walking towards the hemisphere. The sun behind it haloed it in light. 'Garth,' she said, 'we have to get back to the lander.'

'I know.' He continued away. 'I'm just going to leave my wire man. I'll be right back.'

She watched him a moment longer, then turned back to Nadine. 'Garth believes we can communicate with the intelligence behind the sculpture through our own sculpture. He thinks that you should sculpt something to send them a message.'

Nadine got out of the rover. A strip of morning sun fell across the top of her breather and her forehead. 'That's ridiculous. You don't use sculpture as a tool. Sculpture just is.'

Mozden found herself arguing Garth's point of view. A sign, she thought, of desperation. 'Couldn't you make something just to show them we're here?'

Nadine gazed off towards the hemisphere. 'Oh, I think they know. I think they're looking down on us right now and laughing their heads off.' She pressed her palms together. 'I can't sculpt any more. How could I, in the face of this? The artists who created these would have no use for any of my work.' She took several steps back, until the sun spread from her forehead down into her eyes. 'Oh hell. Look.'

Mozden turned. The sun was just clearing the top of the hemisphere. Though it was almost half a kilometre away, she could see now that its surface was covered with a relief of some kind, facets of which shimmered in the sun. From this distance, the relief suggested here vines, there limbs, here a face, there a stone, a complex of powerful forces intertwining with one another, overlying one another, until they formed a solid barrier. The one major feature she had failed to notice through the dark and the activity was a great jagged irregular hole about two-thirds of the way up the hemisphere. Through it protruded a second shape, filling the hole, like a thick twig. It split just outside the hole into narrower branches. The impression was overwhelmingly one of breaking through. The branch-shaped piece had broken through the dome, broken out from under the confining intertwined forces into the air, and life. The branch-shaped piece reminded her of the hand in which the lander sat. It too reached as a plant, or as fingers, would. The positions of the different branches gave a sense of struggling. They did not yearn like the hand, but fought, tense, desperate, trapped, the extension of the arm arrested by the diameter of the hole. She sensed some connection between the two sculptures.

The sun had risen just high enough for it to shine through the crotch of the two biggest branches, like a saving grace they struggled to capture. Along the sides of the branches ran the curving terminator separating light from shadow, tracing lines of desperation. The branches seemed to embody tragedy, to reflect the one most horrible, catastrophic event that could occur, that had occurred. The attempt to break free was noble; the inability struck her with grief.

Yet had she ever even tried, in her life? She thought of all the emotions she'd avoided over the years, desiring always control rather than release. She had taken shelter under that dome, never wanting to expose herself, never daring to live.

Mozden found her jaw clenched and tears running down her face, and in embarrassment she brought her hand up to wipe them, only to have it bounced back by the breather. She looked away, taking a deep shuddering gasp. She was losing control. She cast her mind about, grasping at organisms, enzymes, magma, radiation – nothing could stop the tears. She curled over, chest tight, the pain grasping at the emptiness inside her. What was the matter with her? Christ, this was so stupid. But she couldn't stop crying.

'Garth,' she said, gulping back a sob. 'We have to go.'

He had reached the hemisphere some time ago, but he hadn't turned back.

'The surface is covered with the most incredible work.' From his voice she could tell that he, too, was crying.

For some reason, that helped her gain some control. She straightened, her breath shaky.

'We have to go.'

He turned and started walking back towards them. 'I'm not going.'

'What?' She started towards him.

'When the sun came up, I realized I was never going to see anything as beautiful as this. This is it. There's no need for me to go anywhere, do anything. There's no need for me to make crummy wire sculpture or to follow you around like a dog in heat. We weren't made right. We're a mistake. We can't create. Not like this. But at least I can appreciate it.'

Mozden glanced back, saw that Nadine had stayed behind, near the rovers. She started to run towards him with long strides. 'Garth, this is crazy. You have no food, no water. Your oxygen will run out. You have to come back with us.'

'All my life I've been searching for something. For a while I tried to tell myself it was you, but we both know that isn't so. I realize now this is it.'

'I'm sorry if I – if I was cold to you. That's just the way I am. Listen, you don't want to commit suicide. That's what you'd be doing if you stayed here.'

'I'm not ending my life,' he said. 'I'm fulfilling my life. And you could too, if you'd just open your eyes.'

As they approached each other Mozden slowed her strides carefully, and they stopped facing each other, as a man and a woman in a clichéd old video would, except that in the video he would take her in his arms and swing her around and around. But Garth stood still, gangly arms at his sides, curly hair pressed against his head by the breather, eyes red, cheeks wet with tears. Yet there was a certain dignity in him that she hadn't seen before, his slouching frame now erect. He no longer seemed a clown.

'We need you,' she said. 'You know the most about the organisms.'

'You know that the lander is damaged beyond repair. I saw it on your face. Our window of opportunity has passed.'

Mozden clenched her teeth. 'I don't know that. And you don't know it either.' She didn't know what else to say, but she didn't want to leave him behind.

Garth took her hand. 'You could stay here with me.'

Mozden pulled her hand away. 'By not coming back, you're sentencing us all to death.'

'You don't get it, do you? Don't want to let anything through those defences. It doesn't matter. Death. Life. I'm just a mistake of evolution. I'm an ant crawling over the *Mona Lisa*. But at least I've realized it. This is the most important thing that's ever happened to me. To live without it would be to live a meaningless life. Whether I live a day, an hour, a minute, a second, what's important is that I live it here, in the face of this beauty.'

'But what about your idea of trying to communicate through sculpture?'

'An ant cannot communicate with the *Mona Lisa*. An ant cannot create – beauty like this. All he can do is appreciate it, while there's still time.' Garth turned back to the sculpture, dismissing her.

Mozden tried again to wipe her eyes. 'The longer you live, the more you'll be able to appreciate it.'

Garth shrugged. 'I don't think any of us are really living anyway,' he said.

Mozden sped back towards the lander, Nadine's rover in tow, Nadine in the seat beside her. The sun was already high in the sky, the temperature hot enough to make them take off their coats. She hadn't been able to stop crying, which bothered her no end. She'd reprogrammed her radio to cut Garth out of her immediate communication loop, but she kept expecting to hear his irritating monotone.

'He's a fool,' Nadine said. 'He shouldn't have given in to it.'

'Nadine, would you please shut up.'

'Our lives have significance only in the struggle to catch a glimpse of beauty and meaning and to then attempt to re-create them. Being surrounded by them destroys that possibility, don't you see?'

'If we get the lander fixed,' Mozden said, 'we can go back for him.'

Nadine shook her head. 'He shouldn't have given in to it. It's got to be fought. It's got to be fought.'

They reached the rim of the hand. In its centre sat the ship. Although Mozden could point to no specific change in it from this distance, it had changed completely. The black and grey structure seemed to slump, to be no longer a solid but something in flux. Its straight lines had become curves, its angles had skewed. As she drove closer she saw that the tail section drooped low, and the wings curved downward. The hull seemed to hang on the framework like a wet cloth, as if it were melting, becoming plastic, deforming, transforming. Specks of copper-red glistened over the surface.

Piles of supplies were scattered around the lander. Katrack and Vera must have made the decision to abandon ship, she realized, the fear stopping her tears. A death sentence for all of them.

Vera ran out from beneath the lander to get something from one of the piles and saw them approach. He found a spare breather in the pile at his feet, inspected it, and then performed the same manoeuvre on himself that Mozden had done with Nadine, switching breathers so he would have a fresh transmitter. Nearby on the ground lay a swatch of striped red and white – the American flag, the rest of it apparently melded with or covered by the planet's surface.

Mozden stopped the rover beside Vera as he shrugged on the new oxygen pack. Behind the breather, his model-pouty lips hung askew, and his eyes darted at her and away from her, unable to hold their focus. He snatched up a metal bar. 'Come quick!' He ran back beneath the ship.

As she and Nadine followed, Mozden felt the intense heat of the ground through her thick boots. The damage to the underside of the lander was much more extensive than when they'd left. Wide areas of the black hull looked almost sandy in texture as they crumbled, while large patches of the black had been completely replaced with the shimmering reddish copper that seemed identical to the planet's surface. After breaking down the carbon composite, the organisms were somehow, perhaps with the additional heat, re-forming the carbon into the sheets that formed the planet's surface. She could offer no explanation. Yet there it was.

Vera stopped short and raised the metal bar to pry into the reddish-copper hull beside an odd, pinkish lump. 'Help me!'

Mozden moved closer, not understanding.

'It's Katrack! He got trapped inside the ship!'

She recognized the bald dome of his head now, protruding from the transforming hull of the ship, and as she moved to Vera's side, she saw Katrack's furrowed forehead, and his pale eyes locked on to hers, terrified. The ship clamped around his head was a semiliquid mass, and as she watched, it seemed to pulse, and another centimetre below his eyes was extruded. Someone, somewhere, was screaming.

'Grab his hand!' Vera yelled.

Less than a metre away, another object protruded at an odd angle from the underside of the lander. It was a hand, Mozden realized, and part of a forearm. Again the lander seemed clamped around it, pulsing, throbbing. Katrack's fingers stretched outward, and Mozden was reminded jarringly of the sculpture they had left behind. Nadine grabbed on to the hand and started to pull. Mozden returned her attention to the head. It hardly seemed part of the same body. She locked her hands around Katrack's forehead and pulled. It was hard to get a good grip.

Unable to pry the bar between Katrack's head and the lander, Vera frantically jammed it at the juncture, scraping Katrack's temple. The ship pulsed again, releasing another centimetre, revealing the top half of his nose. There must be something in the chemical make-up of humans incompatible with the organisms. But the process seemed to happen at its own pace, despite their efforts.

Katrack's skin had gone red as she'd been pulling on him, she'd assumed out of fear and stress. But now it was beginning to lose its colour, turning a bluish white. He was suffocating in the grasp of the ship. 'He'll need a breather as soon as his nose comes clear,' she yelled.

Vera threw down the bar and grabbed on to the arm beside Nadine. 'Go get a breather,' he ordered her, using his weight to pull back on the arm. It extended a little.

Mozden readjusted her grip and pulled down harder, her fingers digging into his head. She heard Vera screaming, and realized that she was screaming too. The lander pulsed, another centimetre released. Nadine stopped at her side with the breather, gasping in great, panicked gulps. Between

Mozden's fingers, Katrack's head had gone cyanotic. His eyes had lost their focus. She started wrestling with his head now, yanking and desperately trying to twist it free. Another increment was released by the lander, exposing the end of his nose. 'Get the breather on him!'

Nadine pushed the breather up against his face, still clamped by Mozden's hands, and activated it. It was impossible to fit and seal it properly, but even this way it should be able to provide him with oxygen.

'I don't think he's breathing,' Nadine yelled, her voice high and foreign.

Mozden slapped Katrack's head. His pale eyes stared into the middle distance. Nearby, Vera had got the arm out to the biceps and was pulling in deep, frantic heaves. Mozden took a deep breath and broke the seal on her breather, pulling it halfway off. She brought her mouth up to Katrack's ear. 'Breathe damn it wake up wake up!' she yelled in one long breath, then added, 'Commander! Commander Katrack!' She fitted the mask back over her face and slapped him again. He blinked then, and there was a slight movement to his nostrils. She resumed her pulling, and his colour began to improve. His eyes regained their focus on her. Centimetre by centimetre he was released. Vera moving closer to her as the upper arm drew him closer to the head, she gaining a better grip as more of his head came free, until at last his mouth was revealed.

'It won't take me,' he said, and his face was filled with a terrible loss. 'I want to be part of it, but it won't take me.'

Mozden lost her grip on him and stumbled back. Vera's unchanged expression of horror revealed that he'd known this all along. 'He went back into the lander on purpose. When we knew there was no getting out. He said he was carbon, and he wanted to be part of the sculpture.'

Avoiding Katrack's gaze, Mozden clamped her fingers around his head again and pulled. She could understand why Garth had surrendered to the sculpture: his life had been a search for something to fill the emptiness, for something worthy of surrendering to. But Katrack had seemed so self-sufficient. The sculpture had touched him, though, as it had touched all of them. It had shown him there was something

Negative Space

more. Slowly his chin came free, his neck. It was endless, endless work.

'Why is he shaking?' Nadine asked.

Katrack was trembling. 'Can't – breathe –' His head began jerking in violent spasms, as if he were being shaken by some giant hand. His arm flailed out of Vera's grasp. The breather fell to the ground. Nadine retrieved it and struggled to hold it to his face.

'Pull!' Vera said. 'Pull!'

Mozden wrapped her hands around his neck and pulled as hard as she could, pulled with every muscle in her body, pulled as if she wanted to rip his head off. Vera was right beside her now, the arm out to the shoulder, the beginnings of Katrack's bare chest starting to come free. They were all screaming. Yet they all heard it, when it happened. A firecracker-quick series of snaps like a bunch of twigs being broken.

They all went still.

She tried to deny what she knew, for she couldn't explain how she might know it, but she knew what the sound had been. It had been the sound of Katrack's ribs being crushed. She forced her fingers to his carotid artery, to take his pulse. There was none. Her hands cradled his limp head. 'He's dead.'

Nadine dropped the breather.

They stood there for some moments. The ship pulsed in its own time, releasing another centimetre. Nadine turned and walked away. Katrack's face hung slack, mouth open with the weight of his head, eyes tilted vacantly at the ground. She'd never seen a dead man before. His intelligence, his vitality, his smile still seemed potential, as if they could return. She trailed her hands from his neck, to his cheeks, to his temples, gravity finally slipping his head out from under her fingers. Vera remained clinging to Katrack's arm, his breath sounding, through the radio, rough and hard.

'He used his command override to keep me out of the ship,' Vera said. 'I tried to find a way in.' He held Katrack's hand, his head resting against Katrack's arm. He looked terribly young to Mozden. 'Then he started screaming that he was being pushed out. That it would take the ship, but it wouldn't take him. "Why won't it take me?" he kept saying.' Vera fell silent. The wind gusted past them.

'Why would it want us?' Mozden replied. 'We're polluted materials.' She took his free hand. 'Come on. Let's go take a look at the supplies.'

Rolling his pouty lips under, he looked up at Katrack, who dangled loosely from the ship.

'Come on.'

He released his grip on Katrack and followed.

As they came out from under the lander, they saw Nadine unhooking the tow line between the rovers. Perhaps she had a plan, Mozden thought, though what that plan might be she couldn't imagine, since they were trapped on a planet that wouldn't support them with only minimal supplies. 'Nadine,' she said, 'what's your . . .'

Nadine's head jerked up at the sound of her name, and she ran to the operational rover and started to drive away. She hadn't finished unhooking the tow line, so the second rover followed, slowing her acceleration up the bowl of the hand.

'Nadine, stop!' Vera yelled, running a few steps ahead.

'What did she take?' Mozden's first thought was that Nadine had taken off with all their supplies. But, looking at the scattered piles on the ground, she knew that wasn't true. The remaining four breathers were still there, as well as the spare oxygen packs, several large canisters of water and four cases of food packets.

'I don't know,' Vera said, beginning again to run.

The sense of urgency overtaking her, Mozden ran after him in big, loping strides. Nadine headed up the side of the depression.

She stopped just short of the rim, near two of the great fingers that stretched up out of the ground. She took something long and narrow out of the back of the rover.

'Rocket launcher,' Vera said.

They ran faster. Nadine balanced the launcher on her shoulder and aimed it at the nearest finger, only about fifteen metres away.

'You're too close!' Vera yelled.

Nadine took the launcher off her shoulder and studied it, as if she'd been unable to fire it. Mozden realized she'd forgotten to pull the safety cord. They were only perhaps thirty metres away now, Vera slightly ahead of her.

Nadine pulled the cord, returned the launcher to her shoulder.

'No, Nadine!' she yelled. Vera made a dive for her. Then the rocket launcher went off. Nadine's aim, at such close range, was good. The rocket hit the finger about four metres off the ground, and in a brilliant flash of light and a huge, echoing boom the section around the rocket exploded, shooting out in great sheets and fragments.

A sheet slammed Mozden to the ground, the oxygen pack jamming into her spine. As she lay beneath it, dazed, a hail of shards rained down. She drew her arms in to her sides, her breath coming in hard short gasps. The ground shuddered with a thunderous impact, and she spread her palms flat against the planet's surface, as if to hold on. A huge chunk of the finger must have fallen.

And then came the silence that followed a huge concussion of sound, empty, like deafness. Shaking, she pulled herself out from under the sheet. Nadine lay a short distance away. Mozden crawled through sculpture fragments towards her. 'Nadine! Nadine! Are you OK?'

Nadine pushed herself into a kneeling position, her back curved. Her voice was part murmur, part growl, as her lips chewed out the words. 'I'm going to force them to cast me out. Or I'm going to destroy this place trying.' She picked up the rocket launcher and reloaded. Mozden grabbed the weapon, wrestled it away from her. The arms of Nadine's jumpsuit were peppered with blood.

Nadine grabbed up a chunk of the sculpture and staggered to her feet. Mozden thought for a moment that Nadine was going to attack her with it, but instead Nadine stumbled through the rubble to the mangled, incomplete finger and began to pound on it.

Mozden was about to go after her when she caught a glimpse of Vera. He'd been on the far side of Nadine, and she'd forgotten about him for a few seconds. He lay on his back unmoving, arms and legs tossed in crash-test-dummy positions. Below the base of his breather protruded a thin reddish-copper shard that had sliced through his throat.

Mozden didn't think she would move again. She felt anchored to the planet, as if this were her place, she a sculpture grown out of the planet's surface. The planet turned. The wind blew. The shadows lengthened. The heat faded. She could stay in this cocoon of shock until her oxygen ran out. It would be easy. She had lived a coward's life. Time now to die a coward's death. But there was that constant pounding to deal with. It bothered her. She forced herself to speak. 'Nadine,' she said. 'Nadine.'

But Nadine continued to pound at the huge, broken sculpture. In the twilight, blood soaked the arms of her jumpsuit.

'I'm going,' Mozden said. She found her legs wobbly and undependable, as if she'd forgotten how to use them. But with each step they seemed to strengthen. She unfastened the tow line between the rovers, got into the lead rover, and drove it down the shimmering side of the hand back towards the lander. The echoing pounding followed her.

In the shadow of the setting sun, the ship looked alien. Only scattered patches of black and grey interrupted the smooth, reddish-copper surface. The near side had melted down to the ground, and it looked almost as if the planet had thrown a carpet over the lander, absorbing and subsuming any materials it could not convert. The shape still gave off the vague sense of a nose and a tail, but the wings were totally gone, and the rest had lost the symmetry characteristic of the lander. Although she could still partially see the ship in it, she could also partially see something else, a form still taking shape. In its incompleteness, it seemed to reflect its former occupants: their neediness, their emptiness, their tragic inability to deal with beauty. Her head felt tight and hot, and the tears started once again.

As she drove around to the far side of the ship, still bathed in the setting sun, she saw that this side had not melted into the ground. A hollow had formed under one part of the ship. In it, against the shimmering surface of the ground, lay Commander Katrack's naked body, extruded and avoided by the transforming ship. Human life was foreign to it: incompatible, inferior. Yet not irrelevant.

She had wondered before if the planet even knew they

Negative Space

were here. Katrack had given her the answer. It had rejected him. And in rejecting him, it had acknowledged him.

Mozden packed up all the supplies she thought she might use. They could last her three weeks, if they didn't get infected. If they did, or they already were, she had a few days at most. She didn't know if that would be enough time. She'd sensed it when she'd driven through the sculptures that night with Katrack, and again when she'd seen the hemispherical sculpture – the unity of all the sculpture on the planet. They were not a series of disconnected shapes covering the surface; they were one shape: one massive, complex, multi-faceted sculpture. The desperate hand breaking out of the hemisphere related to the yearning hand here, which related to the figure in pain they'd found beyond the rim, which related to the city of peace. The emotions of each connected to the emotions of the others, combining to create an overwhelming whole. She didn't know enough about art to explain it, but she sensed it, deep in the place where she sensed the planet spinning beneath her, the rush of winds over its surface, the surging heat below, the blooming life of the micro-organisms, the delicate fingers of magma directing them carefully, deliberately. Perhaps those fingers yearned to touch the sky, or fought to break free; perhaps they dreamt a million different dreams in their deep and hidden hearts. She only wished there were time enough to understand.

Nadine had claimed that the viewer of art entered into a reciprocal communication with the piece of sculpture, the artist's subconscious communicating with the viewer's subconscious. If that were true, then in studying enough of the sculpture, she could perhaps begin to understand the artist behind it. The power and beauty embodied in these shapes had touched her, had at times overwhelmed her. If she could only assimilate enough of it, perhaps she could in some small way achieve communion with the planet, the communion she had always sensed possible but just beyond her reach. Perhaps she could break through and grab the hand on the other side. She did not wish to fill her emptiness as Garth had, to surrender in the face of beauty as a passive awestruck spectator. But if sculpture and space existed only in relation to each other, then perhaps she was the emptiness in relation to which the sculpture had meaning.

Tears running down her cheeks, Mozden climbed into the rover and drove up, out of the hand, into darkness.

**Negative Space
Acknowledgements**

I'd like to thank Dr Howard Mayne, Dr Stephanie Ross, Dr Andy Michael, Dr Tom Laue, Dr Gary Day, Dr Paul Viscuso, Dr Eugene Boudette, M. Mitchell Marmel, Tom Thatcher, David Loffredo, Jim Batka, David Fish, Barry Barker and James Harold for sharing their scientific expertise. I'd also like to thank Lee Smith, Mark Stafford, Judith Hardin, Barnaby Rapoport, JoAnn Forgit and Jim Mortimore for their helpful critiques. And thanks to my husband, Michael Flint, for advising me on the artistic aspects of this story.

Dome of Whispers

By Ian Watson

'Welcome to the Dome of Whispers, star-stranger. I am Istinbat. Please let me assure myself that you carry no recording devices or other instruments. The visitor to the Dome of Whispers may bring only himself, or herself . . .

'You may leave your wrist computer here. No one will touch it.'

The burly man shed his bracelet, and Istinbat placed it on a shelf. The shelf was otherwise empty; there were no other visitors yet. Perhaps there would be no others.

Istinbat looked out from the doorway briefly, imagining the splendid view of the Dome, golden in the morning sun, that this stranger must have enjoyed as he approached up the road from Wakil City. The Dome rose three hundred metres at its zenith, and was a full kilometre around its base. The area immediately surrounding it was paved in turquoise marble, well worn by the scuff of countless feet down the millennia – though this was one of those centuries when the number of feet was more easily countable. Just off the marble stood a line of hutches, where vendors – poor brown folk with flashing teeth – were only just now putting up their shutters, to hawk their holopictures, spiced buns, wine flasks, fresh fruit, bowls of spiced goat's-meat stew. Mainly they supplied the guardians of the Dome with food and drink; tourists were only a sideline. A stall concession at the Dome was a rare prize for a poor man; and only to a poor man would it go by tradition. The stallholders would bring the food and drink over when a bell tolled. Istinbat himself had not stepped outside the doorway for perhaps a year.

The burly man fidgeted.

With a shrug, Istinbat turned from the doorway to the outside world. He pulled a cord which would summon another guardian from the catacomb quarters underneath the Dome. Twitching a taper alight, he preceded the visitor down the flight of steps into the long downward tunnel leading to below the mid-point of the Dome.

Istinbat was a tall thin man, with a long nose, thin pursed lips and eyes of a startling violet hue: the face of a sucking insect. His head was shorn, and he had a creamy skin, much lighter than the norm on this world, blanched by long attendance in the Dome. He held the taper high, and thus they proceeded down the tunnel in a cocoon of light.

'Will you be staying in the Dome with me?' asked the visitor idly enough, though the answer obviously mattered to him intensely.

'A guardian has to stay – though not intrude. I shall station myself a fair way off. You may take as long as you like. All day, till dusk. I shall not get bored, with all the voices speaking to me. I have hardly heard the same one twice, in all my years since I was a boy.'

'Hmm,' said the visitor. Obviously the answer pleased him. What private message was he hoping to hear – or to leave – in the Dome? Yet this was no concern of Istinbat's, except in so far as it had been a very long time since anyone had come to the Dome from another world with a specific purpose beyond simple curiosity.

As they walked, a second cocoon of light approached them. A similar tall robed figure – the woman Tasamma – glided past, with a nod to Istinbat, as routinely as an ascending funicular railway cab passes a descending one midway.

The tunnel opened into a large circular chamber, with several brass-bound doors beyond which were the labyrinths of living quarters, and burial places. Once, there had been a hundred guardians. Now there were scarcely twenty.

A well-worn spiral stone stairway led up into the Dome itself. Istinbat held the taper well clear of his body to illuminate the steps; there were a hundred of these.

He noticed that the visitor did not puff or wheeze as he climbed.

As the man stepped up into the centre of the great bare floor of the Dome, Istinbat twitched out the taper. It was luminous enough inside. Light diffused from the translucent eye of the Dome, and from similarly translucent blocks inset at regular intervals high around the walls – or rather, the one wall. Faintly, from that all-encompassing wall, the massed

Dome of Whispers

echo of the whispers came to their ears like the distant susurrus of the sea. Istinbat wondered what the wall would say to him today . . .

In the southern hemisphere of the planet Suf stood this famous Dome of Whispers: famous in the sense that it was the only thing by which most star people remembered the planet Suf these days. Much turbulent history had flowed through Suf down the millennia – and ebbed away again, leaving Suf to its own private weave of events, of which nowadays only a few threads remained. Yet Suf still ticked on, even though the clock (as they said locally) had no hands; and the old Dome endured, though comparatively little visited except by those native to Suf.

While it still stood, the Dome remained one of the most remarkable buildings in all the star worlds; for it had the most peculiar acoustics of any building ever raised.

Whispering galleries existed elsewhere: places where you spoke softly and your companion heard you clearly hundreds of metres away around the building. But in the Dome of Whispers, alone, no utterance was ever lost. Whatever was spoken there continued on around the Dome for ever, quietly, undiminished.

This building of perfect proportions acted as a superconductor – not of electrical current, but of sound waves. Perhaps there really was something superconductive about the unique quartz-veined marble of which it was built – and something piezoelectric too; perhaps the slight compression caused by the impact of sound waves set up a current which stored and reproduced the spoken word again and again around the Dome. Perhaps. The guardians of the Dome had never permitted anyone to take the smallest flake of a sample away nor bring any kind of mechanical or electronic instrument into the Dome. It was all that the Sufish had, this Dome. Better that it should remain a prodigy, a marvel, than be explained away.

For millennia past the people of Suf, both common and uncommon, and intermittently the people of other star worlds (generally uncommon) had come here to whisper the secret of their lives or a confession or a prophecy. They had come to swear a binding oath or a love pledge or a vow of revenge. They had come to immortalize – for as long as the Dome endured – their own insight into the meaning of life.

During periods of Sufish decadence, the Dome had been used as an oracle . . .

Around the perimeter of the floor stood various mobile ladders resembling pieces of ancient siege gear. Their wheels rested on a track running right around the circuit of the wall. These ladder towers leant backward precariously, balanced on a support leg which wheeled along an inner track.

'I expected it would be noisier,' said the visitor. 'Uh . . . should I speak?'

'It's all right to speak here. Beyond the black marble line, three metres from the wall, is where the effect occurs. You can speak anywhere within those three metres, and be recorded at that very point in the air. We don't really know how large the capacity is – certainly not infinite – therefore each visitor may make only one statement, and then he must withdraw.'

'But you said that I could –'

'You may *listen* for as long as you like. With sealed lips. When you remove the seal, you may speak just once. Most people only have one real thing that they need to say.' Istinbat plunged a hand into his robes and produced a strip of adhesive bandage. 'I am accustomed to silence, but I must ask all visitors to seal their lips during the Listening, till they wish to speak.'

The visitor nodded. 'Only one real thing to say . . . or to hear – it's quite true.'

And what is your real thing? wondered Istinbat.

The visitor stared around the Dome. Twelve metres above the floor was a continuous inscription cut in an angular script; it ran around the whole circuit of the wall. The inscription was repeated exactly in the black marble of the boundary line. The visitor pointed at it, sweeping his finger along.

'It is the whole of the ancient poem known as the *Ruby Yat*,' said Istinbat, 'in the old script of Suf. A poem on the theme of mutability and eternity. Very few people can read the old Sufish script these days. Lovers sometimes match up the angles of the letters, above and below on the floor, as a way of marking where they pledged their love. They copy down the piece of text, without understanding it. Even so, it might take them quite some time to find the exact point where they spoke, and the exact angle of their lips.'

'But can you read it?'

'Oh yes, that is something else that we guard: a knowledge of the sounds of those letters.'

'Will you read some of it for me? Please. I will pay you generously.'

'Why should I need money? But I will read it, if you wish. Come, we will walk to the beginning.'

'No, I already know the *Ruby Yat* by heart. I am looking for one particular passage.'

'So, a friend has been here, perhaps? It's unusual, to know the *Ruby Yat* by heart.'

'It's handed down . . . in my family. But this is the only example of the old script left.'

What family would that be? wondered Istinbat. Was this man a scholar?

Historians from off-planet had, from time to time, eavesdropped on one voice, then another, then the one after . . . sifting the equivalent of a ton of ordinary potsherds to find, by chance, one golden brooch or King's insignia, one historic confession or vow. They soon gave up, their heads full of peasant love-words, verbal graffiti, portentous statements by the totally forgotten.

'What passage?' he asked.

And the visitor recited:

' *"Of my Base Metal may be filed a Key*
That shall unlock the Door to Paradise." '

'But that's wrong,' said Istinbat. 'It should be:

"Of my Base Metal may be filed a Key
That shall unlock the Door he howls without." '

The man's face darkened. 'Yes, yes, of course it is. How stupid of me.'

'But if you memorize the whole poem, in your family . . .?

I suppose changes creep in. Corruptions of the text.'

'Yes, yes, they creep in.'

'But you knew you had made a mistake.' Istinbat thought briefly. 'Where the text diverges, is that where you expect to find the message waiting for you?'

'Just show me where those words are, will you?'

'I am doing you a favour, star-stranger . . .'

'And you don't want money. What do you want?'

'Why, I am curious. Events do not happen on Suf these days. I have a feeling that this is an event.' Istinbat felt a curious sensation, of *power*. It was an unusual sensation, and not one that he particularly cared for. This burly visitor was, perhaps, accustomed to power . . . or else he remembered power. Here, however, amidst the tide of voices, he was powerless.

'But aren't you vowed to silence . . . Istinbat?' The visitor had named him, to forge a relationship.

'Yes. But at the same time a guardian feels curiosity about the myriads of voices he hears.'

'If only he could identify one of them, is that it?'

Istinbat chuckled dryly. 'Most people identify themselves. Right here is their immortality. I will show you. Seal your lips. You may reflect upon the phenomenon of the Needle and the Haystack.'

'But you said you would stand a fair way off.'

'And now you have involved me.'

Once across the black marble strip, it was like dialling through the air-bands of an enormous radio, catching a word here, a phrase there, half a sentence – switched away by the least movement on their part. Here was the archaeological deep litter of thousands of years, compressed into three metres of whispering air, every millimetre of which clamoured for attention, begging to be heard.

Yet unlike an archaeological site, here there was no depth yardstick of time. So here was a plea out of the deeps of time . . . perhaps. Here, next to it, was a promise from last year . . . perhaps again. There was no discernible difference in the signal strength. It did not matter whether the original speakers had cried out loudly or murmured most quietly. Each whisper

Dome of Whispers

had the same strength as the next. Nor did they overlap, however crowded together they were. No one talked anyone else down. Each whisper was equal.

The visitor moved as if he was moving through treacle, though actually there was no resistance except for the drag of fascination.

He moved his head in tiny quantum jumps from one whisper to the next. Ah yes, one heard with the left ear or the right ear . . . but never with both at once. One heard *inside* the ear.

'Orelda, thee I love for ever . . .' Dust.

'. . . yaum el-nnushur . . .' Unknowable.

'. . . anda klath impto hoptu vendi saa . . .' What language?

An alien hissing and croaking, never from a human throat . . .

'I swear my vengeance upon Satpat and all his heirs, by all of mine, for as long as our revenge is renewed in this iota of ever-air . . .' How long did that blood feud last for? Or had it merely just begun?

A nervous giggle: *'Well, what do I say?'*

A crisp voice: *'This is Sully Hoberman from Alpha C in the Suf year 5079. The proof of Galois' last theorem, which I have now found is as follows . . .'* Was Sully Hoberman right or wrong? Who knew? Who remembered?

A primping voice: *'I, Marquis Enderby, will now recite my prizewinning ode which placed first in the Concourse of Poetry at Middlestar . . .'*

'I'll marry Lala whatever her dad says . . .'

And on. And on. An infinity of voices.

Well, not an infinity, but very many.

Istinbat let the stranger listen for ten or fifteen minutes, then laid a hand on his arm and nodded him back across the black marble strip. Gently, he detached the adhesive strip from the man's lips.

'Now will you satisfy my curiosity, star-stranger?'

The visitor glanced around the Dome again, confirming that it was still empty but for the two of them. He flexed his hands. Strong hands they were.

'I suppose I shall have to!'

And this the stranger proceeded to do; and it began to dawn on Istinbat that he had put himself in danger of his life. Surely no one would attempt to murder a guardian in the very Dome itself? Still, as the man spoke, Istinbat measured himself against him . . . unable, even so, to bring himself to call a halt to the stranger's words. For this was the Event, and it seemed as though Istinbat had been waiting out his whole life to connect with this moment . . . of History.

The Empire of Tajalam, at its height a thousand years earlier, spanned seven worlds in the Praesepe Cluster, that mass of stars five hundred light years from old Earth for which the fanciful old Earth-Chinese name was 'the exhalation of piled-up corpses'. Regarded with an unromantic eye, Tajalam's Empire seemed amply to merit the Chinese description. Yet, despite his barbarities, Tajalam had been a remarkable character who persisted in sending out expedition after expedition into deepest space long after all other exploration and pioneering had slowed to a snail's pace.

He was searching for no less than Paradise. A Paradise planet, which he believed must exist somewhere among the millions of suns.

Perhaps it had to exist, simply to counterbalance the hell of Praesepe.

And Paradise had been found – somewhere – by the last and smallest expedition. No doubt it spoke volumes for the loyalty that Tajalam inspired, or the terror he induced, that the expedition came back at all to tell him. Probably the former, since by then his Empire was crashing about his head, and he was on the run. Apparently he ran by way of

Dome of Whispers

Suf, before eventually committing suicide with his ritual ruler's sword in the city of Qalb on Usul. From some personal quirk – which those of his descendants who survived the pursuing wolves had enshrined as a tradition – Tajalam had adopted the *Ruby Yat* as the basis of his private battle-code and cipher system.

It was a strict part of Praesepe culture that a dead ruler's sword should be preserved in public for evermore. In Tajalam's case, his enemies might have felt like melting it down – but not when it was stained with his own blood. That final act of his had sealed the sword into the stone of history for ever. Thus his victorious enemies took the sword back with them to Praesepe Prime, where it lay in their central museum these days.

That sword had an inscription on it: the words that had pierced his heart . . .

'We didn't find *that* out, Istinbat . . . not for nine hundred years. We were scattered to the stars, as far from Praesepe as possible, living under new names, often living in poverty.'

'We?'

'The direct line of Tajalam. It's *unusual* for a ritual ruler's sword to have an inscription on it, you see. We believe the words were inscribed shortly before he killed himself, and sometime after he passed through Suf. They were a message to his heirs, which his immediate heirs never received.'

'They were the key to the paradise planet?'

'Exactly. And it's here. The celestial coordinates to Paradise are here. Now I've slaked your thirsty curiosity, perhaps you would tell me –' the visitor gestured impatiently '– *approximately* where?'

'I will have to remain alive afterwards,' said Istinbat, hoping that he did not sound as though he was begging for his life. Though how could he ensure that he remained alive?

No doubt, in the last thousand years, Tajalam's line had become more settled in their ways, less inclined to produce exhalations of piled-up corpses. In some not-unpleasant respects, the human galaxy had run out of energy.

The visitor laughed.

'We shall see, Istinbat. We shall see.'

'You will swear it, by ... yes, by the blood of your ancestors. Or I will not tell you where to listen.'

'Oh, very well. I so swear that you shall live ... if you can call this living.'

'Do not despise the Dome, star-stranger. Has it not kept Tajalam's secret for you for a thousand years?'

'Yes, actually that's the only good reason for its existence! Plus, I suppose, the luring of a few scraps of trade to this backwater.'

Istinbat shook his head.

'There's more than that. Much more. Here is the essence of hundreds of millions of people. Here is the last surviving breath of their souls, now that they are dead. True, some are vain and some are fatuous, but it is what they were. And that's enough.'

'The door, man! Unlock the door. Now!'

Istinbat considered the inscription, then led the visitor halfway around the Dome. With his foot he tapped the end of one word in the black marble. With his finger he pointed to the corresponding word above. With a mocking grin, the visitor retrieved the bandage from Istinbat's hand and stuck it back over his lips. Slowly, very slowly, he moved forward.

Supremely alert, the burly man sifted through a thousand voices – confident, petulant, brash, boastful, yearning – before one harsh, regal voice spoke to him; and he froze utterly. Until now, for an hour and more, he had been moving in infinite slow motion. Now he did not move at all. He was a statue.

'I am Tajalam,' said the voice. 'My son! My heir Tajasanid!'

But Tajasanid, son of Tajalam, was dead a thousand years since – caught by the wolves, in disguise, on Praesepe Prime itself.

'You seek the key that will unlock the door to Paradise, as I sought it too. Meanwhile, the enemies increase. The assassins bestir themselves. The carrion fowl gather. I know you, my son, and I love you. How to save you from yourself, as I was never saved from myself? Let me tell you, Tajasanid, that the forging of an empire is simply *forgery*. It is the production of counterfeit – whereas a single man may become true gold himself. Remember our battle-code command for wreaking havoc and laying waste a world: "Wilderness is Paradise enough!" There is no alien paradise planet to inherit, my son, except for the Paradise that you will make for yourself in the wilderness of exile, and simplicity. Howl now, my heir, but heed my words in time. I hope you will learn how wilderness may be truly paradise enough. I learnt it too late – but I shall write it in my blood for you to find. This is my legacy. Farewell – and blessings!'

The visitor tore the seal from his lips, and howled. He hit out at the air, as though he could strike Tajalam himself across the face, but his blows only met air.

Before Istinbat could intervene, the visitor stepped back across the black marble strip of his own accord.

Controlling himself, the visitor said to the guardian, 'Didn't I say that there was only one good reason for this Dome's existence? Well, didn't I?'

'What did Tajalam say to you?'

The visitor spat on the floor.

'Barbarian wisdom! Now that that single reason has gone, my friend, and now that the reason for my own life has gone together with it . . . well, I did promise you your life, and there's small reason to break my promise now! So be warned, do not remain in this Dome today. This Dome is a trap for fools – for millions of idiots. Here is the temple of folly of all the galaxy. I do not suffer fools gladly, even though I am one myself.'

The visitor strode away towards the mouth of the spiral stairway.

'What do you mean to do?' cried Istinbat, hurrying after him.

'I shall put an end to folly, honourably, as Tajalam put an end to his own folly. Stay out of this Dome!'

'But I *guard* this Dome.'

'Guard it from the outer doorway, then!'

'What can one man do?' Istinbat laughed. He twitched his taper alight again. 'I am a fool too. I thought this was an Event. It is no event at all. Nor are your threats an event. You did not even speak them aloud, so that future visitors can hear and wonder. You only howled like a beast. Your howl whispers round the wall for ever, now, until time wears the Dome away.'

Istinbat reached the base of the stairway, where the visitor was necessarily forced to wait for his way to be lit. Istinbat led him quickly along the tunnel.

'I have told you,' the visitor repeated. 'You, who wish for an Event. I promise you there will be an Event.'

Ignoring the woman Tasamma, sitting inside the doorway, the visitor retrieved his computer bracelet and strode away, brushing aside a few brown people with flashing teeth who rushed to him from their stalls.

Istinbat watched him go. The visitor did not look back.

Half an hour later, still sitting together in golden silence, Istinbat and Tasamma saw a small hyperboat rise up into the cloudless sky from the desert beyond Wakil City. But it did not shrink to a speck, disappearing into space. Instead, it arced above the city on a tight parabola, curving back down towards them.

'It's out of control!' cried Tasamma.

Istinbat dragged her down the stone steps into the darkness of the tunnel. They huddled where they fell.

A moment later came the crash of the explosion: an almighty thunder-shout. The tunnel floor ripped under them. A single brick fell on to Istinbat's back. Dust choked their lungs.

Coughing, they staggered back up the steps again and out on to the turquoise marble space, where vendors were running and crying out, though all apparently unhurt. The rise of the Dome above them was intact. However, as Istinbat and Tasamma ran together around it, keeping a long way from its base, they saw that the whole western quadrant had been demolished. Pieces of marble had been tossed about the sands by the force of the explosion. The remains of the hyperboat, scattered widely, were recognizable only because they were steel, not stone. The Dome was a great yawning cave now – a broken golden egg.

As Istinbat trotted towards the great hole, a voice assailed his ears, fleetingly.

Dome of Whispers

    '*I'll marry Lala whatever* . . .'

    And another: '*Khalwat dar anjuman* . . .'

    And a third: '*I, Seloose of Vega, swear* . . .'

He stopped, appalled, bewildered. Tasamma stopped too, cocking her tall thin head.

The voices were all escaping into Suf, flying out of the hatched egg of the Dome as though from a Pandora's Box, spreading and reproducing themselves throughout the suddenly increased atmospheric volume. The phenomenon was as enigmatic, to Istinbat's mind, as the Dome itself had been.

Alone, he scrambled over the banks of rubble in the face of a tidal bore of voices, into the mouth of the cave.

He was nearly driven back by the pressure of noise, but then quite suddenly the voices became a trickle, and ceased – the flood had flowed past him.

Istinbat stepped down onto the floor of the Dome, and hurried towards the nearest intact stretch of wall. He crossed the black marble strip, and found only silence there.

Which is why the planet Suf is known as the Whispering World, or the Ghost World, nowadays; and why the brown people with flashing teeth wear plugs of wax in their ears and converse in sign language; and why more tourists pay visits to Suf, to be haunted. Generally the constant haunting is too much for the curious tourists, so that after the first five or six hours they will seek refuge in the inappropriately named Dome of Whispers, where alone in all that world there is utter silence.

That silence has its guardians, who will not as a rule let visitors so much as whisper anywhere inside their fractured holy place. Though sometimes, for a truly golden consideration, they will allow a person to shout aloud and hear his or her voice vanish utterly without even an echo.

Nowadays there are a hundred guardians. People are eager to escape all the whispers in the world.

Waters-of-Starlight

By Stephen Marley

The Mississippi, black as night, brimmed with stars.

River Woman, arms upraised, lamented on the muddy banks of the star-reflecting waters. Her grief, arrowed to the keenest aim, launched the funeral canoe out on to the river as she chanted a Delaware death song, her sorrow guiding the death boat downstream on its journey to the sea.

Inside the hide-covered canoe lay the corpse of Voice-of-Thunder, the long, stitched scar on his left breast a testament to his murder – heart cut out by a tomahawk.

Death song concluded, she watched as the funeral craft reached the bend in the river and glided out of sight into the southern shadows.

'Farewell, chief of Twilight Owl clan. Farewell – my husband.'

Pale Wolf, brother of Voice-of-Thunder, sat cross-legged at her feet, arms hugging his naked torso as he rocked back and forth. Distraught with loss, he was all Delaware brave to the last braid of his hair, despite the legacy of a million years of mixed blood in his veins. In the twelve thousand years of his life, this was the first time he had witnessed death, that rarest of events.

Her upraised arms sank slowly. So then – her husband had died after twelve millennia under the suns and moons of the ever-moving river. Of her own eight thousand years, the last three millennia had been shared with him. Voice-of-Thunder had left the small world for which his spirit had always been too large. She was alone.

With salty, reddened eyes she gazed at the Mississippi currents. Her husband had left on his last voyage, and now she must leave on hers. That was the pact they had agreed, two thousand years ago when they had flown with the wings of eagles above the sacred Black Hills of Dakota. The first to perish must be launched downriver, the one remaining must take the final path upriver. That pact had been kept secret, for the survivor would be guilty of the greatest of all crimes against mortals.

As Voice-of-Thunder rides the river to the sea I will voyage upstream to the stars – and beyond, to the edge of the real. I will commit the supreme crime.

She stepped back from the shore, her mind already set on the journey – the secret preparations, the furtive departure. No one must know – especially Pale Wolf.

Goodbye, Voice-of-Thunder. Born four thousand years before me, you lived only one life – the Delaware life. I should have died before you.

With a low sigh, she turned her back on the Mississippi.

A savage howl echoed to the sky.

The sudden outburst of Pale Wolf's anguish stopped her dead in her tracks. She spun round and was confronted with the embodiment of the man's pain.

A prolonged wailing issued from the distended oval of his mouth as his body contorted, its musculature shifting and reshaping, rough grey hairs sprouting from the heaving expanse of flesh.

Within several breaths he had shape-changed into his spirit-animal. A pale grey wolf sat by the river, howling at the stars above the cypress trees.

Raising her own eyes to the sky, she roved its dark and glitter. Another star was missing tonight: another sacrifice to the greedy Waters-of-Starlight. One by one, heaven was losing its eyes.

Time to leave the world.

She stared into the small fire as her fingers drummed out the seconds into minutes.

The flames cast a dithery illumination on the bark-skin walls of the lodge that had been winter home for Voice-of-Thunder and herself. Seated inside the domed lodge, she cast a glance at the open flap. A hundred paces distant, Pale Wolf squatted by the river, gradually reverting to human form: her brother-in-law's shape-changing never lasted long. And in a little while he would be invested as chief of Twilight Owl clan and take her as his wife.

Well, chief he would almost certainly be, but her husband

– that she would never accept. If he had any doubts of her compliance, they were small doubts; she had played her meek and mild role till she almost choked on it. In obedience to Pale Wolf's wish, she waited in her lodge for a brief talk before he left for the ceremony of chieftainship in Smoke Glade, a ritual forbidden to women. She knew what he would demand in that short talk, and she would lie accordingly. It would be easy to lie to the man she suspected of murdering her husband.

Pale Wolf, human shape almost restored, was striding across the grassy soil in her direction. She assumed a placid mask: one last act and the performance was over.

Her gaze roved the interior of the lodge. For her, it was a shell, scooped dry of substance. Inside, a nothing life, with her husband gone. And outside – across Earth's oceans and continents – a nothing life also. There was a giant, human-shaped hole in the world that nothing but Voice-of-Thunder could fill.

She bowed as Pale Wolf halted outside the lodge. 'Enter, Young Pale Wolf, brother of my husband,' she greeted formally.

She noticed, as he sat on the opposite side of the log fire, that a few tufts of wolf hair were still retracting into his flesh. 'You will address me as *Old* Pale Wolf from now on,' he said, twitchy with irritation. 'I have earned the right to become old.'

Still young in physique, lean and lupine, he had, with his brother's death, undergone a major rite of passage towards earning the privilege to be named 'old' – one who has lived life to the full. But for all his years, unlike her, he had seen death only once and experienced a single culture-identity. Four millennia younger than he, she had witnessed many deaths and lived a dozen identities, acquiring the title of *Old* River Woman. That disparity in status rankled with Pale Wolf.

'After you wear the ceremonial headdress, doubtless you will be acclaimed as Old Pale Wolf.' The diplomatic response went some way to mollifying him.

His face, a light-and-shadow play in the flutter of red flames, became introspective. 'We've given vent to our grief,' he said. 'Now let it remain in our breasts. I've lost a brother. You've lost a husband, whose murderer will be tracked down. As for the death-boat ritual, in violation of Delaware burial customs, you know my feelings on that.' He raised a palm at her unvoiced protest. 'Yes, I know – it was my brother's wish. Let no more be said of this.'

River Woman inclined her head. 'Let no more be said.'

'Then – you know why I'm here. I will take you as wife after I don the ceremonial headdress, but first I must hear the words.'

'The words?'

'The words of obedience, and of devotion. You must forget Voice-of-Thunder, and any secrets you shared with him will be shared with me.'

She was moving into hazardous territory. Tread carefully . . .

'What secrets did you have in mind?'

His mouth bent in what might have been a smile. 'Did you two ever talk of journeying on the river of the heavens – the Waters-of-Starlight?'

She kept her expression composed, although her heart missed a beat. Did he know? No – he couldn't have guessed her plans.

'There may have been talk,' she said offhandedly, 'but that's all.'

He gave a slight nod. 'My brother talked to me, too. He'd often muse on the Seven Millennia and the creation of the Waters-of-Starlight. What must it have been like back in those seven millennia of technology – he used to ask – when humans lived barely a century, looking at the stars and wondering if humanity would ever reach them? The thought of death must have been the background of every life in those days.'

She shrugged her shoulders. 'All that was a million years ago. Or two million, or . . .'

He gave a grim chuckle. 'I know – after a million years of recorded history, you stop counting. What's the point? Everything has been said and done a million times. What's there to do in the twilight of the Great World of galaxies and nebulae but dance and hunt and play?'

'Yes,' she replied. 'What else?'

'So,' he said, 'there will be no more stories of the Waters-of-Starlight, and of its final river bend into the crack in the Great World's walls. The Great World of a billion galaxies is truly our mother and we belong with her. What do you say?'

She met his gaze, stare for stare. She sensed that the wrong answer could mean her death at his hands, here, now. 'I'm a true daughter of the Great World Mother. If you forbid all mention of the Waters-of-Starlight, you have my support – as befits a devoted wife.'

'And do you swear that you and my brother never intended to sail the river of the heavens?'

'Even if my husband had voyaged down that river, I would not.'

He broke into a grin. 'Yes, I can see the truth of it in your eyes. I've acquired the insight of the old, I really have. You're wiser than my brother was, dreaming of his unknown worlds. Yes, you'll make a good wife. Half-breed though you are, you've lived many centuries as a Delaware and you know how rich our life is. For us, everything is alive, from boulder to buffalo. Each object has its *manitou*, its intrinsic spirit. We hear the language of the trees and the speech of the rivers.'

River Woman lifted her hands. 'It's a rich life.'

His grin broadening, he rose to his feet. 'I had a small doubt of you, but you've dispelled it. I'll return as chief, and you will be my wife. Remain in the lodge until then.' After a farewell wave, be left with long, loping strides.

She sat with head bowed as his footfalls receded into silence. The silence lengthened. Her fingers resumed drumming out the seconds.

Be patient just a moment longer. Wait till he's well clear.

Her fingers stopped their drumming.

Pale Wolf will be in the southern woods by now on the way to Smoke Glade and the start of the ceremony.

'Now!'

She sprang up and sprinted out the lodge, her moccasins padding the grassy soil fringing the river. She swerved north towards the black congregations of trees.

Run-run-run . . . if you want to keep your heart beating in its chest.

She maintained a rapid pace as she headed for the northern woods. In the deeps of those trees was a canoe secreted by a creek, her way out of the world.

All she needed to break free was an hour. A little hour.

Pale Wolf sprawled outside the ring of Twilight Owl clan elders who huddled in blankets around a blazing log fire in the middle of Smoke Glade.

Lonely Elk the medicine man, head and shoulders draped with antlered elk skin, stomped around the clan circle, mumbling a wordless preamble to the lineage recital. After the brief recital would come the protracted ceremony of conferring chieftainship.

The medicine man halted his muttering and danced into the circle of elders until he was two paces from the fire. Then he began a slow outward spiral as he intoned the lineage recital.

'The time of the Seven Millennia began with the folk of Sumer in the Land of the Two Rivers. Then the folk of Egypt raised their pyramids and man-headed lion statues in the Land of the Nile . . .'

Pale Wolf shifted uneasily. This should have been the shining hour of his life, but he was troubled by a ghost. Behind his eyes, the spectre of Voice-of-Thunder rose from the waters, breast wound gaping, mouth stretched to condemn Pale Wolf as kinslayer. True enough, kinslayer he was, and even though the killing was done out of duty to the Great Mother, the horror of the act was stark and the ensuing grief bitter.

And then there was River Woman. Less than a half-hour ago he had left her lodge, certain that she nursed no suspicion of his guilt. But, despite her black hair and smooth skin and bright eyes, she was old in experience, with the power of the old to outwit and deceive. He had slain Voice-of-Thunder for planning the Great Desertion, fleeing the Mother by way of the Waters-of-Starlight. Could he be sure that River Woman wasn't engaged on the same enterprise?

He was almost convinced of her innocence, but was he *sure*?

No – he wasn't.

Lonely Elk's strengthening voice rose into the night.

'In the fourth millennium the eagle standards of Rome rose and fell and the Han Empire of China reached –'

Pale Wolf sprang up. 'Lonely Elk! Come here!'

The medicine man pulled to a halt, shocked at the flagrant breach of custom. Wary of Pale Wolf's natural authority, the elders restricted their disapproval to a shake of the head as Lonely Elk trudged out of the circle to the young warrior.

Pale Wolf pointed at Lonely Elk's medicine bag. 'Take that magic of yours and send out the Lightning-that-Sees. I want River Woman kept under watch.'

He waved away Lonely Elk's protests. 'It won't take you many moments. Here –' He reached into his pouch. 'Here's a lock of her hair for the lightning to know whom it seeks.'

Run-run-run.

Keep running and don't think of what might be following, she urged herself. Don't think of the punishment for the Great Desertion.

More than halfway to the creek and the canoe.

The trail veered sharply to the right, and through a break in the trees she glimpsed a small glade. With that glimpse daylight memory sun-flashed in the night.

Wind-of-Leaves Glade. It was there, three thousand years ago, she first met Voice-of-Thunder. She had just changed from a Chinese princess of the Empire of Harmonies to a Delaware squaw – although, as he'd pointed out, she was dressed as an Apache. Not that he cared about ancestral dress and customs, whose details were lost after a million years and more. On all the planets the nine root races had reverted to genotypes as the structure of the cosmos began to weaken, seeking solace in dubious racial origins while the Great World ran down to its end.

'Half-breed,' she muttered, recalling Pale Wolf's sneering reference to her.

We're all half-breeds, Pale Wolf. We're Delaware and Iroquois, Chinook and Cheyenne, Sioux and Apache. And we're European and Arabian, Mayan and Malaysian, African and Chinese, as well as blood from the rest of the Nine Races of the Great World.

Waters-of-Starlight

She left the trail, following a jagged path through dense woodland. From here, the ground dipped all the way to her destination. A short distance, then she'd be in the canoe and protected by the *manitou* of the Father of Waters. Her feet padding softly on the loamy soil, River Woman sped lightfoot through the congealed shadows of trees.

The night sky blazed into blinding light, exposing every detail of her surroundings. She shut her eyes against the glare. It was like sheet lightning, but prolonged and lacking the accompaniment of thunder.

It was the Lightning-that-Sees.

Her heart turned to stone and sank. Pale Wolf had ordered that the lightning seek her out. She hadn't entirely fooled him back in the lodge.

'I should have known.'

The glare blinked out and she opened her eyes. Her vision sparked as she glanced up at the sky.

For a time, the sky was calm starlight. Her legs beating a steady pace, she began to hope. A few hundred strides and she'd reach the canoe.

The starry calm was shattered by a soundless stab of forked lightning. It crazed a blue path aimed at her head.

The Lightning-that-Sees had tracked her down.

Lonely Elk kept up a monotonous chant in his slow, spiral dance around the fire.

'In the sixth millennium the folk of Earth left Mother Earth, and walked on the moon and the small world of Mars . . .'

Pale Wolf could barely watch the ceremony. Not until he was certain that River Woman was in the lodge, where she belonged, would his spirit be still. In his groin, his arms, his mouth, he wanted River Woman. And he wanted her *young*. No more title of Old River Woman, for all that she had lived in several myth pools – Crystal Egyptian, Polar Inca, Twilight Celt, Imperial Harmonies Chinese. She was young, and desirable and –

He gave a start as the sky lit up with a sheet of silent lightning.

The medicine man continued his chant without missing a beat:

'In the seventh millennium the folk of Earth met the first of the Great World's other root races, and began the creation of the Waters-of-Starlight, known in those days as one of the wonders of the universe. Then all the Nine Races were united. Thus ended the seventh millennium, the end of technology, and the beginning of thought-shaping. Thus began the time of the Waters-of-Starlight . . .'

Pale Wolf tightened his lips. The Waters-of-Starlight wouldn't be mentioned after he was chief, even though he had once dream-hunted on its earthly branches. The lure of arcing away from the homeworld tributaries on to the high river to the stars that led to the crack in the Great World was too great a temptation. He would remove that temptation by making all spirit-river travel taboo. Then none of Twilight Owl clan could ape the departure of the gods, those of humankind, eons past, who had chosen to become spirit energy, invisible, impalpable. Unhuman. The last of those gods had deserted the Great World Mother through the gap in her walls long ages ago. Let no mortal follow . . .

I had to kill you, brother. Don't you see that? You betrayed the Mother.

He shook from his head the memory of a tomahawk and blood gushing from parted flesh. His gaze strayed to the northern woods, on the lookout for the finger of the Lightning-that-Sees.

Lonely Elk neared the end of the lineage recital.

'A billion stars died in the creation of the Waters-of-Starlight. And with its creation a traveller could journey halfway across the Great World and all its galaxies in a time measured by days. And along the ever-increasing length of the River the craft of the Nine Races voyaged on currents of thought and sails of imagination. Streams and tributaries of the Waters-of-Starlight wended into the rivers of every small world. After a hundred millennia the Waters-of-Starlight interwove every region of the Great World Mother. But the River drained the Mother dry, and she aged before her time. Stars blinked out, one by one. The Great World hastened to its death . . .'

A trail of forked lightning zigzagged to the north, pointing to the whereabouts of River Woman.

Pale Wolf froze at the sight. The finger of lightning pointed well north of the lodge. He understood River Woman well enough to know that she wouldn't defy his commands lightly. She'd deserted the lodge. Was she deserting the clan and the Great Mother?

The crooked finger of light withdrew and swooped to the south, leaving her standing in the dark of the trees, trembling.

'Pale Wolf ... He knows where I am. He knows I'm deserting.'

Recovering her wits, she ran into the deep night of the woods. And there, in the night of the woods, she saw a face pale as the moon. An owl-featured moon. It glided through the trees.

'Silent Owl,' she said faintly.

The apparition in the woods was the painted face of the itinerant shaman who flitted in and out of the clan's existence like an uncanny shadow. His true name unknown, he had been dubbed Silent Owl by the Five Nations because he never spoke and always visited at night. His infrequent visitations never failed to touch her with dread: those probing, yellow eyes of his.

Silent Owl, after his apparition, disappeared into the darkness, but she still sensed the scrutiny of his tawny eyes.

Pale Wolf climbed slowly to his feet, gaze fixed on the northern woods. He was barely aware of the medicine man's chant.

She's leaving – she must be leaving.

'And at that time, there were those among mortals who became sky gods,' Lonely Elk intoned. 'They became as spirits, unseen and mighty, and bent a branch of the Waters-of-Starlight into a crack in the Great World's walls, and departed through it, never returning. But the mortals that stayed behind remained true to the Great Mother and shunned the final river bend out of the Great World. And the Nine Races gathered and decreed death for those who seek to escape the Great Mother on the Waters-of-Starlight. The Great Desertion shall be punished by the ripping out of the living heart from the chest –'

Living heart from the chest . . .

Pale Wolf swung round to the circle of elders. 'She's deserting! Deserting the Great Mother!'

The hide-covered canoe slid out of the creek into the broad expanse of the Mississippi. With an easy motion of the paddle, River Woman swerved the craft upstream, making quick progress against the gentle flow.

Voice-of-Thunder would be halfway to the ocean by now. By morning, his funeral canoe would be carried on the waves of the sea.

She glanced over her shoulder. No sign of pursuit. She might make it – there was still a chance. A few more loops in the Mississippi and she'd be beyond capture.

Ahead, the river meandered, distance on distance, for almost six thousand kilometres to the headwaters of the Mesabi ranges in the northwest of the continent. Six thousand kilometres . . . Her mouth formed a wry twist. She would soon be paddling down a river to the edge of the universe – the headwaters of existence.

The sky lit up at her back. She tensed, then relaxed. The Lightning-that-Sees had been sent out again to find her present location, but its crooked fingers would be scouring the woods: she was now part of the *manitou* of the Mississippi, and invisible to the searching fire.

Expelling a long breath, she fixed her eyes on the way ahead. As the low banks slid by she lapsed into the cadence of paddling, letting go of frets and anxieties.

The rhythmic pulse of the paddle allowed her, at last, the relief of grief.

A part of her soul had departed downstream, with Voice-of-Thunder. His absence was the absolute fact of her being. Even if she paddled to the farthest reaches of the universe, she would never find him. The Great World Mother was, for her, the emptiest of wombs.

All that remained was the pact. The one that dies goes downriver. The one that survives goes upriver, all the way to the mysterious crevice in reality. And beyond that crevice – what? Perhaps nothing. Oblivion. She would welcome that.

If it were up to her, she'd lie down and die right now.

She realized that tears were streaming down her cheeks. 'I've kept my promise,' she said. 'I've set out on the last voyage. And I'll reach that last bend in the river.'

'Where is she?' bellowed Pale Wolf, rushing to the banks of the Mississippi. 'Where has she gone?' He darted a look at the medicine man in the forefront of the assembled clan. 'Lonely Elk, what's happened to your powerful medicine, medicine man? *Where is she?*'

Lonely Elk quailed before the young man's wrath. 'The Lightning-that-Sees can no longer locate Old River Woman in the woods.'

'Then let the Lightning-that-Sees search the river! She can't have gone far.'

Lonely Elk raised his hands in a helpless gesture. 'The *manitou* of the Father of Waters will blind the eyes of the lightning.'

Pale Wolf pushed the old man aside and strode to the river's brink. He stared downstream to the south, at the spot where his brother's funeral canoe had vanished from sight. Then his eyes slanted upriver. 'She's headed for the nearest mingling with the Waters-of-Starlight – upstream.' The line of his mouth hardened. 'The Great Desertion.'

Decision made, he spun round. 'Snow Bear! High Eagle! I want a hunting party launched upstream before I count off the minutes on the fingers of one hand. Two canoes – three if possible.'

Snow Bear and High Eagle hurried about their task as the clan elders spoke in hushed voices of the appalling prospect of a Great Desertion.

Pale Wolf observed the scene with an abstracted air, mulling over the hunt's prospects.

Then Silent Owl appeared.

A thin man who might have been young or old, his face painted with an eerie white mask, seemed to emanate from nowhere, as if the air were a camouflaging cloak he folded about himself.

'Silent Owl,' Pale Wolf greeted in a flat tone, suppressing a surge of unease. 'You always arrive unbidden, and at the most timely hour. Will – will you take the third canoe?'

Silent Owl gave the most infinitesimal of nods, then glided out of sight. Pale Wolf refrained from calling commands after the departing figure. Silent Owl, who had come and gone at will over the long history of the clan, never uttering a single sound, was not one to be commanded.

Pale Wolf returned his attention to the river. With Lonely Elk and Silent Owl in the hunting party, the canoes could traverse not only the Mississippi, but the farthest reaches of the Waters-of-Starlight itself, as sanctioned by the law of the Nine Races. They were now Hunters, tracking a deserter from the Great World Mother, and they were permitted, if necessary, to follow the renegade to the last bend out of the world. Pale Wolf was confident of chasing down his prey long before then, in the tributaries of the Waters-of-Starlight, those earthbound branches he had often paddled down in younger days.

'I'll find you, River Woman.' He ground the words between his bared teeth. 'I'll find you.'

His gaze roved the Mississippi, settling on the southern bow to the nearby Atlantic. After a few moments, he spied a blurred outline that resembled a log floating on the surface.

Then he saw it for what it was, and his blood turned to red ice.

Voice-of-Thunder's funeral canoe drifted around the bend of the river, floating upstream. *Upstream* . . .

Pale Wolf's heart drummed its dread. His voice was a hoarse murmur. 'I'm sorry I killed you. Have you come back to haunt me?'

The funeral canoe glided over the moonlit currents, the waxen figure quiet within.

Noticing the currents, Pale Wolf burst into laughter, dread dispersed. River Woman had overlooked something in her hurry to escape, as had he in the heat of anger.

'Lonely Elk! Sunlight-on-Spear!' he shouted.

The medicine man hurried to his side. 'Yes?'

'Commune with the *manitou* of that canoe out there, and do it quickly. Then follow my orders to the word.'

As Lonely Elk bobbed his head in acknowledgement, Sunlight-on-Spear raced up behind the medicine man.

'Sunlight-on-Spear, hurry and fetch your bow – and

Waters-of-Starlight

prepare burning arrows,' said Pale Wolf. 'I have a task for you before we depart.'

Pale Wolf looked back at the funeral canoe.

'A gift for you, River Woman, with the river as gift-bearer.'

Mourning became as rhythmic as the stroke of the paddle, the systole and diastole of the heart. She could almost hear her sorrow as a kind of music.

She glanced up at the moon. It was past its zenith. Some two hours since she ran from the lodge. She looked ahead at the last turn in the river before it mingled with the path of stars. Ten minutes, perhaps less, before she'd be skimming along a very different river made of memories, dreams, soul substance.

These would be her last few minutes on a natural river of Earth, if this Mississippi could be called natural. It was unlikely that this was a Mississippi recognizable from the time of the Seven Millennia, when the river was first given its Algonquin name, meaning Father of Waters. Like the rest of Earth, like all the small worlds populated by the Nine Races, the river was a re-creation, fashioned almost a million years ago, and artificially preserved. Artificiality was a feature of these latter days. All that lay in the future were moot facsimiles of the remote past. The Seven Millennia had cast a long shadow over succeeding eons.

'Well, goodbye to all the ages.'

The canoe gave a sudden jolt and veered off course before she compensated with a shift of the paddle.

The Mississippi's turgid flow became agitated, not knowing which way to turn. A plethora of bubbles popped the surface. Eddies and tiny whirlpools sent sleek shoals of river fish darting willy-nilly. An eel thrashed its coils, thumping the side of her canoe as the tide doubled the canoe's speed.

She gave a shrug. Of course – the current was reversing. Three times a day the Atlantic intruded deep into the Mississippi delta, driving upstream, bearing creatures of the sea into the river.

Rounding the curve that would steer her on to a tributary of the Waters-of-Starlight, she heard what she first took to be the rustling of leaves. Then the distinct noise of crackling, mounting in volume, impelled her to turn round.

'Great Spirit . . .' she breathed, fear thumping in her breast.

A fiery canoe, borne on the back of the tide, was scudding in her wake And it was moving *faster* than her craft. As it closed in she spotted the arrows stuck in its hull – and in the burning body that lay inside. Someone had fired burning arrows into the corpse and its canoe. Interweaved with the flames was a luminous blue glow, evidence that a medicine man had evoked the *manitou* of the canoe.

'And propelled it at speed up the river, driven by the *manitou* of the Atlantic,' she said under her breath.

The craft was now near enough for her to discern the air rippling in its wake, giving hints of a phantasmal, rolling sea.

The blazing body in its floating funeral pyre swept past her craft. 'Voice-of-Thunder . . .' she murmured, watching the river-borne corpse veer steadily out of view, a bright blaze in the night.

Then came the sound of a drum, slow and steady: *ra-rum . . . rum . . . rum-rum-rum . . . ra-rum . . . rum . . . rum-rum-rum . . .*

The Hunters. Pale Wolf had used the incoming tide and the spirit of the Atlantic to gain on her. Not daring to look back, she swept the paddle in frenzied strokes, rounding the curve of the bank to catch her first glimpse of the Waters-of-Starlight tributary.

Pale Wolf leant forward in the prow of the leading canoe like a beast poised to pounce.

His finger jabbed straight ahead at the smudged profile of a craft, almost blanked out by the curvature of the banks. 'There! There she is! Faster! Faster!'

Snow Bear and Cloud-on-Mountain, the two rowers at his back, redoubled their efforts. Close behind, in the second canoe, Lonely Elk sat in the prow, chanting to the *manitou* of the Father of Waters as the burly figures of Sunlight-on-Spear and High Eagle plied the current with vigorous strokes.

A few metres back, parallel with the second craft, Silent

Owl sat cross-legged, alone in a black canoe without paddles. With two sculpted sticks, he beat a remorseless percussion on the deerskin drum in his lap: *ra-rum . . . rum . . . rum-rum-rum . . . ra-rum . . . rum . . . rum-rum-rum . . .*

Silent Owl, with his features perpetually obscured under a white owl paint mask, possessed strong medicine learnt not only from the Algonquin magical *midewiwin* initiation, but from the Iroquois practice of *orenda*, which extended spirit powers, and a plethora of other arts from all the tribes of the Americas. Solitary, in his canoe, Silent Owl propelled and guided the craft by the sheer power of his spirit.

'Silent Owl!' Pale Wolf shouted, hands cupped round his mouth. 'Can you race on ahead – stop River Woman before she reaches the Waters-of-Starlight?'

Silent Owl, as ever, spoke no word. Neither did he accelerate the knots of his pursuit. The white-faced man in the black boat hung back, as if biding his time. Waiting for the kill.

She drove the canoe in an unerring line, her objective in sight.

There it was. One of Earth's five thousand tributaries to the Waters-of-Starlight. A waterfall – and this waterfall fell upward.

It loomed on one side of the Mississippi, half a kilometre wide and higher than the eye could see. Its translucent waters rushed upward in a diaphanous riot of silvery torrents and milky froth. Yet the ghostly, reversed waterfall was silent as snow. Not so much as a *shush* of a splash.

River Woman attuned herself to the spirit of the waterfall, transmuting her body and the clothes it wore into their *manitou* essence, along with the canoe and the paddle in her grip. She and her craft became soul stuff as they entered the soundless, boiling foam at the base of the waterfall.

Then the canoe streaked up the towering torrents. And the Ole Man River of the Mississippi was left behind.

Pale Wolf felt the wolfish vitality of his spirit animal rise as the canoe and its occupants coalesced into their *manitous* and mounted the flanks of the waterfall. Lonely Elk and Silent

Owl, in the following craft, had worked their magic well. The full hunting party was on the heels of its quarry.

The sensation of rapid ascent began to ease as grey mist enveloped the canoes, thickening with each breath. By the time the steep incline levelled out, the fog was too dense to distinguish the following craft.

Then the fog boiled into a frenzy as the maelstrom hit. Brutal waves, battling in cross-currents, threw the canoe hither and thither.

'Stay calm! Stay firm!' he exhorted Snow Bear and Cloud-on-Mountain, who were near to dropping the paddles in panic. 'This is the confluence of earthly rivers. We'll soon be free of it.'

He was less certain than his words. In all his experience, the confluence had been no more than rolling waves. Were the Waters-of-Starlight beginning to tear apart, as the Great World was coming asunder? He had heard such rumours. It was the Waters-of-Starlight that had violated the Great World's fabric of space and time, and perhaps the Waters-of-Starlight was now unravelling with the Great World. There was raw justice in that.

As suddenly as the storm erupted, it subsided. The waters quietened and the mist lifted.

After checking that the rest of the canoes were still following, Pale Wolf studied his surroundings. They were skimming along a muddy brown river, flanked by the steam bath of a rainforest. At their backs there opened a vast plain, speared by sky-high pagodas. He gave a nod of recognition. That was the Plain of Birds around the Mekong delta back there – and beyond it, the Pacific.

The plantain trees were closing in fast, blocking out the Plain of Birds. The dwindling scent of the South China Sea was smothered in the sultry air.

He loosened his collar, skin drenched with sweat under his buckskins. His companions followed his example. 'We're on the Mekong,' he said. 'The spirit Mekong. She's trying to give us the slip.'

'But how can we be sure Old River Woman is on the Mekong?' queried Cloud-on-Mountain.

Pale Wolf opened his left hand, revealing a lock of hair.

'While I have this, we'll be drawn to the path River Woman takes.' The lock of River Woman's hair, which he had purloined from Voice-of-Thunder's pouch as the body was placed in the funeral boat, would be drawn to the head from which it was clipped.

'She's close,' he said, staring upriver. 'Don't doubt it. Very close.'

She kept up a steady pace, scudding down the Mekong – the River-Mother, in Sanskrit. Had she eluded her pursuers at the confluence? She could only hope.

From time to time, she darted a backward glance at the winding river. No sign of Delaware canoes. No resonance of drumbeat.

The Mekong she travelled on had no physical existence. It was a dream made fluid, distilled from the real Mekong of Earth and the Waters-of-Starlight. And it reflected her own hidden mind. The fantastical became actual on the star path.

The giant, dank ferns, dripping copiously in the humidity, the spreading plantains, the interlacing limbs of liana – all familiar from the actual world. Even the mosquitoes were present in this implicate world, clouding the brown surface of the Mekong and making free with her skin.

Between clusters of plantains, she glimpsed a Greek temple, brand-new as the day it was completed in Eleusis in the fourth millennium. A number of Olympian gods were descending on the temple, their white, vaporous forms streaming in a celestial wind. She spotted Zeus, Athena, Hermes . . .

Then a figure, partially obscured by the steaming vegetation, emerged from the temple's Ionic columns and headed her way.

She gave a slow shake of the head. She had allowed a conflicting reality to get out of hand. A divine and perhaps deadly nonsense was on the loose.

The figure reached the bank, its profile clearly revealed.

'Oh *no* – Apollo.'

An animated statue of Apollo, marble-white, dressed in a black evening suit and patent-leather shoes, walked towards her over the water. He slipped on dark glasses and extracted a cutthroat razor from his pocket. Brandishing the glinting razor in the living marble of his hand, he sauntered the last few paces to her boat, a smile creasing the inhuman perfection of his features.

'I gather you're leaving the Great Mother, River Woman,' Apollo said in a tone like resonant crystal. 'That won't do, not at all. I was never much of a one for Earth Mothers, as you know, but for a mortal to desert the Earth Mother is quite reprehensible, so –' the razor swished, catching the sunlight '– I'll – cut out your heart. Yes, I think that would be best.'

How could she oppose this sinister Apollo? Desperately, she rummaged through all the skills she'd learnt in the many culture identities of her life. Nothing sprang quickly to mind.

Besides, fighting in a canoe presented problems.

Apollo stepped into the canoe, rocking the boat.

Marble, she observed, studying the god's strange flesh. That's the key.

And the means of turning that key to her advantage . . .

Subsonic chant from the Chinese Empire of Harmonies.

'Turn back downriver, woman, or –' Apollo wove the razor in front of her face.

She compressed her lips and emitted a low humming sound, directed at the whiter-than-white god in the blacker-than-black suit. She deepened the humming to subsonic level.

'What – what are you doing, woman?' There was a ring of alarm in the crystalline voice.

She unleashed the full blast of subsonics on the marble Olympian.

The vibrations played havoc with the deity's mineral anatomy. He shook and shook. Fit to burst.

A crack zigzagged up his throat with a loud report. Other cracks swiftly mazed his stony form.

An arm snapped loose, sliding out of the sleeve to splash into the water.

Relentlessly, she kept up the acoustic onslaught.

Apollo exploded out of his evening suit. She ducked as white shards whizzed overhead.

When she looked up, all that was left of the marble Olympian was a torn black suit and a pair of patent-leather

Waters-of-Starlight 297

shoes. The razor and dark glasses had gone the way of the devastated body.

She pressed on, deciding to phase into one more tributary just in case the Hunters had tracked her to the Mekong. If they were on the scent, one more river should throw them off it.

'But they're probably floundering in the confluence or riding a dream Mississippi into intergalactic space.' She smiled to herself.

The smile vanished at a sound reverberating from downstream . . .

Ra-rum . . . rum . . . rum-rum-rum . . . ra-rum . . . rum . . . rum-rum-rum . . .

As she formed the image of a stream in her mind, a corresponding stream instantly appeared in the bank. A few sweeps of the paddle sped her into it.

A few strokes more and she left the browns and greens of the Mekong for the blues and yellows of Crystal Egypt.

As the hunting party slipped down the stream into the broad Nile of Crystal Egypt, Pale Wolf couldn't help peering at the black canoe in the rear.

Silent Owl sat in the prow, motionless but for the hands that pounded the deerskin drum, a relentless pulse. It followed Pale Wolf like the beat of his own conscience. The shaman's tawny eyes gave the impression of blind scrutiny: dead men's eyes that could see into your soul.

Does he know? Does he know I killed my brother?

Well, he reasoned, if he knows of the act he may know of the motive. It wasn't because of my feelings for River Woman, I swear. I swear by Gitche Manitou. His stare lowered to the narrow-bladed tomahawk in his right hand. The blood had been easily washed from the weapon but the stain on the weapon's *manitou* was permanent.

It was a crime, but a necessary crime. Voice-of-Thunder, betraying himself by a thousand little lapses only a brother could detect, had exposed his intention to seek out the crack in the walls of the world, either alone or with his wife. Better his brother die than bring down the shame of the Great Desertion on the Twilight Owl clan. And worse than the shame was the iniquity of deserting the Great Mother, the giver of all.

He squared his shoulders, taking the burden of blame. He had killed for the Great Mother, and would kill one more time.

Up ahead, in clear view on a wide, gentle curve of the Nile, River Woman was using the paddle for all she was worth.

Pale Wolf's grip tightened on the tomahawk.

She tried not to listen to the beat of the drum as she skimmed upstream on the blue Nile of Crystal Egypt.

From the limestone plateaux on each side of the gleaming river there reared pyramids, sphinxes and colossi of vibrant crystal, resonant with internal harmonies. Elegant priests and priestesses processing down palm- and sphinx-lined avenues conducted their hieratic tasks in the slow action of a dream, sweep and sway. Ethereal barges and rafts of floating temples hushed by her on the stately current.

The numinous essence of Crystal Egypt bore in on her, summoning with old names and ancient devotions, but she fixed her inner vision on a liquid blue distance and the first of the cataracts, source of a tributary that soared out of Earth and into the deeps of space.

The Hunters had some psychic means of tracking her, that was evident. No point in sidetracking from dream river to dream river. Pale Wolf would pursue her every stroke of the way to the last river bend in the Great World. It was a simple race all the way to the edge of the real.

The soul of Crystal Egypt swept by, league on ancient league, and the cataract came into sight. Attuning her spirit to the stars, she launched the canoe on to the cataract, which instantly reversed its flow from downhill to uphill. She raced up the steepening slope of rising waters with mounting acceleration. Shred by gauzy shred, Egypt fell away, its antique whispers dwindled.

There was a sharp jolt as she parted company with Earth. A confusion of the senses.

When her psyche calmed, she looked around and saw that she paddled on a silver river with nothing above or below her but the stars and Earth's cloudy blue sphere.

'On the Waters-of-Starlight,' she murmured. 'Next stop the end of the universe.'

The true shape of the Waters-of-Starlight was unknowable to all but the departed gods. To most earthly eyes, River Woman's included, it presented itself as a rippling river of starlight in solution laced with luminescent spray. No wider than the Mississippi, the river wended out of the solar system to the interstellar spaces, a strange trick of perspective extending its vanishing point far beyond Pluto's orbit. In principle, the starry path had an unlimited number of courses, as many as there were directions and destinations. The mind of the traveller picked out one from a myriad.

According to all the legends, the way to the last river bend out of the world was straightforward: keep to the high river and always paddle upstream. On the high river, upstream was equivalent to journeying into the past, downstream into the future.

So keep to an upstream course on the high river, and the voyager travels back billions of years to the crack in the Great World's walls. The crack had been identified crudely in the sixth millennium as an explosion which gave birth to the universe, a notion typical of the ancients' anthropocentric view of time as solely downstream. In truth it was simultaneously the beginning of the cosmos and its end. But what lay beyond the crack was still a mystery.

And why had not one of the gods ever returned? Another mystery.

Her breath misted the air, a luminous spirit exhalation in the black vacuum.

'To the edge of the real,' she said, dipping her paddle in the luminous waters.

With a single stroke she skimmed the canoe past the moon's orbit. She could still feel the influence of Earth's gravity – Mother Earth, as the ancients named it – calling her back with a plaintive '*Stay home, stay home . . .*'

Another stroke and she was at the limit of Earth's reach, surprised by the keen sense of loss in her soul. She gave a last backward look. At this distance, Earth was a small, gentle thing.

'Goodbye, small world mother.' *Perhaps we only love when we leave.*

She bent to the task of paddling into the gulfs between the stars, experiencing a sense of parting from Sol, the sun that birthed and sustained her homeworld.

'To you, too, goodbye.'

Then she was beyond the primordial attraction of the sun and the canoe gathered speed, free of a gravity indistinguishable from nostalgia.

In the interstellar spaces, the canoe's progress increased rapidly. A hundred and more stars lay between River Woman and her home star by the time she had taken a hundred breaths.

The acceleration continued, until each dip of the blade was the passing of a century.

She was no longer Delaware, Chinese, Crystal Egyptian or any other of the cultural identities that had adorned her life, but an ungarnished Earthwoman – a long way from home. Her isolation exalted her to a being of fable. The river was myth, and the paddle strokes stirred the foam of legend from its waters.

It was true, what the old Waters-of-Starlight mariners said: between the stars, you believe yourself alone in the cosmos.

Then she heard a sound, chasing in her wake: *ra-rum . . . rum . . . rum-rum-rum . . . ra-rum . . . rum . . . rum-rum-rum . . .*

She couldn't suppress a rueful smile. She wouldn't be alone, not for one second of the journey across the span of the universe. The Hunters would be always at her back.

She increased the strength and rapidity of the paddle strokes. Her trackers wouldn't slacken in their pursuit, that was sure. Pale Wolf had never lacked determination. She'd have to call on all her resources to maintain distance from the hunting party.

Slowly and smoothly, she sank into a trance of motion, of rising and dipping blade.

Closing her eyes, she rode on heaven's river, and time became strange. She dreamt (or did not dream) that a Flying Dutchman galleon sailed by her on the waves, the face of the captain stark with damnation. And there might or might not

Waters-of-Starlight

have been a floating city of granite and, later, a quinquireme of Nineveh bound for a distant star.

Her meditation was shattered by a sudden turbulence. Surfacing from the trance, she perceived that her craft was speeding away from an outer arm of the Milky Way. The pangs of separation from her home galaxy were severe. The river gave a bewildering twist as it finally scudded free of galactic gravity.

The tumult in her spirit subsided as the canoe skimmed along the river into the gulfs between the galaxies and nebulae. Free of all attraction except the Great World Mother's, she sailed near the speed of thought, the absolute limit of motion.

The paddle was redundant, at least for now. She laid it in the canoe and took a long backward look. The spiral of the Milky Way spun away into the blackness on its solitary dance. Despite the rapid recession of the galaxy, the canoe seemed to ride the river currents at a slow and steady pace.

Although she had travelled back in time at least a billion years, the Waters-of-Starlight's eccentric relationship to the cosmos kept her in her personal present, representing the universe as it was a few days after her departure from Earth. In reality – whatever that meant – behind the stable backdrop, the galaxies were rushing together on their own upriver path, back to the headwaters.

How soon now before she reached those headwaters? Near the speed of thought, it was said, you could cross the universe in a day.

'A day away from the edge of forever,' she said, returning her attention upstream.

She caught her breath as the river's silvery reach trembled and almost blinked out. For a while it was stable, then it shivered again, coming close to dissolution.

'It's dying,' she muttered. 'As the universe dies, so does the Waters-of-Starlight that hastened its end.

'Endure for just one day,' she begged the river. 'A single day for me to keep a vow.'

Speeding from his home galaxy, Pale Wolf smiled at the unravelling of the Waters-of-Starlight. In sharp contrast, his companions in the lead canoe gave vent to cries of dismay, echoed in the following craft. Only Silent Owl preserved his eerie composure, seated in his black boat.

Snow Bear gripped Pale Wolf by the arm. 'We must turn back before the river vanishes!'

Pale Wolf pushed the man away in disgust. 'Turn back from the hunt? Fail in our duty to the Great Mother?' He raised the tomahawk. 'The only way back now is to kill me. Make your choice.'

After some hesitation, Snow Bear backed down. The others followed his lead.

Pale Wolf nodded his approval. 'Have courage. The remaining journey is short. Thought is the swiftest of arrows.'

Rebellion quelled, he turned back to the winding Waters-of-Starlight. Once again, the river trembled, and the canoe shuddered in response. Despite the confident words to his men, Pale Wolf knew there was scant hope of returning to Earth. The lock of hair in his left hand would keep them on River Woman's tracks for as long as the Waters-of-Starlight survived, but the river was on the verge of extinction.

Let it survive just a little while, just a day, until he'd hacked out River Woman's heart.

He folded his arms, stare fixed ahead.

On the long journey there had been no sight of his prey. But if the river didn't fail him he would run her down, even if it was on the last lap.

Yes, if he had to traverse that last loop out of the world to do it, he would offer her heart to the Great Mother.

Time flowed by as the Milky Way diminished into just one more galaxy.

The Waters-of-Starlight gave spasmodic vibrations, increasing in rate and intensity as the galaxies condensed into a background haze, enclosing the world in a sphere of glowing silver.

'We're at the centre of the Great World Mother,' Pale Wolf said in awe.

And yet, he felt he could stretch out and touch those glowing walls.

'We're at the centre of the Great World – and at its edge.'

Waters-of-Starlight

After a long silence, the drum resumed its beat: *ra-rum . . . rum . . . rum-rum-rum . . . ra-rum . . . rum . . . rum-rum-rum . . .*

Abruptly, the river's course became problematic. It diverged into an infinity of possibilities.

Directions abounded. This way was that way was this –

Pale Wolf's wits scattered, bright dust in the void.

Then the Waters-of-Starlight failed.

Unwound into nothing.

'Great Mother!' Pale Wolf screamed.

The dark gulped down the scream.

River Woman, paddling the canoe to the centre and rim of the universe, sensed the closeness of a singularity, a paradoxical everything-and-nothing – a plenum-vacuum.

'Almost there.'

She gave a heave of the paddle, and the ripples circled out into space.

And the river – the river wavered beneath her. And dispersed with a sigh.

Not now! Not now!

She summoned up her final resources. She was River Woman. She could make her own river from traces of the dispersing Waters-of-Starlight. It might survive a little time, until she reached her goal.

'Crystal Egypt,' she whispered, her soul embodying memories. 'The sacred Nile.'

The canoe lurched violently into a living dream of blues and yellows.

Then she was floating up the wide, slow-flowing Nile of Crystal Egypt, from the delta to the cataract, crystal pyramids and colossi gliding past. Below the calm waters she felt the presence of Sebek, the all-devouring crocodile god.

And somewhere up ahead, nearby, the end of the universe.

She reached the cataract and soared up its silent torrents.

Then, from close behind, there came a familiar sound: *ra-rum . . . rum . . . rum-rum-rum . . . ra-rum . . . rum . . . rum-rum-rum . . .*

From despair to elation in a single moment. Pale Wolf grinned.

The pulse of Silent Owl's drum had the resonance of triumph.

From absolute darkness to the blue waters of the Nile. He glanced at the lock of hair in his left hand. Where she went, he went. This version of Crystal Egypt was one of River Woman's realities.

River Woman had found a way to extend the river's last gasp, and the backwash of her river reality had salvaged the hunting party from oblivion.

'Many thanks,' he laughed.

Peering upstream, he sighted a small speck ascending an inverted cataract.

He thrust the tomahawk forward. 'I see you, River Woman. I see you.'

The Egyptian reality fell away and she was paddling down the stifling Mekong, crowded in by a jungle of plantains and interlacing liana and pursued by the rhythm of a drum. The rainforest was suffused with the presence of the nearby crack in the world, hidden beyond the roof of foliage.

She expelled a long breath.

'River Woman!'

She spun round at Pale Wolf's shout. His canoe was rounding the bend in the river. Within a spear's throw.

A vigorous sweep of the paddle sped her canoe on its way. She skimmed along the Mekong for a hundred breaths, then spotted a small creek to the right.

Transforming the creek to a branch into another river, she veered down the branch, which swiftly opened out into the wide, boiling crest of a waterfall. The rainforest faded as she swept over the waterfall's rim.

The canoe dipped and tumbled down the wall of foam. On the long drop she glanced up and glimpsed the three tracking canoes plunging in her wake.

Then she bit the surface in a brawl of spray. She was hurled in any and every direction, blinded by spray. She kept up a determined action of the paddle until, shaking the water from her eyes, she saw that she was clear, out on the open Mississippi under the stars.

Upstream, around the next bend, she could feel the

overwhelming actuality of the gap in the Great World, dwarfing the spirit Mississippi into the tiny dream that it was.

She drove upriver with all her energy.

'The last lap.'

Racing against the current, she barely noticed the Mississippi spectres gliding past, antique memories: a paddle steamer, its great wheel churning the waves, and antebellum mansions rising elegantly on the banks.

The antebellum world was displaced by older ghosts: Algonquin and Iroquois in their spectral canoes. The ghosts of the ancestors.

At length even the ancestors faded as the dark river unwound.

The image summoned up one of the wonders of childhood: the fascination of corners, in rivers or roads.

In her infancy, every corner promised a revelation: *Follow me, and I will lead somewhere you cannot imagine . . .*

But every corner led to another corner, and the beckoning mystery retreated, pace for pace with her advance.

This last river bend, however, was the final corner.

'River Woman!'

She spun round – and moaned with dismay. Two canoes had caught up with her, within a long paddle-reach of her craft. Pale Wolf's lean face was avid with the hunt. The strain of sustaining the river's existence had slowed her down.

But it was still her river, and she could use it against the Hunters.

She evoked a state of inner turmoil, then projected it into the river. The surface bubbled in consternation, sending up spume from mounting waves, rocking her boat from side to side. But the main force was in the backwash.

Behind her, rapids upreared from the previously flat surface. White rapids, growling with a voice of thunder.

The two canoes were tossed high and wild, toppling the hunters into the river. Farther back, Silent Owl's boat seemed to be riding the storm, forced downriver.

She returned to her task with renewed perseverance, scudding over the currents. A hundred more strokes and she'd be there, around the last corner.

There was a slight drag on the craft, a shift of equilibrium. An instinct told her what was wrong, what was very wrong. She tried to ignore it.

The canoe gave a violent tilt. Her arms windmilled as she struggled to maintain balance, and the paddle plunged into the river.

Pale Wolf pulled himself into the canoe, skin streaming with spirit water. Once he was on board, the craft he'd almost capsized quickly stabilized.

He crawled towards her, tomahawk gripped in his right hand. Within touching distance, he halted, holding out his open left hand. A lock of hair lay curled in the palm. 'Your hair won't let you go, River Woman.'

He threw the strand into her lap. And raised the tomahawk. 'Now – give me your heart.'

Pulse thudding, she shrank back. Pale Wolf didn't follow.

The tomahawk was motionless in Pale Wolf's frozen grasp. Dread expunged the hunt hunger in his face. He was staring upriver, his eyes blank as black beads.

'Brother . . .'

She twisted round, and saw a light on that last bend of the river. Red flames. A fiery funeral canoe, impelled by the green tide of a ghostly Atlantic.

The *manitou* of Voice-of-Thunder had preceded her to the last corner of the world.

She looked back at Pale Wolf. Rage had ousted dread from his features. 'The dead who go nowhere can lead nowhere,' he muttered. He glared into her eyes as he hoisted the tomahawk. 'Now, River Woman, your heart . . .'

She lurched to one side as he swung the tomahawk. The canoe tilted perilously, then overturned.

The water hit her with a smack of spray. In a slow spin, she spiralled into the depths. Overhead, she saw the silhouette of the canoe glide out of reach.

Then her floating hair was grabbed and her head yanked back. Her breath escaped in an uprush of bubbles.

Pale Wolf thrust his face close to hers, keeping a firm clasp of her hair, then drew back as he pressed the tomahawk blade to her breast.

She caught the weapon in both hands and shoved it away,

Waters-of-Starlight

her feet kicking furiously as she fought to break free.

At the touch of the blade, she felt the tomahawk's *manitou* – and the spirit blood that stained it. Her husband's blood. And, unless she escaped Pale Wolf, husband's and wife's blood would soon mix.

She planted her foot on Pale Wolf's chest, and pushed with all her strength. On land, the simple manoeuvre would have been ineffectual against a warrior like Pale Wolf. In water, she was in her element.

The hank of hair Pale Wolf held in his grip tore free of his hand as he was propelled downstream.

She struck upward and broke the surface.

Then cried out as a hand clasped her wrist. Pale Wolf . . .

But the hand wasn't Pale Wolf's. And the canoe she'd surfaced alongside was black. Silent Owl's canoe, waiting for her.

With Silent Owl's aid, she eased herself over the side and slumped into the stern.

Downriver, Pale Wolf's head and flailing arms were visible above the current. A current that ran into – nothing. Her river was shrinking.

Pale Wolf made no sound as he fell over the river's crest into nowhere.

Turning from the bleak spectacle, she faced the last river bend. Voice-of-Thunder's fiery funeral canoe was still visible on that final loop of water. And Silent Owl's craft kept pace with it, drumbeat by drumbeat, outrunning the advancing rim of vacancy.

They were soon skimming over the green tide of a ghost Atlantic, narrowed to a river.

Then Silent Owl stopped his drumming, and their progress slowed. He leant his owl-painted face to her, reached out a gaunt hand, and dropped two coins in her lap. The rough coins were inscribed with ancient Greek letters.

She shook her head. 'What is this? What do you want?'

He held out his palm.

She glanced at the two Greek coins, the outstretched hand. 'Is that who you are – Charon the Ferryman?'

She dropped the two coins into his open palm. The fingers closed over them.

Then, with a flick of the wrist, he tossed the coins into the air and retrieved them with a deft catch. He opened his hand to reveal a pair of dice, the surfaces of one die all sixes, the other all sevens.

'You're Coyote – the Trickster,' she said, with less than conviction.

Another turn of the wrist, and the dice were replaced by the coins, which he dropped in a pouch.

She gave a shrug. 'Perhaps you're the most mysterious of all beings – a human.'

Silent Owl's lips bent in a slender smile. He resumed his drumming and the craft sped forward.

Led by the burning funeral canoe on the spirit Atlantic's current, she rounded the last corner in the world.

Leaving the Great World Mother, River Woman spared a final backward glance. The universe of a billion galaxies, she now saw, was a small, tender thing. The stars, those ancient incubators, had done their work, and done it well. Their task was finished.

Now she knew why not one of the gods had returned. They *couldn't* return. It was impossible to squeeze back into such a small, cramped space.

River Woman raised a hand in farewell, then faced forward.

She saw the end of the river, beyond the boat of fire. The river flowed into a sea above the world, a single drop of which could contain the Great World. A sea of massive reality, and one she half remembered from a thousand dreams and before her first memory. She might have called it holy, but that wasn't enough, nor was joy, or wonder.

'I know this,' she murmured. 'I've always known this.'

River Woman smiled as she entered the sea.

'I'm home.'

The Place of All Places

Based on an idea by Nakula Somana

Desert is full of memories. They colour everything: emotive, imperative, a desperate urge. And not just desperation but hope, fear, love, pity, awe, hate, curiosity, poignancy, bitterness, all the understanding God ever made lies here. The land and the sky are so full of experience there is scarcely room for Man.

Man lives among the long dunes, racked on the gulf of sand between ignorance and understanding, far from a childhood abandoned in the search for himself; close enough to death to consider Desert's stories of the dying universe.

Here Man has built his home: a place of mirrors and pumps; a mechanism for easing the burden of living. And in his home Man remembers. He remembers the harijans and how they worked like a machine in the dhobiis ghat to sustain his world; he remembers how a different kind of machine had transformed that world. He remembers Boy's selfish demands for love and Uncle's use of Desert as analogy; he remembers the desperate hunger for experience and growth, all unrecognized for so long.

Man has lived Desert's stories and now he understands.

But Man is in his home among the sands, yellow everywhere, and though he dreams of other palaces this is where he will lay his porous bones to sleep. Desert has her sandy arms about his aged hip and will quench her thirst on his fluids until Man is as dry as the wood that fuels his cooking fires.

And so, as night chases the sun from Desert, Man moves, motionless, into the future, shaping the world and shaped by it, his presence defining Desert's stories as the stories define Desert.

He moves as an amphibian killer destroys cities with dreams, slows as a regiment of artists raid history's corpse, stumbles as men lactate and machines are incarcerated for speaking the truth, dies as understanding deafens a world

with whispers. His life shed in the storm of his own desire.
   His journey ends where it began.
   He has but one question, and no answer.
   The Desert tells stories. The stories are real.
   Will Desert remember Man?

The Authors

Stephen Baxter is the author of seven published SF novels, including *Raft*, *The Time Ships*, *Aniti-Ice* and *Voyage*, and more than fifty short stories. His novels have won the Philip K. Dick Award, the John Campbell Memorial Award, the British Science Fiction Association Award as well as awards in Germany and Japan. His work has also been nominated for the Hugo Awards and the Arthur C. Clarke Award.

Jeanne Cavelos is the author of the *Babylon 5* novel *The Shadow Within*. She has worked as an editor for Dell publishing, where she created and launched several innovative imprints, including Abyss (psychological horror) for which she won the World Fantasy Award. Jeanne teaches science fiction and fantasy writing at the Odyssey workshop, New Hampshire, USA (www.nhc.edu/odyssey/). She has also worked at NASA, in the Astronaut Training Division.

Dominic Green is 29 years old and lives in Milton Keynes. Although his first story was published in *Interzone* only last year, he has been writing for quite some time, and he is very tired now and is going home to bed. If any nice publishers would like to publish his first novel, he will be glad to bite their hands off at the elbow. But be warned: there is Swearing in it.

Paul Leonard is the author of several New and Missing Adventures and his story 'Rescue Mission' appeared in *Decalog 4*. He lives in Bristol, in a flat full of books, computer discs, videos and lots of unread pieces of paper, some of which might hold the secret of eternal life, but are more probably telephone bills.

Stephen Marley was born partly in Derby and partly in Galway (it's a long story) and lived a life of high adventure in the back alleys of Europe, notching up a few academic degrees in his spare time. Succumbing to reckless abandon, he threw aside a career in academe and took up writing full-time in 1988. Since then he has published seven novels, including the dark fantasies *Mortal Mask* and *Shadow Sisters*, and three science fantasies: *Dreddlocked*, *Dread Dominion* and *Managra*. He also pursues parallel careers as a videogame designer and a scriptwriter. At present he lives in Derby, but is planning his escape.

Lawrence Miles wrote the New Adventures *Christmas on a Rational Planet* and *Down*. He hopes to edit a Decalog of his own one day, but his ultimate ambition is to break in to television, and move all the furniture around while no one's looking. Let's be honest, he's a total slut who'd write for *Crime Traveller* if you gave him twenty quid and a packet of chocolate Hob-Nobs.

Jim Mortimore is.

Mike O'Driscoll's stories have appeared in Ellen Datlow's *Off Limits & Lethal Kisses*, Andy Cox's *Last Rites and Resurrections*, in *Darklands 2*, all four volumes of *Cold Cuts*, as well as in magazines such as *Interzone*, *BBR*, *Fear* and *The Third Alternative*. Having won a British Fantasy Award for co-organizing the 'Welcome to my Nightmare' Horror Convention in Swansea in 1995, he would recommend the experience to anyone but himself. He is currently busy not working on a novel.

Elizabeth Sourbut has a BSc in physics and an MA in women's studies. She lives in York and divides her time between writing science fiction, weaving baskets, and listening to classical music. Whenever possible, she does all three simultaneously.

Ian Watson has been a full-time writer for the past twenty years. Among his many acclaimed novels, which have gleaned numerous awards and nominations, are *The Embedding*, *Miracle Visitors* and *The Book of the River* trilogy. He has also published more than eight short-story collections, most recently *The Coming of Vertumnus* (Gollancz, 1994).

His most recent novels are a science fantasy epic, *The Book of Mana*, inspired by Finnish mythology, and a topical fast-paced SF thriller, *Hard Questions*. Just published by Gollancz is *Oracle*, in which a Roman centurion is dragged into the present day and becomes enmeshed in an IRA plot to kill the British monarch.

Neil Williamson is a technical author living in Glasgow. His stories have appeared in *The Third Alternative*, *Territories* and *Shipbuilding*, the Glasgow SF Writers' Circle anthology published for the 1995 Worldcon.